CAT
WINTERS

The Raven's Tale

AMULET BOOKS • NEW YORK

Library of Congress Cataloging-in-Publication Data
Names: Winters, Cat, author.
Title: The raven's tale / Cat Winters.
Description: New York, NY: Amulet Books, 2019. | Summary: Seventeen-year-old Edgar Poe's plans to escape his foster family, begin classes at the prestigious new university, and marry his beloved Elmira Royster go awry when a macabre Muse appears with a request.
Identifiers: LCCN 2018046694 | ISBN 9781419733628 (hardback)
Subjects: LCSH: Poe, Edgar Allan, 1809–1849—Childhood and youth—Juvenile fiction. | CYAC: Poe, Edgar Allan, 1809–1849—Childhood and youth—Fiction. | Supernatural—Fiction. | Inspiration—Fiction. | Authors—Fiction. | Richmond (Va.)—History—19th century—Fiction.
Classification: LCC PZ7.W76673 Rav 2019 | DDC [Fic]—dc23

ABRAMS The Art of Books
195 Broadway, New York, NY 10007
abramsbooks.com

For all the young dreamers of the world.

Astra inclinant, sed non obligant.

PART I

– FEBRUARY 5, 1826 –

And so, being young and dipt in folly
I fell in love with melancholy . . .

—EDGAR ALLAN POE, "Introduction," 1831

CHAPTER ONE

Edgar

ood morning, ladies and gentlemen! I imagine myself saying from the pulpit in the pink sanctuary of our church. *My name is Edgar Poe, and today, for reasons I don't fully comprehend, I'm obsessed with the seventy-two bodies buried beneath us.*

Don't ever forget, my dear friends, I continue with this grim fancy, *that a grisly collection of bones, and teeth, and soot sits below your very feet, even as you try not to think of such horrors. Even when your heart is giddy with evangelical glee this fine February morning, the victims of our infamous Richmond Theater fire still dwell among us down there—or at least what's left of the poor souls—piled together in a moldering mass grave.*

And then I envision myself tipping my silk hat with the coyest of grins and saying, *A happy Sunday to you all!*

Down below the floorboards creaking beneath my knees, deep in the belly of Monumental Church, stands a crypt built of bricks that, indeed, holds the remains of all seventy-two victims of the great Richmond Theater fire of 1811. I kneel beside my foster mother in the Allan family pew, my lips moving in prayer, my hands clasped beneath my chin, but my mind slips down between the cracks of the floor and steals into the depths of that underground tomb that still smells faintly of ashes.

The doomed Richmond Theater stood on this very site. The victims of the fire once breathed the same air I'm inhaling right now. I might have burned along with them if my mother, an actress, hadn't died of illness eighteen days before the blaze—if, as a child not yet three, two strangers, the Allans, hadn't taken me into their home and carried me off to the countryside for Christmas.

The back of my neck tingles with a prickling of dread. My eyes remain shut, but I feel someone watching from the shadows of the church's salmon pink walls. Yes, *she's* watching me—a raven-haired maiden in a gown spun from threads made of cinders and soot—a girl my own age, a mere seventeen—one of the dozens of young women whom the fire trapped in the narrow passageways, whom men crushed beneath their feet in the mad exodus from the box seats. The smell of smoke stings my nostrils, and accompanying it, the stench of the maiden's hair burning.

There! There it is again! Singed hair . . . and smoke! Dear God! Black, blistering smoke that chokes, and strangles, and suffocates—

"Edgar!" snaps Ma in a whispered shout.

I give a start and discover that Ma and the rest of the congregation have returned to their seats. I'm panting, I realize. Every muscle in my body has clenched.

Ma pats the hard slab of the bench and whispers, "The prayer is over. Remove yourself from the floor, please."

I push myself off my knees, the soles of my shoes squeaking with such a fuss that Judge Brockenbrough in front of me turns and frowns like an angry old trout. I slide back onto the bench just as the Right Reverend Bishop Moore embarks upon his sermon, preached from high in a pulpit shaped like a wineglass—a shape, I might add, that likely explains the bountiful quaffing of wine among his parishioners after church every Sunday.

"Renounce 'the pomps and vanities of the wicked world,'" the bishop calls down to us, and his snowy white hair swings against his shoulders. "Silence your muses who linger in fire-light and shadows, whispering words of secular inspiration, muddling minds with lewd and idle aspirations that detract from lives of charity, piety, and modesty."

Ma gulps, and one of my former classmates, Nat Howard, a rival poet, turns his face my way from across the aisle with a lift of his eyebrows that seems to ask, *Is he really giving this same damn sermon again?*

I squeeze my hands together in my lap and gnash my teeth, bracing for yet another tirade against the arts.

"In the dawns of our childhoods"—the bishop's voice softens; the broad expanse of his bald pate sparkles with sweat—"in the midst of nursery games and fairy stories, the sweet voices of muses coaxed every single one of us into joining them on fantastic flights of fancy. As naïve babes, we knew not to ignore them. Yet the strongest among us swiftly learned that to walk the path of righteousness, we must turn away from foolish temptations and imaginary realms before our passions grow unruly and wild—before the world views our extravagance. Silence your muses!"

I flinch, as does Ma.

"To live without sin," continues the bishop, "we must reject the theater and other vulgar forms of entertainment—card playing, waltzing, bawdy music, lascivious literature penned by hell-dwelling hedonists such as the late Lord Byron . . ."

Dear God, this is too much! Not only do I consider insulting the memory of Byron a despicable sacrilege, but Pa yelled at me about stifling my poetic muse just last night. His fists, as a matter of fact, shook like they longed to beat the poetry out of me before I leave for college next week, and he pummeled me with insults.

"Pursuing the life of an artist," says the bishop, "inevitably leads to promiscuous intercourse between the sexes, drunkenness, and other forms of debauchery. Fourteen years ago this past December, God witnessed the debauchery among us. He saw the gambling, the prostitution, the theatrical exhibitions, and the blasphemy among the theater players whom this city welcomed with open arms. Upon this very plot of land, in front of a house packed with adults and children of every stratum of Richmond society—rich and poor, black and white, Christian and Jew—the Placide & Green Company performed a pantomime entitled . . ." The bishop pats his brow with a handkerchief and winces before uttering the name of the show the actors performed when flames engulfed the theater: "*The Bleeding Nun.*"

Ma shakes her head in shame over that unfortunate title, as though she were the playwright who concocted it. Judge Brockenbrough's large frame shudders in front of me. Bishop Moore casts a frown in my direction, and I fight against squirming, for I'm the grown, orphaned son of two Placide & Green theater players—as everyone here knows.

"The Lord punished this town's depravity with fire and suffering," he says, tears shining in his eyes. "He called for us to rise from the ashes and build this house of worship on the very site of the inferno, lest we forget the errors of our ways that wrought that terrible night of tragedy. If we stray from holiness once more, he will smite us down again. He. Will. Smite. Us. Down. Again." The bishop rises to his full height and clutches the sides of his pulpit, as though steering a schooner across the Atlantic. He even looks a mite seasick, his lips pale and puckered, yet he musters the strength to bellow once more, "Silence your muses!"

Ma grabs my left hand, and a horrifying hush trembles across the congregation. Sniffles circulate among the parishioners, who dab liquid eyes with handkerchiefs fetched from coats and purses—the usual aftermath of a Bishop Moore sermon, even when he's not preaching about the fire that killed so many loved ones in Richmond.

And yet, despite the window-rattling force of the bishop's warnings, despite genuine fear for my own soul, despite Pa's commands for me to cease writing my poetry, my mind drifts back down into that basement crypt, to the soot and the bones, and I ponder how many words I can rhyme with "gore."

After the service, when the fine Episcopalians of Richmond gather their hats and coats, Ma steps away to speak with friends about a charity project, and I wander out to the aisle on my own.

"Eddy," calls a familiar female voice to my left.

The weight of the sermon lifts from my lungs when I see, weaving toward me through the other churchgoers, my darling Sarah Elmira Royster—normally a Presbyterian—dressed in a blue satin dress that matches her eyes. She wears her hair pulled back from the sides of her face in smooth sheets of brown tresses, finer than silk, without the clusters of ringlets that tend to dangle in front of the other girls' ears.

I push my own curls back from my face and smile. "What are you doing here, Elmira?"

"I came with Margaret Wilson and her family. I wanted to see you."

I can't speak, I'm so overcome with gratitude that she's here for me. I take her left hand and pull her close, losing my wits to the heady lilac of her perfume.

"Not too close, Eddy." She peeks over her right shoulder. "My father told Mrs. Wilson to watch over me. Will you meet with me in private sometime before . . ." She fusses with the gold chain of her necklace, and her eyes brim with tears. "Before you leave for Charlottesville next week?"

"Of course." I caress the back of her gloved hand with my thumb. "I already intended to call on you later today. I have a gift for you."

"My parents will be home today. I want to spend some time alone with you."

"We can arrange a later meeting in the garden, but may I visit today as well? Pa and I had a fight last night that robbed me of all sleep and sanity. The bishop's sermon only added to my wretchedness . . ."

"Please don't silence your muse," she says. "I don't believe there's anything sinful about writing poems of love."

"I'm desperate to leave Richmond and end this suffocation, but it tortures me to know I'm leaving you, too."

Elmira lowers her face. "I'll going to miss you terribly."

"My heart will bleed the moment we part."

She smiles a wan smile and brushes tears from her cheeks. "I do believe your romantic muse is speaking through you this very moment."

"Shh." I peer around. "Don't let anyone hear that I'm poeticizing in church."

We both snicker.

"Do you see Mrs. Wilson?" she asks. "Is everyone watching us?"

I scan the crowd of my fellow parishioners—the established old families of Richmond, Virginia—fair-skinned, bejeweled, and gossipy aristocrats with blood as exquisite as a fine Bordeaux wine—blood far superior to the rot running through my body, or so I've come to believe.

"No, I don't see her," I say, and our eyes meet.

She gazes at me as though she doesn't see the low-born filth and the ugliness that writhes inside me.

"I'm going to miss seeing those beautiful eyes of yours that can't decide if they want to be gray, or blue, or violet," she says, her voice husky with emotion. "And your smile. You have the loveliest smile when you're not lost in sadness."

I gulp down a lump clogging up my throat and lean my lips next to her right ear. "I want to marry you, Elmira. Will you marry me?"

She stiffens, so I stay in that tipped-forward position, frozen mid-proposal, terrified of witnessing the expression on her face. I close my eyes, brush my cheek against hers, and lose myself in reveries of a future world for us—a cottage by the sea, every room stocked with books, the air rich with the scents of ink and watercolor paints; balmy evenings spent tinkling out tunes on a piano; the soft warmth of Elmira's hand cradling mine as we drift off to sleep, side-by-side.

"My father would never allow an engagement," she says at length.

"I know he doesn't think I'm good enough . . ."

"It's not that. We're both so young. I'm not yet sixteen, Eddy. You're barely seventeen."

I clench my jaw and lift my face. "Your father will change his mind when he sees all that I accomplish."

"I should go before Mrs. Wilson spies me over here." Elmira slips her fingers out of mine. "I'm sorry . . ."

"May I still call on you this afternoon?"

"Yes, before our Sunday dinner, but please, don't mention marriage. I'll never be permitted to write to you at the university if you do."

She scurries away to the Wilsons. I'm still tipped slightly forward, fighting to catch my breath, my fingers sweating against the silk of my vest. Her father may as well have just struck a blow to the pit of my stomach.

A clutch of my friends—Rob Mayo, Robert Cabell, Jack Mackenzie—catch my eye from across the nave and wave me over, but I mouth to them, "I can't. Not feeling well."

Ebenezer Burling, who doesn't quite fit in with the rest of the fellows either, lingers toward the back of the pews with his widowed mother. He offers a small wave, and I give one in return.

I then sidle past a couple of gray-haired old lawyers who glower at me with buzzard eyes, undoubtedly questioning my familiarity with Miss Sarah Elmira Royster. Richmond crawls with dozens of pompous asses just like them. Lawyers. Judges. Congressmen. Senators. Constitutional delegates. Rich immigrant merchants like Mr. John Allan, my Scot-blooded bastard of a foster father.

Yet poets, actors, painters, and other dreamers are growing endangered, it seems.

I fuss with the knot of my cravat—the damn thing's strangling me—and join Ma at the rear of the church. The bishop's sermon gnaws at my gut, and Elmira's warnings about her father's disapproval slices an ax blade of a headache through my brain.

Ma fits her gray bonnet over her auburn hair. "Are you all right, dear?"

I squint from the sunlight boring through the windows in the cupola of the domed ceiling and nod with my lips pressed together.

"Are you certain?" she asks.

"Yes," I say with a rasp, but the ugliness inside me writhes with more vigor, squeezing down on my stomach, knotting around my lungs like a thick cord of rope before rising to the surface of my flesh, where my wretchedness burns and yearns to shed from my body like a rattlesnake's skin.

CHAPTER TWO

The Muse

I awaken in the shadows, ravenous for words, hungering for delicacies dripping with dread.

My poet in the black frock coat kneels in prayer beneath the windows in the ceiling that bathe his head in a weak winter light, bronzing his brown curls and the back of his neck. He bends his face toward the floorboards, toward the crypt down below him, and I will the spirits of the dead beneath him to whisper a song:

> *Once upon a dark December, in a year we must*
> *   remember,*
> *Morbid mounds of ash and ember told a*
> *   gruesome tale of gore—*

Ah, there now—he lifts his face, sensing my presence. I smell the incense of his imagination kindling. A small shudder quivers through him.

In his mind, I'm a girl with ashen skin and raven hair who watches him from the walls with raptor eyes. He smells the smoke that still clings to me from the flames that sparked me to life all those years ago, when his mother drew her last breath in a cold and silent room. He envisions me as a young woman draped in one of the high-waisted dresses all the fashionable ladies once wore—gossamer, Grecian-inspired gowns that fluttered in the breezes of his childhood.

Oh, Lord—how my hunger worsens! How I crave a tale of horror that will appease my groaning soul. Dream again, poet, of your other lost lady—the one you call "Helen," who lies in a grave up on Shockoe Hill.

I slither through the shadows, my skirts swishing, sliding, scented with cinders. I don't quite know for certain whether I truly am a girl, but that's how my poet tends to think of me, and so I lengthen, and stretch, and wiggle curves into my hips. I thrust out my torso and plump up my breasts, reshaping myself into the silhouette of a young woman who hides in the warmth of the wood, and the nails, and the pale pink plaster. I creak and crawl in the wall on hands and knees, unseen, unheard by most, and set Edgar Poe's imagination ablaze by conjuring images that astound and horrify him. I inspire him, and in turn, he offers me stories that strike sparks in the flint of my fluttery fragment of a heart.

The Right Reverend Bishop Moore opens his eyes mid-prayer and gapes in my direction.

He senses me, too—ha! ha!

Perhaps my strengthening heartbeat has loudened.

Perhaps my cravings rumble with thunderous wails through the church and shake the floor beneath the bishop's leather soles.

Perhaps everyone hears the songs I've summoned from the dead in the crypt down below.

Edgar cracks a small smile at that last supposition.

"Silence your muses!" the bishop shouts to the congregation minutes later, and I crouch down in the dust of the floorboards and breathe the tang of anguish and terror trapped inside this haunted temple.

"The strongest among us," says the bishop, "swiftly learned that to walk the path of righteousness, we must turn away from foolish temptations and imaginary realms before our passions grow unruly and wild—before the world views our extravagance."

Unruly.

Wild.

Before the world views our extravagance.

My soul—so cramped, so sore and weary of entrapment in shadows—longs for unruliness, wildness.

I *want* the world to notice my poet. To notice *me*.

Wait until they see what's coming. Oh, just wait and see . . .

The service ceases, and the congregation rises. With some tantalizing little nudges from me, my poet woos his beautiful, beloved Elmira, and then he tugs at the cream-colored cravat strangling him and plods toward the back of the church, his footfalls hammering out a steady cadence—a bold and beauteous trochaic octameter that empowers me to stretch even taller. His violet-gray eyes flit in my direction for the briefest of moments—long enough for me to join him.

CHAPTER THREE

Edgar

Ma and I ride back home in a carriage that rocks us through ruts in a road ravaged by years of trade merchants rolling into Richmond in four- and six-horse wagons. Several inches of snow on the ground worsen the lurching and swaying, and despite our driver Dabney's skilled guidance of the mares, Ma and I cling to the brass straps near our heads to avoid flying off the seat.

"As of this morning," I say through my teeth amid the tumult, "I've learned that my artistic aspirations might not simply stop Pa from sending me to the university next week, but they might also impede me from both marriage and heaven."

"You already knew the bishop's opinion about secular entertainment, Edgar." Ma withdraws an embroidered handkerchief from her purse. "He's been preaching such sermons since the earliest years of Monumental Church. I'm sorry if his mentioning the Placide & Green Company upset you. We both know your late mother was a sweet, lovely soul."

"I see beauty and godliness in poetry." I tighten my grip on the arm-strap. "God gave me this brain that longs to create art."

"I know, my dear." Ma unfolds the handkerchief in her lap. "I don't believe Bishop Moore specifically spoke of your aspirations. You write of the stars in the heavens and the purity of love. Isn't there a holy friar in the first line of your poem 'Tamerlane'?"

I gaze out the carriage window at a drunkard staggering out of the Swan Tavern.

"Yes," I say, "there's a friar, but I don't believe Bishop Moore would like 'Tamerlane.'"

Ma emits a sudden cough that makes me jump. I watch her face redden as she draws a horrifying gasp that sounds like she's inhaling all the oxygen in the carriage, and then she bends forward at the waist and hacks into her handkerchief, her shoulders lurching, shuddering.

"Ma?" I place a hand on her back and endure the convulsions of her spine beneath my palm. "Do you want a doctor?"

She gasps again and forces herself upright by pushing one hand against the seat and using the other to grab the brass strap. "No, darling." Her eyes water and spill over. "I'm fine." She wipes her cheeks with the cloth. A troubling purple hue darkens her lips.

I dare a glance at her handkerchief, fearing the sight of blood—the telltale sign of tuberculosis—the disease that killed my mother.

The cloth looks clean. Thank God!

I hook an arm through hers and sicken with fear that she'll die while I'm away at the university. She pats my hand and bellows a low wheeze that fills my eyes with tears.

Ma and I enter the front doorway of our brick beast of a house.

Our *mansion*, to be precise.

Pa purchased this hilltop Camelot—named "Moldavia" by the original owners—just the summer before, after inheriting an obscene amount of money from his uncle William, who seized up and died one morning in the middle of tea and pancakes. We moved here from a smaller Richmond residence shortly after the purchase.

"Go wish a good morning to Pa," says Ma in the grand hall that amplifies the post-coughing croaks of her voice.

My throat tightens at her suggestion, and again I fuss with my cravat. My Adam's apple lodges above the knot, and for a moment I'm caught in a mad struggle to breathe.

"What are you doing, Edgar?" She pushes my hands away and reties the bow as though I'm still a child. Years of illness—as well as over two decades of marriage to an ass—have darkened the skin beneath her brown eyes and deepened the furrows of her forehead, and yet she's remained a handsome woman, despite all. Her mouth and nose are so petite, they make her husband's face look like an ogre's in comparison whenever his head hovers beside hers.

"I heard you two fighting again last night," she says.

I peer straight ahead without blinking. My arms hang by my sides, my shoulders stiff, the blades aching. I smell Pa's tobacco in every particle of air inside the house.

"Go wish him a good morning, Eddy." She fluffs the bow at my throat. "Set things right."

I swallow. "He accused me again of 'eating the bread of idleness.'"

"He's just urging you to fulfill your potential."

"That doesn't explain all the countless times he threatens to stop me from attending the university. I'm so close to leaving. So damn—"

"Edgar! The Sabbath."

"So *maddeningly* close."

Ma wraps her hands around my shoulders and leans toward me. "It's difficult for him to imagine you receiving the type of education his parents were never able to afford for him. He's giving you opportunities he only dreamed of for himself."

"Then why is he threatening to take it all away? Just look at this place he's put us in." I jerk my head toward the oil portraits glowering from the walls, the bronze statues, the monstrous furniture imported from Europe, the mahogany staircase that winds up to the second floor, where a mirrored, octagonal ballroom awaits. From inside the dining room down the grand hall, I hear the house servants—two of Pa's three slaves, the other being our aforementioned driver. They clank silverware against dishes and speak in low tones as they prepare the room for our Sunday dinner.

"How can he say he may not be able to afford my education," I ask, "when he's rolling around in piles of money? He's one of the richest men in Virginia right now."

"All he wants is for you to show him gratitude for what he's done for you. Please, go upstairs and wish him a good morning. Start the day together on a peaceful note." Ma smooths out the lapel of my coat. "For me."

"He keeps calling himself a 'self-made man.' What a laugh!"

"Go! We have family visiting later today. And Aunt Nancy will return from her visit to the countryside soon. I don't want tension in the house." She backs away two steps and folds her hands in front of the skirt of her gray dress, watching to see whether I'll obey.

I do, for her sake, not because I want to show any gratitude to Pa.

"*The gay wall of this gaudy tower,*" I say in my head during my climb up the winding staircase, my soles sinking against plush velvet runners, "*Grows dim around me—death is near.*"

I linger in the doorway, my fists clenched at my sides, feeling small and insignificant in this cold, garish tomb of a house. Near my right elbow, a bust of Pallas surveys the room from her post upon a marble pillar. A pair of medieval swords hang in a crossed position on the bricks of the fireplace, and above Pa's head, a Revolutionary War musket awaits further action in its wooden mounting on the wall, next to an anxious clock that ticks away the seconds.

"Good morning, Pa," I say, my voice shattering the near silence.

Only his eyes move, shifting in my direction. "How was church?"

I shrug. "Bishop Moore preached once more about God punishing Richmond through the fire."

"How is Ma's cough?"

"It worsened when we rode in the carriage through the snow. She sounds better now, though."

Pa nods with a grunt and returns his attention to his book. The echoes of our shouting match from the night before thrum across the walls, which, just like downstairs, house shadowy oil paintings from centuries past, as well as faded yellow tapestries that smell of dust and mildew. Pa is a ferocious consumer of art—a wolf that feasts on the carcasses of long-dead geniuses. And yet he calls me a disappointment whenever I insist of late that I aspire to make my living as an artist.

I turn to leave.

"Where are you going?" he asks, that Scottish brogue of his making it hard to tell whether his tone is stern or light.

"To my room."

"To write?"

My neck bristles. "I'm simply going to jot down two harmless little lines. They came to me during my climb up the stairs just now." I peek over my right shoulder to gauge his reaction. "I remember what you told me last night about my writing, but it's the revised opening couplet for the second stanza of 'Tamerlane.'"

He closes his eyes with a wince and a belch, as though "Tamerlane" just gave him indigestion.

"Well," I say, remembering Ma's request for peace, "good morning to you."

"You said the lines just came to you?" he asks before I slip away.

"Yes." I turn back around.

Pa sits perfectly still in his chair, but something about the way he's staring at me, his mouth pensive, his mind obviously churning, gives the impression that he's trembling. He lifts his chin with a stare so cold, so devoid of emotion, he injures me more than if he were yelling at me or whipping me.

This is precisely how John Allan keeps me in his clutches. All the pride he once showered upon me when I was his intelligent little pet with long ringlets—his wee, charming fellow, whom Ma dressed in bright yellow trousers and a purple jacket to show off to their friends—drains from his eyes. He glares at me with the contemptuous stare he's honed so well, as though I'm a stranger who's swindled him out of his happiness.

"I never asked for you to bring me into your life," I say.

Well, no, that's not true. I don't actually speak the words aloud. I long to remind him that he—a grown, free, relatively sharp-witted man—agreed to bring me into his home a month before my third birthday. And yet I don't.

"I used to be just like you, Edgar." He points at me with a long, crooked finger that rocks to and fro. "I believed myself a talented god—an artful wooer of women—who could seduce the world with language."

My father, I now realize, is already a tad drunk this fine February morning.

"Yes, I know," I say. "You've told me several times of your talent for writing. You were the next William Shakespeare."

"Just like you're the next Byron."

I respond with a smile to deflect the sting of his barb.

With a lazy, languid movement, Pa reaches out to a candle that burns in a pewter stick on the table beside him. He pinches the flame between his fingers and snuffs it out. The soft sizzle of protest, the sudden whiff of smoke, make me gasp. I recall Bishop Moore's warnings of muses inspiring us from firelight and shadows.

"What are the two new lines of 'Tamerlane'?" Pa then asks, which throws me completely off balance, and before I can even think to hesitate, I respond:

"'The gay wall of this gaudy tower/Grows dim around me—death is near.'"

Pa leans forward in his chair, his head tilted to his right, his elbows creaking against the armrests of his burgundy throne. His jaw waggles back and forth; he appears to swish my poetry around in his mouth and taste the flavor of every syllable and letter. His shaggy red eyebrows rise with interest, and for a moment I believe he might proclaim that he approves of the lines.

"Don't write them down," he says instead.

I blink, confused. "I beg your pardon?"

"We went over this very thing last night, Edgar. Quell the urge to compose these poems of yours. Snuff out your literary ambitions. Do something industrious for once in your life."

"I know you don't want me making a living as a writer, but why must you insist I refrain from at least enjoying the one thing that makes me happy in this wretched life of mine?"

"Oh, please." He huffs and leans back in his chair. "Stop your melodrama."

"It's not melodrama, Pa. It's the truth. I'm not happy unless I'm writing."

"I'm the one who'll be paying your expenses for the University of Virginia. I'm the one who's been pouring money into your future for years. I don't want to see you penning any more lines of poetry."

"But—"

"If I walk into your room later today and find that new couplet penned in fresh ink, you're through with your education. Do I make myself clear?"

My fists again clench. "I don't understand why we keep having this same fight."

"Because you're seventeen years old now. You can't keep wasting your time like this. I refuse to invest in expensive university tuition if you're planning to live the life of a pauper."

"You used to encourage me to write. When I attended Master Clarke's school, you sat beside me in front of his desk and laid out my poems in front of him. You asked if he thought they were good enough for publication."

"You were a child, Edgar. A clever child with a spark of talent, but you're not going to seem so clever and charming when you're a grown man falling behind on your bills."

"But—"

"You're a well-bred Southern gentleman, educated in both London and Richmond, for God's sake. Fight off the urge to write these terrible Byron imitations of yours before you turn into a sickly, filthy burden on society, just like your—"

The word he wants to say hangs in the air between us with a chilling weight.

He longs to compare me to my mother. My poor mother, Eliza Poe, who struggled to ensure that her young children would be sent to good homes as she withered on her death bed. A woman whom less-charitable snobs viewed as a whore because she trod the boards as a working actress.

My foster mother's footsteps whisper across the hall downstairs. She hears us, I'm certain of it. She tries to stifle a cough, but it erupts from her throat like the bark of a dog.

Pa inhales a long sniff through his cavernous nostrils and raises his book back in front of his face.

"Are you referring to my long-dead mother, Pa?" I ask, my chin lifted.

The book remains in place.

"Pa, are you insulting her memory?" I swallow. "On the Sabbath, no less?"

"Edgar!" calls Ma from the bottom of the staircase. "Go out to the kitchen and ask Judith and Jim if they have everything they need for Sunday dinner. They've just finished preparing the dining room."

"Ah, yes," I say as I back away from the Lord of the Manor. "I can see why I should strive to model myself after you, dear Pa. Such a fine, loving gentleman, faithful and utterly devoted to his family."

Pa lowers his book. "Do you want me to kick you out of the house this morning, boy?"

I freeze.

"I'm not legally bound to raise you, Edgar. Don't you ever forget that."

"How can I possibly forget when you constantly remind me?"

"If you don't want to find yourself homeless and penniless today, then shut your damn cocky mouth and show me respect. You're a charity case, and I've been generous enough to raise you like a prince."

I turn and escape down the hall, hurling my coat onto the table outside my room with a flutter of the flame in the agate lamp. I slam my door shut behind me, hard enough to rattle the books on my shelves, and I sequester myself inside my chamber—my library and sanctuary overlooking the Allan kingdom of orchards and terraced gardens that slope down into the fog of the James River valley.

I pull out my draft of "Tamerlane" and, with fresh ink and a goose-feather quill, I scribble down my new couplet, despite that man's threats and games.

The gay wall of this gaudy tower
Grows dim around me—death is near.

A log shifts in the hearth behind me. Startled, I turn around, fearing that Pa followed me into the room. The only movements I detect are the flames in the grate, as well as the dance of shadow and light the fire casts on the maroon fleur-de-lis of my wallpaper.

I turn back around, fetch a clean sheet of paper and a charcoal crayon, and expurgate myself of the restless abominations chewing on my soul by drawing a fiendish young woman in a black dress of mourning. I sketch long, snaking tendrils of ebony hair, smirking lips, a strong chin raised in defiance, and a pair of deep-set eyes that seem to tease: *I dare you to show me to the rest of the world. I dare you to show them your morbid fancies, Eddy Poe.*

The scent of smoke from my hearth—of ashes decomposing—sends me down once more into that basement crypt beneath Monumental Church, and I'm forced to remove my cravat to breathe.

My fantastic lady isn't wicked enough, I realize, and so, instead of adorning her throat with a necklace made of pearls, I draw for her a macabre piece of jewelry that inspires a pleased chuckle from the back of my throat: a necklace beaded with twelve perfectly white, utterly hideous human molars.

I rub a hand across my mouth and ponder what more fineries the lady requires, tasting a smudge of charcoal on my bottom lip.

Something scratches at the wall behind me.

Again, I jump.

Once more, I turn, and I freeze with fear, for the glow of the fire on the shadows of my wall seemingly wriggles and yawns into the shape of a mortal being who sways to the mesmerizing rhythm of the flames. At the center of the figure beats a tiny pulse of light.

A heart.

A silent, beating heart.

"No, that's madness," I whisper, and I return to my drawing, now appalled at what I've just sketched on the paper, my eyes locked on the string of teeth encircling the girl's neck.

What if Ma sees this? Or Elmira? So much horror. Oh, God, the attention—the fretting that would ensue!

Behind me, the lungs of the fire exhale a loud breath, perturbed by the wind stirring in the chimney—perturbed by *me,* perhaps. A sudden rain pelts my windows with a *tap-tap, tap-tap, tap-tap* that heightens my anxiety. The seething clouds in the sky extinguish the sunlight, and all four walls of my chamber reflect the orange of the flames—the radiant, wriggling orange of the flames.

I crumple the drawing into a ball, rise from my chair, and turn for the fire to burn this revolting excuse for art that's

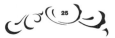

just oozed from my fingers, but my feet come to an abrupt halt.

I've just heard a voice.

A voice in my room—near the fire—just uttered four words:

"*Let. Them. See. Me.*"

I inch backward, my legs stiff, my head shaking in denial, and the small glow of light within the figure on my wall brightens and pulsates with the same *tap-tap, tap-tap, tap-tap* as the beats of the rain.

Tap-tap, tap-tap, tap-tap . . .

The drawing falls from my fingers, dropping to the floor. I clasp my hands beneath my chin, and instead of merely mouthing words of prayer, as I did in church, I call out in full voice, "'Our Father, who art in heaven, hallowed be thy name . . .'"

Another loud breath gusts from the flames, and to my horror—to my wonder—the wriggling reflection of a figure made of fire thickens, solidifies, and steps out of the wall. Yes! A girl in a dress made of soot and black feathers *climbs out of my wall!* Her narrow sleeves and skirts drip with shadows that plunk against the floorboards to the same anxious rhythm as the rain's *tap, tap, tapping.* Her eyes glimmer with firelight; her maroon lips match my wallpaper; her hair hangs to her waist in tangles of inky black curls. Her skin is the dismal gray of ashes, and I gulp in response to the sight of her nails—long, and hooked, and metallic.

My mouth falls open, and the trembling worsens. My pulse throbs inside my ears.

"I'm awfully hungry," says the girl in a low voice that vibrates with a sound like a cello. "I want more words. I want the attention and fretting you've just promised."

My legs weaken. I open my mouth but can't even shriek.

The creature saunters toward me on the hard soles of slippers carved out of charcoal, and with every clomp of her feet, my spine grows colder, colder, colder . . .

My eyes water.

I still can't speak.

She stops right in front of me, the shadows bleeding from her sleeves like gallons of black paint, staining my rug, and the smells of hot coals and charred wood engulf my nose. My knees fail me; my head dizzies. With a *thump*, I drop down to my chair, and the wickedest, the most brilliant lines of prose and verse hum inside my head.

The girl clasps my face in her hands, her palms fiery and firm, and she breathes down on me with a heat that singes the wiry little hairs inside my nostrils.

"Why are you shaking so much, Eddy?" she asks. Rings of fire radiate from her pupils, pulsating out to the edges of obsidian irises.

I squeeze my lips together to suppress the tremors in my chin. My eyes veer toward the necklace clasped around her throat, just inches from my face—a necklace strung with a collection of human teeth that clink together with each of her movements.

"Wh-wh-who are you?" I ask in a strained whisper that pains my tonsils.

"I've been with you for so long, Eddy," she says. "You know who I am."

I shake my head. "You can't be here."

"I'm hungry."

"No, you must leave! Pa could walk into this room at any minute."

"Why are you suddenly so afraid of me?" She cocks her head, and the fire in her eyes dims. "I've been with you every single time a macabre verse or a grotesque image flickers through your brain. I'm with you in graveyards and during bleak midnight—"

"You can't be here!" I grab her wrists and fight to pull her hands off my face. "I'm so close to escaping this place. Please! Get out!"

Her fingers squeeze down on my cheekbones. "At the very least write down my name."

"You have no name. Please, for the love of God! Leave!"

She bends closer, and those teeth at her neck again clatter together. "Don't leave me standing here as a nameless creature, Edgar. I might be able to pass myself off as a decent muse if you christen me with a poetic appellation that falls from the tongue like satin." She glances at the goose-feather quill resting in my brass inkstand, revealing the profile of her aquiline nose—a nose curved into the shape of a beak, even more so than Pa's hawkish proboscis.

"Give me a name that means 'light,' not shadow," she says, "and we may be able to show them there's beauty in horror."

She drops her hands from my face and steps two feet away.

I touch my cheeks, for they now itch like mad. A chalky film of soot coats the tips of my fingers.

The girl fetches my charcoal drawing from the floor, lays it out on the desk beside me, and, with a slap of her left palm against the paper, she says, "Name me."

I scoot around to face my desk, wiping sweat from my brow with the back of my right sleeve. *Naming her might chase her away,* I reason. *If all she wants is a name, then give it to her. For heaven's sake! Give it to her!*

My hand shakes when I slide the gray quill from my inkstand.

"Edgar Poe," she says so softly, and I peer at her once more. "Bestow on me a name that they shall sing forevermore."

Hearing this, I write:

Lenore

Someone raps upon my door.

I leap up from my chair. "It's Pa!"

"Are you certain?"

"Leave!" I grab her by the arms and shove her toward the door that leads from my bedroom out to the upper level of Moldavia's double portico. "Get out!" I swing the door open. "Don't ruin my chances for the university. Please! Go hide somewhere. Disappear!" I push her outside and hear the swish and rustle of all the feathers flocking her skirt. "He'll kill you if you stay!"

I slam the door shut, bolt the latch, and pull the purple curtains shut to stop seeing her stunned black eyes peering in through the glass.

Ma opens the main bedroom door. "Edgar?" she asks. "Were you just shouting?"

I wipe more soot off my cheeks and clear my throat. "I'm sorry. I'm ... um ... I lost my temper over Pa's latest insults and abuses."

Ma stands in my doorway with one hand on the latch, the other at her breast. The sadness elongating her eyes, the redness of her nose that betrays recent tears, pains me to no end, and yet I don't want her lingering here inside my chamber, hearing any sounds that might arise from that ... *creature* I've just thrown outside.

"Where's Pa?" I ask, moving away from the back door, even though I feel the curtains looming behind me.

Ma drops her hand from her chest. "He just stepped out."

My heart jumps into my throat. "He's ... Pa? ... P-P-Pa's somewhere outside?"

"Yes. He went into town."

We lock eyes. Pa's escapes into town typically mean he's visiting his newest mistress, the widow Elizabeth Wills—and yet that disgusting possibility isn't the predicament that horrifies me at present.

He'll see what just emerged from my room.

He'll see her. *Dear God, he'll see my demon muse!*

I wheel around and yank open the curtains, hoping to pull the wraith back inside, to hide her somewhere in the house.

But she's gone.

CHAPTER FOUR

Lenore

Ahhh . . . the sight of my name branded in ink in the whimsical loops of my poet's handwriting has quickened the blood in this odd new body of mine. Down on the snow-covered streets of the city, surges of ecstasy careen through my soul—my flourishing, strengthening soul, stifled no more. I spread out my arms, and my eyes flutter closed at the pleasurable thickening of my bones, my muscles, my organs, my skin . . . My fingernails harden, my lungs swell with air, and the shadows cease dripping from my sleeves.

I smooth out the feathers lining my skirt and say with a pleased sigh, "Let them see me!"

Off I then traipse to a section of the city where clusters of chimneys pipe thick plumes of smoke into the steely winter sky—where brooding brick mansions and acres of land give way to smaller homes built of wood, butted together on streets down the hill from the neoclassical columns of the state capitol building.

A chorus of church bells peals to the north and the east—a clanging commotion I don't care for in the slightest, for it reminds me of that white-haired bishop's pontifications. My shoulders jerk at each bong.

Si. Lence. Your. Mu. Ses!

Si. Lence. Your. Mu. Ses!

A one-horse carriage rolls toward me, its driver an older man with the face of a prune who shrinks down in his seat when he spies me wandering toward him.

"Aha!" I shout, and I raise the hem of my skirt to better clamber through the snow. "You look like you're close to meeting my old friend Death, sir! Not much longer until that rickety heart of yours stops ticking and you slide feetfirst into your grave!"

His eyes bulge from their sockets. "W-w-what did you just say?"

I smile, warmed by his terror. "I said, not much longer until Death fetches you from the comforts of your bed and sends you down into the cold red clay of the Richmond earth!"

The man tightens the reins and sends his horse galloping away with a whistling wind that tousles my hair.

A black cat leaps over a brick garden wall and stops in my path. With piercing green eyes like the two pools of Hades, the beast traps me in a stare that congeals the new blood in my veins.

"What is *that?*" I hear a woman ask from the house connected to the garden wall, and I assume she must mean this foul feline.

The beast arches its back, its ebon hair standing on end, and it hisses with a show of needle-sharp fangs.

I bare my own teeth and hiss back with a breath that sends the cat rolling over, mewling with the cries of a frightened kitten. It then bolts across the street on a blur of dark legs, and I lean forward and shriek from the depths of my belly to ensure that the scoundrel never crosses my path again.

"Oh, God! What is it?" asks the woman again, and I look up to discover small gatherings of men, women, and children—mortals with complexions of black, white, brown,

and pink—huddled together on the stoops and porches surrounding me. The woman speaks of me, I realize. I'm the
dreaded "it."

Everyone watches me, judging me, wondering what I
am, their mouths agape, arms corded around each other.
Again, I lift the hem of my skirt to keep the soot-powdered
fabric from dragging in the snow, and I rotate around for
all to view me, proud of the purple-and-green iridescence
of the feathers on my skirt—impressed with the ability of
my slippers to smear smudges of charcoal across the virgin
white powder.

As I turn I call out:

Beware, a maiden unrefined,
Leapt out from a darkened mind,
Lo! She sees yon gawking faces,
Feed her fear, not charming graces,
Watch her!—creeping, sweeping o'er,
Reaping rhymes of death and horror!

"Who brought this grotesque girl into the city?" shouts a
man from behind me, and I whirl around in his direction.

The Right Reverend Bishop Moore plods toward me in
the snow, his thin strands of white hair blowing against the
shoulders of a gray woolen cloak, a rust-colored scarf coiled
around his neck. A breeze ushers the musty smell of his
church ahead of him.

He balls his gloved fists by his sides and tromps toward
me as though he aims to knock me down. "Who is responsible for her?"

"Come inside," says a mother in a house on the corner up
ahead, dragging her children indoors. "This is far too horrible
for you to see."

"This is all in bad taste!" calls a man from an upstairs window. "We don't tolerate anything bizarre here in Richmond.

And on a Sunday, no less." He swings his shutters closed with a *thwack* that makes me flinch.

"Shall I fetch my musket?" asks the woman at the house beside me, and I notice she's a sturdy specimen of the human race with broad shoulders, massy hands, and shrewd-looking eyes that might excel at focusing on a moving target.

"Whose trick of sorcery are you?" asks the bishop, stomping closer, his voice echoing across the houses. "Did the devil send you?"

I lean forward, my hands clenched on my skirts, and respond with another howl that could summon the dead. Ha! I hope it summons the dead!

Something explodes nearby, and an object whizzes past my right arm with a scream of hot air. I stumble backward, the world brightening, loudening for a dizzying moment, and a metallic taste scours my tongue. When I come to my senses, I find the source of the attack: across the street stands a man in a dun-colored hat who holds a smoking pistol.

"Did you just try to shoot me?" I shout at him.

The fellow doesn't respond. Doors slam shut around me.

I march toward the assassin. "I said, did you just try to shoot me?"

He shuffles backward in the snow, slipping for a moment, his hat sliding down his forehead, then he breaks into a run in an eastward direction. I tear after him, but another gunshot rings out from behind. I dive to the snow, swallowing a mouthful of slush, and the woman who threatened to fetch her musket says, "I almost hit the demon!"

"Leave this city!" calls the bishop. "I don't know who summoned you or what you are, but someone will pay for this egregious sin. Richmond is no playground for devilry!"

Someone throws a stone at the back of my head. My eyes sting with tears. These fools aren't simply frightened—they're violent.

I push myself to my feet and run northward to a place I know well—the Burying Ground on Shockoe Hill—that city of the dead high on the crown of Richmond.

CHAPTER FIVE

Edgar

A path of charcoal footprints leads away from Moldavia, starting in a drift of snow piled next to the northeastern corner of the portico, below my room. I stuff my drawing of Lenore into my breast pocket, grab a spade from the toolshed, and bury her tracks beneath heaping scoops of fresh powder, fearing that Pa will trace the dirty prints back to my chamber—fretting that all of Richmond will know what I've released.

An explosion, like the firing of a pistol, ricochets across the city. I flinch, and then a second blast rings out from the same easterly direction.

It can't be! I keep shoveling. *No! That had nothing to do with that phantasm from my room prowling the streets—or Pa witnessing her out there.*

Perspiration drips from my pores, despite the freezing air. My heart pounds. My arms ache. Too many months have passed since I've had opportunities to run, swim, and box, to exercise my muscles and my lungs—and yet, despite the discomforts of my frantic shoveling, I focus my attention on the University of Virginia, waiting ahead, almost within reach.

Bury this evidence of your macabre fancies, I tell myself with each scoop, *and by early next week you'll be living a three-day's journey away from Pa and the Castle Moldavia, immersing yourself in ancient tomes, feasting on historical research for the epic poem that will inspire everyone to finally appreciate you: "Tamerlane."*

Lenore's footprints journey out to the main street of Richmond and travel into the heart of the city. I cringe at the thought of shoveling snow for the next eight to ten blocks and abandon my spade in our vegetable garden.

Using only my feet, I kick away the charcoal tracks until I reach Seventh, where I realize how suspicious this all must look: that eccentric Edgar Poe, son of strolling players, amateur thespian, writer and reciter of poetry, covering the marks of his guilt in the middle of the street for all to see.

I shove my hands into my pockets and walk like a normal human being—not a desperate, murderous fiend. I'm aware of the cacophony of my boots crunching across the snow and the clangs of a bell on a steamer in the James, but my ears strain to hear any cry or howl that might reveal the location of Lenore. A pall of chimney smoke drapes the city, bleeding into a fogbank that drifts up from the river in a chilling shroud of mist that soon wracks me with shivers. The farther I stalk through the neighborhood, the more the smoke builds inside my nose, and I worry I may be smelling *her.*

"Eddy!" calls my sister, Rosalie, from behind me—a sister I scarcely ever see, even though she lives a mere block from me at Miss Mackenzie's boarding school. The Mackenzie family took Rose in when she was a one-year-old babe in arms, back when the Allans staked their claim over me. And our older brother, Henry—a seldom-seen shadow—has lived in Baltimore with our Poe grandparents ever since our parents left him there as an infant.

This is what happens when artists follow their muses, I think as I observe the approach of my sister—a girl who resembles me in coloring and facial features, from her large gray eyes to her broad moon of a forehead. *Families get torn asunder. Siblings grow up as strangers. Children are forced to rely on the charity of people who may choose to throw them out on the streets when the sweetness of youth sours.*

I shake off this thought with a shudder, shocked at the sudden doubts about my future as an artist—knowing it's Pa talking, not I.

Rose strolls close enough for me to see that she's carrying a pair of ladies' walking boots and a blanket, both an unremarkable shade of brown, similar to the coloring of our hair. Both items are frayed at the seams and obviously well worn.

"Did you hear about the girl?" she asks.

My back muscles tense. "What girl?"

"One of my schoolmates just returned from church with her mother and said she witnessed a fantastic creature—a girl made of ash and raven feathers—tromping and shrieking through the snow. Everyone thought she was a demon. Two people fired at her with weapons."

My legs buckle, but I hold my arms out to my sides to avoid swooning. "They—they fired at her? Did they hit her?"

"No. She ran off. Do you think she might be a muse?"

"W-w-why do you ask?"

"I believe I've had muses of my own slip into the world like weird and wondrous demons. Mary said the girl seemed dangerous. A bit silly, too—but terribly dangerous."

"*Silly?*" I ask.

"Mary said that the girl spoke some sickly rhymes that weren't very good."

I wince and cover my mouth with both hands, mortified at the city's reaction to Lenore.

"What's wrong?" asks Rose.

"Have you seen John Allan anywhere out here?"

She shakes her head. "I just snuck out to leave shoes for the girl, so she won't keep making these charcoal tracks. I worried she might be your muse."

I snort at her assumption and scratch the back of my neck. "I write of romance and epic adventures, Rose. If a muse of mine were to step into the world, it would appear in the elegant form of Calliope, a writing tablet in hand."

Rose frowns. "I know what it's like to be haunted by dark muses, Edgar. My life began in the same manner as yours, remember?"

"I'm not haunted by dark—"

"I try to write poetry," she says, "just like you and Henry, but I don't always feel clever enough. Sometimes I wonder if my muses of poetry once stepped out of the shadows of the boarding school walls, and one of the other girls poisoned them out of fear or jealousy. I imagine them as twins—neither boy nor girl, but something in between—and I think someone poisoned them. I truly do."

My forehead creases at her ramblings; her odd theories—even though, considering the feverish spell of the morning, I think I might believe her.

"John Allan won't let me leave for Charlottesville if I keep writing, so please"—I grab her arms and lower my voice—"please, Rose, don't speculate in front of anyone else that this vision has anything to do with me."

"Do you want to help me deliver these shoes to her?" She lifts the walking boots, which tap together at the heels.

I swallow my frustrations. "I told you, John Allan can't see me searching for her."

"The very least you can do is ensure that no one will hurt her."

"If I can only make it to college, everything will be fine. This will all be fine. No one has witnessed me with her. I'm certain of it . . ."

"Our mother wouldn't approve of you abandoning your poetry." Rose casts a sidelong glance that cuts me to the quick. "Would she?"

"Rose!" I drop my hands from her arms. "What a cruel, unfeeling thing to say!"

"Our mother chased her muse all the way to America from England. And our father gave up his future as a lawyer to follow both Mother and his muse onto the stage."

I brace a hand against my stomach. "I'm not abandoning my muse *or* my poetry. I'm protecting them. I'm ensuring that Pa doesn't see what's spilled from the depths of my depraved brain."

"Come along!" Rose hurries down the path of charcoal, the shoes and blanket bouncing in her arms. "Before John Allan spies her tracks!"

"Oh, God." I groan, for I know she's right—Lenore's prints might lead him to her.

I trail after my sister, my head dizzy, my ears alert for the scraping or squishing of footsteps following behind us in the snow.

The black tracks cease to exist twelve feet away from the tombstones and evergreens of the Burying Ground on Shockoe Hill, a rural field of mourning at the crest of the city, near the poorhouse and the Hebrew graveyard. To my left lies a pair of charcoal slippers, clearly kicked off in haste. Clean prints in the snow reveal Lenore's continued travels—possibly on bare feet—into the hallowed grounds. My toes freeze just from thinking about walking through the powdered ice without the protection of shoes.

"Do you think she's crouching behind one of the stones in there?" asks Rose with a swallow.

I can't answer. An intolerable sadness has just stolen the breath from my lungs, for I know this graveyard all too well.

I stood amid those very tombstones nearly two years earlier, clinging to my friend Rob Stanard, watching a half-dozen men in stovepipe hats feed his mother's casket down into the gaping maw of the earth. The dankness of the soil, the preternatural chill emanating from the hole where they placed that angelic woman, the mourners clad in black like ominous crows, the painful shrinking of my windpipe—every suffocating second of that morning haunts me whenever I wander up this hill. Jane Stanard—my *Helen*, as I call her in my mind—never disparaged my mother for her profession. She never told me my poems were anything less than exceptional. She wouldn't loathe my muse or call her "silly."

A flutter in my heart tells me that Lenore hides behind Mrs. Stanard's grave. In my bones, I know I've fallen under the spell of my dark muse more than once in this field before, when I've held vigils for my Helen with her son—when Lenore dwelled inside the Burying Ground's shadows, supping on the marrow of my melancholy.

"Stay here until I'm safely at the university, Lenore!" I call toward the stones—keeping my distance from them. "Don't come near me. Stay hidden. And don't wear those shoes ever again. My sister brought you a pair that won't leave behind a carbon trail."

At first, we hear not a sound in response. A light wind breathes against my neck, above the back of my stiff collar.

But then a low bellow, like the growls of Cerberus, emanates from somewhere behind the stone markers. Rosalie glances my way, her face pallid, her eyes wide, and my breath leaves my lips as a weak shudder.

"Toss them," I say. "Toss them quickly!"

Rose throws the blanket and boots toward the graveyard, and we turn away and run.

CHAPTER SIX

Lenore

My poet called me by that name.

Lenore.

The name of light he bestowed upon me.

Lenore.

My name forevermore.

I feel almost human—almost wanted—and valued. But then the rest of his words seep into my brain with the sizzling sting of acid.

"Don't come near me!" he yelled.

Don't!

Don't!

DON'T!

I crouch down behind my favorite stone in this city of sleeping souls and growl from the back of my throat with a satisfying rumble that vibrates through the trees and the family plots.

The Poe siblings fly away across the snow, repulsed. Horrified.

"I'm not meant to be hidden, Edgar Poe!" I scream after him, clinging to his darling Jane Stanard's monument with the uncapped urn. "Let them see me, you coward!"

An object of some sort now lies in a heap beyond the graveyard's boundary.

A pile of fabric, dark chestnut in hue.

A sniff of the air assures me that the grounds are free of any whiffs of gunpowder or malice. No one crouches in the evergreens, poised to shoot me.

For luck, I kiss the tombstone and inhale the rose-tinged perfume that drifts from the spirit of Eddy's "Helen." I hope her protectiveness toward him extends to me. His grief for this woman burns in the center of my charcoal heart, as it has for years.

With jarring creaks in the joints of my human ankles, I creep around the tombstone and slink toward the Poe siblings' offering on the soaked feet of my stockings, which match the maroon hue of my poet's chamber walls.

They've left me a cotton blanket and a pair of boots with scarlet socks stuffed beneath the tongues. I sift through the items, in search of a poem or a drawing—*anything* to appease the hunger now hissing inside my belly—but all I touch and see are sublunary nothings composed of leather, wool, and cotton. The boots reek of perspiration. The socks require darning in both heels. Yet I plop down on my rump in the snow and pull the coverings over my feet, relieved by the embrace of warmth around my soles and ankles. I wrap the blanket around my shoulders and cast my eyes toward a fogbank rolling toward me.

A line from Shakespeare's *Macbeth* tumbles from my lips:

"By the pricking of my thumbs,
Something wicked this way comes."

I draw a breath and brace for the chill and the sonorous wind.

A twig snaps.

I jump to my feet, the blanket spilling from my shoulders, and spy a man in a forest-green coat and an umber hat watching me from the fog, several yards away. I can't quite see his eyes beneath the shadow of the hat's brim, but he's just standing there, staring at me, his mouth stretched into a taut line of concern, shoulders hiked. I don't detect any hate emanating from his direction, and yet his presence—his sudden manifestation in the murk—makes my heart give a shudder.

The fog drifts across the gentleman, who, from behind that misty, meandering curtain has acquired a sudden, certain look of a spirit come to warn me of some fast-approaching horror. *Ah*, a luscious rush of shivers chills my spine with thrilling quivers; the small fright this man delivers piques my interest to learn more.

"Show yourself, sir," I implore.

He ambles my way, emerging from the fog with a slight limp that strikes me as familiar. I shrink back, now recognizing the approaching face—the hawkish eyes, the curved nose, the enormous chin punctuating an unfathomably long head. He removes his hat to reveal a whitening crown of coarse red curls.

John Allan.

"I followed your footprints up here," he says in the same deep Scottish brogue he uses to roar at my poet, and it stirs up a tempest of hate and sorrow inside me.

I trip backward over a tree root and take shelter behind a pillar of stone a foot taller than I.

The soles of John Allan's boots grind across the snow, and he asks, in a voice that quavers with an unexpected tremble of emotion, "Cassandra?"

Baffled, I peek around the stone at him.

He steps closer, struggling to clamber over the mounds of powder and ice piled around the graves. "Do you remember me?"

Has he mistaken me for someone else? I wonder. Has he not come to strangle me?

With the brim of his hat pressed against his chest, he stands before me and tilts his head to his right, evaluating my face, which I pray resembles Cassandra's.

"I heard about the sighting of a bizarre young woman down there in the city," he says, his voice breathy, tremulous. "They said she appeared to have sprung straight out of the embers of Hell. I wondered if it might be you—if your appearance had altered after what I did all those years ago. Do you . . ." He rests his hat against his right hip and leans against his good leg. "Do you remember me, Cassandra?"

Knowing it wisest to play along, I ask, "Jock?"—uttering the nickname I've heard his wife and friends call him within the walls of Moldavia.

"*Och!* You do remember!" He smiles and inches closer. "I've often looked for you—even though I've known I shouldn't. I offer my humblest apologies, Cassandra." He bows his head, crinkles his eyes shut, and sniffs with a liquidity that suggests he might drop to his knees and bawl. "Don't think I don't remember your screams when I pushed you into that hearth . . ."

I back away.

"I'm sorry." He edges closer. "I was young. I needed to focus on my work. You were a distraction. A chimera. A dangerous dream."

"I don't thrive on apologies, Jock. Art nourishes me—not guilt." Imagining those hands of his forcing his muse into flames, I leap onto a sarcophagus and call down to him,

"Give me poetry, John Allan! *Now*—before I frighten you so horrifically, I stop that cruel heart of yours from beating."

He wipes his eyes with the back of a sleeve and coughs up two lines of a sonnet:

"*When forty winters shall besiege thy brow,*
And dig deep trenches in thy beauty's field—"

"That's Shakespeare's 'Sonnet 2,' you dirty plagiarist. Give me an original composition, and hurry!" I claw at my stomach, my nails ripping at my dress. "I'm famished!"

He tugs at his collar and squeaks out another attempt at versification:

"*The gay wall of this gaudy tower*
Grows dim around me—death is near."

My face sobers. I jump off the stone and glare at this thief of words.

"That's Poe," I say.

He blinks, clearly startled. "What name did you just say?"

"Poe." The word leaves my rounded lips as a puff of air that makes him blink again and tilts him backward. "Edgar Allan Poe."

John Allan's mouth hardens. "How do you know about Edgar and his poems?"

"I've been watching you from the shadows, Jock." I raise my chin, which I point at him like an accusatory finger. "You're a jealous man. An unkind man. You long to kill another muse—*his* muse—but you shall rue the day you do, for I will ensure, with every ounce of power I possess, that your name goes down in history as the man who harmed and hindered a haunted young genius."

He lowers his face and fusses with his hat. "I will not apologize for the way I choose to raise Edgar."

"Take me to your house for supper. Invite me in. Prove to me you're not an enemy of art."

He grimaces. "I can't do that."

"Why not?"

"You would frighten my wife. She's not well. She wouldn't ..." He inches backward and surveys me from the roots of my midnight hair down to the toes of my borrowed boots. "You're much more unsettling than I remember, Cassandra. Much more shrewish and appalling."

I ball my hands into fists. "What do you expect when you push muses into fires?"

"I already apologized for my behavior." He shoves his hat back on his head. "I'll leave a poem for you later, but only if you inspire *me*, not him. Don't you dare cast an eye toward that ill-tempered thorn in my side. He's been nothing but a damn sulky nuisance for the past two years. I can't wait to be rid of him."

"Bring me one of *his* poems for dessert," I say, and my mouth waters to such excess, a thread of drool spills down my chin.

John Allan winces. "I don't need you badly enough to permit him to write. In fact, never mind about the poems. I want nothing more to do with you."

"If that were true, if you didn't crave poetical inspiration as much as you desire the air you breathe, you wouldn't have groveled and sniveled when you first saw me just now"—I lean forward and deepen my voice to the depths of the lowest bass—"*Jock.*"

An audible gulp slides down his throat, and I witness the shine of horror in his eyes. He turns on his heel and hustles away into the fog as fast as he can, but, thank God, he does not kill me.

CHAPTER SEVEN

Edgar

I splash my hair with water from the ivory basin in my bedroom and attempt to tame my curls with a comb. I'm still breathless from my flight through the city; still dizzy from Lenore. My entire body trembles with a dire need to visit Elmira—to embrace life instead of shadows.

My mirror reflects my agitated state. The grayish eyes that women call "beautiful" and "stirring" strike me as pale and protruding this afternoon. They look like they've witnessed a murder.

"My God, you need to leave Richmond," I whisper to myself, and I scoop water into my mouth to calm my parched throat.

I fetch my gift for Elmira—a purse that the clerk at the shop sealed up in brown wrapping paper and tied with a blue satin ribbon. After bidding Ma adieu, I cross the street to the Roysters' residence—another brick behemoth that occupies an entire city block. Shutters as black and as glossy as granite frame the dozen windows monitoring my approach. Twin pairs of Ionic columns cast their shadows upon me during my climb up the steps to the mahogany front door.

I hold my breath and clang the iron knocker.

One of the Roysters' house slaves, a fellow not much older than I named Arthur, allows me to enter, takes my hat, and escorts me to Elmira and her mother in the reception room with its scarlet walls that squeeze around me like the chambers of a heart. Oil lamps with crystal icicles flicker in silence against the blood-red paper, giving the distinct impression of pulsations. A fire roars in the hearth. Perspiration puddles on my forehead. My eyes stray to the windows, fearful of the return of Lenore, but I force myself to think of only love and goodness.

Elmira alleviates my anxiousness by saying in that rich voice of hers, "Good afternoon, Edgar."

I sit down beside her on the sofa, cradling her gift in my lap. "Good afternoon, Elmira . . . and Mrs. Royster."

Elmira's mother—a paler, older, blond-haired version of her daughter—mutters a listless welcome from a high-backed chair across from us, the family terrier tucked beneath a tartan blanket in her lap. A red rug lies unfurled like a tongue between my shoes and Mrs. Royster's slippers, and I notice that she slides her feet beneath her chair, pulling herself farther away from me.

This cold reception has nothing to do with the manifestation of Lenore in the city. I often find myself wondering, while seated in the houses of friends and sweethearts, if a low-born odor wafts off me, despite the expensive wool of my coat, the embroidered silk of my vest, the impeccable straightness of my posture. Pa paid for me to attend the finest schools for young gentlemen in both Richmond and London. I speak Latin and French, I've been celebrated for swimming six miles in the James River—*against* the tide—at the mere age of fifteen, and I live in a damned mansion, but nothing I do or say will ever erase the stink of poverty these people smell on me.

"So . . ." I clear my throat and hand Elmira the present. "As I mentioned before, I have a gift for you."

"How thoughtful and sweet you are, Eddy." Elmira smiles and shakes the package near her ear. "Hmm—it doesn't rattle enough to sound like a box of candies, and yet it's heavier than a garment . . ."

"Family will be arriving soon, Elmira," says Mrs. Royster. "Please open the package without turning the process into a charade." She pets the terrier's head with firm strokes that stretch the poor dog's eyes into the back of his head.

Elmira lowers the gift to her lap and unties the ribbon, her face bright with anticipation.

My chest suddenly tightens with a fit of panic and self-loathing. Just like at home, I'm surrounded by statues, tapestries, fabrics, fripperies, and furniture hauled out of chalets and castles halfway across the world—luxuries I'll never be able to afford for a wife.

Elmira sets the ribbon aside and unpeels the brown paper. She doesn't notice the way my breath catches in my throat.

I want to marry this girl, but, my God, Pa is right: I *will* struggle to pay bills if I pursue the life of a poet. I'll drag her down into the mire of my abominable penury. Like the father who sired me, the two-bit actor David Poe, I'll turn to drink to survive the pain of watching my life descend into squalor. I'll abandon my darling to the clutches of death while offering my entire soul to my muse—while drowning myself in whiskey and wine until I die.

"Oh, how lovely," says Elmira, and she lifts the mother-of-pearl purse out of the wrappings. "Oh, Eddy! It's beautiful. And what is this?" She leans forward and reads the silver plate mounted on the front. "It's engraved with our initials . . . or . . ."

I blush and squirm, for there's been a mistake with the engraving.

Elmira lifts her face. "Why does it say 'S.P.R.' instead of 'S.E.R.'?"

I fold my hands in my lap and fight off the urge to shrink down into the sofa's velvet cushions. "The engraver made a mistake."

"You weren't intending to give this purse to another girl, were you?" asks Mrs. Royster.

"No! Of course not. He made a mistake. I specifically told him our initials were 'S.E.R.' and 'E.A.P.' I must beg your forgiveness, Elmira. Do you want me to return it?"

(I do not mention that Pa has already refused to pay for the remediation of the error.)

"No, it's still beautiful," says this charming angel. "I'll just pretend it's an E."

Mrs. Royster lowers the dog to the floor. "As I said, the family will arrive for Sunday dinner soon. Time to see Edgar off."

Elmira reaches her hand out to me across the sofa, but her mother's gaze stops me from touching her fingers.

"I intend to study diligently at the University of Virginia and return a success," I say to remind them both that I'm a serious candidate for marriage. To remind myself. The statement sounds rehearsed and forced, even to me.

Mrs. Royster rises to her feet, casting the blanket aside, and states once again, "Family is coming."

"I'll walk Edgar to the door."

"You need to change into your other dress."

"I'll only be a minute, Mother."

Before Mrs. Royster can balk any further, Elmira walks me out to the grand hall. The soles of our shoes clap against the floorboards in unison, and the backs of our wrists brush against each other, but we don't dare hold hands.

"I've been thinking of what you said to me in church," she says in a whisper near the front door.

My heart leaps. "You have?"

With a lift of her slender eyebrows, she casts a glance back toward the reception room. Before I can even blink, she pulls me out to the front stoop and swings the door shut behind us.

"Will you meet me in the garden before you leave for Charlottesville, Eddy?"

"Yes, of course. Will you give me your answer there?"

She slides her fingers around the lapel of my coat and leans her lips close to mine, her breath deliriously sweet and warm. "If I engage myself to you, it would need to be in secret."

For a moment I can't articulate any words—I'm too spellbound by her nearness to even breathe—but, somehow, I manage to say with a stammer, "You're—you're considering my proposal, then?"

She nods and smiles.

I cup my hands around her face and kiss her lips—those soft and gentle rose-petal lips that melt my legs into a pool of wax. Warm little breaths flutter through her nose, and I can't help but sigh against her. We come up for air, and she clasps me to her breast, clinging to the back of my coat. I bury my nose into her neck, inhale her luscious lilac scent, and allow the tip of my tongue to taste her bare skin.

The door opens.

We untangle in an instant.

Mrs. Royster's forehead furrows into a geological marvel of crevices and peaks.

She hands me my hat. "Go home, Edgar."

"Yes, ma'am. Good afternoon, ladies," I say in my finest Virginian drawl, and I scramble down the front steps.

Upon my return to the front drive of Moldavia, a gust of cold air knocks the hat off my head. I bend down to fetch it and detect a strange acridity in the wind.

The ripe pungency of damp earth.

The smell of an open grave up in the Burying Ground.

My heart hasn't yet calmed from Elmira, but now it pounds with a thunderous rhythm.

I stand back up, and against the bleak clouds, Moldavia degenerates into a frail and decrepit shade of its former self. The red bricks fade to gray. The mortar binding them together greens with a film of moss and slime. The white paint of the pillars of the double portico brown up like roasted apples, and I can hear the wood creaking and straining as the columns fight to bear the weight of the house's sagging bones.

I clutch my hat by my side and jog up to the front door before a voice that vibrates with the notes of a cello can call out from behind, *Let them see me!*

Inside the house, instead of my macabre muse, I'm welcomed by the dulcet tones of Aunt Nancy, Ma's sister, conversing with Ma in the reception room to my right. My posture relaxes, and my stomach settles, for the presence of women—mortal, living women who care for me, despite who I am—always soothes my soul like a balm.

At three o'clock, I embark upon a feast beneath the bright Argand oil lamps of Moldavia's dining room with Ma, Pa, Aunt Nancy, and our guests: the late Uncle William's adopted, grown children—William Jr. and James—and William Jr.'s new golden-haired wife, Rosanna. We dine on barley soup, Virginia ham, chicken pudding, peas Francoise, roots a la crème, candied sweet potatoes, puff pastry, fruit, wine, and port.

"Did you hear about the disturbance in town earlier today?" asks William.

I try not to drop my fork.

Ma pales and asks, "A disturbance?"

Pa slices his ham with his eyes fixed upon the meat. "What disturbance might that be?"

"A frightful girl," says William. "Well, not precisely a girl—a ghost, or a madwoman, or a dark harbinger of evil—ran about town, threatening residents with some sort of execrably bad jingle."

Pa's own fork clangs against his plate. "'Execrably bad'?" he asks. "How do you mean?"

I lift my face toward him, wondering why it's the criticism of the poem that worries him about Lenore.

"I don't know," says William, dabbing his face with a napkin. "I simply heard she was both a horrifying spirit and a facile rhymester. The night watchman proclaimed that he'll be walking the streets tonight with bloodhounds and a fellow sentinel, armed with a musket."

"Lock your doors, Jock," says William's younger brother, James, with a low chuckle. "We all know about this sensitive poet over here." He nudges my foot under the table. "We wouldn't want him to fall under the influence of a Gothic muse, if that's what this rhymester was. I heard that Bishop Moore preached against muses just this morning."

"Don't be foolish," says Aunt Nancy. "Who ever heard of a muse running around for all to see?"

"Precisely," says Pa, still sawing at his ham.

William lifts his glass of port and asks, "What have you written lately, Edgar?"

I don't say a word in response—not a word.

"Edgar has put his poems aside," says Pa. "He leaves for the University of Virginia at the end of the week and will cast off such nonsense henceforth. Although I still believe the tobacco business is the route he ought to take instead of the university. I could use him in the counting room while we dissolve Ellis & Allan."

"I've heard you write lovely love poems, Edgar," says Rosanna—another sweet balm to the sting of this house, and I can't help but notice how much the curve of her neck resembles Elmira's.

To *her* I speak: "Thank you, ma'am. That's kind of you to say."

Pa steers the conversation toward the dissolution of his partnership—the most boring and banal topic in the entire history of dinner conversations.

My gaze strays toward the branches of the trees, sleeved in snow, rustling outside the windows. My eyes relax into a lull, and my mind again swims toward rhymes of death and sorrow, of red lips and deep blue eyes like those of Elmira and Rosanna, sealed beneath the lid of a coffin. I tip toward the brink of summoning that "Gothic muse," until Ma breaks into another fit of coughing beside me.

After dinner, we retire to the reception room overlooking the James for music at the piano and more drinking. I hear the low tones of the darkness stealing over the horizon, as I tend to do in the evenings—a foolish fancy, perhaps, but it's what I hear.

Before he settles into a chair, Pa claps a hand on my left shoulder, pulls his pipe from his mouth with a fleshy sound, and leans close to my ear, his breath sour and wretched.

"I need to speak to you after the guests leave," he says, and his words settle into my bones, where they chill and writhe.

"Yes, sir," I say, for Ma sits nearby.

I long to take a swig of the wine that's making its way around the room—the smell of it burns across the air with an incendiary sweetness that tempts—but alcohol, even in small doses, affects me more than it does other people. I can't bear the thought of falling into a stupor in front of the entire family, especially Rosanna, who's just smiled in my direction, a light blush on her cheeks. Pa would chide me again. I'd collapse to the floor or spend the night in my room flopped across my bed, gripped in the throes of a ghastly headache, forgetting everything that happened after I drew the glass to my lips and tasted the first sip.

My God, I can't even drink liquor like a man! I'll never be able to earn a proper living like a man, stave off tears like a man, listen to music without succumbing to emotion like a man, please my family like a man . . .

The Galts depart after dark, but Aunt Nancy stays, for she's resided with us as long as I've been a member of the Allan household. I disappear upstairs to my bedroom and clear my mind of the Galts, the Allans, and that muse up the hill by lighting a lamp and leaning back in my chaise longue with a volume of Horace's poetry.

"Edgar," says Pa.

I give a start and sit upright. I've left the door open a crack and see Pa tottering into my bedroom, his nose flushed with the ruddy shine of spirits. His lips look wet, and the whites of his eyes burn a liquid red.

I set my book aside, my heart thumping, my neck perspiring, despite winter's cold breath beating at my windows.

Pa reaches into his breast pocket and pulls out a crumpled piece of paper.

"What is that?" I ask.

He staggers over to my desk and slams the paper down as though he's killing a spider. He then proceeds to smooth out the page with a crinkling commotion until it resembles a flat sheet of parchment again.

I rise and discover it's my "Tamerlane" manuscript, including the two new lines he instructed me not to write. Amid my ordeal with Lenore, I forgot about the rogue couplet.

Oh, God!

Pa rubs the back of his neck and sighs through his nostrils. "I forbade you to write down those two new lines, Edgar. Why did you disobey me?"

"The lines . . ." I clear my throat and attempt to deepen my voice. "They simply wanted me to write them down. That's how poetry works, Pa. I can't silence inspiration."

He grimaces as though he's just tasted a half-regurgitated piece of ham and brushes a hand through his hair. "My God, Edgar. Your chance to attend the university hinged on your ability to obey me, and you just ruined this opportunity—killed off your entire future—with two insipid lines of poetry. There's no way—*no way in hell*—I'm sending you to Charlottesville now."

I lift my chin and stare him in the eye, and before I can even think to hesitate, I open my mouth, and I finally say it—

"I know you're spending time with another woman across town."

Pa blanches. Once again, he runs his hand through his hair, his fingers now quivering. He seems to shrink five inches. "What . . . what are you talking about?"

"I'm talking about Elizabeth Wills, the pretty widow you visit. I also know you've fathered and financially supported more than one illegitimate child right here in Rich—"

Before I can finish that sentence, he's on me, his hand around my throat.

"Ever since you turned fifteen," he says, the fumes of wine and tobacco pummeling my nostrils, "you've been nothing but a sulky, ill-tempered burden who's making your ma sicker than she already is. You're making *me* sick."

I dig my fingernails into his knuckles and struggle to pry his fingers off me, but his hand is so large, so clamped around my throat.

"I'll send you away at the end of the week," he says, spittle wetting my face, "not because I care a damn about your education anymore, but because I want you out of my house. Forget about poetry, and painting, and all your other nonsense. Study like a damn monk. Make yourself a useful, working member of society instead of a vagabond in the gutter. And after you graduate, I'm not giving you a single penny from my pockets, I don't care how destitute you are. You'll not receive one cent from me. Do you hear me?"

He's squeezing my throat too much for me to speak, so I nod, and gasp, and fight to breathe.

He lets me go, but before he retreats, he twists his knife all the deeper into my heart by saying, "What a disappointment you are, Edgar. Such a disappointment!"

He leaves my room with a slam of the door that makes the lamplight shudder. I rub my throat and attempt to swallow, but the pain brings tears to my eyes.

Pa tromps downstairs, and I hear him shout at Ma and the servants. "Tamerlane" lies in a crumpled heap on my desk, but I don't care. My head spins, and Pa's still shouting at everyone because of me, even though he instigated every single battle in this war of ours when he first climbed into another woman's bed—when he first called me an ingrate—when he ignored the agonizing bout of grief I suffered after Jane Stanard's death.

Ma's crying. Aunt Nancy's pacing the upstairs landing. I throw open my back door to the upper portico and escape into the night.

CHAPTER EIGHT

Lenore

M y poet runs through the lamplit streets of Richmond.

He sprints across the snow in the near-darkness, his pulse surging, feet flying.

From my place of repose on an icy sarcophagus, surrounded by spirits who linger behind tombstones, too frightened by my presence to yet show their faces, I listen to Edgar Poe race through the city below me.

He listens to new lines of "Tamerlane," which emerge in the cadence of his footfalls.

The wordly glory, which has shown
A demon-light around my throne,
Scorching my sear'd heart with a pain
Not Hell shall make me fear again.

I roll off the stone, untangle myself from the webbings of my blanket, and lunge for the city with the swiftness and agility of a lion.

CHAPTER NINE

Edgar

Up ahead sits the cottage of my friend Ebenezer—my boon companion who swam in the falls every summer with me and the other young miscreants of Richmond; who steered me up the James in his sailboat, guiding us on adventures through the wild river islands.

I tear across his lawn, spring into a tree, and climb up the white trunk to the snow-slick shingles of his roof. With a lift of the sash of his gabled window, I slide feetfirst into his room.

Ebenezer bolts upright in bed—not yet tucked beneath his blankets—not yet dressed in his nightclothes—but stretched out with a book atop his cotton bedcover.

"Aha!" He snaps the book shut. "I knew I'd see you here tonight."

I close the window. "Why do you say that?"

"Bishop Moore's sermon."

I bend over to catch my breath, brushing snow off my pantaloons in the process, but I don't yet answer.

Eb swings his long legs around until he's sitting on the edge of the bed. His tawny hair sticks up like matted dog fur from the way he lay on his pillow.

"You looked like you might vomit up your breakfast after the bishop commanded us to silence our muses," he says. "And

I loathed what he said about your parents' theater company. What an ass he was this morning." Eb flinches at his own words and glances at his door. "Don't tell Ma I said that." He snickers. "Or God, for that matter. Forgive me, Lord."

I rub at my throat, still feeling the grip of Pa's fingers. "I'm here because of Pa, not the bishop."

"Oh?" Eb sets his book next to the lamp burning on the table beside his bed. "And what did King John of Moldavia do this time?"

Instead of replying, I make a beeline to Eb's wardrobe, home of a glorious stash of pilfered liquor.

"Oh, Christ, was it 'getting splashed' bad?" he asks.

I dig around in his piles of pantaloons and nightshirts. "If I can only survive until this weekend . . ." My fingertips bump against the curves of a smooth piece of glass. With a smile, I pull out a beautiful black bottle of sherry by its neck. "Oh, God, if I can make it to the university, Eb, I'll be free. I'm so damn close to escaping."

Behind me, the window rattles.

I wheel around, the sherry sloshing in my hands, and I gape at a dervish of tree branches flailing about in the darkness. The window shakes harder, as though it might shatter, and the air in Eb's bedroom crackles with static that raises the hairs on my neck. A palpable force barrels toward me.

Eb jumps up from his bed. "What the devil is that?"

"Keep the window closed."

"What?"

"Keep the window closed!" I toss him the sherry, lunge for the window, and hold the sash down. The windowpane buzzes against my right ear, and then—*oh, hell!*—I feel the force of a firm set of hands fighting to raise the sash.

"She's trying to open the window!"

"Who is?" asks Eb.

I push down with more strength and close my eyes—unable to bear the sight of her again. I know it's her. It must be her, for Ebenezer's room just turned shadowy and cold, and I'm clammy and panicky, as though trapped in a coffin, buried alive. I can't breathe!

"What the devil is happening, Edgar?" asks Eb.

"I'm not letting anything confine me here in Richmond!" I yell, gasping for air. "Go away, Lenore! Go away! Pa will see you! He'll trap me in Ellis & Allan!"

My shouting is futile—my strength inadequate.

The window flies open, and the smell of smoke rushes in.

CHAPTER TEN

Lenore

My poet fought to keep me out in the snow.

He FOUGHT to KEEP me OUT in the SNOW!

I force the sash open, hard enough to knock him backward to the floor in a room I do not recognize, papered in a sickly shade of yellow.

I slide through the window and land on my feet.

Edgar crawls crab-style away from me, and the owner of the room—a pimple-marked scarecrow with bulging brown eyes—gawks at me while clutching a black bottle.

"W-w-what is she, Edgar?" asks the fellow, the liquid sloshing in the bottle, and he leaps onto the bed. "What is she?"

"I told you to stay hidden, Lenore," says Eddy, rising to his feet. "I told you—"

"*You* call *me* to you, Eddy." I shove my right index finger against my chest and march toward him. "You're the one who summons *me*."

"N-n-no." His back smacks against a wardrobe with its doors hanging open. "No, I wouldn't call you to me when Pa's threatening to—"

"Stop it!" I grab him by his cravat and yank him toward me, hard enough to jerk his head backward on the hinge of his neck. "Stop saying how much you fear that *Pa* will see me. Stop shouting for me to go away because of him. You summon me *because* of Pa. He's already seen me, in fact. You wanted him to view me, because you know precisely how powerful I am."

Eddy's face blanches. "He's seen you?"

"He thinks I'm his muse. He promised to bring me poetry, but he lied, and I'm starving!"

"Edgar, is she your damn muse?" asks the other boy from up on his bed, his voice rising to a squeak. "Your—your muse is something you can see, and it looks like *that*?"

Eddy purses his lips and fidgets beneath my grip, but he does not respond to the boy.

"Are you ashamed of me?" I ask, and my eyeballs prickle, as though someone's sticking them with needles.

My poet lowers his eyes beneath his dark lashes, his breath choppy, his posture wilting.

"Are you?" I ask again, strengthening my hold on the knot of silk tied around his neck.

He gulps, and with a nod, he answers, "Yes."

The walls of my throat thicken and tighten.

I let go of the unfaithful wretch. "If I could nourish myself I would! If I could pen my own poems—"

A temptation catches my eyes from across the room: a speckled quill, resting on a table below a map of the world.

If I could pen my own poems—make my own music—dine on my own delectable art, I would. Oh, I most certainly would.

I pounce at the table and gaze down at the quill, eager to feel the brush of the plume against my skin, to dip the nib into the depths of a fragrant pot of ink and write down my own words.

What would happen if I touch it? I wonder, for the quill hums and sizzles, as though sparks might snap from the veins of the feather. *Would it hurt? Would I die for questioning my station?*

The flame of a tallow candle bends toward me with a hiss, and for a moment I fancy that a rival muse inhabits the light—a muse jealous of my ability to put pen to paper. I blow out the flame and grab the quill.

The plume burns!

My God!

I scream and let the thing drop to the floor, my right palm scorched and throbbing, a streak of red emblazed across my skin. Blisters bubble across this fiendishly fragile new flesh of mine, and I cry out in pain, dropping to my knees, mourning my fate, forever bound to a poet who rejects me.

With a wail of rage, I push over the desk's chair.

"What was that?" calls a woman's voice downstairs. "What are you doing up there, Ebenezer?"

"Get her out of here, Edgar!" shouts the other boy—this *Ebenezer*—and he jumps off the bed and calls outside his room's door, "Edgar is here, Ma. We're reciting *Julius Caesar*."

"Well, stop all that hullabaloo within the next five minutes," calls the woman, "so I may go to bed."

"Yes, Ma." Ebenezer slams the door shut.

I scream again and grab a leather-bound book from a shelf next to the desk—a book that I promptly hurl at my poet, who's still frozen by the wardrobe.

"I will not be useless!" I fetch a second text to throw. "I will not be ignored and secreted away like something shameful."

Edgar deflects each book with his left shoulder and calls to Ebenezer, "Give me the bottle!"

"Are you going to hit her over the head with it?"

"Uncork it and give it to me, Eb! Now!"

I tear the map off the wall and stomp the world beneath my feet. Something pops behind me, but I ignore the distraction, yank *Robinson Crusoe* off the shelf, and pitch the book at Edgar's head.

He catches it in his left hand, takes the bottle in his right one, and then he tips back his head with a tousle of his curls and gulps down a long swig.

Oh, no!

Oh, no, no, no!

Something's suddenly not right.

A rush of fumes stings my throat and blurs my vision, and my head floods with the sensation of drowning in a stupefying liquid. A heaviness, a fogginess, bears down on my brain, and I wobble on my feet, my arms swaying like pendulums I can't seem to control.

Eddy hands the bottle back to his friend, who immediately takes a drink, and then my poet's eyes do a curious thing: they peer straight ahead and go dead. Two vacant gray voids. *Just look at them!* My own eyes grow exhausted and bleary just from staring at him. His chest rises and falls, his arms hanging by his sides, and his lips, now rosy, fall open. A moment later, his eyes roll back into his head, and mine, on their own accord, do the same.

He collapses to the floor.

As do I.

CHAPTER ELEVEN

Edgar

My tongue tastes pickled this incomprehensibly cold morning.

My eyes ache. If I crack them open, I fear they might bleed.

I've awakened flat on my back, sprawled across the floorboards of Ebenezer's room, which reeks of cheap sherry. Sunlight turns the backs of my eyelids into burning scarlet drapes that further fuel my concern that my eyeballs might bleed.

I shiver and roll onto my left side, where I rub my legs together like two pathetic sticks of kindling. The bare floor beneath me remains a block of ice.

The sudden *click-click-click* of someone striking flint against steel inspires hope that either Eb or his mother bends over the tinderbox at this very moment, preparing to light a much-needed fire in the hearth. The kind individual then blows on the tinder for a minute or two, coaxing a small flame that will soon ignite a match—or so I hope. I tuck my chin to my chest, curl into a ball, and sigh in relief at the sound of a match sizzling to life with a sharp whiff of sulfur.

"You two gentlemen made a fine mess of your room last night, Eb," says his mother, now whooshing air onto the fire through a pair of wheezing bellows. "I should have known you were drinking when I heard all the shouts and the thumps."

Ebenezer responds with a guttural grunt. I peel open my right eye and find my boon companion facedown on his bed, his shirt untucked, his thicket of hair again standing upright on his head. He's only wearing one sock.

A trail of something wet runs between the bedroom door and the boots beside his bed. I pray that the liquid is either water spilled from a glass or melted snow, not piss.

"Edgar," says Mrs. Burling, "do your parents know you're here?"

"My parents are dead," I say without thinking.

My declaration silences her. I lower the lid of my peeled-open eye and hear her jabbing at the logs with a poker. The urge to vomit attacks, but there aren't any pails nearby, so I bring my knees to my stomach and go absolutely still.

Little fingers of warmth from the fire soon touch my face, reaching across my right cheek and stroking my ear. Mrs. Burling walks toward me in shoes with soft soles, and a breeze from her skirt rustles near my head.

She leans down and pets my hair. "Are you unwell, dear?"

I manage a small nod.

"Is there trouble at home again?"

Another nod, and I burst into tears that would infuriate Pa, but her fingers are so gentle, and her voice tinkles with such concern—I can't help it. I bury my face into my hands and weep.

You're seventeen years old! A near-grown man! For God's sake, you don't need to behave so sensitively all the time, Edgar.

"Damn that John Allan for doing that to him," says Eb. "The man's a cold snake."

Mrs. Burling withdraws her fingers from my curls. "Stay here as long as you'd like, darling."

From behind my palms, I cough up a strained "Thank you," sniveling, sniffing, my hands salty with tears. Another round of nausea strikes. I clamp my mouth shut to keep from spewing the wine from my stomach across Mrs. Burling's feet.

She leaves the room, and, once I'm certain I won't vomit, I drift back to sleep.

The next time I awaken, I remember Lenore.

A lift of my head confirms that Eb alone currently dwells in his chamber with me. He's kneeling in front of the fireplace, his back facing me.

"Where is she?" I ask. "Where's Lenore?"

Without turning around, Eb says, "God, she was awful, Eddy. So awful." He shudders.

Something moves inside his wardrobe.

I wriggle myself up to a seated position while eyeing the closed cedar doors, fearful that Eb somehow crammed my muse inside.

Eb rubs his hands together in front of the fire with a vexing *swish, swish, swish.*

I push myself off the ground and stand upright.

The noise in the wardrobe resumes: a scratching—a clawing.

I step closer, my legs no firmer than reeds bending by the river. Eb keeps rubbing and rubbing his damn hands.

I take a breath and reach for the wardrobe, imagining the worst—a dismembered and decapitated Lenore, still somehow alive, still furious. Before my courage falters, I swing open both doors.

Two stunned black eyes greet me.

Small, beady eyes.

A field mouse, not Lenore, crouches in the folds of Eb's beige nightshirt, holding a cracker Eb must have stored with the wine.

I exhale and turn to Ebenezer. "Eb, where is the girl?"

Eb stops his infernal hand warming. "That *girl*—if that's what you call her—collapsed to the floor the same instant you did, even though she didn't drink a single drop of the sherry."

"Where is she now?"

Eb rises to his feet. "I didn't know what to do with her. I couldn't just leave her lying here for Ma to see. So"—he runs his hands through his hair—"I got myself drunk enough to go near her, and then I picked her up and carried her out to the snow."

My jaw drops. "How far into the snow?"

"Just"—he swings a hand toward the window—"out to the side of the road. Not far enough, now that I think about it."

I lift open the sash, poke my head into the cold, and locate an ash-coated, human-shaped indentation in the snow, out by the street in front of his house.

"She's not there!" I pull my head back inside. "*When* did you leave her there?"

"I don't know." Eb scratches his scalp. "About fifteen minutes after Ma went to bed."

"She was out there all night?"

"Why are you so worried about her, Eddy?"

"Because if she dies—or if anyone finds her—I don't know what will happen to me."

Eb shakes his head and emits a small laugh. "That's clearly not your muse, my friend. I don't know what she was, but . . . did you see those teeth she wore around her neck?"

I wince. "Yes, but—"

"You're so damn good at writing wicked satire and epic poetry. If you care what everyone thinks of you, the way you're always talking about, you can't write about *her.*"

"I know that!" I slam the window shut. "But I don't want her to die. I simply want her to hide."

"She's clearly unrelated to your genius with words. And how could you ever think of marrying a girl like Elmira Royster, princess of Richmond, if something like *that* is lurking in your shadow?"

I wrap my arms around myself, not even daring to consider how Elmira would react to Lenore.

"This macabre muse of mine," I say with a sniff, "might actually exist in most every word I write, Eb, even if you don't quite see her." I bite down on my bottom lip, absorbing the truth of my own words, and then I button up my coat.

"Are you going home?" he asks.

I head toward his door. "Ma will be worried."

"Will I see you again before you leave for Charlottesville?"

"I'll make sure to visit later this week."

"Thank you." He puts his hands on his hips. "I didn't mean any offense. I wasn't trying to sound like Bishop Moore, commanding you to silence your muse. I'm just worried for you. I've been praying, for your sake, she was simply a bad hallucination that swam out of that bottle of sherry."

"You're right, Eb."

His shoulders relax. "She *was* a hallucination?"

"No." I open his door. "I do care what all those asses think of me, regrettably."

The imprint of Lenore's body in the snow offers no clues as to her whereabouts. Soot marks the spot where her dress once pressed against the earth, but the surrounding snow is clean.

And yet I do spy footprints, *several pairs*, leading to and from her indentation. I envision a mob hunting her down in the dark, hauling her away, killing her, throwing her into the river . . .

I stagger toward home, shoving the heels of my palms against my temples in a frenzied attempt to concoct a line or two of a poem—to ensure that my muse still exists, as much as I've repelled her. My brain swims under the spell of the lingering sherry, and I realize how impossible it is to walk in a straight line, let alone to construct words of poetry, which requires the sharpness of a mathematician's mind.

One block away, the local blacksmith, Gilbert Hunt—a slave and hero of the theater fire—clanks his hammer against his anvil. His steady beats have served as the percussion of Richmond's symphony since my earliest days, but this morning old Gilbert may as well be hammering my skull.

The wind shifts, and the sour smell of hops from the riverside breweries overpowers the air. My stomach lurches. A carriage rolls around the corner, but I'm suddenly too sick to care who sees me at my worst, gag too much to fight what's coming, which leads to a wretched and pitiable moment of dropping on all fours and throwing up the contents of my stomach into the snow.

Nearing home, I stop first in our kitchen—an arsenal of cooking tools and crockery with dried herbs and roasting meats sweetening the air—one of several wooden outbuildings built behind the main house. Pa never visits the kitchen, and because of his absence, as well as the fire that perpetually blazes in the open hearth and the company within, the room is the warmest and most welcoming realm on the entire property.

"Good morning," says Jim, our gray-haired servant with a voice rougher than sandpaper. He chops up an onion at the worktable in the center of the room, and the fumes bring about more queasiness.

"Good morning, Jim," I say, my voice as gravelly as his.

Our other house slave, Judith—the tall and sturdy woman who raised me whenever Ma fell too ill to do so—peeks over the right shoulder of her dark orange dress while stirring one of the pots bubbling over the fire. Just like Ma, she wears a white cap of sheer muslin whenever she's on the grounds of Moldavia, but the ruffles don't fall low enough to hide the concerned crinkling of her forehead or the puckering of the skin between her brows.

"Did you drink a glass of wine last night?" she asks.

"The drinking involved nothing as a civilized as a glass," I say with a grin.

Judith glowers, unamused.

I brace my hands against the worktable and hang my face over the tops of carrots and radishes piled in a heap of massacred greens. My stomach gurgles.

"Are you about to get sick?" asks Jim.

"I'll be better in a moment."

"Your absence was noticed at breakfast," says Judith.

"With glee or sadness?"

"The ladies, as usual, fretted about you."

I raise my face. "And Pa?"

Judith passes behind me and pats my left shoulder. "He expressed concern about you, too."

The eerie trill of a bird outside brings gooseflesh to my arms. I glance toward the window and see the piercing yellow eyes of a screech owl with feathers that blend into the bark of the closest tree. That same bird alights in those branches most every day and night, all four seasons of the year.

Judith pours a cup of water from the pitcher at the cabinet by the window. With a tremble of its throat, the bird hoots at her in its strange screech owl manner that resembles the whinnying of a horse.

Judith presses her dark brown fingers against the pane and says with a coo, "Not now, Morella dear. There's work to be done. I'll tell you a story tonight."

I swallow down the bile in my throat. "Do you tell that owl the same tales of graves and restless bones that used to frighten me when I was young?"

She withdraws her hand from the window. "Don't those tales frighten you anymore, now that you're older?"

My knees buckle from the sherry, and my left hand slips off the table.

"Please, go lie down," says Jim. "You're not well."

"I need a little more strength before attempting that Matterhorn of a staircase."

"Drink this water." Judith places the tin cup in front of me. "You look paler than Death."

I test out a small sip, and my throat reacts like a cracked desert floor absorbing its first drops of rain in a year.

Judith unwraps a loaf of bread from a cloth at the table near the brick oven.

"That strange phantasm that ran amok across the city yesterday," I decide to tell her, believing she might understand, "is my muse."

"I know," she says.

My mouth falls open. "You do?"

She fetches the bread knife from a hook on the wall, her back toward me.

"*How?*" I ask. "H-h-how did you know?"

She polishes the long, thin blade with the cloth that covered the bread and says, "I've taken care of you since the Allans first brought you home all those years ago. I watched that macabre and melancholy spirit of yours forming and squirming in the shadows before I even told you a single tale of haunts."

"Did you know she'd one day possess the power to climb out of the shadows?"

"I'm surprised she hasn't done it sooner."

I gulp down another sip. "What do you suggest I do about her?"

"You're a free young gentleman, Master Eddy." Judith carves the heel off the loaf. "You can follow any muse you want; create whatever art you desire."

"Not according to Pa."

"You'll be on your own soon."

"Even then, what would people think of me if I were to write of demon possessions and corpses returned from the grave?"

"There's nothing wrong with tales of fright and horror told late at night." Judith lays the slice of bread on a stoneware plate decorated with paintings of cobalt-blue daisies. "They make your listeners appreciate waking up in the morning, discovering they're still alive."

I breathe a short laugh in agreement.

She sets the plate in front of me and wipes her hands on her apron. "Sometimes muses follow us around when we don't want them. But other times they're not there when we need them." She leans a hand on the worktable and bends toward me, rubbing the cowrie shells of the necklace she wears. "When you drink liquor . . ."

I lower my head in shame.

". . . you silence your muse," she says, "more than your father ever could. You're a bigger threat to your creativity than that man will ever be."

I nod, even though I'm not entirely certain I believe her.

She reduces the volume of her voice. "We carried her to our quarters last night—Jim, Dab, and me."

The bread slips from my hands and drops back to the plate.

Judith lowers her voice to a whisper I can scarcely hear. "She's out there in my room. Dead asleep. We found her lying in the snow."

"How did you know where to find her?"

She returns to the cast-iron pots hanging over the fire.

I shift around to better see her, even though my body insists on sagging against the table. "Judith? How did you know she was out there?"

"I listen to my muse," she says, swirling the spoon through a pea porridge. "You ought to thank the Lord that Morella told me where to find that poor spirit of yours before anyone else came along and either stole her or killed her—or before she froze to death."

I wrinkle my brow. "Did you say 'Morella'?" A peek back out at the tree reveals that the screech owl has vanished.

"She started off as a wild and wicked one, too," says Judith of the bird, or so I assume. "She made me tremble late at night, stirring up all sorts of stories in my brain—stories that I knew would shock the others if they heard them pass through my quiet little lips. But I kept her close to my heart and nurtured her well—just as you ought to do for your spirit out there."

She nods toward the window. "As soon as you're rested, go take care of her. Allow her to evolve."

"I'm on the verge of escaping Moldavia."

Judith shakes her head. "You'd be a fool to let something like that perish."

"I'm about to enter a highly prestigious university."

"Your muse has the power to soar far and wide if you let her."

"But—"

"Your muse," says Judith again, more slowly, "has the power to soar far and wide if you let her. Don't ever take such freedom for granted."

I sip more water.

"Are you listening?" she asks.

I choke on the liquid and wipe my lips with the back of my right hand. "Everyone who saw her in Richmond reviled her. If I nourish her and flaunt her, they'll hate me, too, even more than they already do." I shake my head. "I can't pursue my fascination with the macabre. It would spell the end of me."

Judith sighs and returns to her stirring, muttering an apology to Morella and that "poor lonely raven."

CHAPTER TWELVE

Lenore

I have two pieces of advice for you, Raven Girl," says a lush and warbling voice that could be either male or female.

I open my eyes, my tongue parched, my soul famished, and discover two yellow orbs with enormous black pupils peering down at me from overhead. They belong to a face, half-human, half-screech owl—a curious visage with the bone structure of a woman and a fuzzy covering of mottled brown feathers. Two tufts of feathers stick up from her round head, giving the impression of horns.

"*One*," says the owl through a pair of small, gold, human-shaped lips, "do not let young Mr. Poe near a bottle ever again. This is vital. Do you understand me?"

I blink but cannot speak.

The owl creature bends closer with a rustle of the feathers at her throat. "That boy sends you into stupefying slumbers every time he sips the juice. It happened even when you were still incubating in the shadows. I'm surprised you don't remember."

I sit upright on a mattress that crinkles with hay, discovering myself in a room not much bigger than a shed, furnished with the bed, a washbasin, and a small chest of drawers. Wreathes of dried flowers hang from the bare planks of the walls, and the air carries the hickory wood scent of Moldavia's kitchen.

"Where am I?" I ask, my pulse drumming in my ears.

"*Two*," says the owl, and she smacks the back of my head with an arm swishing with feathers, "move on from this vulnerable, mortal-like stage of yours—now! What were you thinking, prancing around for all to see?"

"I don't know who you are, but I'm magnificent. I want the world to see me."

The owl creature scowls and tuts. "You vain, prideful creature. Most of us would never even think of entering this showy form you've inhabited. We don't care about proving how magnificent we are. We simply evolve."

I cast a look of doubt. "I don't believe that."

"Believe it, greedy girl! The pleasure of orchestrating art is all we need to flourish."

I rub the back of my head and eye this odd, judgmental owl person, who sits on the headboard of the bed in a body the size and the shape of a woman's. From her neck to her ankles, she's draped in a thick cloak of feathers that mimics the ragged browns and grays of the barks of trees. Around her neck hangs a necklace strung with small bones, perhaps the femurs of mice.

"Who are you?" I ask.

She stretches her neck. "My artist calls me Morella."

"Who is your artist?"

She drops down to the pillow, where she sits with her knees pulled to her chest beneath the *whoosh* of plumage. "My artist is older than yours—far wiser than yours—and she's terrified for you. She saved you from freezing to death and hid you here in her cabin, so you owe her respect. Most of us hide in the shadows and firelight until we feel the shift."

"What shift?"

The owl again tuts. "This is why you don't run around pell-mell! You know nothing."

"What is the shift?"

"The sacred moment when our artists commit themselves to us. When they finally declare, 'Discouragement be damned!'—and they pledge in their hearts to follow their passions until their dying day. That's when we evolve into our spiritual form." She leans closer, her planetary pupils expanding beneath a pair of eyelids with ghostly white lashes. "And then no one can kill us, not even our artists. But by strutting around in this poodle-like stage of pomposity"—she flicks the back of my right wrist—"you'll be dead within a week."

Hunger stabs at my stomach. I bend over at the waist and clutch my belly. "I'm starving."

To my shock, Morella shoves me off the bed.

I land on my back with a *thud* and a grunt.

"What is the matter with you?" she asks. "I'm speaking to you of matters most urgent."

"I don't understand what you're saying. How am I any different than you?"

"Aside from my artist, mortals can't see me the way you're seeing me now. They think I'm a simple bird. They only hear my owlish trills, but more importantly, they listen to me speak through my artist's stories." Morella crouches down on the floorboards beside me. "And no one can kill me, because I'm fully formed. My artist will forever hear me, feel me, and *need* me, even when she's lying on her death bed, gasping her last breaths. That's how powerful I am. I waited to evolve until she was just as ready as I."

I snort. "My artist will never be ready. He's too concerned about the opinions of his damn father. I'm famished!" I roll over on hands and knees and crawl toward the door.

Morella tackles me from behind in a tangle of arms and legs. Elbows clunk against floorboards, and my left cheek smacks wood.

She lodges a knee into my spine. "My artist has taken care of your artist for years," she says into my right ear, her voice buzzing through my skull and my teeth. "She loves him like a son, even though he's not her flesh and blood, even though her bondage is barbaric, unnatural, and stifling to the soul. Respect my artist, even if you do not respect your own. She wants you to stay in this room and avoid getting killed until the young gentleman leaves for college. She will feed you stories of graves and ghouls far more delicious than anything Eddy Poe can offer—for her tales are a part of his."

I stop squirming and go still, intrigued, for I think I know the tales of which she speaks.

Morella loosens her grip and takes her knee off my back. "You are too wild and naïve, Raven Girl. You don't appreciate what you have."

"I'm neither a raven nor a girl."

"You're obviously meant to evolve into a raven."

I sit upright and rip a splinter out of my thumb with my teeth. "My artist named me Lenore."

Morella chuckles. "That's too pretty for you. You're the ugliest thing I've ever seen."

"Ugliness is beautiful."

Those golden lips of hers break into a smile, and she smooths down the tufts of feathers sticking up from her head. "Then I must be Helen of Troy."

I snicker and allow this beauteous, bizarre being to help me to my feet, lulled by a soft trilling in her throat and the clicks of the bones hanging around her neck, which are almost as decadent as my necklace of teeth.

"Will you promise to hide?" she asks, her hand warm around mine. "If you survive, if you do manage to evolve and devote your existence to art, I promise you, you will be able to slip into realms fit for a god. You will roost in a sumptuous world wrought from your artist's imagination and experience unprecedent spiritual pleasures, of which no mortal has ever dared to dream."

A small sigh leaves my lips, and I stand up taller. "Is this true?"

"I do not lie, Lenore." She kisses my cheek, and for the breadth of a second, my blood thrills with the thrum of the ecstasy to come. "Survive this week without dying, and you shall soar forevermore."

"I'll hide," I say, even though my hunger sears.

"Wise choice." She raises her arms and swallows me up inside her wings.

Within the folds of that earthy cloak, against the sturdiness of Morella's feathered chest, I hear whispers of stories I remember from the shadows of Eddy's childhood—stories that a woman with beautiful black skin and a voice like velvet told in front of a kitchen fire—tales of demon visitations and ghosts that grabbed the arms of little boys in graveyards at night, pulling them down into the cold and musty ground. And the music of the children's screams in the stories strum through my head like a Viennese waltz.

CHAPTER THIRTEEN

Edgar

Something stirs within the cabin where Judith, Dabney, and Old Jim reside.

Ma and Aunt Nancy knit scarves for the poorhouse up in Ma's bedroom, and Pa has been working at his mercantile since morning. Judith and Jim labor in the kitchen, and I hear Dabney cleaning the stable down the way.

Yet I sense movement and breath within the wood-framed structure standing before me.

In my right hand I carry a heart-shaped necklace, dug out from a box of costumes and stage jewelry from my old Thespian Society days with schoolmates, before our parents shut down our theatrical endeavors. The red stone cut from glass grows warm from my hand, and the silver chain slips out from between my fingers.

In my head I carry ten lines of a poem I've been struggling to compose while resting from the sherry.

I walk up to the door of the cabin and breathe through a nervous bout of light-headedness.

The screech owl—"Morella"—lands upon the peak of the pitched roof with a flap of her striped wings. I ignore the mournful sound of her whinnying, avert my gaze from those shocking yellow eyes, and rap upon the door.

No one answers.

A glance over my shoulder confirms that I'm still alone and unobserved, save for the owl. I turn the latch, enter the quarters, and close the door behind me.

In the main room, where Jim and Dabney sleep, stand a pair of plain wooden beds, covered in gray woolen bedcovers, butted against the bare planks of two of the walls. A table occupies the room's center, its three chairs all pushed in, with no signs of recent use.

I walk across the floor, drawing groans from the bellies of the unvarnished boards. My eyes drop, and I spy soot sprinkled across the braided yellow rug in front of the toes of my shoes. More patches of the fine black powder trail off toward the door to Judith's bedroom, which stands slightly ajar. The closed curtains, coupled with the gloom of the sky outside, transform the room beyond into a dark abyss.

With my left hand squeezed around the glass heart, my gaze focused on that door, I dare to tread two more steps. My back tingles with the same flood of chills that used to wash down my spine whenever Judith spun her stories for the other servants and me. Her voice, how it rumbled, every syllable enunciated to dramatic effect, and her face, how it glowed such an extraordinary shade of orange from the shine of the flames snapping in the kitchen's fire. Whenever she finished sharing her fantastical feasts of folk tales, she would tuck me into bed, and I would yank my blankets over my head until I struggled to breathe. More than anything else in the world, I feared that a cold phantom hand would reach out and grab me from the darkness, or that I'd open my eyes to the ghastly face of a ghoul breathing against me.

"Lenore?" I call toward Judith's doorway.

No voice, nor breath, nor creaking floorboard responds.

Nonetheless, I offer an olive branch to my muse by speaking the opening lines of the new poem I'm composing:

"Thy soul shall find itself alone—
Alone of all on earth—unknown
The cause—but none are near to pry
Into thine hour of secrecy.
Be silent in that solitude,
Which is not loneliness—for then
The spirits of the dead, who stood
In life before thee, are again
In death around thee, and their will
Shall then o'ershadow thee—be still . . ."

Nothing stirs in reply to my words. My poem simply thudded against the walls.

I consider leaving, but before I swivel my shoulders toward the exit, the bedroom door cracks farther open.

I freeze and hold my breath.

"Write the words down," says a voice that reverberates within my rib cage.

More chills run down my spine, leaving in their wake a cold sweat that spills out to my shoulders.

I see her—*Lenore*, that living shadow wrought from the embers of my soul. She sidles around the door. Her maroon lips still match the chamber wall from whence she came, and I now detect the fleur-de-lis pattern of my wallpaper etched across the curve of her bottom lip. Her ashen complexion looks more cadaverous than I remember, which magnifies the protrusion of her round, jet-black eyes. Her broad forehead, I realize, resembles mine, framed by that long and tangled hair so desperately in need of combing.

"Write the words down," she says again, more slowly.

"I—I can't." I inch backward. "Not until I'm safely gone from Moldavia. But I intend to call the poem 'Visit of the Dead.' What do you think of it so far?"

She nods toward the silver chain dangling from my left fingers. "What are you holding?"

I open my palm and reveal the glass heart, which shimmers a red so dark, it almost resembles her eyes. "It's for you."

She turns her chin to her right and casts a glance that tells me she does not trust this material offering.

"I must beg your pardon for my initial reaction to you," I say. "And for drinking. Please, accept this gift as an offer of my humblest apology."

She rubs those maroon lips together. "You speak as though you've been trained to say pretty words when behaving like an ass."

I can't help but laugh a little. "Yes, I have, indeed, been trained to speak in such a manner, but the apology is sincere. Someone more knowledgeable about muses than I showed me the error of my ways."

With cautious footfalls, Lenore approaches, her eyes fixed upon the sparkles of the glass.

My hand quakes.

The chain jangles.

Those mortifying molars strung around her throat chatter as though they're lodged inside a human skull.

She lifts the heart from my palm and sniffs the stone, so seemingly pleased by the aroma, that her eyes flutter closed, and a sigh pours from her lungs.

"It smells like a theater," she says, her voice softer, warmer, easier to absorb.

I sigh, as well. "I fetched this beauty from a box of costume pieces."

Her eyes reopen, and the fires of creativity throb around her pupils.

"The chain is long enough," I say, my voice squeaking, "that you can simply loop the necklace over your head, without my needing to help you clasp it."

She lifts the necklace over herself—no need for me to touch her, thank heaven! She pulls her hair out of the back of the chain and settles the heart against the soot-powdered fabric of her bodice, several inches beneath the string of teeth. The stone shines scarlet against the sable backdrop of her bosom.

I clear my throat. "You may follow me to the university this weekend, Miss Lenore . . ."

She snorts. "'Miss?'"

"Yes." Again, I clear my throat and straighten my posture. "But only if you work to assimilate into the world of the university, which, as you may or may not know, only permits male scholars."

Her jaw stiffens. "You should have imagined me as a boy, Eddy."

"Well, we shall figure out a clever way to—" I purse my lips, unsure how to complete that thought, wondering how the devil I'm supposed to hide this oddity in the middle of the University of Virginia—an institution reserved for the South's most refined and promising young gentlemen.

"Perhaps . . ." I gesture toward my neck and grin with a show of my teeth, hoping she'll understand that I want her to remove that disgusting string of molars without my having to actually articulate the request.

"'Perhaps . . .'?" she asks, peering at me from the tops of her eyes, as though she does understand but wants me to say it.

"Perhaps you could remove that other necklace."

Her glare turns menacing, and she seethes like a bull, but I persevere with my requests, for they're vital to our survival.

"And . . . and maybe wear your hair up in the style of modern young women. And perhaps refrain from destroying my friends' bedrooms . . . or frightening townspeople . . ."

"You"—she steps forward—"are not"—she pushes her face into mine—"my master."

"I don't claim to be your master."

"We are supposed to work as collaborators."

"We . . ." I lean away from the heat and the stench of her hell-furnace breath. "Are we?"

With a growl of frustration, she grabs me by my shoulders. "You do *not* get to tell me how I should appear and act"—she backs me toward the front door—"when *you* created me to look and behave this way. If you want me docile and dull, then resign yourself to forever writing those anemic love poems you've pilfered from Lord Byron!" She slams me against the front door.

"You sound just like Pa," I say through gritted teeth.

"That's because *Pa* and I both know you can do better. But the difference between us is that John Allan fears your potential, whereas I'm the electricity igniting it."

I turn my head at the sound of hooves squishing through the snow that's melting out on the street.

"I should go," I say. "Pa might return."

"How am I to follow you to the university, Edgar? How do you intend for me to get there when you're so ashamed of me—so terrified of people seeing me?"

I shake my head. "I—I don't know. Can't you travel in a non-corporeal manner? Or seep back into the shadows?"

"No! I'm meant to be seen now. There's no going back."

The hooves travel nearer. I pray that they don't belong to the mares pulling Pa's carriage.

"Well"—I swallow—"then a boat might be best. Stow away on a vessel heading north on the James, then somehow find your way up the Rivanna River into Charlottesville."

Her eyebrows relax into regular brows, as opposed to two clashing sabers.

"Would you like me to write those directions down?" I ask.

She shakes her head and says, "North on the James, and up the Rivanna River."

"Pa cannot know that you're out here. Please hide well until I leave for the university. Do not make a sound."

She backs away, her narrow skirts swishing. "I shall be as quiet as a dead mouse."

"No, that's not how the saying . . ."

She turns her head an inch to her right and narrows her eyes, daring me to try to correct her mistake in adding "dead" to the idiom.

"I'm much obliged," I say instead.

"Do not try to change me."

"I wasn't . . ."

"I'm the best part of you, Edgar Poe."

Oh, dear God, I hope that's not true.

I shake my head. "I don't . . ."

"'Discouragement be damned' is what you need to say. That's all you need to do to save me. Pledge yourself to our art until your dying day, or else . . ." Her eyes flood with tears—a strange sight on one who doesn't seem to feel much in the way of sorrow. She clutches the glass heart hanging around her neck and blinks as though she doesn't quite know what to do with her emotions. "Or else you'll lose me," she says, her tone so frail, so human, I forget for a moment what she is.

I snicker softly. "I don't think I'm apt to lose someone like you too quickly."

She watches me for a moment without speaking, and then she says in a voice that reaches straight into my soul, "I'm obsessed with death but terrified of dying."

My lips part with a gasp.

I'm obsessed with death but terrified of dying.

This astonishing creature has just put into words what my heart has longed to speak ever since my mother ceased breathing. My throat fills with a pain more lacerating than the blade of a razor, and before I know what's happening, a paroxysm of silent, tearless sobs shudders through me, my stomach convulsing, my lips trembling.

"I understand," I say in a strained whisper, curling my hands into balls by my sides in a desperate fight to regain my composure.

A tear spills down Lenore's right cheek, etching a trail of soot. "Then pledge yourself to me, and I will never smolder out and die on you—not as long as you shall live."

"I must go." I open the door and slip outside.

"Eddy—"

I close the door and say through the wood, "I'm sorry. Pa's due to return home."

I then scramble back to the main house with the swiftest stride I've ever walked without actually running, for I cannot pledge myself to something so strange, so singularly unsettling, when I, too, am an oddity who's only pretending to belong.

CHAPTER FOURTEEN

Lenore

Church bells chime five o'clock.

Two hours have passed since my poet shut yet another door in my face.

Morella brings me a sheet of white parchment, addressed to "Cassandra," which she found in an emptied box of tobacco, wedged into a lump of snow at the entrance of the Burying Ground on Shockoe Hill. I pluck away pine needles and unfold the paper, and then I swallow down the syrupy sweetness of John Allan's imitation of Shakespeare's "Sonnet 18."

May I compare thee to a winter's morn?
Thou art colder and wilder in temper,
Harsh winds blight fair roses sleeping 'mid
    thorns,
And winter's beauty fades past December . . .

"By the pricking of my talon," I say, digging the sharp curves of my right fingernails into the parchment, "something wicked named John Allan fetters Poe with fears of failure while Jock knocks on pleasure's door. Edgar Poe will never choose me; much too frightened, he shall lose me—'You have now ceased to amuse me!' Allan shouts and slams the door."

Says Morella, "Hush, Lenore."

She crouches on her knees at Judith's window, her head ducked beneath the yellow muslin draping the pane, and she whispers, "Here comes John Allan now."

I crawl to her side and peek through the window with only my forehead and eyes raised above the sill.

John Allan marches toward a tree that's languishing near the carriage house, his chest so puffed with peacockish pride that his back slopes unnaturally backward. His brass walking stick squelches through the slush.

Even though he's several yards away, even though he's pre-occupied with the blight of the tree and isn't coming for me, I feel the pressure of his fingers squeezing around my trachea.

I glance at Morella for comfort, but she, too, rubs her throat with a grimace of pain.

CHAPTER FIFTEEN

Edgar

S omehow, I survive the week leading up to the Day of Departure.

Somehow, my muse remains quiet and concealed.

Thank heaven! I'm packing—preparing at last. My time in Moldavia is almost time past!

By the eve of the grand exodus, a Saturday, mid-February, I've crammed my trunk full of clothing, taken one last stroll beside the whispering waters of the James, and bidden adieu to most everyone in Richmond whom I care about—except for my beloved Elmira.

My darling and I meet an hour before sundown in a tract of land we call the "Enchanted Garden," an Eden of linden trees and winter-slumbering vines of roses, jasmine, and myrtle, tucked behind brick garden walls. Pa's partner, Mr. Charles Ellis, created the grounds to test seed samples sent to Ellis & Allan, but everyone in Richmond knows that if young lovers crave privacy, they only need to meet among the lindens.

Elmira takes both my hands in hers and gazes at me with wide, watery eyes. "I cannot believe you're leaving tomorrow, Eddy. February used to seem so far away."

"I know." I kiss the back of her gloved right hand. "Thank you for meeting me here."

"I wish we could have been together every day of this week."

"Before I go, I want to do something properly for you."

Her cheeks pinken. She knows what I'm about to do, and yet she kindly feigns surprise by asking, "What is it?"

My heart rate triples, and I thrill with the same sense of terror and elation as when I stood on Ludlam's Wharf at the age of fifteen and prepared for my swim on the James. I hold my breath and take a leap by bending down on one knee, the ground wet enough to dampen my pantaloons, but I don't care a fig about the cold.

A nervous laugh passes through Elmira's lips, and she tightens her grip on my hands.

"Miss Sarah Elmira Royster . . ." I peer up into her deep blue eyes. "I do not mind if our engagement needs to be made in secrecy. I love you as no man ever loved a woman, and when I finish my education at the University of Virginia, nothing would make me happier than returning home to the wittiest, the prettiest, and the most loving of brides that anyone could ever wish for. Will you do me the honor of becoming my wife?"

She smiles in that bedazzling way of hers that sparks a mischievous glimmer in her eyes and draws dimples to her cheeks.

After a lengthy and weighty exhalation, however, her eyes sober; her smile wilts.

My heart stops.

"It would, indeed, need to be a secret engagement, Eddy."

"I know."

"I'm sorry, my love, but my parents can never learn anything about this until we're older. They would say I'm too young and forbid me to see you or write to you ever again."

"I know."

"And my father . . ."

My jaw tightens, for I'm aware of Mr. Royster's opinion of me.

"I don't believe," says Elmira, unpeeling the delicate outer layer of my heart with each syllable she speaks, "that he would ever consent to me marrying a poet."

I lower my face, my shoulders heaving, and, without even trying, I concoct anagrams that corrupt the name of her father, *James Royster*.

Mayor Jesters

Arrests Me Joy

Mrs. Joy Eaters

Meet Roy Ass Jr.

"Please stand up, Eddy." Elmira gives a soft tug of my hands. "Your knee will get sore down there on the freezing ground, and I want to speak to your beautiful eyes, not the top of your head."

I do as she asks, and she steps close to me, brushing a hand through my hair, above my left ear, sending tingles down that side of my neck. The floral tones of her perfume bring the garden into full bloom, even though the vines have yet to start budding.

"I'll betroth myself in secret to you, Edgar," she says, "as long as you promise to write me from Charlottesville and assure me of your love when we're apart."

I wrap my arms around her. "I promise to write you every day."

She snickers. "You won't have time for your studies if you're writing me every day. And I won't have time for mine if I'm always reading your letters, which I know will be the length of novels."

"I'll write you every week, then," I say, entranced by the nearness of her mouth, her breath, her ethereal irises.

"I'd be happy with every week. I'll send you a reply just as often."

"Is this a 'yes,' then? Will you marry me?"

"Yes." She kisses my lips. "I will wait for you while you're gone, my sweet, romantic dreamer. I shall marry you, and one day"—another kiss, one that sends my brain into amorous intoxication—"we'll live together in a kingdom by the sea."

I grin like a drunken fool during supper, my head tipsy from the way Elmira's fragrance lingers in my clothing. The lamps of Moldavia burn more brightly than ever before; every rose and lily embroidered in the tablecloth grows more vivid in color. The mutton tastes divine.

"You look positively jubilant, Edgar," says Aunt Nancy from across the table, her tight sausage curls wobbling against her cheeks as she slices her own wedge of meat. "You must be eager to depart for the university tomorrow morning."

Ma cups her hands over her face and bursts into tears.

Pa frowns.

Aunt Nancy reaches out to her sister and says, "Oh, Fanny, I didn't mean to upset you."

My secret proves tortuous. I long to tell Ma, *I know you're weeping over the pain of losing a son tomorrow, but I've just ensured that you'll one day gain a beautiful daughter!*

"Take care to contain your exhilaration in front of Ma, Edgar," says Pa, which inspires Ma to cry all the more.

At night I sit on my bed and unlock my wooden writing box to ensure I've packed enough paper, sealing wax, quills, ink, charcoal crayons, and other necessities. My penknife seems to have gone missing, but after some lifting and shuffling, I locate it beneath the stack of paper.

Ma coughs in her bedroom.

I close my box and listen to her muffled sputters and hacks.

She sounds worse. So dreadfully worse.

With a candle in hand, I navigate my way through the throats of the night-shrouded corridors. One of the servants has already extinguished the oil lamps, and each time Ma coughs, the shadows of the walls contract around me.

I rap upon her door. "Ma?"

She waits a moment before calling out, "Come in, Eddy."

I open her door and find her propped up by pillows in her canopied bed, drowning in the sea of her burgundy bedcover. Her face looks as small as a child's in the middle of all the ruffles of her white nightcap. The herbal oils and rose water she uses to soothe her coughs saturate the air.

"Come, sit down." She scoots over and pats the mattress beside her.

I close the door behind me and go to her right side, trying not to flinch when she coughs yet again. The flame in the crystal lamp next to her bed wriggles at my approach. I set my candlestick beside it.

"Sit down," she says from behind a handkerchief she's pressed to her mouth.

I obey her wishes and sink into the downy depths of her bed.

"Eddy..." She wraps a hand around mine, her fingers shockingly cold, but I endure the chill without pulling away.

Her voice drops to a feather of a whisper. "Even though it's hard for me to let you go, I know the university will allow you to find success in this world."

I sigh through my nose. "Pa tells me quite the opposite."

"I know what Pa says."

"He called me a disappointment." I glance toward the closed door. "I still worry he won't take me to Charlottesville tomorrow."

"He *will* take you. I'll make sure of it. And he is not disappointed in you. He simply does not know how to raise a boy with your vast intellect and passion. You baffle and perplex him, which heightens into frustration and anger."

"Oh, I know all about his frustration and anger."

Ma scoots closer. "I will be proud of you no matter what you choose to do with your life, my darling. Don't ever be ashamed or afraid to follow your muse."

I contemplate what Ma's reaction might be if she were to meet my muse face-to-face.

"Would you still be proud of me"—I look her in the eye—"if I were to write of darker topics?"

Her forehead puckers. "What darker topics do you mean?"

The tremor in her voice answers my question.

"Never mind." I give a small shake of my head. "I don't want you to fret about me."

"Why would I fret about you because of something you wrote?"

"Please forget what I just said. There's no need to worry." I wrap my free hand around our clasped fists. "I'm going to make you so proud at the university, Ma."

She relaxes against her pillows. "I don't doubt that you will."

I smile, and we slide into a silence weighted with sorrow, our hands piled together, the hearth fire crackling. Ma's lungs wheeze with a high-pitched whistle like the wind in the chimney.

The church bells of Richmond, in unison with the clock down the hall, chime the nine o'clock hour in a chorus of clanging—in a chorus that sings of time rushing forward.

A hound howls in the distance.

I can tell by Ma's watchful gaze that she's transcribing every feature of my face onto the canvas of her memory.

I can't bear to look at her, for I see yet another dying woman.

"I'm going to miss you," I say.

"I'll miss you, too, my love." She pulls me against her and entraps my face in her cap's splay of ruffles, but I do not mind, for she clasps her arms around me with the same strength of affection that she always used to soothe me whenever nightmares crowded my brain.

"I'm forever thankful for the day you came into my life, Eddy," she says, "with your big gray eyes, your beautiful brown curls, and your clever manner of speaking. Before that moment, I never truly understood what it meant to love another person. I don't know what I would have done without—"

She erupts into sobs that stop her from forming another word, and the sobs build up to another round of coughing—the most violent fit I've heard from her yet.

I fetch her a glass of water, tuck her blankets around her legs, and pump air into the fire with the bellows in a mad attempt to rouse the flames and warm away the chill clinging to her chamber.

Ma wipes her eyes and thanks me, but I must leave her, for now I'm crying, too. Her lips have turned so pale and waxen; her cheeks look as sunken as a corpse's. Her lungs won't stop that hideous whistling and wheezing.

I retreat to my bedroom, my candle's flame whooshing next to my ear, light streaking across the green walls.

"Edgar," calls out Pa from behind me.

I stop and pivot toward him on my right heel.

His massive figure fills up his entire doorway. He's just standing there, winding a silver cravat around his neck, squinting at me through the dim corridor, no doubt noticing my bloodshot eyes and tearstained cheeks.

I will not allow him to emasculate me tonight.

"I bet you blubbered like a bairn when your ma lay dying in Scotland, you bloody bastard," I say in a low growl.

Well, no, I don't actually say those words aloud. I will if I need to, but for now I simply stare at him with unblinking eyes, my candle sighing in my hand.

"Please remember the frailty of Ma's health when you write to her from college." Pa ties the cravat in a knot at his throat. "Do not distress her with requests for money or tales of your troubles and homesickness. I know how dramatic you are when you pen your letters . . ."

"I do not intend to distress her, Pa."

"Address such concerns to me alone."

"Yes, sir."

He swivels back toward his chamber.

"Why are you dressing like you're about to leave the house," I ask, "when we're departing early tomorrow morning?"

He pauses, standing halfway inside his bedroom. All I see of him are the back of his green coat and his head of coarse curls.

"My activities are of no concern to you, Edgar," he says. "Go to bed."

He swings his door shut.

I sigh and continue onward to my bedroom.

Behind his closed door, Pa likely proceeds to comb his hair and trim his side-whiskers for another visit to Elizabeth Wills. I wonder, with a queasy rolling of my stomach, if tonight he and the widow Wills will celebrate ridding themselves of me. I wonder if they'll snicker together in her bed and say, *Good riddance to that troublesome little piece of tripe!* Meanwhile, Ma lies in her bedroom, struggling to breathe, and I curl beneath my blankets, listening to the clocks counting down the hours of the night, as I bid a silent farewell to all the women I'm leaving behind, both aboveground and below.

As for my muse, I wish the James River would swallow her up this dark hour, as cruel as that may sound. I long to arrive in Charlottesville as a regular student with reasonable ambitions—an eager young scholar with talents that please and inspire, not horrify and sicken—a liberated soul who'll soon never need depend on John Allan again.

CHAPTER SIXTEEN

Lenore

With a gasp, my eyes fly open in the stark chill of Judith's bedroom.

The heart cut from glass hangs around my neck and glows in the firelight of the hearth beside me. I'm curled on my left side on a braided rug, while Judith, my far-too-generous protector, snores in her bed above, bone tired from toiling away in Moldavia. Her clothing and hair carry the spices and smoke of the kitchen into her bedroom, and I daresay she never truly leaves that kitchen except through her stories spun after dark.

Morella has slipped off into another realm—her reward for the tales told.

The stone heart beats against my breast with a low and ominous pulse. *You will not belong in Charlottesville, it seems to warn. He'll reject you; neglect you, even worse than he does here. Go, soak up the spirits of Richmond tonight. Absorb every morsel of your poet's memories of this city so you may pour them back into his soul when he no longer lives here—when he struggles and avoids you—so the two of you may reap a bounty.*

I tiptoe out of the cabin and leap into the night.

The red earth of Richmond bleeds through the slush of the roads. I wander through the muck and the cold toward the city's oldest public cemetery, the churchyard of St. John's.

Drink up the memories, says the wind that lures me to the hallowed grounds up another hill to the east, *until they drench your heart with a deep and dreary darkness. Drink up the memories until you can't bear another dismal drop.*

Amid the headstones and footstones and the tabletop markers that protect the graves of St. John's, linger the souls of old Richmond, their forms gauzy and glimmering in a pale, pearly blue, almost white, but not quite. They emit the scents of mist and rosemary, of sorrow and revival, and I taste the bittersweetness of their deaths on the back of my tongue.

The spirits stir when they see me and stare at my approach. A bewigged man in a cocked hat dives back into his grave with a yelp, as though I'm the devil incarnate, come to drag him down into the putrid bowels of hell. Several spirits straighten their posture and smooth out the wrinkles in their clothing, as though they understand what I am—as though they know I possess the skills to allow the living to remember them, to celebrate them, to immortalize them in the potent blood they call "ink."

A girl near Edgar's age in a dress with a full skirt reaches out her right hand and asks, "Will you inspire your artist to tell my story?"

She's so pretty and poised, he just might want to tell her tale, but I walk onward to an unmarked grave at one of the farthest edges of the churchyard.

A beacon of light and fog awaits in that region. The nearer I travel, the more the luminescence forms into the shape of my poet's deceased mother, the actress Elizabeth Arnold Hopkins Poe, dressed in a Grecian-inspired gown with a sash wound around her ribs, beneath her bosom. Her eyes resemble my poet's eyes, and she and he have the same hair, but Eliza Poe's curls fall well past her shoulders.

His mother observes my approach, beaming as though she recognizes me, emitting a love so mighty, so maternal, the force of the emotion knocks me to my knees. I kneel before her, my eyes closed, humbled, speechless, my soul satiated by her outpouring of affection, so different than even Morella's concern. I'm bathed in the fragrance of cinquefoil petals.

"Edgar?" asks his mother.

I peek up at her, uncertain whether I heard her correctly.

She leans forward and squints through the light of her own celestial mist. "I don't always see the living all that clearly, but you look like . . ." She stretches her neck. "*Yes . . .* you most certainly look like my younger son."

"Do I?" I ask with a swallow. "What do you see?"

"A somber young man, collapsed on his knees, dripping in shadows that spill from his soul." She steps off her plot of land, a hand pressed to her heart, her eyebrows pursed. "Edgar, my dear, what has happened to you?"

I gaze down at myself to see what she sees, finding my body altered, now dressed in my poet's black frock coat and cream-colored cravat, as well as his narrow gray pantaloons, stretched over a pair of muscular thighs. Vaporous shadows, indeed, seep from my sleeves and my hands—*his* sleeves, *his* hands—drifting to the ground as heavy plumes of smoke that pool around my legs.

"Mother," I say, my voice shifting into Edgar's soft Virginia drawl, "tomorrow I'm leaving Richmond to attend a university. What should I do about my dark muse while I'm amid scholars who might hurl stones and insults at her?"

Eliza Poe blinks several times, as though confused. "I did not know you follow a dark muse."

"I'm ashamed of her. I asked her to alter her appearance so she won't humiliate me. Even you sounded appalled by the idea of her just now."

"You look like you've been ravaged by sorrows, my darling." Mrs. Poe trembles, the warmth of her affection shifting into cold fear. "Your muse should elevate your sufferings into works of art, not add to your worry. Together, you ought to create poetry and music that lift you out of your pain and struggles, even if only for a short while. That is the beauty of art." Eliza clambers over a tree root and walks toward me. "Where is this dark muse of yours?"

I back away on the ground. "I don't want you to see her."

"Where is she?" Eliza reaches out and grabs my right wrist. Her lips part with a gasp, and her eyes expand as though she now views me for who I am. Her fingers chill to frost on my flesh, and the light of her spirit dims to a pale pewter gray that makes my ears ring, my teeth buzz.

She lets go of me and shrinks back. "Who are you?"

"He named me Lenore," I say, my voice small, no longer sounding like his. "I'm your son's muse—his macabre spirit—his poetic obsession with madness, and weirdness, and the most delicious horrors."

"When did you emerge in his life?"

I avert my eyes from hers. "You don't want to ask me that question."

She wraps her arms around herself, her shoulders hunched, her head bowed, folding into herself as though she understands that I first sparked to life in the firelight and shadows of a strange house—a cold house—when she died in a bed in front of her wee boy.

The other spirits, obviously affected by her pain, either hide behind headstones or breeze toward another section of the churchyard, the air souring as they leave.

"Eddy could have suffered a far worse fate," I say to his mother, "than to have developed a dark muse."

Eliza Poe turns away from me and weeps with the sound of the wind in my ears.

I venture closer to her. "I intend to make his life extraordinary, Mrs. Poe, if he'll only agree to commit himself to his art."

She still will not face me.

"He can give everyone what they so desperately crave: hope for life beyond death." I inch even closer. "Love poems fall out of fashion over time, often turning maudlin in the ears of future listeners. Humans' enjoyment of satire and humor is equally fickle, and epic adventures stop seeming so epic when new heroes accomplish new feats. Yet mortals' fear and bewilderment of death will never die—not as long as people keep dying."

At that, Eliza Poe turns around.

"I can't soften my appearance and change who I am, because this"—I slap my palms around my cheeks—"is already a more palatable façade that hides what I am. I'm not a young woman. I'm a shadow."

Eliza Poe nods in understanding. "If you're what his muse needs to be, then, I agree, you should not alter one thing about you for the sake of what others might think."

"How did your muse convince you to pursue your art?" I ask.

"Ah . . . *my muse* . . ." Edgar's mother smiles a wistful smile, and her color brightens to a cerulean glow. "My mother was an actress, so I wasn't frightened at all when he made himself known the very first time I performed on a stage. I was nine, and during the music of the applause, he stepped out of a candelabra—a *beautiful* creature, radiant and angelic, with a wry grin that hinted at his humor. He transformed into a nightingale before my eyes."

I blink. "It happened that suddenly?"

"Everyone told me thereafter that I sang like a nightingale."

A sense of panic seizes me. "*How* did it happen that suddenly? Why didn't it happen to me that quickly?"

Eliza returns to the site of her unmarked grave. "He allowed me to experience the incomparable rush of elation—the pure joy and the pleasure of performing in front of an audience. The moment he showed his face, my art turned vital, and I forsook *everything* else to pursue him." She sits down on the mantle of snow that blankets her bones. "That's why I left my first-born son, Henry, with his grandparents in Baltimore all those years ago. I couldn't live without my muse. He was too much a part of my blood and soul, even more than my own flesh and blood." She lies down on that cold patch of earth. "This conversation saddens me too much. I'm too tired to speak of such memories anymore. And you shouldn't wander the city in that delicate state. Go home, Lenore, and transcend the sorrows of this world with my dear Edgar."

I step forward to inquire whether she has any advice for surviving Edgar's new life at the college, but she fades from view while singing the opening verse of "Nobody Coming to Marry Me"—an English theater ditty I've often heard Eddy whistle.

I journey up Shockoe Hill to visit Jane Stanard's spirit, intent on absorbing her appreciation of Eddy's poetry—to drink up her chaste admiration for him—perhaps even to imbibe more draughts of his sorrow that lingers at her gravesite.

A night watchman calls out, "Ten o'clock, and all is well!"—one block to the north. Dogs snarl and bark from the same direction.

Oh, God!

I abandon my plan and break into a run back to Moldavia, afraid to encounter either man or beast, glancing over my shoulder to be sure no one follows.

I slam into something hard.

A pair of hands grab me in the dark.

"Cassandra?"

I shake out my head to regain my senses and discover I've crashed into none other than John Allan. He clutches my forearms and gazes down at me.

"Were you looking for me?" he asks.

I pull out of his arms, repulsed by his odors of perspiration and tobacco. His forehead gleams with a slick layer of sweat, and the gold buttons of his vest are fastened all wrong, as though he dressed himself in a hurry.

"Ten o'clock and all is well!" the watchman again calls, now closer. Footsteps both animal and human pad through the slush in the streets in the dark.

"I must hide," I say, covering the teeth around my neck. "Hide me!"

"Hey!" calls the watchman from behind. "Is that the same monstrosity that ran through town the other day?"

John Allan's eyes bulge. He's been caught with a muse—a fate he clearly can't bear, for his mouth stretches into a grimace.

"Hide me, please, Eddy," I say, ducking behind him.

"Eddy?" he asks.

My blood chills at my mistake.

"Is that the demon?" asks the watchman.

"Please, Jock," I say. "I didn't mean to say Edgar's name. Please don't—"

"Yes!" John Allan clasps me by my elbows and swings me around. "This putrid little serpent just tried to attack me."

He shoves me toward the watchman, who lifts his lantern and recoils at the sight of me. At his side a ruddy-cheeked companion, armed with a musket, helps him wrangle a pack of bloodhounds straining at the ends of their leashes. The curs bark and snarl, tails down, ears laid back, teeth bared, eager to rip at my flesh—this hideous, constricting human flesh I should have never inhabited. I should have never rushed to be seen.

I push John Allan aside and bolt toward the south.

"Get her!" shouts the watchman, and the men set the dogs free.

The bloodhounds chase me down a sloped street, a quagmire of snow and mud.

My poet is a runner, thank heavens, so I have his ability to sprint with the swiftness of Atalanta, but the dogs bear down on me with velocity and power, snorting and growling, their paws pounding the ground behind me. I fly through the night in my borrowed brown boots, raising my skirts up to my hips so my legs may stretch to their full length, and I whimper and wheeze, desperate to reach the sanctuary of the James—terrified of slipping and falling.

The smell of the wharf emerges—the sharp scents of tar, pitch, and water.

I splash through puddles in alleyways, dart between warehouses and breweries, the darkness thickening, mist clinging to my skin. The dogs bark at my heels, so close!

Oh, God! So close!

Up ahead, moonlight shimmers across black waters. My heels pound across the planks of Ludlam's Wharf, where my poet once escaped my shadow—fled his grief for Jane Stanard—took on a naysayer who wagered he couldn't swim all the way to Warwick—all by diving into the river in front of a crowd of dozens and swimming six miles beneath a blistering June sun.

Following his lead, I hurtle myself off the end of the wharf, and with a deadening splash that floods my head and lungs with a torrent of freezing water, I plummet—confused, disoriented, weak, and groaning—down into the depths of the James.

PART II

– FEBRUARY 12, 1826 –

From childhood's hour I have not been
As others were—I have not seen
As others saw—

—EDGAR ALLAN POE, "Alone," 1829

CHAPTER SEVENTEEN

Edgar

Pa and I leave the house at daybreak, and the eastern sky greets us with a banner of fuchsia and gold that makes my chest swell with hope. I taste freedom in the breeze.

Out on the front drive, Old Jim shakes my hand, wishes me well, and says, "You'll be missed."

"I'll miss all of you dearly," I say, gulping down the emotion that cracks through my voice. "Thank you, Jim." I give his hand an extra pump, for he's agreed to deliver a parting letter to Elmira, in which I've assured my secret fiancée of the constancy of my heart.

I climb into our carriage and settle in across from Pa, adjusting my frock coat to avoid sitting on a lump of fabric. Dabney shuts the door behind me.

Ma watches us from the reception room window, flanked by Judith and Aunt Nancy. During our parting embrace, Ma sobbed until she swooned. Judith ran for the smelling salts, while Aunt Nancy and I draped Ma's limp body across the crimson cushions of the couch. I nearly lost my breakfast. Pa sighed over the delay in our departure.

Dabney nickers to the horses, and the carriage rolls forward. My trunk and writing box shift overhead.

"A three-day's journey, then?" I ask Pa.

He unfurls the morning newspaper across his lap. "I think we can manage the excursion without killing each other."

I smirk at his remark and lean back against the black leather seat, bidding adieu to my beloved women, the sweeping porticos, the columns, the orchards, the gardens, and the vistas of the green river valley in the Kingdom of Moldavia.

For two and a half long days Pa and I rock about in the carriage. Dabney carts us northwest on the Three Notch'd Road that runs from Richmond to Charlottesville, and we sleep two nights in the upstairs rooms of taverns alive with fiddle music and card games while we breathe the aromas of the South's strongest ales. We dine on mutton, geese, and hams brined in excessive coatings of salt that chap our lips, as well as fresh countryside cheeses and jams. And, somehow, we, indeed, manage to avoid killing each other, possibly because most of our hours entail our reading in silence or gazing out the carriage at creeks and glorious mountain ranges painted across the sky.

We don't speak of my poetry. I'm half convinced my dark muse somehow disappeared, for my thoughts seldom veer into the realm of melancholy out here on the highway that propels me toward liberation.

We arrive in Charlottesville during the afternoon of February 14, 1826—St. Valentine's Day. Before the Academical Village of the university even rises into view, Pa pulls out his leather pocketbook.

"I'll not stay long," he says. "Just enough time to ensure you're headed in the correct direction. I'll give you your money for expenses now."

I frown at the idea of him scarcely taking the time to stop the carriage and let me out. His knobby fingers pluck a stack of money out of the pocketbook, and he counts and recounts the bills with care.

"It's one hundred ten dollars." He hands the money to me. "Spend it solely on university expenses. Be prudent and careful."

"Thank you," I say, and I tuck the cash into my own leather pocketbook.

"I've requested special permission for you to attend the lectures of two professors instead of three," Pa decides to then add.

My hand freezes on the pocketbook that's half-stuffed back into my coat. "Why would you do that? I'm an advanced student, Pa. Attending the lectures of three professors is the normal requirement."

"We don't have the money for you to attend three professors, Edgar." He fetches his pipe and silver tinderbox from another coat pocket.

A wound inside me rips open. All I can see is the garish opulence of Moldavia—the bronze statues, the mirrored ballroom, the rosewood chairs Pa just imported from an eight-hundred-year-old castle in Germany. Pa strikes flint against steel, igniting the char cloth in the tinderbox. He then lights a match and sets a flame to his pipe, filling the carriage with the fragrance of the finest fire-cured tobacco in the entire state of Virginia. My eyes lock onto his jeweled cufflinks, the gold fob of his pocket watch, his new coat, his polished shoes with gold buckles . . .

We don't have the money for you to attend three professors, Edgar.

He exhales a puff of smoke, and his aging, red-rimmed eyes meet mine. He's watching me, waiting to see if the "sensitive" burden sitting across from him succumbs to tears, but I don't give him that satisfaction. I return his stare and breathe without a sound, and I think, *Good Lord, man, if you want to turn me into a feral monster and a criminal, just push me out of the carriage right now and be done with it. Don't continue to abuse me by fooling me into thinking you're providing for my future.*

It's with unsteady feet, therefore, that I climb out of the carriage at the University of Virginia.

Two other students have also just arrived, both accompanied by parents and their servants, the latter of whom hoist trunks of belongings across the Lawn—a terraced stretch of land blanketed in two inches of crystalline snow. When it thaws, the area would make an exquisite field for challenging schoolmates to foot races.

Ten white pavilions, connected by pillared brick colonnades, form the perimeter of the Lawn, and at the far end rises a Rotunda-in-progress, barricaded in scaffolding that can't hide the fact that the university's founder, Thomas Jefferson, modeled this architectural masterpiece after the Pantheon in Rome. Carpenters hammer at the Rotunda, and I envision the completion of the structure's Corinthian columns and glorious domed roof.

My mouth hangs open far too long as my brain attempts to digest the idea that this bastion of hope—this neoclassical palace of knowledge—is to become my new home.

"Wait here with the carriage, Dabney," says Pa. "I won't be long."

My stomach sinks again at the idea that he's ridding himself of me so quickly.

I shake hands with Dab, who's roughly the same age as Pa, forty-seven, but the compassion in Dab's brown eyes makes him seem ten years younger.

Without further ado, Pa leads me across the Lawn with my writing box tucked beneath his left arm. I lug my trunk, which bangs against my right leg. The other fellows and their escorts migrate toward a two-story pavilion on the western side of the Lawn, so we follow, assuming we're trooping off in the right direction. Pa puffs on his pipe and spoils the crisp February air with his tobacco.

A large man with white hair and long ears steps out from the pavilion.

"Welcome, gentlemen," he says, enunciating each letter with great care. "I am the proctor, Mr. Arthur Brockenbrough. Follow me please, so that we may enter your names into the matriculation book."

"I'll say goodbye to you out here," says Pa before we've even reached the brick terrace of the colonnade. "Study hard, Edgar. Complete all your assignments. Attend every class."

"Won't you at least stay until my name's been logged into the book?" I ask, lowering my trunk to my side. "Do you truly need to run off so quickly, Pa?"

"You're a grown man now. You don't need your 'pa' leading you by the hand into college." He hands me my writing box, rattling the contents with his brusqueness. "Good luck. Behave well. Make Ma proud."

"Of course I will."

"Yes, I'm sure."

After a swift parting embrace, he turns and leaves me standing there with my belongings. I watch him retreat across the Lawn, his pipe smoke curling into the air above his tall umber hat. His tobacco lingers in my nose—the odor of thick leather ledgers, counting-room coins, and candles burnt down to nubs during late-night transactions. The smell of a world in which men worship stacks of money more than their own families and feed the imagination of their youth to the jaws of the fires burning in their grates.

When it's my turn to step up to the proctor's desk, I say to the gentleman, "I heard you mention that your name was Brockenbrough, sir. Are you perhaps related to Judge William Brockenbrough of Richmond?"

"He's my brother."

"Your brother?" I raise my eyebrows, comforted by the notion that I'm speaking to the sibling of someone I know, despite my longing to sever ties to Richmond. "Well, then it's my pleasure to meet you, sir. Your brother owns the church pew in front of my mother's."

"No doubt our paths have crossed at some point, then." He dips his pen into the inkwell. "What is your name?"

I submit my name ("Edgar A. Poe"), my birthdate ("19 Jan: 1909"), my parent or guardian's name ("John Allan," although I think the proctor spelled Pa's surname as "Allen"), my place of residence ("Richmond"), and I elect my schools of study: Ancient Languages, taught by Professor Long, and Modern Languages, taught by Professor Blaettermann.

Mr. Brockenbrough instructs the two other new students, who now look a little lost, to go back outside to meet their "hotelkeepers," who'll escort them to their rooms. He then sends me over to the desk of a Mr. Garrett, the bursar, who's to collect my fees.

Mr. Garrett—another white-haired gentleman, one with wooly brown eyebrows and an astoundingly large chin—sifts through the papers on his desk.

"'Poe,' you said?"

"Yes." I fetch my pocketbook from my coat.

The man pulls my list of fees to the top of his stack. "Well, Mr. Poe, I have listed here fifty dollars for board, sixty dollars for the attendance of classes of two professors . . ." He glances up at me. "You're enrolled in only two schools of study, is that correct?"

I nod without speaking, and my heartrate doubles, for he lowers his head to read off yet *more* fees, but he's already reached one hundred ten dollars—the total sum filling my pocketbook.

"Fifteen dollars for room-rent, twelve dollars for a bed, and twelve dollars for room furniture." He lifts his eyes again. "That brings us to a total of one hundred forty-nine dollars, due immediately."

I swallow, and rock backward, nearly fainting, for the air's grown so horrifically thin.

"My foster father, John Allan, sent me here with only one hundred ten dollars."

The man puckers his caterpillar eyebrows. "Are you certain?"

"Yes, he counted the bills in front of me several times." I back away with my pocketbook cradled in my hands. "Let me go see if his carriage is still out there. He might not be gone just yet."

"Please do."

I cross the planks of the solid wood floor in relative silence and wait until I step outside the building before breaking into a run across the Lawn.

He's gone.

Pa's carriage is nowhere to be found.

"I must beg your forgiveness"—I slink back over to Mr. Garrett and his accounting books, my soles squeaking against the floor—"he's already left. I'll write to him immediately."

"Are you certain he has the proper funds waiting at home?"

"He's one of the richest men in Richmond. You may write to the proctor's brother, the honorable Judge William Brockenbrough, if you don't believe me. Yes"—I raise my chin—"John Allan has the funds."

Mr. Garrett eyes me as though evaluating the weight of my worth with some sort of measuring device in his eyes. He sniffs, perhaps searching for any traces of the stink of poverty wafting off me, but I hold my head high, my posture straight as a rod, my face stoic. He then dips his quill into his ink with an audible *plunk* and writes down something on my page of fees, but I can't read his upside-down scribblings.

"Pay the one hundred ten now," he says with another sniff through his fluttering nostrils, "but do, indeed, write to him immediately. You'll owe thirty-nine dollars after today's payment."

"Yes, sir." I pile the money that I do have onto his desk, and like Pa, the man counts and recounts each bill, his jowls drooping with a frown of concentration.

"Again, I beg your pardon, sir," I say. "There must have been some mistake on his part."

"You'll need to purchase books, as well." Mr. Garrett scratches more notes about me across his paper. "And you're expected to deposit one hundred fourteen dollars for your uniform and related clothing, not to mention your pocket money. Surely, your father knew of all these expenses."

"I'm not certain, sir. He gave me the one hundred ten dollars just now; that's all that I know."

"Wait outside with your belongings." He hands me a piece of paper that lists my debts. "A hotelkeeper will fetch you and take you to your room. Classes are already in session for this term. You may start attending lectures tomorrow."

"Thank you, sir."

Mr. Garrett wrinkles his nose as though he, indeed, detects a foul stink. He knows I'm part of the lower class—he might even guess I'm the son of strolling players—and he doesn't care a damn about my foster father's wealth.

I leave the Rotunda, clasping my trunk and my writing box by my sides, my pocketbook empty, my pride shattered.

No more than a minute later, however, an antidote to my humiliation arrives: the sudden clamor of students exiting their lectures in the pavilions. Their voices ring across the air. They stride down the colonnades with ease in their steps, dressed in the light gray coats and striped pantaloons of the university's uniform.

A man of sizable girth approaches me—a fellow too old and shabby of dress for me to mistake him for one of the students. His cheeks are rosier than a sunburn; his eyes, the murky blue of a swimming hole.

"Good afternoon," he says. "I'm one of the hotelkeepers, Mr. George Washington Spotswood"—he tips his leather hat—"distant cousin of *the* George Washington."

"I'm Edgar Poe," I say with a shake of his hand, wondering if he always introduces himself with a mention of his famous cousin, or if I look the type to be impressed by presidential relations—which, in fact, I am.

"Let us travel to your dormitory, Mr. Poe."

"Thank you, sir."

I trail the man down the brick path of the western colonnade, passing white Tuscan columns on the left side of the walkway and cucumber-green doors framed by matching shutters on the right.

Halfway down the Lawn, Mr. George Washington Spotswood unlocks one such door using a jangle of keys. "There's to be no card playing or drinking in here. The faculty and the sheriffs swear on God's teeth they'll punish any more gamblers or drunkards with suspensions and expulsions."

"Yes, sir."

He swings the door open, the construction so new, the joints don't even creak. "Make yourself comfortable, Mr. Poe.

You'll take your meals in the hotel. Either the hotelkeeper for the West Lawn or one of his servants will be in your room around six o'clock in the morning to light your fire and bring you water. I'll speak to you about payments for firewood, washing, and so forth in the coming days."

I clench my teeth at the mention of more payments. "Thank you, sir."

"Good day to you."

"Good day."

Mr. Spotswood leaves me behind in a simple chamber with white plaster walls, a fireplace with no logs, a twelve-dollar bed, and a twelve-dollar table and chair set I cannot afford. I'm reduced to the status of "pauper" before I've even commenced my classes.

But, still, I'm a pauper untethered from the presence of the Great John Allan.

Before I can close my door to unpack, a beanpole of a fellow with blond hair hanging in his eyes raps on my doorframe.

"Welcome to the Lawn," he says. "I'm Miles George from Richmond."

"Edgar Poe." I shake his hand. "Also from Richmond. You weren't in Master Clarke's school, were you?"

"No, but I've heard of you—a writer, right?"

I smile. "That's correct. A writer for now, at least."

Miles pushes his hair off his forehead, revealing a pair of striking green eyes above a flawless nose that ends in a sharp point. "Have you heard about today's expulsion yet?"

"No."

"A student named William Cabell—"

"Oh, I know several Cabells in Richmond," I say.

"Virginia is packed full of Cabells. Last month, Will Cabell was riding around with friends in a carriage, reeling drunk, when he saw a group of professors walking with a lady friend. Well, he decided to—" Miles turns his head to his right and barks a short laugh. "The drunken ass stuck his head out the carriage window and asked the lady, 'Why would a woman with such a fine face and beautiful breasts waste her time letting those damned European professors bugger her?'"

My eyes widen.

"And today," continues Miles, his face blushing to the color of pickled beets, "those 'damned European professors' sentenced him to expulsion."

"A University of Virginia student shouted *that* at a lady?"

"Yes." Miles laughs again. "Haven't you heard about life here in Jefferson's grand experiment of mating the core ideals of the American democracy with a classical, European education? Old Tommy Jefferson trusted that we scions of the South could all self-govern ourselves with our high moral standards. Ha!"

"I've heard it's a bit wild here."

"Oh, it's more than 'a bit wild'—it's bedlam! Be prepared to hear blasts of gunfire at night, especially outside the West Range dormitories, which we call 'Rowdy Row.' And be careful when you drink. The faculty is on the hunt for anyone who's splashed. At the very least"—Miles again sweeps his hair out of his eyes—"be a quiet drunk who doesn't insult the professors' lady friends or piss in Jefferson's gardens."

"Thank you for that advice," I say with a smile that belies my fears of what I might actually do while splashed here. "I will do my best not to sully the gardens."

"Yes, no sullying!" Miles pats my left arm. "Nice to finally meet you, Poe. I'm looking forward to reading your writing."

"Later this week, after I'm settled in, bring over some of your friends. I'll give a reading of some of my satires."

He raises his eyebrows. "Will you?"

"Yes," I say with a nod, deeming my ridicules the best fit for a collegiate setting. "And after I meet these 'damned European professors,' I'm sure I could perform a weekly reading, inspired by their lectures."

Miles chuckles. "I have a feeling you'll be an interesting addition to this place."

"Thank you."

He gives a short wave. "I'll see you soon, Poe."

"Goodbye, Miles."

I close my door as Poe the Satirist.

Miles George strolls away knowing nothing of Eddy the Romantic . . . or Edgar the Master of Macabre Fancies, who glances at the shadows of his new room with a wary eye, dreading the sight of Lenore almost as much as he fears expulsion because Jock Allan was too damn cheap to leave enough money.

CHAPTER EIGHTEEN

Lenore

My poet is a swimmer, so I fight my way out of the tangled darkness of river grasses and rise above the surface, where I swim past ships and steamboats that creak and rock in the docks like arthritic old men. I swim around forested islands with slick granite shores that rise from the water as ashen mounds, lit by the cockeyed grin of the moon.

The water I swallowed during my plummet into the James engorges my body—a body already weighted down with Edgar Poe's memories. Such heaviness would drag a weaker swimmer down to the river's bottom—the chill of the James alone would freeze a more delicate soul—but I am neither weak nor delicate. Despite the burdens I bear, my arms plow through the night-blackened waters, and I kick my legs like a champion, with scarcely a splash or a fuss of foam in my wake. The farther I travel north, the less brackish and polluted with sewage the James tastes on my lips, and I soar out of the ugliness of the past.

For days and nights, I push upriver to the mouth of the Rivanna. A screech owl flies overhead, guiding my journey with outstretched wings gilded in sunlight and silvered by the moon, until I part ways with the James and travel northwest to Charlottesville, and Morella turns back home. The cadence of the water lapping the shores and the occasional music of a fiddle drifting through the winter-bare trees appease some of my hunger for art. Too often, however, I'm so ravenous that I don't see straight, and I find myself briefly ensnared in fishing nets or patches of ice that slice like knives.

Sometimes I lie down for a rest amid the naked foliage on the river's edge and listen for the sound of a heartbeat that tolls like a bell in the distance.

Hear that throbbing, thumping bell—tempting bell! *What* a life of liberty its melody foretells.

I won't drown within this river, even though I'm short of breath, even though I shake and shiver, I will not give Pa one sliver of the pleasure of my death.

No!

I *will not* give old John Allan the satisfaction of killing me, and so I swim on, and on, and on, and on, lured by that distant, beating, haunting, taunting, palpitating poet's heart—that muffled, melodious bell, bonging, longing for tales to tell.

CHAPTER NINETEEN

Edgar

A European professor, indeed, reigns over my seven o'clock Italian lecture in the school of Modern Languages—a German fellow named Blaettermann of rough build and sweaty orange hair.

It's so agonizingly early that dawn hasn't yet broken. The fire in the hearth yawns and stretches as much as we do. A corps of candles and wall sconces illuminates the room, perfuming the pavilion with a scrim of smoke that hangs between us and the professor.

"We are going to concentrate on the poets of Italy this month," he says in a harsh Saxony accent, his round head weaving and bobbing in and out of the shadows.

A student at a back table mimics the professor in an exaggerated version of his accent, clipped and guttural, with a barrage of buzzing Zs.

The other students in the back howl with laughter. Professor Blaettermann curses at them in German and shakes a fist in their direction, but then he proceeds to list on a blackboard the Italian poets we'll be reading. The students shake their fists back at him, mocking his shouts, and someone throws a shoe that bounces off the board in a shower of chalk.

I bend over my notebook and write down the poets we're to study, so anxious about my outstanding fees that I don't dare risk expulsion due to a poor disciplinary record. Most every other student in the classroom wears the light-gray coat and striped pantaloons of the university's uniform, but I'm sitting here in my black frock coat and brown trousers, unable to pay for any such garments.

My stomach groans. Breakfast won't be served until the eight o'clock recess of the lecture.

Someone throws another shoe—a fine, polished black one that would probably pay for my uniform and more.

The flame of the candle burning on my table sizzles and bends my way.

Do you think these fellows all believe themselves better than you? I wonder with a glance at my classmates. *Do they know you're the orphaned son of an actress and a drunk? Do they smell the stink on you? Can they detect that directly after class, you'll need to write to a man in Richmond who despises you—a man who's never even legally adopted you—and beg him for money, pleading with him to pay the remainder of your fees so you won't be hauled away in shame?*

I focus my full attention on Professor Blaettermann's voice and pray for my survival in this madhouse. Despite the chaos writhing within the white walls of this pavilion—despite the explosions of either fireworks or gunfire that woke me up late last night—I would prefer, without a doubt, to live here instead of Moldavia.

Dear God, please don't let anyone drag me away before the session ends in December.

I swiftly make friends, at least—Miles George, Thomas Goode Tucker, William Burwell, Zaccheus Collins Lee, among others. A few of these new chums also claim that they're runners, so I challenge them to foot races across the Lawn during the afternoons after the lectures, never mind the snow and the tumbles we take when our feet slip out from under us.

None of these fine lads know that I've written to Pa with a request for more money and a detailed account of the expenses incurred, so Pa won't think I'm inflating the amount. They don't even know that I've mailed a letter to Elmira Royster that expressed the ardor of my passion, and they most certainly aren't aware that I'm secretly engaged to her, a girl whose father believes I have the marriage potential of a horse turd in the street. I can't risk gossip about my engagement traveling back to Richmond. Miles might know Elmira—or have acquaintances who know her family.

Saturday night, after a long week of lectures and settling into my surroundings, I invite Miles, Tom, and Will to my room to test out their opinions of my work. The fellows pile into my dormitory, freed from their gray uniforms, clad in coats of their own desired colors and styles, which they peel off and toss onto my bed.

Tom Tucker, a pasty fellow with short black hair and the face of a twelve-year-old, pulls a decanter filled with liquid out of a pocket in his overcoat. "Do you like peach and honey, Poe?"

"I've never tried it."

"You're not a true University of Virginia student until you do." Tom plunks the decanter onto my table, directly in front of where I'm sitting.

Alcohol the color of liquified gold sloshes before my eyes. Tom pulls out the glass stopple, and the fumes of a sweetened peach brandy consume my nose.

Miles and Will dig crystal snifters out of their coat pockets on the bed.

"Where did you get those?" I ask with a laugh. "Your grandmother's cabinet of heirlooms?"

"You're not far off," says Will, the shortest of our group, but his lion's mane of red curls adds at least three inches to his height. He lines the snifters on the table as though they're delicate jewels.

"Shall I pour," asks Tom, "or would you prefer to do the honors as our esteemed host, Poe?"

I eye the golden temptress waiting in the glass before me, unsure whether I'm yet comfortable enough to quaff spirits in front of these gentlemen.

I push the decanter toward Tom. "You pour. I'll wait to drink until after I pay homage to dear Professor Blaettermann on my wall."

"On your wall?" asks Miles, brushing his blond hair out of his eyes again.

I nod. "On my beautifully bare wall."

"Oh, I can't wait to see this." Miles takes a seat on the floor next to the pile of firewood that's run me several more dollars into debt.

Will sits down beside him and removes his socks and shoes, as though settling in for the night.

Tom pours the peach and honey.

I slide open the drawer of my writing box and fetch a charcoal crayon. The flame of my tabletop candle wriggles in anticipation of my eminent performance.

"Gentlemen," I say with a leap upon my bed, brandishing the charcoal like a nubbin of a sword, "I present to you an ode to the esteemed professors of Jefferson's university."

"Here, here!" says Miles with a raise of the glass he's just received from Tom. "Shower us with your brilliant criticism of asses that I've heard so much about in Richmond."

I grin and blush. "Oh, you've already heard about my satires, then?"

"Our young Edgar Poe here," says Miles to the others, "is famous for chasing a bastard out of town when said bastard insulted him."

"Did you challenge him to a duel?" asks Will with a rasp after taking a swig of his drink.

"No, it was no duel," I say, digging my feet into my mattress, steadying my balance. "I ridiculed the ass with an anonymous poem—a rapier-sharp lampoon that I named 'Don Pompioso' and plastered across the city."

The boys snort into their brandies. Tom scoots the chair away from my table and plops himself down on it while taking a drink. Liquor dribbles from his chin to his pantaloons, and the aroma of alcohol overpowers the air.

"Is everyone comfortable and ready?" I ask.

"Yes!" says Will after another gulp.

I clear my throat and lift the charcoal crayon with a theatrical flourish, envisioning myself on a stage, candlelight shining down on my head from a brass chandelier.

"Here's a thing I've wondered since I was quite small and young," I say. "Why are we enamored with the sound of British tongues? Why are our professors all imported from abroad? All they need to do is belch, and, God, we all applaud!"

The fellows clap and whistle while balancing their brandies on their laps, and the flame of my tabletop candle stretches five splendiferous inches into the air. In fact, every lamp in my room burns with more vigor, illuminating the canvas of my wall.

I draw Professor Blaettermann's round head on the plaster.

"Keep going!" calls out Miles.

"More! More!" shouts Tom.

With a smile, I draw a droopy pair of eyes, a turned-up nose, and wild patches of hair, and I proceed with my versification:

"Latin spills like satin from those European lips,
'We don't care if they can't teach, just send them
> *on your ships!'*
That's the rule of bon ton fools in Yankee Doodle
> *Land,*
'Lord help any child taught by a Yankee Doodle
> *man!'*
Even though we broke from England in a
> *bloody war,*
British education is the method we adore,
Some say Southern accents tear the classics into
> *shreds,*
I say, 'That's a damned, old lie embedded in your
> *heads,'*
So, I ask again—and I will shout it from my
> *lungs—"*

I pause to draw three plump little hairs sticking out from Blaettermann's chin mole. Then I turn toward my audience, arms raised in the air, and call out:

"Why are we enamored with the sound of British
> *tongues?"*

"Huzzah!" shouts Miles, smacking his palms together, and the others follow suit, whooping and belching from the brandy.

I bow from atop my bed, my right hand pressed flat against my stomach, but I freeze at a troubling *whoosh* that intrudes upon my room—the sound of a sudden surge of fire.

I lift my face, and my mind muddles. My brain, for some reason, insists on miscalculating the number of young men seated inside my room, and I wonder if I've already swallowed a draught of the brandy without my realizing. I straighten up and count their heads once again.

Tom sits on my chair, but three fellows, not two, now occupy my floor.

I jump off the bed. "Who's that sitting next to Will?"

The lads cease applauding and look to their left. They've all drained their first glasses, so no one even attempts to offer a coherent explanation for the sudden appearance of this fourth person, who's clad in the university's uniform, his face tipped downward, his eyes hidden beneath the low brim of a gray silk hat with the feathers of a mockingbird sticking out from a black band.

"How did you get in here?" I ask.

"You invited me," says the stranger in a voice not unlike my own.

"Who are you?"

"Garland O'Peale."

I shiver at his name, although I'm not entirely sure why.

"Do I know you from Richmond?" I ask.

"The question is," says the stranger, "does Richmond know you from me?"

He raises his face, and I witness a ring of fire radiating from his pupils, throbbing out to the edges of a pair of amber irises.

My legs give way. I stagger over to my table and fall against the wood, nearly knocking over the glass of peach and honey waiting for me.

"Are you all right, Poe?" asks Tom, rising to his feet. "You seem used up already. Did you drink before we got here?"

I dare another glance at Garland and see a clean-shaven face that resembles my own, with the same long but sufficiently good nose, narrow chin, and uninspiring mouth. His eyes, like mine, are large and framed in jet-black lashes, but their bright amber hue looks inhuman. I know what the fire pulsing inside them signifies, but I want nothing more to do with muses clamoring for attention.

I grab the snifter and dump the brandy down my gullet in a single gulp that stings my tonsils.

"Bravo!" says Will, and another round of applause ensues to revere my bold drinking style. No one else seems bothered by Garland O'Peale.

I pound my glass to the table and brace my hands against the wood, enduring a disorienting wave of dizziness that makes me rock back and forth. The world tastes of peaches and fire.

Garland belches, which irks me. I've just suppressed my own belch by pinning my lips together and holding my breath, and yet he has the gall to go and belch for me.

"Edgar?" asks Miles with a nervous laugh. "Are you ill?"

A gust of wind slams against my window and whistles beneath my door, and the atmosphere shifts. My bitterness eases, yet my passions awaken. I gaze up at the plastered wall above Miles's head, noting its blankness, its possibilities, and I believe I see, staring out at me from the shadows, the eyes of Jane Stanard with their heavy lids and pale lashes. With my charcoal crayon in hand, I plod across the floorboards, the air a thick stew that hinders the movements of my legs, and the gentlemen on the floor part to let me to pass.

I draw my Helen's eyes right there on the wall, and then I add her slender brows, her petite lips, her regal nose, and the curves of her cheeks and chin, but her eyes are out of proportion—much too large for her face. She's staring at me in anguish, in agony. She's the version of Mrs. Stanard I only heard about from her son, my younger friend Rob.

I think my mother might be going mad, he told me before we entered Master Clarke's school one autumn morning when I was fourteen. *Something's wrong with her brain. She's not well at all.*

Using my crayon, I immortalize the soft curls of her hair that fell across her forehead like clusters of hyacinths, but my hand soon rebels and turns her locks into a frenzied mass of black tangles that snake away from her head. She's wild and tortured, not at all the gentlewoman who invited me into her garden with her son and asked me about my poetry.

"Once I loved a woman, whom they buried in the ground," I say, my voice whispery and deep. "During the splendorous spring of my darling's short life, she invited me inside her garden walls and asked me to sit with her in a bed of lilies."

My charcoal crayon has now desecrated my angel into a rotted specter, resurrected from the grave, reminding me that beauty is fleeting, death conquers all—it *always* conquers all. I can't bear to see her this way, so I thicken her brows and her mouth and shorten her slender neck by drowning her throat in a sable collar. She's not Mrs. Stanard—my Helen—she's someone sinister, sensuous, beguiling . . .

"And when she died," I continue, darkening her lips, "she invited me inside her churchyard walls and asked me to sit with her in a bed of lilies. She pulled me down into the ground, into the chilling, charmless churchyard ground, thrilling me, killing me, robbing me of breath, and there I now lie, beneath a bed of lilies."

I finish my creation and sink back on my heels, my fingers smutted with charcoal, my soul a pound lighter.

Behind me, the green door of my dormitory now stands ajar—I know this for a fact without even turning around, for the wind snuffs out two of my candles, and my teeth chatter from the briskness of the air. I hear gasps of horror circulating among my friends.

"What is that?" asks Miles, the timber of his voice higher than usual, and I imagine the expression of disgust on his face.

The charcoal falls from my hand and chips against the floor. I press my forehead against the wall, and without turning around, I feel Lenore standing in my doorway, her arms hanging at her sides, river water dripping from her river-grass hair, the glass heart of her necklace beating, bleeding against the soot of her dress for all to see.

CHAPTER TWENTY

Lenore

My poet's heartbeat drew me to his door.

From across a field of snow lit by a waxing moon, less than two hundred feet from his presence, I detected a change in the air—a bitter chill, as though another form of art—biting and ugly—consumed his attention. Despite my fatigue from my swim, I charged his way, and now I'm standing in his doorway, the glass heart palpitating against my bosom to the rhythm of the heart that beats inside the breast of Edgar Allan Poe.

I clasp the sides of my head and release a silent scream, freeing the essence of Jane Stanard from my soul. The air ripples with her energy, and Edgar draws her on the wall with heavy strokes of charcoal. I close my eyes and direct my artistic vessel to breathe the dankness of her grave, to climb inside her casket with her, to suffer the suffocation of a premature burial, to remember the luster of her light brown curls and the glory of her voice. The candlelight shivers, and Edgar speaks of his dead love and a bed of lilies with beauteous prose in a mournful, whispery tone that floods me with rapture. I remember Morella's promise for the evolution of beings like me:

You will be able to slip into realms fit for a god. You will roost in a sumptuous world wrought from your artist's imagination and experience unprecedent spiritual pleasures, of which no mortal has ever dared to dream.

I reach out my hands, so close to touching such a realm.

". . . and there," says my poet, "I now lie, beneath a bed of lilies."

The palpitations of the stone slow to a gentle ticking, and a wind from the open door blows out two of the candles in the room. Through bleary eyes, I see the slumped shape of my poet, his forehead shoved against the wall. He rubs the back of his head of curls with fingers smeared in charcoal.

"What is that?" asks an emerald-eyed blond boy from down on the floor, a note of awe chiming in his voice. He gawks at me with his head tilted backward, and his right foot twitches, knocking over an empty glass.

Three other young men gape at me with expressions of both fear and befuddlement, their eyes glassy, their mouths dangling open, their faces flushed and damp. They're too stunned to hurt me, and they smell intoxicated, so I don't fret for my life like I did on the streets of Richmond.

My head tingles and itches, as though something wants to burst free from the roots of my hair. To make room for whatever it is that longs to grow, I grab two clumps of my hair and rip them straight out of my scalp.

A boy sitting in a chair tips over backward and crashes to the floor.

Edgar turns around, and his face blanches at the sight of me.

"I've had quite a lot of . . . quite a lot of time to think, Eddy." I drop the hair to the floor and step toward him, my boots squelching with river water, my tongue swelling up to the size of a brick. "I'm here to show you the joy of your art. The unadult ... unadulter ... unadulterate ..." I shake out my head when the word just won't come. "The *pure* joy of concocting grotesque masterpieces." I shove the heels of my palms against my temples and squeeze my eyes shut. "Did you drink ..." I sway. "Did you drink again, Eddy?"

"How did you get here?" he asks. "You know you can't be here."

"No! Don't say that again!"

"I'm hosting guests!"

"Don't you dare throw me out. If I don't belong here, Edgar, then you don't belong either!"

"Oh, holy God of Abraham!" says the blond boy on the floor with another gasp of awe. "This is the most entertaining night of my life!"

One of the other fellows—some dandy in a silk hat with gray-and-white feathers—leaps to his feet and hooks a clawed hand around my left arm. I wince with pain, but before I can say a word, he pushes me outside, slams the door shut behind us, and shoves me out to the snow in the Lawn.

"Edgar doesn't want you here!" says the brute.

I struggle against falling. "Who are you?"

"I know exactly who *you* are." He marches toward me, his eyes orange and ablaze with flames that pierce the darkness.

I back away. "I don't understand ..."

"Poe isn't meant to become a purveyor of the macabre," he says in my face, his breath sickly sweet. "Horror is for the lower classes. Horror isn't art!"

His words slice a tear in my upper left sleeve.

I leap backward and cover the rip with my right hand, my forearm freezing, stinging. "How did you do that?"

"Go!" He stomps his right foot, as though I'm an animal he can scare off. "Go haunt a ten-year-child—that's who ghost tales are for, not university students. You're nothing more than a theater effect, and you reek of cheapness. You're drivel!"

My right sleeve tears, exposing the skin of my elbow.

"Who the devil are you?" I ask, retreating further still.

"I'm Edgar Poe's muse."

"That's not true."

"Oh, but it is, little spider." He walks closer, wiggling his fingers, mimicking the movements of scuttling arachnids. "So, go crawl back into the shadows and cobwebs from whence you came and leave inspiration to me."

"Don't stape . . ." I grab my chin, attempting to move my mouth in a manner that won't melt my words into nonsense, for my tongue's just gone numb. "Stape sass."

The bully in the hat blinks and sways. "Don't I know what you're saying. I don't know . . . what . . ." He clasps his face in his hands, his mouth as seemingly broken as mine.

The same nauseating, liquid sensation that knocked me to the floor of Ebenezer's bedroom again saturates my brain. I throw my arms straight out to my sides to regain my balance and totter away.

"That's right, go, spidery spider!" says that counterfeit muse from behind me, his words slurred and punctuated by a hiccup.

I dread the idea of the two of us collapsing together on the Lawn in the dark, so I round the far corner of the colonnade, where it meets up with a curved brick wall. With loud grunts and more rips in the fabric of my dress, I climb up and over the wall, landing on my feet in a moonlit patch of snow near a building that exhales the fiery exhaust of a smokehouse.

My knees buckle.

The ground tilts.

I stagger three more steps and collapse into a snare of brambles, drifting into a brandy-induced haze in a bed of thorns—a far cry from "realms fit for a god."

CHAPTER TWENTY-ONE

Edgar

The first sight I witness in the lacerating light of day is my distorted rendition of Jane Stanard, sketched in thick strokes of black charcoal on the wall opposite my bed.

I cover my eyes, my head throbbing, on the verge of imploding, and I recall my behavior during the previous night's bacchanalia with my new companions. I flaunted my poetry, exposed my grim imagination in front of those well-bred boys, and they saw *her*.

I bolt upright in bed, suddenly panicked that I'm late for one of my seven o'clock classes.

I remember that it's Sunday and lie back down with a grunt. As soon as my head slaps the pillow, however, a dire urge to vomit sends me tumbling out of bed.

I trip over a pile of hair, coiled like a nest of black racer snakes on my floor, swing open my door, and lunge for the Lawn, where the contents of my stomach explode across the sunlit snow. I crouch on the ground and gasp for air, and the glare from the blinding field of white drills holes through my pupils. My eyes water and leak.

Behind me, some witness of this volatile regurgitation clears his throat.

I glance over my shoulder.

Oh, God!

Garland O'Peale, that new shadow of mine, reclines against the green shutter on the left-hand side of my door.

"I've been watching you and her from the firelight," he says.

I pant for a moment before I'm able to ask, "Watching me and *whom?*"

"You and your Lady of the Dark who appeared in your room unannounced, sopping wet. That ghastly Naiad from the River Styx."

I kneel there in the snow on hands and knees, my stomach convulsing, and, as hard as I fight against it, I throw up again, repulsed by the foul sweetness of the peach brandy in its acidic resurrection. My face hovers over the mess fizzing below me, and with a groan, I pledge to God aloud, "I will never drink again."

Garland snorts. "Southern gentlemen drink like fish, Poe, and you need to fit in. Could you perhaps learn to drink better?"

I sink back on my haunches and twist my torso toward him. "Who the devil are you—telling me what to do?"

Garland rises to his feet and brushes a thin layer of ash off the stripes of his pantaloons. "I'm your ticket to pleasure and prosperity, my friend. Bring me *anywhere* with you, and you'll be the wittiest king of the crowd. Isn't that what you want: to stand above the pompous masses and rally the world into worshipping your genius?"

Ignoring the roiling of my brain, I push myself off the grass and stagger over to him. "I don't need another muse running around in front of everyone. One was bad enough, and you, quite frankly, are an ass."

Garland smiles. "No, it's that other one who's your problem, Poe. *I'll* behave for you. *I* won't show up unannounced. I'm happy to wander the streets of Charlottesville and observe the performances of the foul and the foolish in the courthouse, or I'll pore over books in your dormitory, attend your lectures for you—whatever you want me to do. I'll leave you alone as much as you desire while you fight to better yourself in the halls of this university, *if...*" He raises an index finger and lifts his chin. "*If* you continue inviting me into these private little soirees in your chamber. There's nothing that strengthens me more than bathing in the bliss of the applause you receive from people who adore you."

I rub my parched lips together and contemplate this offer, finding his terms startlingly reasonable compared to anything Lenore has ever proposed.

And yet, this Mephisthophelean mockingbird troubles me down to the marrow of my bones.

"'And so, being young and dipt in folly,'" he says with a side-long glance, a knowing grin, "'I fell in love with melancholy...'"

I shudder. "Why did you just say that?"

"I wonder if you might be in love with that wraith that weighs down your soul with obsessions of death. Do you actually feel an affinity to something so depressing?"

"I'm not in love with her..."

"You can't risk associating with a specter like *that* when you're not even certain how Pa will respond to your request for more money."

My blood congeals. "H-h-how do you know about my letter to my father?"

Garland removes his hat from his head, revealing a head of short gray hair, slicked back from his forehead—a startling contrast to his youthful face. "Your *father*, King John Allan, dangles you from the end of a silk thread. Who's going to be the one who cuts the string?" He cocks his head. "You or the king?"

I shrink away. "Please put your hat back on so no one questions what you are. No one respectable at this university has muses gallivanting about."

"That's because no one else here craves fame and attention as much as the young genius Edgar A. Poe, praised by many, yet loved and understood by none."

"How do you know about my letter to Pa?" I ask again through gritted teeth.

Garland leans forward, his eyes more piercing than even the sunlight. "Because I helped you to write that letter, my friend. I've been incubating in your candlelight, inspiring your writings ever since you first realized precisely how much the gentry despises people like you."

"Well, I didn't ask for you to incubate."

"Yes, you most certainly did! You encouraged me to flourish when you wrote your ridicules of Richmond asses and worked yourself into a frenzy to prove you're not only equal to the bon ton—you're *better* than they are."

I shake my head.

"Don't shake your head at me, Poe. You're meant to be a satirist and a literary critic. Your destiny isn't love poems and nonsensical tales of the grotesque. So, go chase that horrible, hackneyed other muse away. Snuff her out!"

I recoil at his suggestion and cast a glance toward the open Lawn for any traces of a figure clad in a black dress.

Garland gestures with his head toward the south. "I last saw her stumbling around the corner at the far end of the colonnade." He grips my right forearm, his hand feverishly hot. "Those friends of yours worshipped you last night." He peers into my eyes with those troubling irises, so swollen with firelight. "They *worshipped* you," he says again, "until you slipped under her influence and repulsed them all with those miserable ramblings and drawings."

I push his hand off me and back out of his reach. "I don't want the world to see me as simply a man with a barbed pen," I say, pounding a fist against my chest. "That's not why people revere legends like Byron."

Before Garland can spit out any more opinions, I turn and march toward the southernmost corner of the colonnade, fretting over Lenore's whereabouts after last night's bout of drinking, knowing that no one from home could help her this time.

Garland O'Peale calls after me in a voice that echoes across the Lawn, "You're not Byron, Edgar Poe! And you never will be! Be something else."

From behind a serpentine wall built of bricks, a warbling alto voice sings the final verse of an Irish poem I recognize and adore—Thomas Moore's "Come, Rest in This Bosom."

"Thou hast call'd me thy Angel in moments of
*   bliss,*
And thy Angel I'll be, 'mid the horrors of this,—
Thro' the furnace, unshrinking, thy steps to
*   pursue,*
And shield thee, and save thee,—or perish there,
*   too!"*

Through some miracle of strength, I manage to overcome the debilitating effects of my recent stomach woes and hoist myself up to the bed of mortar topping the wall.

Down below in the snow lies Lenore, flat on her back, her legs caught in a web of dried-up brambles. She's missing patches of hair above both her temples, and a dark layer of fuzz that reminds me of the down of a gosling fills the gaps on her scalp. She stares at the sky with eyes dazed and dulled.

Judith's admonishment from back home haunts me:

When you drink liquor, you silence your muse, more than your father ever could. You're a bigger threat to your creativity than that man will ever be.

I swing my legs over the wall and jump down to the snow, peeking around to ensure that the professor who manages this tract of garden land isn't pressing his nose against a window in his pavilion home overlooking the space.

Lenore raises her head two inches off the ground, gazes at me over the length of her supine body, and sings the first verse of the Thomas Moore melody:

"Come, rest in this bosom, my own stricken deer,
Tho' the herd have fled from thee, thy home is
     still here;
Here still is the smile, that no cloud can o'ercast,
And the heart and the hand all thy own to the
     last."

She then plops her head back down on the snow and sighs. "You drank again, Eddy. Stupefied me again. Shunned me again. And, even worse, you summoned another muse to usurp me—a vicious one at that."

I bend down and untangle her legs from the brambles, pricking myself on thorns as I pluck the vines from her clothing. Stinging drops of blood pool on the surface of my fingertips, but my guilt over Lenore's pitiable state stops me from wincing or cursing at the pain.

She wears a pair of stockings dyed in the maroon fleur-de-lis pattern of my walls back home. A pang of homesickness for Ma stabs at my heart at the sight of them.

"I am not going to alter my appearance for you," says Lenore, still lying there, her arms stretched out to her sides. "I followed you here, swam two rivers for you, all to leap straight into the lush and lyrical literary offerings we need to create together as artist and muse. But I don't have the energy to fight your shame of me. That's what weakens me most of all: your utter humiliation."

I pull the last of the thorns from her stockings. "I'm not ashamed of you."

"That's a lie. You know it as well as I." She clenches her hands into fists against the snow. "I spoke to the spirit of your mother the night before you left Richmond, right before Pa and the night watchmen tried to drown me in the James."

Tingles of fear shoot down my arms. "Her *spirit?* They tried to *drown* you?"

Lenore pushes herself up to a seated position and shakes snow from her hair. "Your mother told me, 'If you're what his muse needs to be . . . then you should not alter one thing about you for the sake of what others might think.'"

Blood drains from my face. "No one has ever claimed to have spoken to the spirit of my mother—not even I. And what did you mean when you said Pa tried to drown you in the James? What are you talking about?"

Lenore leans toward me. "If you want people to stop seeing me in this crude, undeveloped form, if you want your naysayers to cease their attempts to silence me, then commit yourself to your art, Eddy, as I asked you in Richmond."

The voices and footsteps of fellow students travel by on the other side of the wall. My heart ceases beating for a second at the sound of them. The fellows laugh and speculate about the edibility of the food they're about to encounter in the hotel.

Lenore takes hold of my left hand, her metallic nails sliding against my skin, and a strain of music, low, and lilting, and lovely, seems to pour from her fingers into my heart.

"If you pledge yourself to your macabre writings, Edgar, then the others won't see me in this human form anymore.

I'll mature into a spiritual entity, most likely taking the form of a raven or a crow, and we'll travel into sumptuous worlds wrought from your imagination. I will direct the course of your art, inspire you, and speak divine truths through you, but you must stop shunning me. And you absolutely cannot replace me with that sharp-tongued *serpent* that chased me out of your room, whatever the devil he was."

"The other muse," I say, dropping my voice in case he's listening from behind the wall, "calls himself Garland O'Peale."

Lenore furrows her broad forehead. "Edgar Allan Poe."

I open my mouth to continue telling her about Garland, yet I stop and ask, "Why did you just say my full name?"

"Rearrange *his* name."

I withdraw my hand from hers, for the music she emits while touching me slows my ability to focus on Garland O'Peale.

Garland O'Peale.

Gar, like the end of Edgar.

Lan, like the end of Allan.

I cringe. "He anagrammed my name!"

"He *stole* your name, the filthy thief. Look what he did to my sleeves with his damned sharp tongue." Lenore bends her right arm, exposing a rip in her sleeve so damaging, her naked elbow pokes through the fabric. "He's dangerous, Eddy. He's the one who'll turn companions into enemies, not I."

"Oh, no . . ." I jump to my feet. "I can't have the two of you fighting and begging me to silence the other. I don't have time for this!"

Lenore stands, as well, but before she can speak, I tell her, "Pa didn't leave enough money for my expenses here. If I can't finish my education, he'll force me into his counting room for the rest of my life. I'll pore over ledgers until my eyes weaken and my brain numbs, and I won't have a single second left for even the most uninspired of writing, let alone anything divine."

Without warning, Lenore clutches her throat and jerks to and fro, wracked with a sudden fit of convulsions.

I inch toward her. "What's wrong with you?"

"John Allan's hand travels far," she says, her voice a frog's croak. "I feel his grip on my throat. He's trying to strangle me through your debt." She shuts her eyes and endures a greater bout of spasms, as though an invisible hand is wringing her neck.

I stare at her a moment, stunned and anxious by her behavior, yet also suspecting she may be duping me into pledging myself to her version of art.

"Stop that," I say.

She gurgles and purples.

"Stop your melodrama, Lenore!" I say. "Stop it immediately! You're far too old for that sort of ridiculousness!"

As soon as my command tumbles from my lips, I realize how much I sounded like Pa.

Lenore's eyes fly wide open, and she lets go of her throat with a gasp.

I grab my own throat, appalled at the phrases that just flew out of it.

She bends over at the waist and catches her breath. "What did you just tell me?"

"I didn't mean to sound like him. I thought you were using histrionics to fool me into—"

She snaps the silver chain that I gave her off her neck and stands upright, exposing a gruesome stain on her dress—a bloodstain the shape of the heart made of glass, as though the necklace somehow animated itself and seeped across her bodice.

"Oh, God," I mutter, but before I can recover from my shock from the blood, she throws the stone at me, hitting me on the chest.

Without a word, she then lunges for the wall and scales the bricks.

"Lenore?" I call after her. "Don't run around out there while angry. Please, find a safe place to stay. I'll call for you if I need you."

She whips her head toward me from the top of the wall, her teeth bared, her spine curved. "If you call for me," she croaks in the deepest voice I've ever heard from any creature, "I won't come."

Another throng of students clambers past the wall out there, and Lenore jumps down into their midst. After a brief pause of stunned silence, the fellows shriek like children witnessing an atrocity.

"What was that?" they ask after Lenore must have run away.

"It looked dead!"

"What was that?"

"A corpse?"

"My God!"

"What was that?"

This is the most entertaining night of my life! I remember Miles declaring in my bedroom in the throes of activity the night before, and his praise of Lenore somehow muffles the other fellows' horror.

I pick up the heart necklace from the ground, unexpectedly warmed by its touch, soothed by its beauty.

Actually, my recollection of Miles's admiration allows me to suddenly *enjoy*, and *relish*, and *appreciate* these other schoolmates' reactions to my Gothic muse.

I wait behind the wall for the students to gather their wits, and a smile that must look wicked and as pleased as can be spreads across my face. With my back pressed against the cold bricks, I clutch that crimson heart, which neither beats nor bleeds in my hand, but I imagine all the diabolical details and evocative phrases I would use were I to write about a lifeless human heart quickening back to life—shuddering, shaking, resuscitating with a low, dull *thump-thump, thump-thump, thump-thump* . . .

CHAPTER TWENTY-TWO

Lenore

Yes, indeed, I'm quite beguiling; there's a reason Edgar's smiling—yes, I kissed a kiss of dread into the heart I wore before—the stone heart I doffed afore, and he shall see what I've in store, if he follows his Lenore . . .

"Lenore!" I shout into the wind from the Lawn, tasting the name that curls around my tongue like chocolate shavings must melt in the mouths of mortals. The students of the University of Virginia dart back into their dormitories and watch me from behind cracked-open doors, fearful yet curious.

Oh, so curious.

Their fascination fortifies my soul, fans the fires flowing through my blood, and sends another tingling sensation of impending growth tickling across my scalp, urging me to rip out more of my hair to make room for the feathers. *They must be feathers!*

I stop in the snow in front of the northern rooms of the East Lawn and yank out every strand of my hair from my head. Yes! *Every single strand!* The process of tearing out fistfuls of tresses—that unnecessary glamour impeding my evolution—feels absolutely divine and causes no pain.

A young man gawks at me from the shadows of a Tuscan column. I pay no attention to the features of his face, for my eyes lock onto the outward-curving crown of the tremendous black hat that climbs into the air nearly two feet above his head. I rub my fingers across the downy fuzz encasing my scalp. The breeze chills me.

The young man seems frozen in Parian marble, and yet I approach him.

"May I have your hat, sir?" I ask in my politest of tones, knowing that university gentlemen don't often receive requests from hairless creatures in outmoded mourning dresses.

"W-w-what did you just say?" he asks, his chin quivering, eyes watering.

"May I have your hat? In exchange you may have my hair that's lying over there in the snow."

"I don't want your—" He abruptly stops himself, his eyes protruding from his sallow face, as though he fears he's just made a horrid mistake by rejecting my hair.

"Please"—I loom closer, my hands on my hips—"my head is freezing. May I have your hat, sir?"

Without speaking, he whisks his hat off his head of golden curls—the fellow could have stepped straight out of Rubens's *Cherubs* painting—and hands the chapeau to me.

"Thank you. I am much obliged to you for your generosity," I say, for I am not a monster like that usurper Garland O'Peale. My manners are as appealing as my madness.

I fit the hat over my head, thrill at the warmth of the satin lining sliding across the curves of my scalp, and with a tip of my head to my generous benefactor, I dash off for the city of Charlottesville, in search of artists who will offer me scraps of nourishment while my poet learns he needs me.

CHAPTER TWENTY-THREE

Edgar

Lenore invoked such a palpable sense of terror on the university grounds that I hide away in my room for the rest of the day to keep from admitting I had anything to do with the spectacle. I sleep off the brandy with fitful naps full of nightmares about my penury.

By suppertime, my schoolmates still murmur of the "specter."

In the hotel where we dine, I sit myself next to Tom Tucker, who himself looks cadaverous this evening, his eyes bruised, his cheeks gaunt.

"Do you know what everyone is talking about, Poe?" he asks with his head sagging in his hands. "I don't remember a damn thing that happened between knocking at your door and waking up a few hours ago."

I chuckle. "You look like the brandy punched you in the eyes."

"I think Will and I might have gotten into a fight." Tom shakes out his head. "I don't recall why."

Miles joins us, also claiming to suffer from peach-and-honey–induced amnesia, although I catch him studying me out of the corner of his eye at one point as we dine on our pink slices of beef, as though he remembers . . .

On Monday morning, Garland waits for me at the pavilion door of my Latin lecture. A pair of green-tinted spectacles conceals the unearthly glow of his eyes.

"Good morning," he says, pinching the brim of his gray hat between his right thumb and index finger.

"Where did you get those spectacles?" I ask.

He shrugs, which I interpret to mean, *I stole them, of course.*

"I need to concentrate on this lecture." I walk past him. "I don't have time to converse."

He grabs my left shoulder and stops me from entering the pavilion. "She caused quite a sensation."

"She showed me the rips you made in her sleeves."

"May your tongue remain sharp, Poe, and your enemies, dull."

"Why do I get the impression you're one of my enemies, O'Peale?"

"Au contraire. I'm your salvation. I'll liberate you from your desire to write nonsense."

I wriggle out of his grip. "I may write nonsense, but at least it's exquisite nonsense."

Garland coughs up a laugh that draws the attention of John Lyle, one of Miles's well-mannered chums from the East Lawn. I lower my face as John slips into the pavilion behind me.

"I need to devote all my thoughts to my studies," I say to Garland. "I'm still waiting to hear Pa's response to my request. I shall see you Saturday night, and no sooner."

Garland tips his hat with a wobble of the feathers in the band. "I'll go walk among your fellow humans, then, and observe the eccentricities of your kind."

"Observe unobtrusively please."

"I'll be as quiet as a rat."

He scuttles away before I can remark that he's botched up the idiom, remembering that Lenore once also skewered that same phrase.

❦

Pa's response to my letter arrives at the end of that second week at the university. His correspondence bears his scarlet seal of wax, monogrammed with an ornate *A*—a sight that fills me with both hope and uneasiness. I sit down at my table in my room and draw a series of long breaths before gaining the courage to break the seal.

I unfold his crisp parchment.

My stomach sinks.

In his letter, addressed, at least, as "Dear Edgar" and not a cold "Dear Sir," Pa berates me for asking for more money.

He chides me for not contriving to manage to pay one hundred forty-nine dollars with one hundred ten!

I will enclose an additional $40, he states toward the end of the letter, *but no more. Do not write to Ma and trouble her about the money. She is confined to her room with a bad cold. I will order a uniform in Richmond and send it to you instead of paying the university's exorbitant prices. Be more prudent and careful.*

The harsh scent of tobacco drifts from the pulp of the parchment, and I envision Pa hunched over the paper, puffing on his pipe, the shadow of his head seeping across his handwriting.

I pick up the bills he enclosed with the letter.

He left me with only one damn dollar for pocket money—a dollar that will disappear as soon I answer the university's demand to be paid for a packet of books.

Oh, and there's Mr. Spotswood banging on my door again, about to tell me I owe him money for the use of his servant, and for the washing, and for the firewood so I don't freeze to death, and a thousand other necessaries . . .

"Poe!" calls Mr. Spotswood through my door. "I need to speak to you about your fees . . ."

No more than an hour later, I'm standing in a smoky little lending office in Charlottesville, signing an agreement to borrow money at a rate of interest I'll never be able to afford. My neck sweats, and my heart won't stop twitching. Mr. Blumenthal, the lender helping me with the paperwork, peers through his wire spectacles at me with a look of disdain, as though he holds no pity for an Anglo-Saxon, Episcopalian boy dressed in the finest wool and satin that money can buy. John Allan accomplished his goal of presenting me to the world as an ingrate—as an eater of the bread of idleness.

But I refuse to leave the university.

I'm doing too well in my classes.

I depart the lending office with my hat in my hand, my borrowed cash tucked away in my breast pocket, a sharp pain digging at my chest beneath my sternum. The snow has melted, and the windows of the city reflect a warm sunlight, but rain clouds brew in the distance, threatening to drench me by the time I reach the university grounds if I don't hurry.

With my arms wrapped around myself, I walk down a street that squishes with mud, my optimism drained, and I pray for the seraphim in heaven above to send me a respite from my troubles—to free me from my trepidations about the money, so I may concentrate on my education and finally live.

Around the next corner, a song reaches my ear—Thomas Moore's "Come, Rest in This Bosom," the same melody Lenore sang in the professor's garden. A soprano with the voice of an angel now sings the tune within the white walls of a wooden tavern across the square.

> "Oh! what was love made for, if 'tis not the same
> Thro' joy and thro' torment, thro' glory and
>   shame?
> I know not, I ask not, if guilt's in that heart,
> I but know that I love thee, whatever thou art."

On the mossy shingles of the tavern's sloped roof, two and a half stories into the air, stands Lenore in her high-waisted black dress with the heart-shaped bloodstain. I don't see her long ebon hair, but a tall silk hat that matches the hue of her dress rests upon her head. She braces the soles of her boots against the shingles, her hands planted on her hips, her face directed my way—an unsettling silhouette that reminds me of a crow perched on a roof or a funereal weather vane.

Now she turns her head away, facing the western storm clouds sagging over the hills and mountains, and the soprano within the structure beneath her breaks into the Scottish ballad "Barbara Allen"—a tune that's apt to bring tears to my eyes even more than "Come, Rest in This Bosom."

Too moved by the singer's voice, too tempted by curiosity, I cross the square, daring to tread closer to my runaway muse. Lenore's face remains turned away, yet I sense that she's watching me, which makes me shiver.

A deep porch welcomes visitors to the tavern, and at the far end of it, to my left, a white man—a peddler of saddles—barters with a black man who specifies that he's been a free man since birth, and he knows "what is and isn't a fair price." I step onto the boards at the opposite end and peek through a tall window.

A brunette in a green-and-gold dress that offers a plentiful view of her bosom sings amid tables constructed of long planks of wood. She's surrounded by an audience of men with pink faces—drunkards who somehow have time to spend afternoons imbibing beer instead of working. Two whiskered musicians, one playing a fiddle, the other strumming a guitar, accompany the woman, and, by God, even though she has gaps in her teeth and pock marks on her face, the lady's voice—the way she sings Barbara's plea to her mother to make her own coffin, so she can die like the man who loved her—reduces me to tears right there on the porch.

I shift away from the peddler and his potential customer and wipe my face with a sleeve, planning to tell the men that I miss my fiancée if they question my crying. Out of the corner of my eye, I glimpse the shadow of the tavern's roof, stretched out across the street, as well as the silhouette of Lenore atop it. A breeze flutters her skirt, but her torso and head, topped by that unfathomably tall hat, stay so chillingly still, it could be the shadow of a statue.

Her shadow head turns, and I shudder, wondering if she sees that I'm crying over "Barbara Allen." She's arranged all this, I realize. Lenore stole that soprano from some other muse who's probably flitting around, panicking about its singer—a singer more likely attuned to the "bawdy songs" that Bishop Moore railed against in his sermons.

Lenore's shadow crouches down on the roof and slides out of view.

I round the tavern.

"Lenore!" I call with my hands cupped around my mouth, traveling around the perimeter of the building. "Where are you?"

She neither answers nor shows her face.

I drift back to the front of the tavern, where I hear the soprano now singing "I Am the King and Prince of

Drinkers"—a much more appropriate ditty to pour from the windows of an alehouse than a tragic ballad.

"Are you looking for someone?" asks the customer on the porch.

"Are you crying, lad?" asks the peddler.

"I just buried my fiancée," I say, wiping my cheeks once again, my tears renewed by the lie that just slipped from my lips. "Since my love died for me today, I'll die for her tomorrow."

The men's foreheads wrinkle—they're too stunned to even speak, so I bid them farewell and saunter away, wondering if they'll realize I just quoted "Barbara Allen."

I return to the university, my hands crammed in my coat pockets, my head stuffed with the tale of Barbara and her lover, the sad tune on my lips, and it's not until the clouds dump rain on my head near my dormitory door that I realize *she* answered my prayer.

Lenore was the seraph that allowed me a respite from my troubles with money.

I'd forgotten all about John Allan, even though his surname galloped through the ballad.

CHAPTER TWENTY-FOUR

Lenore

If I were to describe in mortal terms the sensation of illicitly eliciting art from another muse's artist, I would say it's comparable to nibbling crackers in the house of an acquaintance when you'd rather be dining on a feast you've prepared with a loved one. Some nourishment results, but fulfillment is impossible.

Performers come and go in the Eagle Tavern of Charlottesville, in which I now reside in the attic above the lofty ceiling of the dining room, unbeknownst to the owners and the entertainers and muses. The musicians and singers rally crowds with boisterous songs about drinking or lust—or lusting while drinking—and the boozers howl along to the music and stamp their feet to the beat, stirring up great clouds of sawdust that make me sneeze. The songs bestow on me no pleasure or sustenance. The smells of beer and perspiration twist my stomach into knots, but I don't get drunk when anyone other than my poet drinks, so I keep my wits about me.

I often peek down on the performers' heads through the attic floor. I puff up my cheeks and blow through the cracks in the boards with breaths tinkling with ice, and the singers cease singing. The musicians stop strumming. They wipe their eyes, now shining with tears, and switch to a repertoire of Irish and Scottish ballads steeped in heartbreak.

On the day my poet wandered into town (not to look for me, I should add!), I poured "Barbara Allen" through the voice of a soprano and soaked Eddy's malleable sponge of a heart with a sorrow that leaked through his eyes. My own heart sparked and quickened—flint struck against steel—and my poet *thrummed* with inspiration. The sky above transfigured into a mystical phosphorescence that hinted of the beauty yet to come.

And now when I rub my hands over my skull, I stroke a plush layer of feathers, blacker than ink, that runs from my forehead down to the bones of my neck. A tarnished mirror stands in one corner of my attic roost, amid trunks and empty crates, and I use it to gauge the progress of my evolution.

My nose curves further into the bill of a bird and possesses great strength of character, like the noses of kings and prophets. My sleek head also looks regal, and the chain of teeth strung around my neck, the heart-shaped bloodstain on my bosom, show the world I am rooted in human life, despite my garments of mourning and soot.

My right hand bears a scar from the quill that burned me, and my sleeves have not mended from the sharpness of Garland O'Peale's tongue. I still taste river water from the night the dogs chased me into the James, and occasionally I spit up sludge and sneeze silt.

And yet I persevere.

I evolve—but not quickly enough.

A new set of musicians breaks into song down in the tavern hall. I peek down through a hole in the floorboards and spy another fiddler, a girl younger than Eddy, with red ringlets coiling down her back—and a singer, a beautiful young man with skin a light brown. He sings out a drinking ballad, "Here's a Health to the Company," inciting cheers and applause from the tavern patrons, who clink together glasses frothing with beer.

I recall the lifeless stupor of Eddy's eyes when he quaffs liquor—the ensuing heaviness of my head—the death of art. I resent that handsome singer down there calling out, "Let us drink and be merry all out of one glass," even though a sense of dread pervades the ballad—a lament that the drinkers may never meet again. I round my lips and blow down my cold breath, and the fiddler and the singer stop mid-verse and switch to a ne'er-heard-before song about someone's true love who's buried in a cemetery on a hill overlooking the James. The singer closes his brown eyes and cries out a chorus about the lover's corpse climbing out of a grave that wriggles with maggots and conqueror worms.

The glasses cease clinking, and cheers wither on lips. Feet tap to the rhythm of the strumming no more.

I fear I may have gone too far this time, for someone thumps up the staircase.

The attic door crashes open.

I lunge for the window, but a pair of celestial creatures—two blurs of peacock green feathers and flashing eyes—pin me down on the floor, pull my right arm around my back, and yell, "Go mind your own artist, you thief!"

CHAPTER TWENTY-FIVE

Edgar

Elmira hasn't yet written.

I've now been in Charlottesville for a month.

It's mid-March. I last saw her before Valentine's Day.

She hasn't written once!

I lie in bed before my Saturday class, lazing in my night-shirt and cap, and I chew my nails over her lack of correspondence, convinced that she's found someone better. She *must* have found someone better. She's Sarah Elmira Royster!

I obsess over the idea that I've never seen what she looks like when she unpins her hair. Ever since I met her last summer when we moved into Moldavia, she's always worn her brown locks parted down the middle and plain in front, with an elaborate knot pinned to the top of her head in back.

With my eyes closed, my hands clasped above my head on my pillow, I push away all the whispers of doubt and imagine Elmira—*my* Elmira—unfastening her hair on a bed built for two in our cottage by the sea. Waves sigh against the rocks down below our chamber, and she sings a dreamy song, while I sift my fingers through each strand that she frees from the pins—strands of pure silk that sweep down past her shoulders. My lips crave the warmth and the pressure of her mouth on mine. I want nothing more than to lay my cheek on the

curves of her satin-soft breast, perfumed in her lilac scents, while her hair brushes my skin, while the waves sigh, and she sighs . . .

Someone raps on my door.

I jump out of bed, flushed and flustered, expecting to find a hotelkeeper or a servant—or to hear more demands for money.

Instead, I open the door to the bespectacled face of Garland O'Peale, his eyes again shielded by those green lenses.

"Shall we have another go at a gathering in you room tonight?" he asks, leaning his pointy right elbow against my doorframe.

I blink and fuss with my nightshirt. "Umm . . . yes, I suppose. Miles said he'd come, and he might bring his chum John Lyle, who's a little more refined than the others. I'm not certain he's even a drinker."

"Good. You need less drinking. Keep distracting your friends with new caricatures on the walls whenever they offer you a glass." Garland nods toward my budding collection of charcoal sketches of professors before adding, "If this Lyle fellow joins you tonight, tell him tales of the five years you spent in boarding schools in London and Stoke Newington. Most of these provincials have never even left Virginia. You've led a far more varied life than them. Flaunt your experience."

"Elmira hasn't yet written," I say, even though I've never confided in Garland about anything before—certainly nothing of romance.

He shrugs. "Maybe she's as fickle as you when it comes to love."

"I'm not fickle."

"Ha! Before Elmira, you wrote love letters to every single girl in Miss Jane Mackenzie's boarding school, and I'm sure you had sweethearts in England, and even *before* England, when you were a spoiled brat of six."

"Catherine Poitiaux was my sweetheart at age six, but"—I wave away the long list of girls who've enraptured me over the years—"no one compares to Elmira. If I lose her, I'll die."

Garland groans in disgust. "You probably said the same of little Catherine Poitiaux."

"If Pa or Elmira's father had anything to do with this . . ." I rub at my face, which needs a shave. "Her father thinks I'm not good enough for her. I believe he once lent Pa money. He knows of my background."

"Ridicule these asses in essays instead of crying over girls, Poe. You really need to learn to swallow down these sentimental fancies of yours. They're not attractive." Garland steps away from my door. "I'll see you tonight. Let's make the show a good one."

We do, indeed, make the show a good one, as we do every Saturday night.

I draw unflattering portraits of the Reverend John Bransby, who ran the school I attended in Stoke Newington from the ages of nine to eleven, when Pa established the firm Allan & Ellis in England. Most of my stories about the reverend aren't as true as they could be, and I pepper them with far more offensive oaths than I probably need to, but my friends bend forward at their waists on my bed and laugh, and laugh, and laugh.

Garland sits on my chair, his legs crossed, his posture impeccable, and he nods in encouragement whenever my energy lapses. Even though he wears his green spectacles, I see the fire of his amber irises blazing into an inferno behind the lenses.

A sense of hollowness plagues me, despite the laughter and the praise. The applause sounds tinny. Something's missing—and not just Elmira.

My monstrous drawing of Mrs. Stanard lingers in the corner of my eye, and my mind strays.

Garland and my companions file out of my room around midnight.

Left to my own devices at last, I pull my sketch of Lenore out of my writing box and loop the glass heart necklace over my head, the silver chain cold to the touch.

I step onto my bed with a charcoal crayon in hand and invoke my macabre muse by quoting the Irish poet William Hamilton Drummond's *The Giant's Causeway*:

> *"Come, lonely genius of my natal shore,*
> *From cave or bower, wild glen, or mountain*
>   *hoar;*
> *And while by ocean's rugged bounds I muse,*
> *Thy solemn influence o'er my soul diffuse."*

The chill of the March night settles over my skin, along with the weight of shadows. The imagined outlines of weird and whimsical wonders rise to the surface of my walls.

Explosions of gunfire echo across the Lawn, and drunken fools push each other against my door. Yet during the entire midnight hour, amid the din of dissolution, I draw whatever my heart asks of me, caring not what my schoolmates might think or what criticism Garland might spew—or even what Pa might comment if he were to stop by for a visit when his business brings him to Charlottesville, as his latest letter implied it might do.

I decorate the wall over my bed and the ceiling above it with sketches of demons, and dragons, and other grotesque and fantastic creatures—wraiths, and Naiads, and the most beautiful women ever witnessed by mortal eyes. And I fall asleep with the scarlet heart dangling around my neck, drifting into a labyrinth of dreadful dreams.

CHAPTER TWENTY-SIX

Lenore

Like the classic poets he studies to exhaustion—Homer, Milton, Virgil, and all those other dead and venerated versifiers—my poet formally invoked his muse.

My poet invoked *me*.

His voice swept through the purple midnight air and traveled over the Elysian hills of Albemarle County, reaching my ears in a parish churchyard—my new home after the other muses attacked me, when I found no proper cemetery in Charlottesville.

"Come, lonely genius of my natal shore,
From cave or bower, wild glen, or mountain
  hoar;
And while by ocean's rugged bounds I muse,
Thy solemn influence o'er my soul diffuse."

The words were the work of the poet William Hamilton Drummond, but the passion of the plea behind them belonged to Edgar Allan Poe.

Yet I remain in the churchyard, ignoring Poe's summons.

Even though I know he cannot hear me, I call back to my poet: "You have that stone heart, filled with a drop of my soul, and that's all the help you'll get from me. I want them to see me, and you want me to remain your secret, you frustrating, stubborn boy!"

During the afternoons in my new graveyard home, a choir gathers to practice their hymns of celebration inside a steepled church so pure, so white, it looks like the angels sliced a piece of heaven like a cake and laid it down on the plate of this green river valley. A flock of muses in dove form perches on the roof of the church whenever the singers meet, and with watchful, glossy eyes, they stare down at my resting spot on a sepulcher below them. They know I'm a thief of artists, but they're too polite to chase me away.

With my eyes closed, my silk hat resting on my breast, I inhale the choir's hymns, as airy and as sweet as meringue, or so I assume, and I fight the urge to refashion their songs into frightful funeral dirges.

At night I roam among the light of the churchyard spirits, who beg me to convince my artist to tell their stories, but none of them pull at my heart quite like the spirits of Richmond.

One night in either March or April, when a full moon beams its silvery haze across the graves, a young gentleman spirit steps around his tombstone. He wears his hair tied back with a bow on his neck, and he's dressed in a ruffled cravat, a short coat with a long tail, and breeches that end beneath his knees, revealing a pair of silk stockings that stretch down to buckled shoes.

"May I kiss those red lips of yours, my bonny darling?" he asks me through his own lips of misted blue. "You've been tempting me with your beauty every night you wander among us."

"Are you certain you believe I'm beautiful?" I ask, removing my hat so he can see my sleek head of feathers. "Aren't you terrified of me?"

He shakes his head. "Nothing terrifies us here, miss, except for the fear of being forgotten. Look at poor Betty Randolph's stone over there. Her name is almost gone."

I investigate the thin gray stone he means, seeing the faded indentations of letters. I rub my fingertips over the dips in poor Betty's name, worried that this same fate might befall our beloved Jane Stanard, despite the grandeur of her monument. A lump swells in my throat.

"The kindest thing you can do for the dead," says the young man who requested the kiss, "is to weave their names into art."

With a nod of understanding, I don the hat once more and scale a tree that leads to the bell tower of the church, where I warm myself for the night.

And I wait, and I wait, and I wait, and I wait for my poet to cast off his fears of his fate . . .

CHAPTER TWENTY-SEVEN

Edgar

On a Thursday afternoon early in May, Miles, Tom, and I stroll back to the university grounds after spending hours browsing the shelves of a bookseller in Charlottesville. The earth has thawed, and frost no longer cakes the Lawn and roofs each morning, and yet I plunge deeper into debt for the firewood I still need to burn off the chill of the nights.

Nevertheless, I'm flourishing in my classes, so my mood is light, and the warmth of the sunlight burnishing my cheeks adds to my sense of wellness. I even treated myself to a copy of Byron's *Childe Harold's Pilgrimage* at the bookseller's, paid for on credit, of course. Tom and Miles tote their own newly purchased books of Byron's poetry.

"Did one of us step in horse shit?" asks Tom when we reach the West Colonnade. He lifts his right boot for a peek underneath.

I raise my left foot and gag at the stench of a ripe lump of dung, comingled with fibrous grasses, clinging to my sole. "Aw, bloody hell!"

Tom and Miles cough up laughs and wave away the smell, while I scrape my sole against the grass, muttering curses so inflammatory, they would melt poor Ma's ears.

"Oh, God, that stinks like hell, Poe," says Tom.

Miles laughs. "And here I thought that was just the stench of your theater heritage."

I freeze.

An unbridled surge of trembling, volcanic rage, the likes of which hasn't gripped me since Richmond, shoots through my veins. His words replay in my head.

And here I thought that was just the stench of your theater heritage.

I throw my book to the ground and punch Miles in the pit of his stomach. He doubles over, a string of drool spilling from his lips, and I throw an undercut into his chin, my old boxing instincts reawakened. The ass drops to the grass, and I'm on him like a feral dog, struggling to swing at an eye, but he fights me off and braces his hands on my shoulders, grunting and breathing his hot breath into my face. I'm only five feet, eight inches tall, and he's close to six feet, so the bastard clasps his giraffe legs around me and flips me onto my back, and now he's on me, squashing my stomach, forcing air from my lungs. I struggle to wrestle him off me, but he grips my wrists and pins down my arms, so I twist and raise my hips in a desperate attempt to catapult him off me.

Tom shouts our names, either cheering us on or yelling at us to stop.

"Let's end this," says Miles. "I'm sorry. I shouldn't have insulted you."

"You're an ass, Miles," I say, thrashing my legs and my elbows about. "I'm not ending this until I knock out your damn teeth in your damn ugly mouth, you pompous son of a bitch!"

His right fist sails toward my face, exploding against my nose with a sharp burst of pain, and when he raises it again, I see my blood shining across his knuckles.

Miles looks at his fingers, sways at the sight of the blood, and slides off me, his hands raised. "I'm done."

I roll onto my left side and emit a whole host of guttural sounds. My nostrils blaze as though I'm inhaling hydrochloric acid.

Miles flaps a handkerchief into my face. "Can you breathe?"

I can't yet speak, but I manage to plug up my nose with the cloth.

"I'm heading back to my room, gentlemen," says Tom, hustling away. "Please don't let the professors see the blood. Don't get expelled."

"Do you need a doctor?" asks Miles.

I grit my teeth and shake my head, praying for a swift surcease of the burning and throbbing.

Miles sits down beside me.

"I should have never said that about your parents," he says. "I apologize, Edgar. I simply get so jealous of you sometimes."

I glance up at him without moving anything other than my eyes. "Why the devil are you jealous of me?"

"Why?" He snorts. "Have you met yourself, Poe? You're brilliant. Not only can you recite every damn poem we need to learn for our classes, you know *everything* about the poems' histories. You spent five years of your life immersed in English culture, for God's sake; you've never had any fears about wooing women, according to Richmond lore; you're handsome as all hell; you're a damned fine athlete, as your ferocious fist just proved . . ." Miles rubs his jaw and attempts to waggle it, his movements stiff and pained. "And you have superabundant talent, the likes of which I could only dream of acquiring."

I close my eyes and groan through the pain. "And yet I'm nothing more than the son of theater people."

"That makes you even more fascinating, to be most honest." Miles exhales a quiet laugh. "Richmond forces us to believe that theaters are the realm of the devil, rebuked by God, but I know that's a lie. I beg your forgiveness."

I nod. "I forgive you. But don't ever insult my parents again."

"I won't."

"And don't tell the other fellows what I come from. Pedigree means everything here, and I'm a charity case."

"Thank God you were taken in by generous and wise people, though."

I open my eyes. "Every day of my life my 'wise' foster father reminds me that he could throw me back out to the streets at a moment's notice. He wishes I would kneel before him, kiss his rings, and grovel in gratitude for his benevolence."

"Oh." Miles shifts his position on the ground, subjecting me to a view of the welt my fist left on his chin. "I didn't realize it was like that. I'm sorry."

I shut my eyes again.

"Hey." Miles clasps my left shoulder. "When are you going to bring back your Gothic muse?"

His question stuns me even more than his insult about my heritage. Using both my elbows and hands, I push myself up to a seated position, breathing through a wave of dizziness. The handkerchief clings to the clots in my nostrils, so I don't even need to touch it to keep it attached to my nose.

Miles snickers at this feat. "That's disgusting."

"My Gothic muse, you mean?"

"No, your muse is a wonder. You should share more of your fantastic and grotesque stories with us."

I bend over at the waist and peel the cloth from my nose, breathing away the light-headedness. "I didn't think any of you would want to hear my tales of the grotesque. I thought you'd all prefer the humorous pieces."

"There are so many people trying to sound humorous and witty around here, Poe. But only you can silence a room by casting us under your strange, whispery spell. Bring her back."

"I sent her away."

"Find her."

"It might be too late."

"You're a man skilled with words." Miles rises to his feet with a slight wobble and offers me his hand. "If anyone can invoke a missing muse, it would certainly be you, my friend."

CHAPTER TWENTY-EIGHT

Lenore

The skies they are opal and restless;
>   The trees they are verdant and gleam—
>   The trees they are wakening and gleam:
It is noon, in a May young and breathless
Near a pool in the Valley of Dreams:
There are charms in this tarn of the pinelands,
In the misted and mountainous hills:—
It is here 'mid the poplars and pinelands,
Where a poet seeks fate in the hills . . .

CHAPTER TWENTY-NINE

Edgar

The afternoon following my pugilistic encounter with Miles, after I'm recovered from my pain and my wounded pride, I roam through a ravine forged through the hills beyond the university—a lush and lulling land of sod and trees reawakening from the depths of winter. Leaves of caterpillar green burgeon on each bough above my head, and songbirds serenade my journey.

The locals call this sloping Eden the "Ragged Mountain."

My wanderings take me through a veil of mist, and when I emerge through the other side, a burbling creek leads me to a pond surrounded by pines.

I remove my shoes and socks, jump upon a log, and, with my hands cupped around my mouth, I call across the water: "Lenore! They want to see you! Where are you? They *want* to see you!"

My shouts disrupt a group of mallards that quack and laugh at my clumsy invocation. With a haughty lift of their tail feathers, they turn their backs on me and swim into a thicket of grasses, where the males' emerald heads shine like baubles in the reeds.

I proceed to launch into Homer's invocations of his muse from both *The Iliad* and *The Odyssey*, all spoken in Greek, and I follow up with John Milton's invocation in *Paradise Lost*:

"Sing heav'nly Muse, that on the secret top
Of Oreb, or of Sinai, didst inspire
That shepherd, who first taught the chosen seed,
In the beginning how the Heav'ns and Earth
Rose out of chaos . . ."

When nothing stirs in reply, other than a breeze and a squirrel shaking needles in the treetops, I plunk myself down on the bark of the log and gaze across the water, my legs stretched out in front of me. My bare toes wiggle into a grainy bed of soil that lodges beneath my nails. The wind toys with my curls and dries my lips.

Out of the corner of my eye, a shadow moves beneath the water.

I sit upright, remembering, with a shiver, the story of the Lake of the Dismal Swamp, a Virginian tale of a young man who goes mad after the death of his sweetheart. He insists to everyone that his darling isn't truly dead, but that she, instead, journeyed to the Dismal Swamp. He follows her to the lake—and no one ever hears from him again.

I stand up and unbutton my vest, my eyes focused on the part of the pond where I saw the shadow. I fancy that a girl was swimming down there in the murk of the tarn, but . . . 'tis only a fancy.

"Lenore!" I shout, pulling the vest off my arms. "I offer my sincerest apology, my sweet, supernatural sister of the soul. Please return. I long for lyrics of tragic lovers and a watery grave. Come, swim in the darkness with me."

I strip off the rest of my clothing and dive into the water with a plunging, rushing roar, swimming deep beneath the shore.

The purls and murmurs of the underwater world sing around me, and my eyes drink in the pond's green lumines-cence, alive with drifting clouds of silt and the silver dances of minnows. Not since the previous summer have I swum in a river or a creek, and despite the chill that numbs me, I float in the water's firm embrace, lulled by a rhythm that ripples into lyrics:

In youth's spring, it was my lot
To haunt of the wide earth a spot
The which I could not love the less;
So lovely was the loneliness
Of a wild lake, with black rock bound,
And the tall pines that tower'd around.

A figure manifests in the water in front of me—a girl with radiant skin of lavender and river-blue eyes like Elmira's. Coiled curls of ink undulate from her head; her lips are a flushed and feverish red. She stares at me with the gaze of the dead . . .

This violet vision of beauty and death drifts toward me, the skirts of her pale purple gown billowing like kelp around her legs. She cups her hands around my cheeks and kisses my mouth—a cold and clinging kiss that sucks the last of the oxygen from my lungs.

I untangle myself from her grip and swim upward, my chest tightening, legs kicking, a bubble of panic screaming from my throat. My right fist punches through the surface, and I raise my head for a gasp of air, wheezing like a walrus. Terrified that fingers will grab my ankles and pull me back under, I launch myself toward the shallows and stumble ashore, panting, tripping, dripping with pond water. I then lunge for my clothing, which I throw over myself in haste while catching my breath.

Before my brain settles from the blood pulsing through it, a blaze of poetry ignites in my mind as bright bursts of light flashing with lurid visions.

But when the night had thrown her pall
Upon that spot—as upon all,
And the wind would pass me by
In its stilly melody,
My infant spirit would awake
To the terror of the lone lake . . .

I plop down on the ground and pull on my socks and shoes with my gaze fixed upon that plutonian pool.

"It's May," says a voice that hums across the pond.

With a shriek, I jump up and spin around.

Upon the log where I previously lounged now sits Lenore with the tall, curved hat of black perched upon her head. She peers at me with her obsidian eyes, her posture erect, her legs crossed, her hands clasped around her right knee. She conveys both the regal mien of a queen and the calculating air of a schoolmistress about to torture her most delinquent pupil.

"It's *May*," she says again, this time with added emphasis on the month.

I stand up. "I know."

"You last called for me in March, and we last spoke in February. That's an appallingly long time for you to ignore me."

"I must beg your pardon for the delay, Miss Lenore, but"—I brush away the wrinkles in my coat, the water from my hair speckling the fabric—"you did say you wouldn't come if I called."

She exhales a sigh of frustration.

I comb my fingers through the tangles in my curls and offer words that I know will appease her: "My friend Miles George wants to see you. He asked to hear more tales of the grotesque."

A glimmer of interest flares in her irises.

"Will you do me the honor of making an appearance in my room tomorrow night?" I ask.

She narrows her eyes and pulls at the threads of her torn right sleeve. "What about Mr. O'Peale? Will he be there?"

"I'll tell Garland to stay away."

"He'll pounce on me as soon as I leave your room."

"No, I'll make an arrangement with him. He can return next Saturday."

She rises to her feet, removes her hat, and exposes a covering of short black feathers in place of her hair.

My mouth falls open at the shock of her avian scalp—so far open, in fact, that a gnat lands on my tongue. I spit out the damn thing with a hop of disgust that I worry Lenore will misinterpret as repulsion toward her.

"A gnat just flew into my mouth," I say, so as not to offend.

"I know." Lenore rolls back her shoulders. "I sent it in there."

Again, my jaw plummets.

"I'm evolving, Eddy," she says. "And yet I'm also not. I haven't progressed since I last left you."

I inch forward. "Miles called you a 'wonder.'"

My God! Lenore actually smiles at that comment—a smile that produces dimples just like Elmira's.

"Is Miles George perhaps in need of a muse?" she asks.

I chuckle, even though I do not intend to lose my muse to Miles George.

Lenore replaces her hat on her head and strolls toward me. "Tell me, Eddy Poe, what did you see eddying down in the waters when you were swimming in the darkness?" She offers me her right hand, her metallic nails glinting in the sunlight.

I step backward and neither answer nor touch her, yet I cast a brief glance toward the tarn.

"What did you see?" she asks again, her arm outstretched, her elbow poking through the tear.

I look once more at the pond and shiver from the remembered kiss.

"'Death was in that poison'd wave,'" I say with a swallow. "'And in its gulf a fitting grave.'"

Another smile spreads across Lenore's face, this one beaming up to her eyes. Her chest expands with a sigh of rapture, and her sleeves no longer appear ripped. In fact, they seem to be patched with a coating of feathers.

"Was that girl in the water your influence?" I ask.

She lowers her arm to her side. "I told you, I'm evolving. And I'm relishing my talents."

"Well, I must say, I'm impressed." I offer her my hand. "Please, I implore you, be so kind as to collaborate with me in front of my companions tomorrow night."

"Will you embrace me before I do?"

I shrink back. "Do—do you mean 'embrace' literally or figuratively?"

"Both," she says, stepping closer, tipping her hat back from her forehead. "As I've said before, the others won't see me as this peculiar girl anymore if you simply declare, 'Discouragement be damned!' Dive into worlds both natural and unnatural with me, Eddy." She takes my hand, her touch somehow cold and iron hot. "Let us weave memories of the dead into works of art and render our Helen—our *beautiful*, loving Jane Stith Stanard—immortal."

My heart beats faster at that offer.

Lenore leans toward me, her breath sweet pansies. "I want to fly across this earth on ebon wings and see everything with you—*everything* this world has to offer. Let us drink up beauty, sing out for all to hear, love like the gods, and immortalize our

Helen forevermore." She cocks her head. "Please, Edgar, will you embrace your Gothic art?"

"Yes." I nod, thinking of Mrs. Stanard's memory emblazed across the world. "Oh, God, yes!" I clasp Lenore to my chest, knocking her hat from her head, and my left cheek brushes against her crown of soft, silken feathers.

She squeezes her arms around me, her heart thumping against mine, and she whispers, "Finally! Thank you. Good gracious—thank you!" She shakes against me, half-sobbing into my left ear, undoubtedly waiting for the earth-trembling shift that will transform her into whatever she's meant to become.

I shudder, as well, unsure how such a metamorphosis will unfold—anxious that it might involve pain, or the unleashing of diabolical horrors, or hideous, squawking cries.

In case it might help her, I offer more words of my poem: "'Death was in that poison'd wave/And in its gulf a fitting grave/For him who thence could solace bring/To his dark imagining . . .'"

What are you doing? I imagine Pa asking if he caught me embracing my muse in the wilds of the woods. *You're seventeen years old now. You can't keep wasting your time like this . . . you're not going to seem so clever and charming when you're a grown man falling behind on your bills . . . Fight off the urge to write these terrible Byron imitations of yours before you turn into a sickly, filthy burden on society, just like your dead mother!*

Lenore lets me go and wipes her eyes with a sleeve that smudges soot across her face. "Go home and write down these lines that emerged from the lake—quickly! Before you lose them."

I back away, surveying her appearance, from her feathered head down to the ashen hem of her dress. She hasn't changed whatsoever.

"I don't know why you didn't just evolve . . ." I shake my head. "I don't understand . . ."

"I think you do. Now go." She waves me away. "Hurry! Don't forget those lines until you forge them in ink."

"I ask once again, will you do me the honor of visiting my room tomorrow night?"

She wraps her arms around herself and gives a small nod. A tear rolls down her right cheek.

"Is something the matter?" I ask.

"Go, Edgar!" she says with a force that rocks the ground beneath my feet and blusters through the pines. "Go write down that poem, you foolish, stubborn boy!"

I turn around and break into a run, propelled by the urgency and ferocity of her command. I bolt through trees and mist and push back branches that scratch at my face, and the harder my feet pound against the forest floor, the more I hear my own voice chanting in the rhythm of my footsteps—

Death was in that poison'd wave
And in its gulf a fitting grave . . .

CHAPTER THIRTY

Lenore

Is something the matter? he asks.

Why didn't you evolve? he wonders.

I shall answer this simple riddle with a simple name: JOHN ALLAN!

That man's voice rings throughout the entire state of Virginia, frightening my poet to death!

CHAPTER THIRTY-ONE

Edgar

I throw open my dormitory door, primed to spring at my table and write down my poem from the lake—but I'm not alone.

Pa occupies my chamber, his back toward me, his attention focused on my drawings on the walls.

"Pa?" I ask.

He turns around with—my God, can it be?—*tenderness* in his eyes, along with a small semblance of a smile. For a moment I forget the battles waged between us and the putrid subject of my debts. For a moment, I'm six years old, and he's escorting me to my first day at Mr. Ewing's school in Richmond with that same "there's my bright lad" expression illuminating his face.

"It's good to see you," I say, and I close the door behind me. "What are you doing here?"

"Business bought me to Charlottesville, as I said it might. Why is your hair damp?"

I touch a hand to my head. "I went swimming."

"Is the weather warm enough yet?"

"I found the water invigorating." I remove my coat with an eye on my quill, which shall not be touched this afternoon. "How are Ma and Aunt Nancy?"

Pa slides the chair away from my table and sits down with a sigh, his knees creaking. "Ma is sick again."

"How sick?"

"The usual coughing. The fretting. The complaining."

"Has a physician seen her?"

"Yes, of course. As always." Pa leans an elbow on my table and rubs his giant forehead, which, I swear, has stretched two inches taller since February. "Are you studying hard?"

"I am." I seat myself on my bed, aware of the fragrance of the river on my skin. "Professor Blaettermann singled me out for praise last week, in fact. He challenged us all to a translation of a poem by Tasso, and I was the only one who attempted it. He paid me a high compliment for my performance."

"You're not getting distracted by other pursuits, then?"

"What other pursuits do you mean?"

He nods toward my dragons, and the wraiths, and the tortured grimaces of the fantastic creatures scattered across my walls, and his voice deepens when he asks, "Do you spend as much time on your studies as you do on these troubling . . . *drawings?*" He speaks this last word as though he shouldn't even classify my artwork as something as normal as a drawing.

"Yes, Pa. I'm doing quite well here. I believe I'll end the session at the top of my classes."

He casts me a sidelong glance. "That's not just boastful talk, is it, Edgar?"

"No, sir. I'm flourishing here." I fold my hands in my lap. "But . . ." I swallow. "I do owe more money for fees."

With a grunt, Pa rises to his feet. "We'll talk about money later. Come, show me the university grounds. It looks like the Rotunda is progressing."

With a bitter smile, I nod—not in agreement about the Rotunda's progress, but because I knew he would challenge me about the money.

"The Rotunda is, indeed, coming along," I say. "They're in the process of moving the library books into it."

He reaches for the latch. "Let's step out for a bit of fresh air, then. You've got this place smelling too much of charcoal crayons. You're not writing your poems in here, too, are you?"

I turn my face away from my quill and bottle of ink.

In youth's spring, it was my lot/To haunt of the wide earth a spot . . .

"Edgar?"

"I'm keeping up with my studies. That's all that matters."

With a hesitant tread, he steps toward my grotesque rendering of Mrs. Stanard with her thickened eyebrows and bulging, anguished eyes. Each clomp of his boot against the floorboards is a footstep stomping across my heart.

The which I could not love the less/So lovely was the loneliness/Of a wild lake with black rock bound . . .

He touches the wall and then looks back at me. He wonders what sort of sickness has rotted my brain. He ponders the depths of my depravity.

"You're such a strange boy, Edgar," he says.

I can't help but smile at that observation.

"Did something influence you to draw these horrors?" he asks.

"You're looking at me as though I'm mad, Pa."

"Was that creature that ran through the streets of Richmond in February, that feckless and hideous ghoul, your"—he grimaces—"*muse?*"

In my mind I retreat from the room. I stand up from the bed and walk backward out the door and backward across the Lawn.

GRAVE-ting FIT-a GULF-its IN-And.

Backward I continue to the far reaches of the university's land and up, up, up into the hillside hickories and poplars, immersed in rhythms and rhymes, conscious only of lyrics of death and longing—of my beauteous new poem, "The Lake."

"I believe the wraith of Richmond was a legend, Pa," I say, "just like every good tale of terror. No one inspired me to draw these grim and fantastic whimsies here. This is all my doing. It's how I relax from the demands of my studies. I could be engaged in far worse habits."

His head dips with a slight nod. "Yes, I suppose you could. You're not drinking much are you?"

I shrug. "A glass now and then. I know my limitations."

"Good lad."

"The other fellows say it's a well-known fact that Southern fathers will forgive their sons for one major scrape here at the university."

"I'm not a Southern-born father," says Pa with his Scottish burr trilling in the back of his throat to emphasize this point. "I do not share in their encouragement of debauchery."

"I know, Pa." I sigh. "I know." I stand and grab my coat. "Shall we go see the Rotunda?"

A fight breaks out near the colonnade we're traversing. Two students whom I recognize from the cheaper Rowdy Row dormitories wrestle each other to the ground, their uniforms wrinkling and staining with grass, their language coarse enough to draw a blush to Pa's cheeks.

"That reminds me," I say to Pa, "I still need a uniform."

"It's being made in Richmond. I'll send it soon."

"Thank you."

One of the wrestlers hollers in pain and yells, "Stop biting my ear! Oh, God! Stop biting!"

Pa flinches.

I stifle a laugh, entertained by the callous businessman's terror of young intellects.

Up ahead, a figure in a feathered hat darts across the colonnade, and I give a shiver, for I fear it's Garland.

"What is it?" asks Pa. "You just turned pale."

I've come to a stop in the shadow of one of the passageway's columns, I realize. Pa gawks at me, and he's so conceited, and yet so damn ugly—ugly on his pestilent insides. God knows how many of his bastards run around Richmond by now. Who knows how much money he's sending to schoolmasters for the education of his illegitimate offspring, like redheaded Edwin Collier, who attended Mr. Ewing's school with me years ago. All those other parents at the school whispered about Edwin resembling my foster father, and how interesting it is that little Edgar doesn't look a thing at all like the man he calls "Pa," but Edwin Collier is almost a miniature version of the gentleman.

I've forgotten all the words of "The Lake." A foul taste coats my tongue, and all I can think about is writing a nasty little piece about Pa, which I'll call "The Business Man."

I am a business man, it'll say. I am a methodical man . . . If there is anything on earth I hate, it is a genius. Your geniuses are all arrant asses—the greater the genius the greater the ass—and to this rule there is no exception whatever.

"And so, yes . . ." I scratch my forehead and press onward down the colonnade. "They're moving the library to the Rotunda."

"Are you unwell, Edwin?" asks Pa.

Again, I stop. "What did you just call me?"

"Edgar, of course." He wrinkles his brow. "What's come over you? Are you sure you haven't been drinking?"

I swear he just called me Edwin, like the name of his son. I swear to God.

I rub my arms to keep warm from a chill that's overtaken me. "I owe so much money for fees, Pa. Sometimes I can't even think straight because I'm so preoccupied with fears of—"

"For God's sakes, Edgar, I'll send more money!"

"Can you pay the bursar for the outstanding fees now?"

"I'm not carrying spare cash."

"Will you please send it as quickly as possible, then?"

"Yes!" He waves a fly out of his face. "I'll send the damn uniform and the money!"

The boy with the bitten ear screams once more.

"Thank you," I say, and again, I walk. "Anyway, they hope to finish building the Rotunda by the end of summer . . ."

Before Pa can step into his carriage, I inquire about another subject weighing on my mind.

"Is Elmira Royster well?"

"I assume so." Pa pulls his tinderbox out of a coat pocket, his pipe sticking out from between his pink lips. "Why? Are you still keen on the lass?"

"I am. I've been writing her letters, but she's not answering them."

"Don't rush women, Edgar. You're always in such a rush for everything."

"If you see her—" I wait to finish that thought until he stops striking the flint and steel together and at length produces a flame in the char cloth. "Will you tell her I've inquired about her?"

"If I remember, I will." He lights a match and ignites the nest of fire-cured tobacco crammed into the bowl of his pipe.

"Behave yourself here. No frivolous spending. No drunken waggery. I don't want to hear about you getting into 'scrapes.'" He tucks his tinderbox back into his pocket.

"Give my love to Ma and Aunt Nancy," I say. "And to my sister if you see her. I've written Rosalie a couple times, but I'm sure she'd appreciate knowing you saw me in person."

"Of course." Pa reaches out and pats my left my shoulder. I'm convinced he lit the pipe as an excuse not to embrace me.

I want to tell him that the lining of my dyspeptic stomach boils and simmers every night when I lie in bed, dreading how many hundreds of dollars I now owe to the lenders in Charlottesville, and how my chest aches beneath my sternum when I breathe.

But he whisks himself into the carriage and closes the door before I gain the courage.

Dabney nickers to the horse and offers a warm wave, and the vehicle lunges forward, rolling back toward the Three Notch'd Road.

I rub my sternum, feeling years stripping off my life.

On the ground beside me, a shadow with a mockingbird-feather hat stretches across the dirt. The sudden urge to rip people to shreds with lacerated words pricks at my tongue.

"So, he's left me here a debtor," I say, "at the mercy of collectors, never knowing when a sheriff might come knocking at my door . . ."

"'I am a business man,'" says Garland in an impressive imitation of a Scottish brogue, his hands stuffed in his coat pockets, his chest thrust forward like Pa's. "'If there is anything on earth I hate, it is a genius. Your geniuses are all arrant asses . . .'"

I tilt my head backward and sigh. "I may need to take to gambling, O'Peale. I should move to the Rowdy Row dormitories, where I can dwell among people more like me. Rumor has it the students are all deep in debt over there."

"The blue bloods of the West Lawn are already talking about you, Poe. They know you owe money. They know you're not one of them."

"I know."

Garland removes his hands from his pockets and inhales through his nose. "Why don't you come meet an influential young gentleman named Upton Beall, one of the residents of Rowdy Row?"

"Ah, yes." I nod and gaze up at the hills. "I've heard of him."

"He could introduce you to the most discreet card players on the university grounds; escort you to his favorite tables in Charlottesville. He's a fellow admirer of peach and honey, come to think of it."

"I need to remain sober if I'm going to gamble." I turn away from the hills and head back toward my dormitory.

Garland catches up and falls in with my stride. "Let us go write that satire, then."

"There's something else I want to write first."

He snickers. "What can be more pressing than a lampoon of John Allan?"

I come to a halt. "I'm afraid you'll need to refrain from joining me in my room tomorrow night, O'Peale."

"Why?"

I gulp. "Miles asked to see my Gothic muse. I've invited her to join us."

Garland plants his hands on his hips and snorts like he doesn't believe me. "Miles George does not want to see your Gothic muse."

"I don't know how much longer I can be friends with Miles and the others. If nothing else, I want to give him what he wants so he might not think so poorly of me during my inevitable fall from grace."

Garland steps closer and picks at his fingernails, which, much like Lenore's, appear pointed and metallic. "Her words may sound prettier to your ears, Poe, but that Gothic witch of yours will lead you faster to your fall from grace than any night of gambling ever will. Do not allow her into your room."

I hesitate before speaking, weighing my words with great care.

So lovely was the loneliness/Of a wild lake with black rock bound . . .

"I plan to snuff out her light after she and I perform tomorrow night," I say with a swallow. "Think of this as a farewell performance to both the West Lawn and my macabre fancy."

Garland cocks his head. "Are you telling the truth?"

I refuse to let my gaze drift back up to the hills that hide my "Gothic witch," as he called her. He will not touch her. He may tempt my cutthroat side that does, indeed, crave biting burlesques of buffoons who disparage me or garner praise where none is warranted, but he will not stop me from swimming in the darkness and immortalizing Helen.

"Yes." I pat his left shoulder. "You'll be in high demand on Rowdy Row, O'Peale, I'm certain of it. No need to be jealous of Lenore's last bow. Please, go amuse yourself until I've moved."

He offers his hand for me to shake, his face all seriousness. I clasp his fingers in the most confident grip I can muster and endure the squirming sensation in my gut that I'm sealing a deal with the devil. Garland's skin simmers as though he's just baked his hands in an oven.

He then turns and swaggers off toward Charlottesville, whistling with the chirps of a mockingbird, which draws the attention of two professors walking along the East Lawn.

I return to my room alone, and I write "The Lake" while breathing the smell of Pa's tobacco that now clings to my walls like mold.

CHAPTER THIRTY-TWO

Lenore

My poet is a boxer, so I use the strength of my arm muscles to dig a grave into the ground of the university Lawn—fully prepared to fill said grave with a body later tonight if Mr. Garland O'Peale proves problematic. A wind howls at my back and stirs up the soil and the dank fumes of the earth. Despite my coughing from the dirt I've sucked into my lungs, I complete my task without assistance.

I wedge the toes of my boots into the wall of mud and climb out of the hole with my spade, borrowed from a shed beyond one of the serpentine walls. Once I'm back aboveground, I shake out my hat and clothing and tromp through the darkness, pushed forward by that easterly wind that hurls me toward my poet's ticking heart.

Some inebriated fools shout crass and blunt propositions about what they'd like to do to my female body when they glimpse a figure in a dress on the grounds. I growl in their direction, and they stumble onto their faces, their bottles rolling across the colonnade's bricks.

My poet's forest-green door appears ahead, beyond a set of Tuscan columns. A sudden case of strung nerves slows my step, but I press onward nonetheless, wringing my hands, swallowing deep breaths.

I approach his room and lean my right ear next to his door.

Within his dormitory, to my relief and exhilaration, Edgar recites a longer rendition of the poem from the pond:

"*. . . Yet that terror was not fright—*
But a tremulous delight,
And a feeling undefin'd,
Springing from a darken'd mind.
Death was in that poison'd wave
And in its gulf a fitting grave
For him who thence could solace bring
To his dark imagining;
Whose wild'ring thought could even make
An Eden of that dim lake."

Applause clatters across the room. I bend down and peek through the keyhole, spying five young men seated on the bed. Eddy bows in front of a fireplace stocked with meager sticks of kindling that wheeze with flames no taller than my fingers.

I place my lips next to the keyhole and breathe a warm breath across the room that enlivens the candles and firelight.

My poet's hair shivers in the breeze, and he turns toward the door.

"Let them see me," I whisper through the keyhole.

He steps toward me, the heels of his shoes brushing against the floorboards, his left hand pressed against his stomach. His eyes glisten with a violet incandescence.

"Let them see me," I say again, and I further unsettle the atmosphere inside the room with another stir of my breath.

"Once upon a midnight frightful," says Edgar, his voice deepening, "'mid a windstorm fierce and spiteful, something wicked and delightful perched outside my chamber door . . ."

He treads closer and softens his tone. "Hush now, listen closely—hear her, sighing sighs of sorrow—fear her.

Hush! Her wintry words grow clearer. Gentlemen, come meet"—Edgar whisks the door open—"Lenore!"

A stunned and wondrous wave of silence rushes against my ears. The boys on the bed shrink backward, pale and trembling, yet mesmerized by the sight of a maiden bathed in moonlight with the taste of death about her.

I step across the threshold, willing the candles to shimmer taller and to cast a glamour upon me. In the breadth of a heartbeat, my mourning dress brightens into a gown of crimson satin with ruffles and ribbons that bloom in place of the flocks of feathers. My hat shrinks down into an arrangement of rich black hair worn "up in the style of modern young women"—as my poet once requested of me. Ringlets dangle in front of my ears like clusters of flowers dipped in the indigo tinge of the night. And the string of teeth clasped around my throat, of course, transfigures into a necklace of freshwater pearls imbued with the softest blush of pink.

I'm a vision of ideal feminine beauty, with just enough scent of the sinister to inspire the audience to hold their breaths, waiting to see what I might do.

I stroll to the opposite end of the room, rest my right palm upon the windowsill, and say, with my face raised, "Let us dance to the tale of the Usher children from Richmond."

"Ah, yes . . ." Edgar's candlelit face breaks into a devilish grin, and he rubs his hands together. "An excellent suggestion." He turns toward his audience, and the shadow of his figure stretches up to the ceiling.

"In Richmond," he says, his voice whispery and low, "many years ago, there appeared a pair of theater players by the names of Mr. Luke Noble Usher and Mrs. Harriet Ann L'Estrange Usher—two better names I couldn't have invented myself."

The boys chuckle, their laughs tight, trapped in their throats.

"The Ushers had two children," continues Edgar, wandering to his right, his arms crossed over his chest, "James and Agnes—two wan and nervous waifs—orphaned in the tender years of their youth. What you are about to witness, my dear friends, is their strange and shocking tale, set in the insufferable gloom of the mansion they inherited from their wealthy benefactors . . ."

A strain of music sings across the air when my poet embarks upon an embellished story of the peculiar Usher siblings, the real-life orphaned children of two of his mother's actor friends. The poor dears were plagued by neuroses and, according to Edgar's dramatic rendering of their lives, met grim fates involving murder and madness.

The audience listens with rapt attention, but they're not shivering with terror. Their eyes haven't yet widened with wonder, even though my poet waves his arms about in a theatrical fashion and raises his voice, fighting with all his might to disturb these boys.

"Let us dance," I say again, under my breath, "to the tragic tale of the Ushers."

The walls covered in charcoal sketches clear away, revealing a ballroom with varnished mahogany floors, lit by the handsome brass chandelier that sparked the great Richmond Theater fire of 1811—yes, the fateful lamp of the theater fire! Eddy pauses and peers at the vision around him, his eyebrows arched, his mouth agape.

"Let us dance," I sing out at the top of my lungs, "to Edgar Poe's tragic tale of the Ushers!"

Out of the emerald-and-onyx sheen of the ballroom's walls step five young women in dresses of black barege silk with short, capped sleeves and coiled rope sashes. They wear ebony gloves that reach up to their elbows, and black jewels drip from their ears and necks. Feathered masks designed to look like ravens conceal all five of their faces.

The young ladies approach the gentlemen seated on the bed—now a settee of purple velvet—and they each offer a hand to the young man whose hair corresponds to the color of their own. A blonde for Miles George, a redhead for William Burwell, and so forth.

Next to a roaring fireplace with flames as tall as I, an orchestra strikes up a discordant waltz, harsh to the ears yet stirring to the heart. The musicians' muses buzz above their heads as a cloud of hummingbirds with bewitching coats of turquoise and sapphire that twinkle in the rays of the fire. The longer the firelight flickers against the musicians, the clearer it becomes that their faces lack flesh. These musical accompanists to the risqué revelry are mere skeletons with talent in their bones!

One of the cellists—a willowy woman in a vermillion dress—strums the main melody, and if you listen quite carefully, you can hear her weeping with a percussive *beat*-beat-beat, *beat*-beat-beat, *beat*-beat-beat.

The young men and women *step*-step-step, *step*-step-step, *step*-step-step to the rhythm of the waltz, while my poet sings his dreary song of the tragic Ushers—a dreary yet ravishing song. And *oh*, how his imagery causes the rich blue blood to flow through the university boys' veins! The waltzers spin and glide *quick*-quick-quick, *quick*-quick-quick, *quick*-quick-quick until they fall to the floor, exhausted and sickened, for my poet just sang out such a grisly exclamation:

"James Usher sealed his sister's dead body into the wall!"

The musicians cease playing and wait for me to react, bows raised above quivering strings, hollow eye sockets directed my way. I lift the hems of my swishing skirts, and with my feet bedecked in red satin slippers, I step over the masked girls and university boys strewn across the floorboards and clamber toward my poet, who loosens his crimson cravat by the flames of the fire. He's breathless from his tale, his handsome face shining in the light of that theater chandelier that once lit the fair face of his mother.

"Do you feel the elation?" I ask of him.

Edgar nods, his pupils dilating from the intoxication of his own imagination, his eyes so violet, so luminous, I see creativity pulsating throughout his irises.

I offer him my hand, my fingers clad in a black glove that conceals my nails.

The members of the orchestra straighten their postures. A breath of anticipation gasps from the fire. I nod, and the musicians resume the same discordant waltz, amplified to twice its previous volume. The floor beneath my soles trembles with music.

My poet and I entwine ourselves together and launch into a dance that travels around the entire room. We stare each other in the eye, not missing a single *beat*-beat-beat, *beat*-beat-beat, *beat*-beat-beat with our *feet*-feet-feet, *feet*-feet-feet, *feet*-feet-feet. Our shadows whirl across the walls, gliding, growing, transmogrifying into a pair of ravens—while young Usher seals his sister's corpse into the wall, while our audience freezes in horror on the floor, while I *try*-try-try, *try*-try-try, *try*-try-try to evolve into my future self before the music stops.

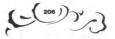

CHAPTER THIRTY-THREE

Edgar

The enchantment of the night washes out of my room with the flow of my friends spilling through my door. I'm left in silence to blow out my candles, afraid to let the tallow burn too long, unable to afford any new candles soon.

Lenore remains in the room with me, again resting her right hand on the windowsill. Her presence warms me yet unnerves me; comforts yet disquiets.

"I feel you evolving," I say while bent over the candle that lights my table, not yet blowing that one out.

"As do I," she says. "Glorious feathers are sprouting down the nape of my neck as I speak."

I pull a piece of charcoal from my writing box and sketch the face of Agnes Pye Usher on the wall above the table. The tallow of the remaining candle wafts a beefy odor into the air that makes my stomach growl.

"I don't know what my future holds for me anymore." I thicken the folds of skin beneath Agnes's eyes. "I doubt I'll have much more time to write."

"What are you talking about? We're just now finally getting started."

"Pa visited me yesterday after I left the hills."

Lenore hesitates before asking, "He's not dragging you back to Moldavia just yet, is he?"

"Not yet." I sigh, and my chest aches when I breathe—or, rather, fail to breathe. My inhalations are so shallow, so asphyctic, that my ears ring with the warning peals of impending unconsciousness. "I've fallen into a debt so deep and vile . . . He said he'd send more money. I don't believe him. He yelled at me for even talking about the fees." I rest the charcoal on the table, leaving Agnes's face suspended on my wall without a body, and I strive to inhale heartier breaths. "I'm moving to the West Range. Rowdy Row. A haven for students in similar situations. They won't frown upon gambling, if that's what I'm reduced to."

Lenore doesn't answer. For a moment I believe she's left me, but when I turn, I find her watching me, the sharp sting of betrayal blotting out the fire in her eyes.

"Mr. O'Peale will be joining you in this new endeavor, won't he?" she asks.

I avert my eyes from hers. "I'll need my wit to survive at the card tables. I owe so much money to so many people . . ."

"What about your Gothic art? What about tonight?"

I stifle a laugh. "There's no place for Gothic art in the world of gambling and debt, unless I can earn my fortune from selling that"—I choose a word that seems apt for the situation—"*nonsense.*"

Lenore's hand falls from the sill. "What did you just call it?"

"I know we entertained the fellows tonight, but the fervor of such fantasies can't last forever."

She seethes, but I ignore her and put the charcoal crayon away.

"Eddy," she says, and when I refuse to turn around, she continues: "The biggest success John Allan will ever have in his life is convincing you that you'll turn into a 'sickly, filthy burden on society' if you write your poems and stories."

I clench my jaw and endure the ghastly beat of my pulse inside my ears. "Don't say that."

"He's winning this battle."

I slap a hand on my table. "Don't you think I know that? I hear his doubts in my head every single day, but it's impossible to ignore him when he holds my future in the palm of his hand."

Lenore marches over to the fireplace, where she pesters the kindling with the poker. "You should publish your poems. Let the world see them."

"They're not good enough."

"That's John Allan talking again."

I sigh. "They still need work. 'Tamerlane' isn't even finished. That's Edgar Poe talking."

Somehow, she coaxes the sticks in the grate into a crackling conflagration. The flames gild the cadaverous hue of her skin.

"I agree about 'Tamerlane,'" she says. "The poem needs more scenes of suffering and heartbreak before we can share it with the world, but, oh, some of the other poetry will haunt their souls! And if we concoct anything even half as brilliant as what we created tonight . . ."

"Naturally, you believe that 'Tamerlane' requires more suffering."

"It lacks passion and originality."

"I know." I tug a handkerchief from a pocket and wipe away the charcoal from my fingers. My gaze strays back to my sketch of Agnes Usher, another child of actors whose parents died and abandoned her to Richmond.

"You have more riches than you realize, Edgar," says Lenore, her voice seeming to crackle with the fire. "You simply need to decide what to do with what you have."

I shake my head. "But I would trade *all* that I have—the intellect, the talent, the expensive education—*all* of it—if I could have just grown up in a home with my own flesh and blood. Or at least with a family that doesn't long to cast me off." I rub a hand through my hair, my head now throbbing, my eyes smarting. "They used to dress me up—Ma and Pa. They put me in yellow linen trousers, red silk stockings, a handsome purple coat, and a velvet hat—transforming me into a fine little dandy—and they'd stand me on a table, where I'd recite Sir Walter Scott's 'The Lay of the Last Minstrel' to all their friends. And even then, when I was a child no higher than their knees, I was trading my talents and intellect for affection."

A draft of cold air nips at my neck. I crumple my handkerchief into a ball on the table, my fingers still dirty, and I gaze again at Agnes Usher.

"They all hated that I hailed from the world of the theater"—I lick my right index finger and blot away a smudge on Agnes's cheek—"and yet they loved me and praised me *because* I entertained them. They devoured my theatricality. But I would give anything—I would sacrifice all my muses, all my intellectual riches—if I could shake off this feeling that I'm always alone—that something is *always* missing."

I clasp my hands around the back of my neck and tell myself that I still might have Elmira, even though she doesn't write. And my life might not end if I move away from my friends of the West Lawn to live in a cheaper West Range room. I might not lose at the card tables—might not find myself expelled for gambling. Pa might send that money after all.

The sudden sense that I've just suffered yet another loss grips me.

I swivel around and discover that Lenore no longer accompanies me, as though she wandered into the flames of my fireplace and sizzled away. Another cold draft of air hits my face.

I possess no urge to create.

I possess nothing at all but a temporary room scattered with drawings of nonsense.

CHAPTER THIRTY-FOUR

Lenore

A face that resembles my poet's peers through Eddy's window. For a moment, I wonder if Eddy somehow duplicated himself and locked his other self outside.

The figure turns away from the glass, and moonlight scampers across the crown of a retreating gray hat adorned with striped mockingbird feathers. I pounce at the window, but Garland O'Peale disappears into the night.

Edgar withdraws into himself over at his table.

"I would trade *all* that I have," he says, "the intellect, the talent, the expensive education—*all* of it—"

He doesn't notice me lifting the sash and climbing outside, even though a cold draft of air slips past me and dishevels his hair. I slide the window shut behind me and dash down an alleyway between garden walls.

Out on the Lawn, I spy the glint of the spade lying next to the open grave up ahead.

"Did you hear the terrible tale of the Ushers, Mr. O'Peale?" I call into the wind, and I skip across the grass toward the hole gaping in the ground. "Oh, my—how our poet springs to life when he's conjuring tales of madness and mayhem! You should have witnessed his ingenious passions sparkling in his amethyst eyes."

"I knew he was a liar," says Garland from somewhere behind me. "He told me he planned to snuff out your light tonight."

His voice rips across the air with a tear of my silk hat. I grab the brim and spin around to face him.

"Why would he snuff out a light," I ask, creeping backward toward the grave, "that beams from his own two eyes?"

Garland steps out of the darkness and stalks toward me in his pretentious coat and pantaloons that mimic the grays and the stripes of the university's uniform. He also wears a curious pair of spectacles that hide his eyes.

I continue slinking backward. "Your type of art is fine for a brief laugh, Mr. O'Peale, but I offer sumptuous feasts of words that the world shall savor for centuries."

Garland balls his hands into fists and breaks into a run.

I swing back around and lunge toward the grave, and just as the devil reaches my heels, I take a flying leap over the six-and-a-half-foot-deep pit.

Garland drops down into the ground behind me.

After the initial *thump*, he goes silent.

I lift my spade and scoop up a pile of mud and mulch, which I promptly dump onto his head.

Garland shrieks and claws at the walls of dirt, flailing around in the dark like an ant.

"You may have a tongue that cuts like a knife, Mr. O'Peale," I say while scooping up another serving, "but I can bury you alive."

"No, don't!"

I throw the dirt against his hat and his back.

"Stop that!" he calls out, hunching down. "Help me out of here."

"Oh, I'll help you out"—I toss in a nice, damp patch of earth crawling with plump pink worms—"if you listen to my proposal and stop ripping me apart."

He squeals and slaps away the worms.

"Did you hear me?" I ask.

"What proposal?"

"You and I both share the same two adversaries." I shovel yet another helping and dangle the spade over his head without yet dumping it, although the wind insists on showering him with a light dusting. "And those two adversaries are named John Allan and Edgar Allan Poe."

"Poe isn't our adversary."

"Ha!" I sprinkle down a few drops of soil onto his mockingbird feathers. "What you don't realize, my fine sir, is that we're not meant to be prancing around in these human forms. We can't even pick up a pen and write on our own terms. We're meant to evolve directly into spiritual beings, immune to harm and death, whirring with creative energies. Our artist knows this, but he's not fully embracing his art. He's clinging to the threats and insults of John Allan and leaving us trapped out here, vulnerable and underdeveloped."

"I feel neither vulnerable nor underdeveloped."

I release the dirt onto Garland's hat, and he panics again, slapping his palms against the wall.

"Let me out of here!"

"You feel vulnerable, you liar," I say, "which is why you want to rid yourself of me. But I can't think of any reason why an artist couldn't work with more than one muse."

"You distract him from his satires and comedies."

"Dark works of art require great wit, and satire sips from uncomfortable emotions. We should collaborate, Mr. O'Peale. I propose we work together."

He gasps. "How?"

I thrust the blade of the spade into the ground and lean against the handle. "Watch over Edgar when he moves to

Rowdy Row and assure that he remains healthy, alive, and enamored with words. If he dies, I fear that we may die, too. If the college expels him, he's told me that John Allan will force him to spend all his time working in the counting room of Ellis & Allan. Keep Eddy safe and intellectually stimulated."

Garland squints up at me. "And what will you be doing?"

"Strengthening myself in the wilds, developing my repertoire. During his direst moment, bring him out into the hills. Let us show him the power of his art and evolve together, before John Allan takes him away."

Garland removes his hat and picks dirt from the feathers. The moon scarcely reaches him down in that dank pit, but a sliver of light illuminates him enough to show me a downy layer of feathers encasing his skull.

"I accept your offer," he says, to my utter shock.

"Do you?"

"Yes. I will accompany him at the card tables."

"Keep him safe."

"I will. You have my promise." Garland lowers the hat back down on his head. "Now help me out of here please . . . *Lenore*, is it?"

I hesitate at first, rehearing Garland's promises in my head, sifting through his tone for any indications of insincerity and danger.

"The sheriff's coming!" shouts a student who bolts across the Lawn. "Get back in your rooms. Blow out your candles. He's looking for card players."

"Hurry!" Garland digs his fingers into the wall and attempts to climb his way out.

I grab his wrists and help to hoist him up, and after much wriggling and grunting, he clambers to his feet on solid ground, still clinging to my arms.

Before I regain my balance, however, he swings me around with a surge of unexpected strength and pushes me down into that hole.

I land on my backside with a force that jolts my neck. Clods of dirt rain down from the sides of the grave and pelt my face.

I spit out soil. "Why did you just do that?"

"As I said"—Garland leans his head over the pit—"I'll keep him safe. You have my promise. And I'll start by protecting him from you."

I wipe the filth from my eyes and push myself up to my feet. My neck and tailbone hurt like mad.

"*You* are his greatest adversary, Lenore," calls down Garland. "The gravest dangers for a man tormented by death are constant reminders of the grave!"

His words slice through my hat, knocking the top half clear off. The decapitated crown lands in the darkness behind me.

I hear a rumble of footsteps and more shouts of "The sheriff's coming!"

"Thank you for telling me of your vulnerability, Madame Macabre," says Garland, his spectacled face still looming overhead. "If you do manage to crawl out of this hole, you had better, indeed, run far into the hills. If I ever see you again on the university grounds, if I catch you calling to Poe from the hills, I'll gladly silence your melancholy voice, so my artist can at long last live!"

His voice tears a rip in the left shoulder of my dress, and the chilled and humid air of the tomb laps at my skin.

Garland bolts away just as I hear a man who must be the sheriff pounding on dormitory doors.

I slouch down in that cold slip of earth and wait for the world to settle above before I dare to dig my feet into the graveside walls and make my escape. My stomach cramps with unfamiliar pangs of human emotions.

Guilt.

Concern.

Sympathy for my poet.

I suddenly fear that Garland may be right: *The gravest dangers for a man tormented by death are constant reminders of the grave.*

CHAPTER THIRTY-FIVE

Edgar

The week following Lenore's sudden disappearance from my room, I receive a package from Pa. He sent me a uniform coat, six yards of striped cloth for the uniform's pantaloons, and four new socks, which, yes, I need, but he didn't enclose a single penny in his package. The bills pile up on my table. The amount of interest I owe on loans robs me of sleep. My brain refuses to produce a single line of poetry, but I don't have the time or the energy to search for my muse.

I study until my eyes blur and attend my lectures with sober attentiveness, yet my studiousness is rewarded with debt and a loss of respect from my West Lawn neighbors.

I pack up my trunk and move to a more affordable room in the West Range, a long arcade of dormitories unattached to any grand pavilions, unadorned by Tuscan columns.

"Welcome to Rowdy Row," says a stocky, hazel-eyed fellow at my door. "I'd like to formally invite you to a gathering of kindred spirits in my room later this evening."

I recognize his round cheeks and his smile wrought with mischief: He's the card player Upton Beall, the fellow Garland mentioned. He's also one of about fifty students included on a recent Grand Jury list of known university lawbreakers. My courage to acquire money through gaming falters.

"Thank you, Beall, but—"

"Poe, is it?"

I nod. "Yes. Edgar Poe."

"I've heard you've fallen on hard times."

I cringe and peer down at my new coat Pa sent. It doesn't quite match the coats worn by the other students—the gray is too pale; the buttons are a dull brass; the fabric scratches. Upton isn't even wearing the uniform, however, and might not care a damn about my clothing.

"No need for shame, Poe." He cups a hand over my left shoulder. "Many of us over here have run into financial predicaments due to youthful extravagance. Come have a bit of fun with us."

Youthful extravagance! If only that were the source of my "financial predicament"!

"Are the hotelkeepers oblivious to these 'gatherings of kindred spirits'?" I ask.

"Hardly." Upton snorts. "They're often sitting right there with us, shuffling the decks. Spotswood. Richardson. They 'accidentally' drink with us, too, as they put it."

I rub my lips together and calculate my debts, which are mounting to well over three hundred dollars. "I'll consider joining you."

"I hope you do." He pokes his head through my doorway. "I've heard your walls are a marvel to be witnessed."

"I haven't yet had a chance to decorate this room."

He pats my arm. "Bring your friend O'Peale along tonight. Some of your other friends say the two of you together are the reigning lords of satire."

"Perhaps," I say.

Instead of joining the card game, I sequester myself in my new room and read books I've borrowed from the library to help with my classes.

Garland knocks on my door and calls in, "Aren't you coming out tonight?"

"I'm not ready for that yet," I call back without even opening the door.

"I thought you moved over here to be with your own kind and earn money through cards, Poe."

"I'm not ready for that yet!" I say again, and I return to my studies.

Miles and Tom venture over to my room Saturday evening, but my other friends from the Lawn refrain from joining them. Some West Range fellows—Philip Slaughter, William Creighton, and Thomas Gholson—also wander in, carrying a punch bowl for brewing up peach and honey. Garland strolls in behind them, wearing his odd green spectacles. A patch of gray feathers now covers the nape of his neck, which I pray the others don't see.

Tom leans back on my bed and sighs at my bare walls. "Your walls are in need of your caricatures, Poe."

"Yes," says Garland with a clap of his hands, "let's christen your room with a sketch of Professor Long."

Philip stirs a ladle through the liquid in the bowl, churning up the soothing scents of sugared spirits.

Out of the corner of my eye, I see my imposter of a uniform slumped over the footboard of my bed and wonder how Pa can bear to sleep at night, knowing that I'm sitting here, miles from home, tearing at my hair, debating whether I should pay for food or firewood this week. And I wonder what the Rowdy Row fellows in the room would do if I broke into one of my poems about heartbreak instead of giving them the caricatures they want. I imagine Lenore stepping out of the gasping flames of my fire and reciting "Visit of the Dead."

Thy soul shall find itself alone—
Alone of all on earth—unknown
The cause—but none are near to pry
Into thine hour of secrecy.

"Poe's plotting," says Tom with a smile. "Give him a moment."

Pa probably isn't even home right now, I realize with a scratch of my head. He's off impregnating the widow Wills, and he's not even thinking of me or Ma. Ma's likely coughing alone in her chamber, too weak to leave her bed, while Aunt Nancy paces the landing, and the servants huddle around the fire in the outdoor kitchen, escaping Pa's kingdom through tales of the dead.

I throw my arms into the air. "'*Vivamus, moriendum est!*'"

"Is that Virgil?" asks Philip, scooping streams of the golden nepenthe into a crystal glass.

"No—Seneca," I say, taking that glass and dumping the brandy down my throat. I then exhale a fireball into the air and translate the phrase: "'Let us live—we must die!'"

"'*Vivamus!*'" says Miles, raising his own glass.

And the other boys chant the phrase with me as I leap onto my bed and draw a sketch of Professor Long's wide-open mouth with his gargantuan gums and giant horse teeth, and out of the man's fleshy lips springs our song of the evening: "'*Vivamus, moriendum est!*'"

CHAPTER THIRTY-SIX

Lenore

I climb out of the musty bowels of the grave I dug on the Lawn, trembling with guilt over the damage I've inflicted upon my poet, and I pledge to immerse myself in love and beauty.

Love and beauty alone.

No more horror and death for now.

The gravest dangers for a man tormented by death are constant reminders of the grave.

Back in the country churchyard, I allow the spirit who wears his hair in a bow at his neck to court me, and, yes, even to kiss me beneath the swollen May moon. His lips are airy and scented with rosemary, and his hands mist the feathers of my head. His coat bedews my bosom and stomach through the fabric of my dress, and his ruffled cravat tickles my throat. He smells like wet grass. He likes to call me his "bonny darling," a name that makes the feathers on the back of my neck bristle, but I do my best to fall into this world of love and beauty.

Love and beauty alone.

I find myself more enamored with a spirit named Jane—a vision of vaporous blue who wears her hair in a ribbon snood, just like Jane Stanard. Her moonstone eyes set my soul afire. Her rosebud lips look as soft as perfumed petals.

One night during a mood of boldness, I perch beside her on a tombstone carved of smooth white marble and ask, "May I kiss you?"

She offers her hand for me to kiss, but she won't turn her lips my way.

My heart cracks into a thousand pieces.

I suddenly understand the agony Eddy suffers when he pines for the women he can't have. Every inch of me aches.

I spend the rest of the night in the bell tower, lost in longing, unsure what to do now that I've allowed myself to taste the potent flavors of love and beauty.

Springtime steals into summer. Sunlight slices through the trees on balmy afternoons, and the Blue Ridge range to the west displays the stirring blue haze of its nomenclature. I wander the hills surrounding Charlottesville and familiarize myself with every ravine and hillcrest, every craggy oak and maple, and I learn who farms the lands, from the European immigrants to the descendants of Revolutionary War heroes to the free black families who've owned their properties since the century before. I glide behind the trees, so no one sees me, but I know from their shudders, their startled eyes, that they feel me roaming out here.

My poet, too, searches for beauty in the hills. His heartbeat gallops through the foliage, but O'Peale trails behind him during every excursion. Garland's clumsy clods for feet snap apart twigs and trample down leaves, disturbing the peace of my Arcadia.

One July afternoon, when the bells of the university toll a gloomy dirge for the death of its founder, Mr. Jefferson, my poet journeys to the pond where I inspired him to write "The

Lake." I watch him from the upper boughs of an evergreen that towers over the forest. He's carrying his portable writing box in his arms, a sight that piques my interest.

Garland creeps behind him—a gray panther on the prowl—a pest in paradise.

I climb up two more levels of the branches and hear Edgar invoke me in the pine-sweetened wind. Again, he recites the opening lines from William Hamilton Drummond's *The Giant's Causeway*:

"Come, lonely genius of my natal shore,
From cave or bower, wild glen, or mountain
hoar;
And while by ocean's rugged bounds I muse,
Thy solemn influence o'er my soul diffuse."

"At the far end of a garden path made of stones," I say into the breeze as a whisper intended for Edgar's ears alone, "stands a woman in a white dress that clings to her legs. Her alabaster hands hold an azure plate covered in seeds, to which pigeons flock, and perch, and dine while they coo with rippling throats. The woman—this living Grecian statue—wears a ribbon snood over her brown curls, and she peers up with a smile and says in a tone that stops you from breathing and nearly renders you unconscious, 'So, this must be Rob's friend. I am delighted to meet you, Edgar. I admired your talented mother. I saw her but once on the stage, when I was a girl, but I remember her lovely face and voice. Come farther inside the garden.' She lowers the plate to a bench and beckons with a wave. 'Come meet Rob's rabbits and pigeons and tell me all about your poetry.'

"A blaze of golden light flares in her direction," I continue to whisper, "and the snood falls from her hair; her clusters of curls break free from their trappings. The garden blooms into the sunlit shores of ancient Troy, and again Helen beckons, while the salt from the sea sprays your lips and gulls cry overhead."

Beside the pond in the pines, my poet dips his quill into a pot of fresh ink that spreads a rich and regal fragrance across the hills. Despite the merciless shadow of his satires stalking behind him, Edgar leans over his writing box, which he's opened at the hinges and transformed into a lap desk, and, my God, he purrs the most exquisite lyrics I've ever heard:

"Helen, thy beauty is to me like Grecian . . . no,
 Phoenician . . . no . . .
Helen, thy beauty is to me
Like those Nicean barks of yore,
That gently, o'er a perfum'd sea,
The weary way-worn wanderer bore
To his own native shore . . ."

CHAPTER THIRTY-SEVEN

Edgar

I wait until a midsummer's Saturday night before joining Upton and his fellow gamblers at the card table in his room. A broad-shouldered blond fellow named Samuel, whom I've met once or twice, lets me in, a gold snuff box in hand.

"Do you take snuff, Poe?" he asks.

"No, I was raised by a tobacconist. I'm trying to escape the world of tobacco while freed from his dominion."

"Understandable." Samuel kicks the door shut while pinching snuff from the box. He then sucks the wad of tobacco up his left nostril and offers a sniffled "Welcome."

"Thank you."

"Welcome, Poe," says Upton, hopping up from the table and shaking my hand. "So glad you finally decided to join us."

"There's the Poet to a *T*," says Philip Slaughter, slapping my back from the chair beside me. He reaches around to take a pinch of snuff from Samuel's box and snorts it up his red-rimmed nose.

"Welcome, Mr. Poe," says one of the players at the table—none other than the hotelkeeper George Washington Spotswood—who's shuffling the deck, an emptied glass of brandy parked at his right elbow.

"Have a drink," says Upton. "Pull up a chair. We're just about to start a new hand."

"Thank you, gentlemen. I'm much obliged."

I dip a cup into Upton's punch bowl but force myself to wait to take a sip until I've won a little money. The libations smell less sweet tonight—more likely to numb my brain with astounding swiftness. I pull up a chair and rest the glass as far from myself as I can.

"How are you at loo, Poe?" asks Upton with a dimpled grin while he raises his drink to his lips.

"I've never played it," I admit, but the others gladly teach me.

Before we officially commence playing, Garland glides into the room amid a round of cheers from the other fellows, who apparently adore him. He plants himself in a chair behind me. He has no money for wagers, for reasons obvious to me, so he simply watches me toss my borrowed-on-credit dollars into the pot.

Between hands Garland leans forward and whispers near my ear, "You're better than this dissolute rabble, Poe. You're smarter than the lot of them. You can win this and save yourself from your impecuniousness."

During the second hand, I lay down my five cards—three of them spades—and grind my teeth over the superior flushes unfurling around me on the table's scratched surface. Upton wins the pot, and William Sewell to his left deals next.

A wind bangs the shutters boarding Upton's window, and the flames in the lamps dance in the draft. The dimming of the light turns everyone's faces into the golden visages of phantasms with hollowed-out eyes. The transformation, for some reason, brings to mind a student named Sterling Edmunds, who recently returned to the grounds. The faculty suspended

Sterling for whipping a schoolmate—whipping him brutally several times with a cowhide—over cheating at cards.

We're all nothing more than beautiful young monsters, I realize as I glance at the faces glowing around me, *one small step away from killing each other.*

I'm forced to keep passing—luck fails me at every hand—and I watch my schoolmates, as well as Mr. Spotswood, scoop my coins and bills into their piles of winnings. I nip small sips of peach and honey, letting the brandy soothe my nerves, but I remain careful—*oh, so careful*—not to slip into incapacitation.

The clock strikes midnight with hellish clangs that dent my eardrums. I totter out of Upton's room, my pockets empty, my brain dulled, my knees wobbly.

Upton grabs my left arm and keeps me upright. "Maybe next time luck will smile upon you, Poe."

"Thank you, friend." I slap him on his back and cling a moment to his shirt and vest to avoid falling. "But I must stay cautious. John Allan is watching." I bend forward, close to his doughy face, and I say in a slow and measured voice, so he'll understand me, "John Allan is *always* watching."

Upton purses his brows. "Who the devil is John Allan?"

"I don't know," I say, rocking to and fro. "That's an excellent question. Who is John Allan, and why does he plague me like a—*plague?*" I laugh at the cleverness of my phraseology, which I foolishly mistake for a pun.

Garland yanks me backward by my collar and escorts me to my room. He slams the door shut behind us and flings me down on my bed.

I hit my left knee on wood and cry out in pain.

"Maybe gambling and drinking isn't such a good idea," he says, sounding far too much like Pa. "Maybe we should stick to hosting fellows like Miles and Tom in your room and reading your work aloud for them. You're a terrible gambler, and your drinking makes me sick. Do you know how hard it was for me to pretend to keep my wits about me in there?"

I dig the heels of my palms into my eyes and groan. "Miles and Tom are my only two friends from the Lawn who'll even speak to me now, and they laughed the last time I read them a story. They said I overused the name of my protagonist, Gaffy."

"I know. I was there and watched you fly into a rage and throw the story into the fire. See the singe marks on my arm!"

Garland pulls back his shirtsleeve and shows me a scaly black patch of bubbles on his inner forearm that makes my stomach lurch. He then backs away, and his eyes lose their luster. His voice sharpens to the lacerating blade of a scythe. "Don't ruin this, Poe. You're doing too well in your classes. You just joined the damned Jefferson Literary and Debating Society. You're thriving here when you're not worrying about money and John Allan."

"Tom calls me Gaffy Poe."

"Who cares what Tom calls you! My God, Poe!" He yanks his hat farther down on his head with both hands, his knuckles whitening. "I'm losing my patience. Stop hesitating and feeling sorry for yourself. Pick yourself up and write."

"Not now."

"Write!" yells Garland, and he leans down over me on the bed and roars with a force that rattles the walls: "WRITE!"

I scramble off the mattress, grab a sheet of paper so recklessly, it tears, and write deep into the night—about what I do not even know. I ramble on and on about injustices, and poverty, or some other subject that's chewing at my brain until my eyes water and my hand goes numb—and Garland's looming there behind me the entire time, his shadow lengthening into the shape of a bird on the wall, squawking, "Write! Write! Write!"

The gambling continues.

The losses accrue.

Garland's oppressiveness worsens.

Pa's lack of financial assistance endures.

Ma writes that she's suffering from another cold.

Elmira still won't respond to my letters.

I toss all my earlier manuscripts, the ones I brought from home—as well as my work on "Tamerlane," "The Lake," and the beginning threads of my ode to Helen—down into the cobwebs of the floor beneath my table.

And all throughout the humid heat of summer, my friends in the West Range view me as their source of entertainment—a theatrical teller of tales in a candlelit room pungent with charcoal, ink, sweat, and booze. But if they look deep into the eyes of the drawings spreading across my new walls, they'll witness what I truly am. They'll learn I'm not just the laughing boy who challenges fellow students to foot races in the Lawn and impresses his professors. They'll understand I'm not the carefree wit they think they know.

I'm lonely. I'm terrified. I'm penniless. I'm haunted.

And I could take down every single one of them with a few swift strokes of my pen, for I see the ugliness inside us all.

CHAPTER THIRTY-EIGHT

Lenore

Something is wrong with my poet.

Whenever he journeys through my forests, he no longer walks with a lightness in his step. Instead, he stumbles into the hills with his hands crammed into his coat pockets, his elbows jutting out from his sides at mismatched angles, his shoulders tense. His violet-gray eyes have faded to the smoky hue of skies in bleak December. Side-whiskers grow in fuzzy patches on his cheeks, lending him an older appearance, and a grave one at that. He looks more like a tobacco merchant than a carefree dreamer.

He invokes me no longer. He simply kicks aside pine cones and sits in silence beneath the trees, staring out at the world below him. Garland doesn't even follow him, and I wonder if O'Peale, too, has weakened. The rogue should have collaborated with me.

Feathers have ceased sprouting from my neck and my spine, and my hunger for words gnaws at my stomach until I feel empty and sick, until I no longer possess the strength to wander through the trees. Cobwebs dangle from my forehead and creep across my dress in sticky clumps that cling to my fingers whenever I fight to brush them away. Spiders crawl down my arms on spindly legs. My throat often aches,

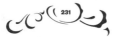

as though John Allan grips my neck in his hands. I even smell the scent of his tobacco in the forest air.

Some nights I fall flat onto my face in the churchyard, as drunk as a lord, and the spirits rush to pick me off the ground and lay me across the sepulcher where I now sleep with my misty Jane, who no longer fears holding me against her.

I still haven't ever tasted a single drop of alcohol.

I *know* who's blurring my brain with peach and honey down at the university.

I know who isn't thinking of his poetry.

CHAPTER THIRTY-NINE

Edgar

A bloody fight erupts outside my room one steaming September night when the dormitory rooms refuse to cool.

Charles Wickliffe from Kentucky pounds upon a shirtless classmate whose face I can't even see at first, and once Wickliffe tires his competitor out, he sinks his teeth into the fellow's left arm and bites him from his shoulder down to his elbow. By now I can view the anguished expression of the victim, who squeals with a sound akin to a pig in a slaughterhouse, but then, even worse, he goes utterly silent, his mouth stuck wide open in a muted version of his squealing, his face blanching, lips purpling, eyes rolling into the back of his head. I rock back on my heels, on the verge of a swoon, just from watching his agony.

Two professors pry Wickliffe off him and bark out the word "expulsion." One of the professors examines the damaged arm—a bloodied, bruised, and mangled mess that again makes me light-headed. It is likely that pieces of flesh as large as my hand will be obliged to be cut out to save the limb. Blood soaks the bricks outside my door, and a professor calls for the janitor to fetch a mop and warns me, "Be careful not to slip."

I close the door and lay down on my bed, cradling my left arm as though I've myself been bitten. The victim's squeals echo through my head.

What would such barbarity feel like? I wonder, and to investigate such pain, I free myself from my clammy shirt and bite my own flesh to a point just before the breakage of skin. My teeth leave an imprint.

I bite again, daring myself to go further, but can't do it.

Once my pulse slows, and the dizziness dims, I stand back up and resume a task I'd been undertaking when I first heard the scuffle outside my door. Using my dwindling lump of charcoal, I climb onto my chair and recreate an illustration of a winged giant from Byron's *Childe Harold's Pilgrimage* on my ceiling—my latest masterpiece.

My thoughts soon return to the student's mangled arm.

So much blood!

So much gore—strips of flesh just hanging off the victim's gleaming wounds!

My preoccupation with his injuries, coupled with the book of Lord Byron's writings lying open before me, leads me to ruminate on Byron's death during the Greek War of Independence, just two years earlier. I recall all the printed accounts of the ceaseless bloodletting his physicians employed to cure him of illnesses. They bled Byron dry, turned him feverish, and he perished in Greece, not yet even forty years old.

Oh, Byron. What brilliance would you have showered upon us in your years of Eld had ye lived to a hundred!

My mind then strays to the death of Pa's uncle William in the middle of tea and pancakes—not a bloody or a heroic demise, to be sure, and yet still a troubling one, according to Pa, who witnessed it—which leads me to an epiphany.

I shall try appealing to Uncle William's son James for a loan.

"Yes, yes, yes!" I declare, jumping off the chair.

I pen a letter then and there, and my hope escalates.

Perhaps I can pay off my debts before the session ends in December.

Perhaps I can sleep better at night, knowing for certain I'll return for a second session in February.

Mr. Spotswood knocks on my door and asks again about the money I owe for the servant he's lent me, and I say, "I'm working on a letter to remedy this problem right now, Mr. Spotswood. And watch out for the blood on the bricks."

I close the door and fetch a stick of sealing wax and my seal from the drawer of my writing box.

Someone else knocks, and before I can even rise to my feet, a band of neighbors barges into my room.

"Tell us about the fight," they say.

"Spare no details," they urge.

"You're the perfect person to have witnessed the gore, Poe. Describe it all in that whispery, eerie voice you like to use."

I hide my plea to James Galt beneath a library book.

"Once upon a stark September . . . ," I say, turning to my audience, but the lack of blood in my brain from the previous spells of dizziness continues to silence my macabre muse. Or maybe she loathes that my poems lie in a jungle of cobwebs on the floor . . .

"Poe?" asks Tom. "Are you unwell?"

I look down at my bare left arm and envision the limb caked in blood from puncture wounds made by my own teeth. I imagine what Pa would say to all of this—the exploration of pain for the sake of my art, the desperate letter to his cousin, the glassy-eyed boys packed into my room, begging for a show, the punchbowls brimming with mint-sling and peach and honey, and the debts.

Oh, the debts.

The debts.

The debts.

The debts.

I swoon right then and there in front of my fellow students, which entertains the lads far more than any of my stories or drawings ever have. I come to at the sound of them all applauding what they believe to have been a performance.

"Bravo!"

"Well done!"

"A nice touch with your temple smacking the floor."

My brain rolls about in my head, and once my vision clears, the first items I view down there on the floorboards (which smell like brandy and my own feet) are my manuscripts, lying in dust and spiderwebs like a pair of winter boots crammed under a bed for the summer. I close my eyes again, even at my friends' urgings to stand up, for this life of mine tires me, and I simply want to sleep.

Cousin James Galt sent me a short, cordial letter to say he cannot offer me a loan. I don't blame him in the slightest, for I have no collateral to offer, and we're not especially close, even though he's a mere four years older than myself.

"But, really, James," I say, crumpling his fine white stationery into a ball between my hands, "would it have inconvenienced you so terribly to assist a cousin in need?"

I hurl the letter into my fireplace, grateful for the free kindling, and the flames consume his rejection with sharp snaps of their jaws.

In early November, I tear open a letter sealed with Pa's scarlet wax and find one hundred dollars enclosed with a note from Pa that tells me the money ought to cover my outstanding expenses. I press my elbows against my table with groaning creaks of the wood, scratch my forehead, and laugh in exasperation, wondering how I can possibly turn one hundred dollars into the two thousand I now need to pay off my debts without some sort of sorcery—without more gambling.

And so—yet again—I pay a visit to the card tables, armed with the crisp set of bills.

"Sorry, Poe," says Upton Beall—yet again—when my money disappears into other students' pockets. "It seems that Luck is simply no friend of yours."

The days shorten. Each morning when I hustle to my seven o'clock class, frosts coat the paling grasses of the Lawn. Up in the Ragged Mountain, the trees shed their crisped leaves, and the hills soon rise above Charlottesville as sere and bristly mounds that no longer call to me. The sky clouds with plumes of hickory smoke piping out of hundreds of dormitories stocked with stacks of firewood—and yet the only substance passing through my own chimney is the whistling wind that ices my bed and my blood. I wear three pairs of socks each night to keep my toes from numbing and bluing.

I study, and I gamble, but I do not write what I wish to write. My poems—the ones that aren't meant to entertain the university masses—remain on the ground beneath my desk, abandoned to my studies and my fretting, peppered in dust, entombed in cobwebs.

There isn't any time to tend to my muse.

There isn't any use.

CHAPTER FORTY

Lenore

O n a clear and soundless night in late November, starved and weary of my life without my poet, I venture to the arcaded West Range building of the University of Virginia. Chalky layers of dust and grime cake my skin and parch my throat. A thick wall of air—my poet's resistance—pushes me backward on the Lawn, but I lean my right shoulder forward and plow through the barrier, which smells of the bitterness of defeat.

With silent footfalls, I cross the bricks of the arcade, my ears pricked for any signs of my poet.

"Where are you, Eddy?" I ask in a voice that, I admit, some might call rather menacing. My eyes scan each closed green door. "And where is Garland O'Peale?"

My feet halt before a door.

Behind the green wood, a heart beats with pounding palpitations.

Tick. TIck. TICk. TICK.

Over the waves of muffled male laughter surging from the dormitory within, I hear each thumping valve and chamber of my poet's heart.

I turn the latch and enter the bruised and dented walls of a booze-drenched room squirming with a dozen young men who chat and chortle around square card tables. They hold

plain-backed cards in front of their faces, splayed out like ladies' fans, and they guzzle down glasses of a clear liquid with sprigs of mint floating around in the bubbles. Coins clank against tabletops. Laughter amplified by alcohol bellows across the chamber, cresting into high-pitched waves that shriek across my brain. One of the players—a potbellied man with fuzzy auburn side-whiskers—can't be any younger than fifty.

Edgar sits among these gamblers, his own hand of cards fanned in front of his mouth. His skin bulges beneath his eyes, signaling his lack of sleep.

With a startled blink, he catches sight of me and lowers his cards.

Not now, he mouths. *Go!*

Another batch of cobwebs entangles my nose. I brush at my face and ask over the roar of the crowd, "Is this why you're ignoring your poetry?"

Edgar widens his eyes.

The other players grow silent and whip their heads around to me, freezing at my presence.

"This is the card playing you told me about?" I ask. "*This* is your solution? To get expelled and shipped back to Richmond?"

The older man with the potbelly pops up from his chair. "What do you mean, 'expelled'? Is the faculty on its way?"

"Oh, God!" says one of the boys, also jumping to his feet. "Everyone, grab your winnings and run!"

Knees bang against tables, and cards and liquor cascade to the floor. The gamblers reach out and grab stacks of money, stuffing papers and coins into pockets, cursing and whimpering—a whirlwind of greed and fear that makes me perspire just from watching. They leap up, chairs tipping over behind them, and push each other out of the way in a mad exodus to the door, their mouths twisted with terror, not

caring a fig about me—the grim specter among them. In fact, I'm forced to jump aside to avoid getting trampled.

Edgar races past me in the crowd.

I run after him.

Before I can even call my poet's name, someone clasps me from behind and throws me to the grass beyond the arcade. The assailant yanks my severed hat from my head.

"I told you to stay away," he says.

I flip myself over on the ground and find Garland standing over me in his green-tinted spectacles, holding my hat—the hat *he* mutilated.

"Does anyone have a pistol?" he calls out, and he spins toward the last of the fleeing students. "I require a pistol at once!"

A door swings open behind him, and a red-cheeked fellow whom I saw at the card tables reaches out and grabs Garland's left shoulder. "Thought I heard you out here, O'Peale. Hurry! Get inside Poe's room before you're caught."

The fellow pushes Garland into the room, and I follow them inside, slamming the door shut behind me.

Edgar tenses by his bed when he sees me, a gray coat half-unpeeled from his arms.

"No!" He drops the coat to the floor. "These two can't be together. Upton, get them out of here!"

"My God, Poe," says the other student—this *Upton*—backing away, a hand clasped over his mouth. "Is this—is this your Gothic muse? The one rumored to have prowled the grounds before? The one Miles raves about?"

Eddy peers at me with pleading eyes. "Go back into the hills—*please*. I'm so close to finishing the session. I need to survive the examinations. I must complete this first year, so I can retain some semblance of honor."

"I'll strangle her for you," says Garland, lunging toward me.

"No!" Eddy throws out a hand and pushes him back by his chest. "Don't hurt her."

"But—"

"I said, don't hurt her!"

The Upton fellow continues to gawk, but he does manage to lower his hand from his mouth, which ends the muffling of his words. "Why have you been hiding her, Poe? She far surpasses anything I've ever witnessed before."

"She wouldn't have been welcome at the card tables," says Edgar, and he averts his eyes from mine. "I see the cobwebs dangling from you, Lenore. I apologize for my negligence." He swallows with a painful-looking ripple of his Adam's apple. "I've missed you."

I react with a startled blink. "Have you?"

Garland throws my hat at me. "He hasn't been himself. Don't feel excessively flattered by that confession."

Upton inches closer and observes the feathers lining my scalp with a quiet gasp of awe. "She's a gem of art. I would have paid the price of admission to see the two of you perform together."

Garland snorts at such an idea.

Edgar arches his eyebrows. "You would have?"

"I told you, dear poet"—I lower my hat to my head—"I'm ready to be seen. Your shame of me is unwarranted."

"I beg to differ," says Garland.

"I don't care a damn about your differing, Mr. O'Peale."

"Stop quibbling!" Eddy kicks aside his coat on the floor. "I'm planning to destroy the both of you tonight, so there's no point bickering with each other! Don't make this worse."

My blood runs cold.

"What are you talking about?" asks Garland.

Eddy sinks down on his bed.

"Edgar . . ." I say over the hammering of my heart. "What do you mean by 'destroying' us?"

He rubs his arms and looks toward his table. "If I'm to keep myself warm tonight . . . I'll need to . . ." He clears his throat. "I'll be forced to burn my manuscripts."

Garland and I lock eyes. My nemesis's face blanches to the color of bleached bones, and my blood simultaneously drains from my head.

The flames in the hearth choke and sputter behind me, but I don't dare look at them.

"I'm sorry," says Eddy, "but I can't afford another stick of firewood. I'm terrified of falling ill before the examinations. I just gambled away my last dollar."

"But . . ." I shake my head. "I saw every person at that card game grabbing up piles of money like they didn't care who it belonged to."

"Do I seem like a lucky man to you?" asks Eddy. "I was so terrified of getting caught and expelled, I didn't touch one cent that wasn't mine. It's getting so damn cold at night, and a pile of flammable paper sits under my table . . ."

"No, no, no!" Upton heads for the door. "I'll bring you some of my own logs, my friend . . ."

"No, please don't!" Edgar leaps to his feet. "I don't want charity yet again. Please forget this."

"I'm not going to let you freeze to death, Poe," says Upton.

"Bring over another glass of mint-sling to keep me warm if that makes you feel better. But please don't view me as a beggar." Eddy pushes a smile to his face and sits back down. "Best be off now, Beall. I feel a mood coming on, and I can't bear the thought of you thinking me both poor and mad."

"Send away Madam Melancholy." Garland gestures with his head toward me. "And your mood will crawl away with her."

"You're wrong, Garland." Eddy picks up his coat from the floor and slides it back over his arms. "Lenore pulls the demons from my head. Since childhood's hour, she's the only thing that has ever kept me sane."

A small murmur of surprise bleats from my lips. So touched by his words am I that my human-esque eyes blur with a film of tears, and my mortal chin quivers.

Eddy crouches down to the floor and crawls beneath his table. "Don't hurt her, O'Peale. Good night to you, Beall. Oh, listen to that!" He chuckles from down in the cobwebs. "I *am* a Poet to a *T*."

Upton opens the door and turns to Garland. "Should I go? Is he all right?"

"I'm coming with you," says Garland, "I need an ax."

My heart stops. "An ax? For what?"

Without replying, Garland breezes out the door with Upton.

Eddy backs out from beneath his table while hugging a pile of manuscripts tangled in cobwebs. A spider dangles from the bottommost page on a thread.

"If cobwebs cling to me when you toss your beautiful poems of sorrow beneath your table," I say, "then what do you think will happen to me if you throw the poems into the fire?" I raise my hands, convinced that I see wisps of smoke emanating from the tips of my fingers. "My skin already tingles as though it might burn."

"I don't want to burn my work, Lenore, but, my God, what am I supposed to do? Pa literally left me here to die."

Garland hurls open the door and hoists a hatchet into the air.

I scream and lunge for the window. Eddy drops his manuscripts.

"Stop screaming!" says Garland. He lowers the blade into Eddy's table with a force that makes me jump. "Clean off this table and break it down into kindling."

Edgar gasps. "I can't chop up my table."

"You've paid for the furniture, Poe. You still have your portable writing desk. Chop it up and leave your manuscripts alone. You are not going to kill your muses." Garland glances at me. "Not even *that* one."

"That's an excellent idea," I say, and I grab a pile of books from Edgar's table and tuck it beneath his bed.

Garland removes the writing box to the corner of the room farthest from the fire, and Edgar and I transfer stacks of papers to the space beneath his bed, where the drafts blow arctic cold against my face.

"I hear your molars clacking together," I tell my poet when we're kneeling down there together.

"I thought that was your ghastly necklace," he says with a laugh edged with pain. He clasps his mattress above, bows his head, and murmurs three new lines of "Tamerlane":

"For I was not as I had been;
The child of Nature, without care,
Or thought, save of the passing scene—"

My poet then rises to his feet, yanks the hatchet out of his table, and knocks the furniture onto its side with a shove of his right foot. With a blow swift and measured, he hacks off one of the table's legs with a startling *thwack*.

Garland joins me at my side during the ensuing whacks.

"I'm much obliged for this idea, Mr. O'Peale," I say, "even though it galls me to compliment you. I admire your quick-witted thinking."

"That's my forte," he says, removing his hat and his green-tinted spectacles.

I step back, for his face reminds me of Edgar's. A strange, mockingbird rendering of my poet with short gray feathers for hair.

"Good gracious," I say. "You look like him."

"I always have. As do you."

Edgar throws the fourth leg aside and proceeds to chop up the body.

"I genuinely still believe we might work well together," I say out of the corner of my mouth to Garland, "if you stop bullying and threatening me."

Garland tucks his hat beneath his left arm. "I'm going to Maryland with Upton Beall after the session ends."

"Are you? Why?"

"I'm fond of Beall. He's extraordinarily fun. And I'm tired of waiting for our brooding Mr. Poe to embrace me. The fire inside me is sputtering out."

Garland looks me in the eye, and, 'tis true—not a single spark illuminates his irises, which now appear a dull yellowish-green instead of amber.

"He'll never stop fretting about John Allan," he says as our poet splits the table into two.

I brush a cobweb off my chin. "Working with other artists isn't the same at all, Mr. O'Peale. I've tried it. It won't satiate the hunger."

Garland rolls up his right sleeve and shows me a horrifying black patch of singed skin on his inner arm. "He's already burned some of his humorous pieces in my presence. His threat to destroy more of his work just now made me realize you were right: Poe is our greatest adversary. You can have him."

"I don't know if he'll be the same without you."

"That's a risk I'm willing to take."

"You might perish without him."

"Another risk I'd rather face than to suffer this frustration." Garland offers me his hand. "Adieu, Madame Melancholy. Good luck back in Richmond. I don't envy you for facing John Allan while there."

I shake his hand, and my heart quivers over his words about Pa—a man I'd hope to never encounter again while inhabiting this vulnerable frame.

Garland slips out of the room, as do I, while Edgar Poe finishes murdering his furniture.

CHAPTER FORTY-ONE

Edgar

I t's true, I've desperately missed my Gothic muse.

My soul strengthens in her presence, and the darkness lifts from my brain.

While my chopped-up table burns in the hearth behind me, I tuck my beloved manuscripts into my trunk and murmur to the wall of art in front of me, "I need to concentrate on my examinations these next two weeks, and then I'll bring you home with me to Richmond."

"You had better," a voice whispers behind me, but when I turn around, I find myself alone.

Again.

The examinations commence. Each night I'm a beggar fighting to warm himself in the glow of the dismembered corpse of his table, but during the daylight hours I'm a scholar trumpeting his knowledge of languages and literature, of ancient lore and lost translations. My professors never see the desperation thrashing about inside me. They don't detect the shivering that never ceases, even when I'm seated in lecture rooms heated with howling fires and throngs of bodies perspiring from nerves.

On the eve of the second week of examinations, Miles George appears at my door with a small table made of cedar.

"You said you lost your table in a drunken wager," he says, "and I can't imagine studying without some sort of desk."

My face flushes with guilt over the lie I told about my other table—and with shame over his pity for me.

"I can't accept your charity," I say. "And I have my writing box."

"I don't need two full-sized tables, Poe."

I shake my head. "No, this is an unnecessary kindness."

"Please, take it!" Miles scoots the table toward me and pushes back his hair, which now hangs long enough to reach the middle of his nose. "It was a foolish purchase I made at the beginning of the term when I thought my dormitory was understocked. I won't have room for it in the carriage ride home. You'd be doing me a favor."

"Well . . . thank you," I say, and I maneuver the table through my doorway.

"Good luck with the last week of examinations."

"Good luck to you, too, Miles."

I long to tell him I'll likely not return the next session but can't bring myself to do so.

Instead of leaving, Miles leans a shoulder against my doorframe. "I wish I could see more of that astounding muse of yours. Do you think she originated by crawling out of your head?"

I plunk the table down in the center of the room. "I beg your pardon?"

"If that's what's inside your head at the age of seventeen, my friend"—Miles cracks a wry grin—"I can't wait to see what's yet to come."

"You're far too generous." I run my fingertips across the table's grain, envisioning how best to slice the wood.

"I'm sure you'll finish at the top of your classes." Miles pushes himself off the doorframe. "I'll see you around."

"I'm thankful I met you, Miles."

He smiles. "I'll be sure to say only good things about you when someone inevitably interviews me about our time here together, years from now."

I chuckle. "Then everyone will think you're a teller of tales, too."

He snickers and meanders away, and I scoot the desk over to the space where my former table stood. I won't slam a blade through it just yet.

Let's save the wood for a night when the cold turns tortuous.

On the fifteenth of December, we're freed from our studies, liberated from examinations, and I learn that my name appears on the lists of students who excelled in both the senior Latin class and the senior French class.

I celebrate at the private house of a friend in Charlottesville and converse at length with the university's librarian, Mr. William Wertenbaker, who's also a student, albeit one twelve years older than myself. He attended my Italian, French, and Spanish lectures with me. We get along so well, in fact, that upon our return to the university grounds, I invite him to my room.

"I hope you don't mind sitting on my floor," I say as I light three tallow candles on the mantle.

"Not at all."

Mr. Wertenbaker lowers himself down in front of the unlit fireplace that's nothing more than a wasteland of ashes. I'm conscious of the candles' black smoke blowing around the room.

The librarian tips back his head to view my drawings on the walls and whistles in appreciation. "Fascinating! I think I recognize the illustration on the ceiling from a collection of Byron's poetry."

"Yes!" I lift a hatchet off the floor, tip Miles's table onto one side, and hack at one of the legs with blows that produce satisfying cracking sounds. "That's precisely what it's from."

"What are you doing to your table there?"

"Kindling." I chop off the leg and admit, with a sigh, "I'm a man deep in debt. I owe over two thousand dollars to various individuals, some of them fellow students and university staff, some of them lenders in Charlottesville. Others are nefarious creatures who want me either jailed or dead. You should see the threatening letters I've been receiving." I nod toward the ashes of said letters, lumped in the grate.

"Oh, Edgar." Mr. Wertenbaker sucks air through his teeth. "That's not a safe way to live."

"I intend to do the honorable thing and pay off every cent."

"How?"

"I don't know." With a grunt, I slam my blade into a second leg. "How large of a blaze do you think we can build with this table?"

Mr. Wertenbaker stands up and brushes sawdust from his trousers. "You'd have the warmest room on Rowdy Row. It's so bitter cold tonight, you might even be able to charge admission."

"I wager we'll have a bonfire before long."

He titters. "I'm not going to wager, but I'll happily help you demolish the table."

We fetch a second hatchet from the janitor and break up the wood until poor Miles's beautiful cedar table splinters into sticks small enough to ignite with a match in the grate.

We stoke the infant flames.

We even toss in two of the tallow candles, and our efforts aren't undertaken in vain, for Hestia rises up in her robes of gold. She swells into an inferno that smells of sweet cedar and meat. Her flames flash bewitching patterns of light and shadow across my walls, and my charcoal illustrations wriggle and squirm, wiggle and worm. Sparks shoot out of the hearth with startling pops that nip the backs of our hands, and we laugh and whoop in appreciation each time we're singed—so proud are we of our conflagration.

Out of the corner of my eye, I see a figure in black dart past my window, and I remember a line of poetry that once flitted through my head back in Monumental Church.

Once upon a dark December, in a year we must
remember,
Morbid mounds of ash and ember told a
gruesome tale of gore—

"Have you heard of the Richmond Theater fire of 1811?" I ask the librarian over the roar of the flames, and I wipe the perspiration pouring from my forehead with a handkerchief.

"Of course, I've heard of it," he says. "The fire affected most everyone in Virginia."

"I attend a church that was built over the crypt that holds the remains of all seventy-two victims. Every Sunday of my youth, I've worshipped above the ashes and bones of those poor, wretched souls."

The librarian cringes. "Oh. God."

"My mother died in the fire," I say, even though it's a lie. It's simpler, and more likely to elicit sympathy, to attach her death to our infamous American tragedy than to say she was an actress who wasted away from tuberculosis. "My life ended that December, before it scarcely began."

"I'm so sorry, Edgar."

"Thank you, Mr. Wertenbaker. You're a good man."

I throw the last of my candles into the flames and watch the final pieces of my life at the University of Virginia sizzle into oblivion.

On the morrow, Pa arrives at my dormitory, and I confess to my debts and my gambling.

He responds with a sigh that crushes me down to a nubble of a man. "I sent you that extra one hundred dollars."

"What alchemy was I supposed to use to turn one hundred dollars into thousands?" I ask. "The university billed me for the cost of books and a thousand other expenses throughout the entire year."

"What possessed you to think that gambling was the answer?"

"What else was I supposed to do?"

Pa covers his eyes, as though my recklessness has blinded him, and again he sighs with a cutting breath. "Haul your belongings out to the carriage. I'll settle the sums of the university fees, but the gambling debts are yours to pay."

"I owe too much to pay them off on my own."

"You should have thought of these consequences when you first sat down at a card table, Edgar."

He shoves his hat over his head and leaves my room to pay my university fees (at long last!). I cart my trunk and writing box out to Dabney and the carriage waiting at the south end of the Lawn, but I see no signs of my muses anywhere on the grounds. A sense of panic grips me and throws off my step.

But, let's be honest, I tell myself, *Pa would never allow Lenore or Garland to climb into our carriage and accompany us back home. He'd kill them if he saw them.*

I hand my trunk to Dabney and bid a silent farewell to my neoclassical Eden, to the sage and exasperated professors, to the Rotunda and pavilions, to my cohorts in dissolution, to the Ragged Mountain, and most distressing of all, to my future.

PART III

– DECEMBER 16, 1826 –

Ah, distinctly I remember
it was in the bleak December;
And each separate dying ember wrought
its ghost upon the floor.

—EDGAR ALLAN POE, "The Raven," 1845

CHAPTER FORTY-TWO

Edgar

During our journey back to Richmond, Pa tells me that he, indeed, intends to stick me into the Ellis & Allan counting room.

"You'll learn accounting, bookkeeping, and commercial correspondence," he says from his side of the carriage, his arms folded over his chest. "You'll be industrious. Disciplined. This is precisely what you need."

I peer out the window at the passing trees, whittled of their leaves, and admire the chalky texture of the sky, the muted blues of a lake, the graceful flight of a gaggle of geese reflected in looking-glass waters. Beauty stirs in winter's pall and draws tears to my eyes. Perhaps Lenore is following me home, after all, coursing down the rivers with astonishing speed.

Pa picks up a three-day-old copy of the Richmond newspaper the *Compiler* from the seat beside him. "What are you looking for out there?"

"Industriousness," I say instead of admitting that I've just been moved to tears by scenery. "Discipline."

He flaps open the newspaper with flicks of his wrist that tell me my answer vexed him, but I care not. He's won his war.

He'll have none of my respect.

Ma greets me in Moldavia's front hall with an embrace that lasts far longer than Pa can tolerate. I catch him shaking his head at our huddle as he retreats upstairs, but my concern lies with Ma and how thin and frail she feels against me. When I let her go, my hands slide against the ridges of her shoulder blades that jut out from beneath her dress.

She brushes a lock of hair off my forehead, her eyes bloodshot and liquid from emotion. "I missed you dreadfully, Eddy."

"I missed you, too."

"Your letters from college were so polite and comforting, but how did you truly fare on your own?"

I inhale a breath that causes me to choke on the stench of the whale oil burning in the lamps—a fishy odor that's never sickened me before. Pa's pungent tobacco lingers on the edges.

Ma's forehead furrows. "Are you ill?"

"No." I clear my throat. "Just tired. The ride was long and uncomfortable. More importantly"—I glance at the hollowness of her cheeks—"how are *you*?"

"I'm doing a little better at the moment. Please, don't fret about me."

"Are you certain?"

She clasps her hands around my arms. "Go upstairs and rest from your journey. You look exhausted."

I peek over my shoulder at the morning reception room. "I wrote to Elmira while I was away."

"I'm not surprised. You've been calling on that girl since we moved into this house."

"Did you see anyone else calling upon her while I was gone?"

"I'm not in the habit of pulling back the drapes and spying on the Roysters, my dear . . ."

I break away from Ma and peek out the nearest window.

A pair of delivery wagons sit in the Roysters' front drive. I see servants carrying bottles of wine and baskets full of flowers into the house.

I rake a hand through my hair. "She never responded to any of my letters these past ten months."

"Oh . . . Eddy . . ."

"I wrote to her every single month."

Ma comes over and places a comforting hand on my back. "Surely, there must have been some mistake."

I crane my neck forward to better view the activity at Elmira's house. "Are the Roysters hosting a party today?"

Ma peeks out the window. "It appears that they are. I remember they hosted a grand holiday soiree last year. Didn't you attend?"

I drop the curtain back into place. "Should I go?"

"We didn't receive an invitation, but that may be because the neighbors know I'm not well enough to socialize."

"I think I'll go."

"Are you certain you're not too tired for a party this evening? Perhaps you should stay home . . . invite your sister to join us for dinner . . ."

"I've missed Elmira terribly. I want to surprise her."

"Of course." Ma helps me out of my overcoat, her movements so gentle, so different from all the elbow jabs and back slaps I experienced in the thunderclap world of collegiate men. "I'm sure your appearance would make for a lovely surprise."

I gulp down my fear that it won't.

Ma wheezes before adding, "Go upstairs and rest for a while before washing up. You still have plenty of time to change into evening clothes. Are you hungry?"

"Famished."

"I'll ask Judith to bring you a tray of food."

"Thank you. I'd be much obliged. I've missed Judith, too."

Ma drapes my coat over her left arm. "You behaved while you were away, didn't you, Eddy?"

I nod and back away. "Yes, ma'am. I behaved the best I could for what I was given."

Her gaze strays up toward the top of the stairs, in the direction of Pa's chamber, as if she knows what Pa did when he left me on my own, miles away from home.

"I'm sure you did," she says. "You've always been such a good and loving boy."

The Roysters' front door looms above me, beyond the twin pairs of Ionic columns that support the white roof of the stoop. On each side of the door, cast-iron lanterns blaze with the fury and grandeur of torches mounted on castle walls. I envision myself crossing a moat to palace gates barred with rods of steel. From the window above, the flutters of violins, threaded with the deep sighs of cellos, sail into the darkness of the night. Vivaldi's Trio Sonata in D Minor accompanies my approach to the Fortress of Fate.

I climb up the front steps in new clothing I purchased from a merchant in Charlottesville for the express purpose of impressing Elmira—garments that I charged to Pa's account, not caring if he complained. The tail of my coat of superfine blue cloth brushes the backs of my knees, and the gilt of the coat's buttons gleam from the fire of the lanterns. I've also donned a new vest of black cut velvet, light brown pantaloons, and an ebony cravat that's tied with great care at the base of my throat. I'm wrapped up in fineries—a debtor in disguise—and I pray my destitution doesn't peek through the cracks.

The Roysters' servant Arthur opens the door and welcomes me inside, and I ascend a rosewood staircase to the ballroom above. A six-foot-tall mirror hangs on the azure wall halfway up the steps, and my reflection within the glass betrays the trepidation beating inside me—the doubts and the fears that dim the violet grays of my eyes to the murk of puddles.

Upstairs, the gentry of Richmond mingle and drink glasses of wine. None of them are suffocating beneath mounds of debt that crush their backs and their souls.

Or so I assume.

None of them have waited ten breathless months for a word of affection from their secret betrotheds.

As in Moldavia's ballroom, mirrors line every wall—mirrors that seem to fill the room with hundreds of aristocrats. *Hundreds of them*, dressed in silk and velvet jewel tones, sipping blood-red libations, singing songs of their fortunes and their vast tracts of land—and yet there's only one of me.

In the mirrors, despite the bright blue of my coat, I appear a grim and ghastly raven wandering in their midst.

And then I see her—*my Elmira*—and I grow a mite bolder.

She's conversing with a clutch of friends near a table topped with golden cakes and pink punch—lovely Elmira, dressed in a gown of midnight-blue satin interwoven with silver ribbons that remind me of light skating across a river during the gloaming. She's sixteen now, almost seventeen—more woman than girl, her beauty magnified by time, and yet her eyes remain those ethereal blue Elmira Royster eyes I know and love so well. My head goes tipsy at the sight of her, and my despair over her lack of correspondence melts into the floorboards.

I cross the room to her, wishing I held a bouquet of scarlet roses. My heart beats with each husky strum of the violins, as if Vivaldi wrote this piece for the precise moment when a young student, returned from the land of academia, crosses a room to reunite with his lady fair.

"Elmira," I say, my voice breathier than usual.

She spins my way with a start, and her eyes grow enormous. "Eddy! What are you doing here?"

"I saw that you were hosting a party. I just returned from Charlottesville this afternoon . . ."

"You shouldn't be here."

My stomach drops. "Why not?"

The other girls fall away from her sides and glide to other parts of the room—leaves scattering from the prelude to a storm, or so it seems.

"What's wrong?" I pull at my cravat. "Why did they run away? I've been in agony without you, Elmira. Why are you acting as though you don't want to see me?"

"Eddy"—Elmira places a hand against her throat, and her eyes swim in tears—"why didn't you write to me when you were in Charlottesville?"

"Why didn't I write?" I step forward. "What are you talking about? I wrote to you every single month—sometimes more often. Didn't you receive my letters?"

"No."

"Why didn't you try writing to me?"

"I did." She blinks away tears. "I wrote frequently."

"But . . . I never received anything from you either. I—" I wheel around and attempt to locate her father in the crowd. Her damn, discriminatory father.

"Edgar." Elmira places a hand on my left sleeve. "I think you ought to leave. The dancing will commence soon, and—"

"Could your father have intercepted the letters?"

She shakes her head, her lips quivering. "I don't know."

I spy Mr. Royster drinking with the Marshalls near the orchestra. "Ah, there's the devil now. Perhaps the time is right to formally announce our engagement . . ."

"No!" Elmira squeezes my arm with an urgency that prompts me to swing back toward her, and I find her eyes brimming in apologies. She ages ten years right there in front of me. Wrinkles of worry sprout across her skin.

My throat grows dry. "What is it? What's wrong?"

"Edgar, I'm engaged to Alexander Shelton now. This is our engagement party."

I pull my arm away, and the floor tilts beneath me. I sway backward into a man built like a boulder who nudges me away and says, "Steady yourself, son. Watch how much you drink."

"I'm sorry." Elmira wrings her hands. "I thought you'd forgotten me. My father . . . he made the arrangements. I'm so sorry."

I clench my teeth to avoid bawling in front of her—in front of everyone—for I'm aware of the attention we've now drawn. Alexander Shelton, crowned prince of the Shelton transportation industry, struts our way, his heels clicking against the waxed floor, his chest puffed up like a cock's beneath a midnight-blue vest that matches the precise hue of Elmira's dress, as though they're already coupled for life.

My name circulates the room with ugly, deadening thuds: *Poe.*

Poe.

Poe.

Tongues cluck. Eyes gawk. Heads shake in disgust. The son of the actress—Gaffy Poe, the debtor of Charlottesville—is making a fool of himself in front of *everyone.*

I turn and abandon the scene with Vivaldi's crescendo strumming through my head.

CHAPTER FORTY-THREE

Lenore

My poet is a swimmer, so yes, I swim again, back down the Rivanna and the James, prepared to face either my death or my resurrection in Richmond.

I waited in the shadows during Eddy's examinations.

I outlasted Garland O'Peale.

I survived ten long months in this fragile, mortal form.

John Allan *will not* ruin everything by caging my poet in a counting room.

At the end of my journey, on a biting December night, I hoist myself out of the freezing river and onto Ludlam's Wharf, where these travels commenced back in February. I lost my hat early on in my swim, so water drips from the exposed feathers of my head to the boards where I kneel in the darkness to catch my breath.

To my left—*to my horror*—lies a body, motionless, in the middle of the wharf, the soles of its shoes directed my way. The sight of the thing chills me down to the marrow of my bones, not because I believe it to be a dead man, but due to the clicking palpitations emanating from its bosom.

There's only one heartbeat, aside from my own, normally audible to my ears.

"Good gracious, what now?" I ask, and I force myself to my feet, my lungs heaving, my legs heavy.

I teeter closer to the body. The figure doesn't stir at the sound of my approach.

A lantern hangs near enough for me to see my poet's face, as I feared. He's dressed in a blue coat and a black velvet vest with a raven-hued cravat shimmering at his throat.

His eyes are closed.

He's scarcely breathing.

"I'm sober, so I know you're not drunk," I say.

He shakes his head.

"Are you sick?" I ask.

"I have no wish to live another hour," he says with an earnestness and a depth to his voice that takes me aback. His eyes remain closed, and his lashes look wet and matted, as though he's been crying.

"What happened?" I ask.

"I have nothing," he says through his teeth. "It's all gone."

I turn toward Richmond, where a repugnant orange haze hangs over the west side—over Moldavia and its neighbors. The music of a quadrille rises from that direction, and a disquieting carnival quality pervades the song.

"What happened?" I ask again.

Edgar covers his eyes with his right arm. "Elmira engaged herself to Alexander Shelton."

My stomach drops, and my body thrums with rage. My ears interpret his words to mean *I've encountered yet another obstacle that will preoccupy my mind too much for poetry.*

"She did *what?*" I ask.

"She never received my letters. I think her father intercepted them."

"Did you explain that you wrote her?"

"Of course."

"And yet she still remains engaged to Mr. Shelton?"

He moves his arm and gazes up at the constellations above, his irises reflecting the oily sheen of the night. "They always leave me."

"We don't have time for any more tragedies and obstacles."

Edgar's voice turns heavier and colder: "I have no desire to live and *will not.*"

I turn around and jump straight back into the river.

Down in the dark and icy depths of the James, I squirm and kick with my hands squeezed around my head, and I question my entire existence.

I'm bound to a soul who doesn't even want to live.

I'll never soar across the earth or love like the gods.

I pull the demons from my poet's head, but who will release the demons from me?

I scream with a deafening underwater howl that expels a flood of shadows from my lungs. Faces manifest in the torrents of gloom shrieking from me—faces with sinister eyes and contorted, shockingly wide-open mouths. The figures expand into shades that reach out to the heart of the river with hands clawed and withered. They cry out in unison with my wails, screaming and streaming into the distance on my waves of agony. Their expulsion from my soul leaves me weak and dizzy.

A firm arm clasps me beneath my armpits and hauls me up to the water's surface, where I stretch my mouth open for a long breath of air.

My poet, it seems, has decided to live after all, and to save me as well.

With his arm tucked around me, he swims me back to the wharf amid the roar and the swell of the James. The river batters our heads and engulfs our noses, and yet my poet musters the strength to pull me onto the boards of the wharf.

I push myself up to a seated position, clasp my arms around my knees, and gasp for air, while my howls of horror keen in the waters. The docked ships bob and sway in the lingering tumult.

"I don't want to lose you, too," says my poet from beside me.

"You're going to need to choose between John Allan and me. *He's* why I can't finish evolving."

"I know."

"You've already lost Mr. O'Peale, Eddy. Garland traveled home to Maryland with Upton Beall."

Edgar swallows near my ear. "I hadn't realized he was gone."

I sigh. "Precisely."

The screams of my shades fade into the night, and I'm left as a shivering, feathered wretch who suddenly doesn't feel strong enough to swim a river ever again. Ice shines in the moonlight on the crest of the shore, and I tell myself I'm merely weak because of the freezing temperature.

Eddy drapes his blue coat around my shoulders, the fabric so dry, I assume he must have doffed the garment before diving into the river. His shoes, also dry, lie on their sides nearby.

I push the coat off me. "You're the one who spent three weeks in bed for swimming the James the other winter. You wear the coat. Don't catch your death of pneumonia."

He hangs one half of the coat over my left shoulder and keeps the other half for himself.

I accept this compromise and scoot closer to him to battle the chills shivering through me.

"What time does Pa retire for the night?" I ask.

"Half past ten or so—or at least that was his habit before I left for college."

I nod. "Go back home and warm yourself in front of the fire in your room. Rest from the shock of this evening. And at midnight, open your door to the upper portico."

"Why?"

"Because, dear Edgar, if I don't at least grow a set of grand and glorious wings tonight, I'm going to slip into John Allan's chamber early tomorrow morning and smother him with his pillow."

My poet stiffens beside me.

I sit up straighter. "We are going to do the wisest thing possible while you're trapped in this mire of Elmira-induced pain."

Edgar clears his throat. "And what might the wisest thing be?"

I turn toward him and look him straight in the eye, our faces so close, I feel his breath fluttering against my cheek. "What do you think?"

He shudders. "We're going to turn her into poetry?"

I smile and nod. "And, oh, what poetry it shall be."

CHAPTER FORTY-FOUR

Edgar

My muse holds me up during my journey back home, and I clutch her to my side to keep her safe from harm. She's too stubborn to wear my coat, so the garment warms me instead, but she at least agreed to fit my hat over her shorn and shaven crown.

Up ahead, I hear the echoes of hoof steps and the jostling of a carriage. I grab Lenore by the hand and hurry her around the next corner, where we press ourselves against the shadowed bricks of a wall and hold our breath. We both shiver from the river, and I struggle not to cough.

Once the carriage drives off, and the danger of discovery passes, we round another bend, and I walk us northward on Fifth—a route that will avoid the sight of the dancing silhouettes in the upper windows of the Royster mansion. The music of the soiree slithers through the streets and leaves a putrescent taste on my tongue.

I tighten my grip on Lenore's hand. "I'll take you to Judith's cabin."

"No, don't."

"Why not?"

"I refuse to risk Judith's safety again," she says. "If John Allan discovers me in her quarters—"

"There's nowhere else for me to hide you."

We both jump at the sudden splash of bathwater dumping from an upstairs window across the street.

I avert my face and lead Lenore onward.

"Hey!" calls a gruff male voice from the window. "I just saw the unholy shine of your eyes down there. What in heaven's name are you?"

We let go of each other's hands and hasten into a run.

"I'll stay in the rafters of the carriage house," says Lenore.

"There'll be no fire to keep you warm in there."

"Allow me to orchestrate a grand feat of inspiration at midnight, and then we'll see if I'm able to escape into realms fit for a god."

A dog barks from a yard up ahead.

Lenore breaks free of me and bolts toward the outbuildings of Moldavia.

No one witnesses my slinking and waterlogged entrance into the house, thank God. I squeak upstairs in my dry shoes and drenched socks and change into fresh pairs of shirtsleeves and pantaloons, not yet ready to crawl into my nightshirt and resign to the night. I lie in my bed beneath the glow of the lamps, and the whale oil continues to assault my nostrils, which, apparently, grew accustomed to the tallow candles of my dormitory. My discarded clothing hangs over a chair, smelling of the river, yes, but also of Elmira's house, as though the water couldn't rinse the humiliation from the beautiful new fabrics.

The lamps burn well into the eleven o'clock hour. I lie against my pillow, buried in blankets to calm the shivers, and I massage my forehead while gazing up at the shelf of books that once allowed me to escape my sorrows.

In my mind's eye I see Elmira, dressed in blue satin and lace, standing at the altar of her wedding ceremony. Alexander Shelton bends his face toward hers to kiss her lips, but Elmira catches sight of me watching her from the back of the church.

She blushes. *Oh, how she blushes!*

And in that blush, I know she remembers what we shared.

She'll regret this decision until her dying day.

And in that blush—

A clock down the hall strikes midnight, yanking me out of that train of thought.

With a groan, I roll out of bed, doubtful that inspiration is what I require to heal. I totter toward the door that leads from my bedroom to the upper level of the portico, not drunk, merely unstable.

After heaving a sigh, I yank the curtains aside with both hands.

Light blinds my eyes.

I wince from the glare.

Outside, the world shines as though I'm experiencing noontide in June instead of midnight in December. I throw open the door, stumble out to the portico, and brace myself against one of the wooden columns, careful not to fall over the low rail. Below me, a vision of the interior of a church without a roof has replaced our terraced gardens, and the gentry of Richmond fill the pews.

In front of the pulpit stand a bride and a groom, their hands clasped together, their backs facing me. Reverend Rice from the local Presbyterian church presides over the nuptials, and his voice chugs through the church as a charmless chant.

"*. . . for richer for poorer, in sickness and in health, to love and to cherish, till death us do part . . .*"

The longer I stare, the more the silk of the bride's pale blue dress warms to the lascivious pink of a blush.

"*. . . with this ring I thee wed, with my body I thee worship . . .*"

On the left-hand side of the aisle, amid the crowd of guests, sits a woman in a black bonnet who now, quite curiously, pats her lap in an iambic, eight-meter beat.

pat-PAT-pat-PAT-pat-PAT-pat-PAT
(*pause-pause-pause-pause-pause-pause-pause-pause*)
pat-PAT-pat-PAT-pat-PAT-pat-PAT
(*pause-pause-pause-pause-pause-pause-pause-pause*)

The rest of the wedding guests join her in this bizarre rhythmical patting, as though encouraging the creation of a poem or a song set to the beat. The meters of my poems often drum inside my head as I write them, but this is an amplified version of such a rhythm.

pat-PAT-pat-PAT-pat-PAT-pat-PAT
(*pause-pause-pause-pause-pause-pause-pause-pause*)
pat-PAT-pat-PAT-pat-PAT-pat-PAT
(*pause-pause-pause-pause-pause-pause-pause-pause*)

When the next round commences, the woman in the bonnet shifts toward me in her seat and says to the beat, "'I saw thee on the bridal day . . .'"

She turns away just as my brain absorbs the fact that Lenore's unmistakable nose and cadaverous complexion peeked out from beneath that ruffled bonnet.

The groom—no other than fish-lipped, locust-eyed Alexander Shelton—reels toward the commotion of the guests, but, despite his hisses and glares, the drumming continues.

pat-PAT-pat-PAT-pat-PAT-pat-PAT
(*pause-pause-pause-pause-pause-pause-pause-pause*)
pat-PAT-pat-PAT-pat-PAT-pat-PAT
(*pause-pause-pause-pause-pause-pause-pause-pause*)

The bride—Elmira—*oh, God! Elmira*—peers over her right shoulder, and her eyes swell at the sight of me watching from up in the portico.

Lenore turns toward me again from the pews. "'When a burning blush came o'er thee . . .'"

"'I saw thee on the bridal day!'" I call down to Elmira, hugging the column with my right arm, leaning over the railing. "'When a burning blush came o'er thee/Tho' Happiness around thee lay/The world all love before thee.'"

Lenore jumps to her feet and jerks a hand at Elmira. "'I saw thee on the wedding day!'"

"'When a burning blush came o'er thee . . .'" I leap back into my bedroom and scramble to locate a fresh sheet of paper on my table.

The guests *pat-PAT-pat-PAT-pat-PAT-pat-PAT*.

"'I saw thee on the bridal day,'" I say in a whisper, dunking my quill into my inkstand.

"'Tho' Happiness around thee lay . . .'" shouts Lenore down in the church, and the rest of the wedding guests echo: "'*Tho' Happiness around thee lay . . .*'"

"'The world all love before thee.'"

"'*The world all love before thee.*'"

I sit down and pen the stanza, tapping my right heel to the beat so my poem doesn't stray from its metrical feet:

I saw thee on the bridal day;
When a burning blush came o'er thee,
Tho' Happiness around thee lay,
The world all love before thee.

"'I saw thee on the bridal day . . .'" chants the crowd outside.

I dash back out to the railing. "'And, in thine eye, the kindling light . . .'"

"'And, in thine eye, the kindling light . . . ,'" say the guests, and they cease patting for a change in the meter.

"'Of young passion free . . . ,'" I say.

"'Of young passion free . . .'"

Elmira buries her face in her hands, so clearly remembering our passion she's tossed aside for the dandy standing next to her.

I yank at the roots of my hair. "'Was all on earth, my chained sight . . .'"

"'Was all on earth, my chained sight . . .'"

"'Of Loveliness might see.'"

"'Of Loveliness might see.'"

The drumming commences against skirts and trousers.

I write down the lines in my bedroom, again tapping out the beat with my feet to make certain every word, every syllable, fits into place.

And, in thine eye, the kindling light
Of young passion free
Was all on earth, my chained sight
Of Loveliness might see.

"'I saw thee on the bridal day!'" calls Lenore, sounding as though she now stands on the roof above the portico. "'When a burning blush came o'er thee . . .'"

I burst through my door. "'That blush, I ween, was maiden shame . . .'"

"'*That blush, I ween, was maiden shame . . .*,'" says the crowd with their pat-pat-patting.

"'As such it well may pass . . . ,'" Lenore and I cry out in unison.

Elmira raises the hem of her pink skirts and staggers down the aisle toward me. Her blush of shame tells me she still loves me. She wants me, and I want her, but I'm not good enough. I'll *never* be good enough!

pat-PAT-pat-PAT-pat-PAT-pat-PAT

"'Tho' its glow hath raised a fiercer flame,'" I call down to her, "'In the breast of him, alas!'"

"'Who saw thee on that bridal day . . . ,'" says Lenore, and her shadow from the roof claps to the meter.

The wedding guests stand and clap along with her.

"'It's glow hath raised a fiercer flame,'" I say, pounding the beat against the sides of my head, "'in the breast of him—alas!—who saw thee on that bridal day . . .'"

The audience claps and chants, "'In the breast of him, alas!/Who saw thee on that bridal day.'"

"'When that deep blush *would* come o'er thee,'" say both Lenore and I while watching Alexander escort Elmira back to the pulpit.

I shuffle backward toward my door. "'Tho' Happiness around thee lay. . .'"

"'*Tho' Happiness around thee lay . . .*'"

"'The world all love before thee.'"

"'*The world all love before thee.*'"

And everyone together, myself and Lenore included, clap and shout, "'I saw thee on the bridal day!'"

I scrawl the last lines of the poem in the lamplight of my room, and the world grows intolerably silent.

CHAPTER FORTY-FIVE

Lenore

In the loft of the carriage house, I kneel in the darkness, buckled over in a sudden onslaught of pain.

My upper back churns and burns, as though a dozen fists are pushing beneath my skin in a frantic fight to rip through my flesh. My poet's poem for Elmira drums in my head, but the words and the rhythm provide no relief, and in fact, the more the poem beats against my brain, the harder the fists struggle to break through my skin.

My dress tears above my shoulder blades.

I groan, so confused, so scared.

"Do not panic, Raven Girl," says Morella's voice from somewhere nearby, and a lantern flares to life.

I dig my forehead against the floorboards and grunt through clenched teeth, my molars rattling, aching. The air thins. The pain heightens. The fists punch with a ferocity that makes my ears ring. I rise up on hands and knees and arch my spine, and the loft shudders and creaks from the violence of my shaking.

All I can do is moan and pray for a swift death, and the moment I believe I'll collapse, my back bursts open with a satisfying surcease of my agony. Something flaps into the air behind me.

I drop to my stomach, exhausted, drenched in sweat, still inexplicably confused. A blanket of feathers falls against me.

Morella crouches down in front of my head. The light of her lantern swings across the backs of my closed lids.

"Lenore," she says in a voice that intrigues me enough to open my eyes. "I've never seen such ravishing feathers as these." Her own feathered head nods to something behind me, and she guides me up to a seated position, despite the buttery consistency of my body.

I manage to twist around, and my lips part in shock at the sight of my shadow on the wall—the image of a girl with a bald head, *yes*, but from her back there now rises a pair of wings.

Voluminous, voluptuous wings, varnished in the velvety sheen of night.

CHAPTER FORTY-SIX

Edgar

In the misty, mid-December morning hours, Pa and I leave Moldavia for the counting room of Ellis & Allan. A wheel needs mending on our carriage after our travels from Charlottesville, so we're to walk the nine blocks to the office, out in the open, offering everyone a view of Pa ushering me into the life he's planned for me.

Our breath fogs up the air in front of us, as though we're puffing on pipes.

Our footsteps fall in the same meter as the poem I penned the night before.

I saw thee on the bridal day . . .

I peek across the street at Elmira's house, which exudes the exhausted air of a night well spent. A lost glove loiters on the lawn. Broken glass winks from the front drive. Smoke sighs from the chimneys with little coughs of fatigue.

Up ahead, a piece of paper flutters across the road. We pass it, and I spy a title written in the heading of a handbill: "The Prodigal Son of Richmond."

I pay the thing no heed, until I notice similar papers posted to various doors around the city, and a twinge of dread pinches at my stomach. Once upon a time, I distributed my poem "Don Pompioso" around town in such a manner to lambaste a fellow who told me he wouldn't associate with the son of itinerate theater players. And I did so again with "Oh, Tempora! Oh, Mores!" a satire that ridiculed an ass of a clerk named Robert Pitts, who both insulted me and stole one of my sweethearts.

On the door of Ellis & Allan, Tobacco Merchants, hangs another copy of the handbill, the paper a burnished cream.

"'The Prodigal Son of Richmond'?" asks Pa, ripping the page from the nail. "Is this another one of your satires you've posted across town?"

"No! I haven't had time for any such thing. I just arrived home yesterday."

Pa frowns down at the thing, and the more he reads, the deeper the wedge between his eyebrows puckers. He raises his eyes. "This appears to be a poem *about* you."

I grab the paper and read, aghast, a poorly penned mockery of my shameful return to Richmond. The poem pokes fun at my debt and my "excesses," as well as my failed romance with Elmira. Our names aren't mentioned, but I'm identified as the "moody child of strolling players," and she "the Richmond lady fair with riches beyond compare." Briefly, I fear that Garland followed me into town and devised this attack as some sort of revenge for my infidelity as an artist, but I realize that a hack with an underdeveloped prune for a muse obviously vomited up this twaddle.

"Who wrote this?" I ask, spitting as I speak.

Pa unlocks the door. "Someone whom you surely insulted in the past."

"Did you or James Galt speak about my debt publicly?"

"Why would James know about your debt?"

I gulp at my mistake of bringing up James.

"Did you write to him about your problems?" asks Pa.

I lower my eyes back to the letter.

Pa shakes his head in disappointment. "Let this be a lesson to you about begging family members for money."

"Do you think he would have told people about it?"

"Let this, furthermore, teach you the dangers of ridiculing anyone whom you believe inferior to your intellect in a public and demeaning manner."

Pa rattles the latch and pushes open the door. "Come inside. Light a fire, so you may burn that monstrosity. We're already wasting time."

I crouch down in front of the grate, throw this attack on my character onto the firewood, and grab the tinderbox to strike a spark in the char cloth. I make a dozen failed attempts before a flame huffs to life. Two men pass by the window, chuckling, so I stay down on my knees, stoking the fire long after it needs stoking, so no one will see me, laugh at me, mock me for my fall from grace.

My spirits wither in the stacks of ledgers and dust. All I smell, all I *taste*, is the tobacco smoke embedded in the knotty panels of the walls from the thousands of pipes Pa and Mr. Ellis smoked in this room to sample the product and to survive the strains of their business. Pa doesn't need the mercantile anymore, now that he's sitting on his fortune from old Uncle William, but during the more difficult years of the business, oh, how Ma fretted! How Pa snapped at all of us and paced his chamber late into the night as he battled bills and plummeting profits.

Merchants and tradesmen are gamblers, too, I remember.

It is not just poets who risk financial ruin.

By noon, the weather darkens. Rain bats at the window beside me, and I see my soul standing out in the mud of Tobacco Alley. She wears the feathers of a raven and answers to the name "Lenore," but I recognize an intimate part of myself in her eyes.

Kill her, and you shall kill me.

She places a finger to her lips, as though she wants me to remain quiet, and then she rotates around to face the brick wall of the mercantile across from me. My stomach leaps, for a pair of wings—a tremendous expanse of pitch-black feathers that would put the Morrigan to shame—drape her frame from her shoulder blades down to the backs of her knees.

Pa taps the ledger in front of me. "Stop daydreaming, Edgar."

I gasp. "I'm sorry."

He cranes his neck and peers out the window, but my Psyche has flitted away.

Whenever I'm not writing, time trudges forward with the maddening pace of a funeral procession.

On Christmas day I'm called away from my desk in my chamber and asked to join the family at the dining room table, where I sit as a ghost of the former inhabitant of Moldavia known as Edgar A. Poe. Surrounded by Ma, Pa, Aunt Nancy, and the late Uncle William's grown children—William Jr. and James—along with William Jr.'s wife, Rosanna, and their infant son, I feast on oysters on the half shell, roast beef and Yorkshire pudding, mince pies stuffed with beef suet and apples, candied sweet potatoes, baked celery, spiced cranberries, plums soaked in wine jelly, plum pudding, and port.

No one speaks to me.

I don't speak to them.

Pretty Rosanna avoids looking at me, as though the gloom dripping off me makes her uncomfortable—as though my melancholy might splatter onto her and stain her dress.

James catches my eye over the plum pudding but flinches, perhaps remembering the loan he denied me—or perhaps he's, indeed, the hack who wrote that twaddle about me and posted it around town. He shifts toward Aunt Nancy and tells her about his recovery from a recent case of the mumps—a conversation involving ghastly swollen glands and sweat stains on his pillow—a topic, evidently, more palatable than conversing with the beggar at the table.

Whenever I'm not writing, time trudges forward with the maddening, mortifying pace of a funeral procession.

During the daylight hours, I toil under John Allan's thumb, without any wages. If I ever complain or ask him to help me obtain some other position outside of this Gehenna, he shows me letters from creditors, shopkeepers, and Mr. Spotswood, demanding payments of my debts.

"You owe me years of work for what you've done, Edgar," he tells me. "Years!"

I seek respite in the drawing room of Miss Mackenzie's boarding school with my sister and her schoolmates. Rose enjoys playing music on the piano for me and tells me, "I've embraced my muse of music, Eddy," and she nods to a bright yellow warbler with a mask of black feathers, perched outside the window. Rose prefers—and she's much better at playing—somber melodies that pluck at the heartstrings rather than compositions of joy, so I leave the boarding school wiping my eyes with a handkerchief. My sorrows stick to my lungs like tar.

I receive no comfort from my Richmond friends, who shun me for my recklessness.

"He isn't home this morning," their servants or mothers say at their doors every time I knock. "I'm sorry, Mr. Poe."

Whenever I'm not writing, time trudges forward with the maddening, mortifying, miserable pace of a funeral procession.

My mind strays in the counting room. I feel a tug on the right leg of my pantaloons and discover Lenore crouched down beneath my desk, her wings cloaked around her like sable robes, her skirt a mound of feathers that reminds me of the stately ravens of the Tower of London.

"'In visions of the dark night,'" she says, "'I have dream'd of joy departed—'"

"You can't be here." I scoot back the chair with a jarring screech of the wood. "My God! Pa will kill you if he sees you. What are you doing here?"

"As I told you before, it's either him or me, Eddy. Hiding stifles me. I'd now rather risk death."

Pa lingers nearby, just outside the doorway to the mercantile, discussing terms with a supplier.

"'In visions of the dark night,'" he sings in his Scottish brogue, "'I have dream'd of joy departed—'"

And his supplier echoes in the high-pitched pipes of a tenor, "'I have dream'd of joy departed—'"

I attempt to ignore the seeping of the poem into the world of Ellis & Allan and return to a piece of correspondence I'm penning to the editor of a periodical Pa sells. Pa hovers in the fringes of my vision, and I catch him glancing into the counting room, his eyes narrowed, suspicious.

And yet the poem unfurls inside my head.

In visions of the dark night
I have dream'd of joy departed—
But a waking dream of life and light

Hath left me broken-hearted . . .

Pa turns away. I flip over a page of weeks-old correspondence and jot down the lines. Lenore sneaks out the window and crouches down behind the pane, yet I continue writing, dreaming, fleeing to an imagined principality in which rhymes and meters possess more worth than gold—where art and literature rule the land.

Pa wanders into the counting room, in search of a ledger. "Are you paying attention to your work?"

"Yes," I say, for my work is poetry, and I am most certainly paying attention.

Weeks pass. I grow a mite older. My eighteenth birthday trickles past me.

And I pay off my debts every single damn day and pretend not to see the occasional satire of me posted on lampposts in the dung-covered streets of Richmond. I pretend not to see the way my former friends turn their backs on me each Sunday at church. I try not to feel as though the counting room of Ellis & Allan is a place meant for counting down the days until, at last, I can die and get shoved into a box, so my eyes no longer need to strain over ledgers.

At night, though—*ah, yes, sweet Lady Night*—you will find me stepping outside my back bedroom door and onto warm mosaic tiles in the ancient city of Samarcand, where Tamerlane once reigned.

> *Look 'round thee now on Samarcand,*
> *Is she not queen of earth? her pride*
> *Above all cities? in her hand*
> *Their destinies? with all beside*
> *Of glory, which the world hath known?*

Stands she not proudly and alone?

Whenever I'm not writing, time trudges forward with the maddening, mortifying, miserable, morose, moribund pace of a funeral procession.

And so, I write as often as I can.

CHAPTER FORTY-SEVEN

Lenore

On a still and soundless night in the middle of March, I stroke my wings in the loft of the carriage house and ponder what more it will take until the wings allow me to fly.

"What more can I do besides killing John Allan?" I ask Morella. "I taste the ambrosia of realms yet to come, but then . . ." I crawl to the loft's round window and peek out at the candlelight shining through the windows of Moldavia. "But then *Pa* appears like an executioner in a black hood and drops the blade of a guillotine on my progress."

Morella polishes the bones of her necklace with the feathers of her wings. "Convince young Mr. Poe to fly away from this house and never return. That's the only way to end this battle between father and son—and father and muse."

I stretch out on my back and gaze up at the rafters. "I'm thinking of wooing the spirit of Jane Stanard tonight."

Morella lifts her face. "What would be the purpose of that?"

"My poet's lovesickness steals into my blood every time that I play with his imagination. And I miss my misty Jane in the Albemarle County churchyard. My lips desire kisses."

"Kiss your poet, then."

"He hasn't yet earned a kiss from me."

"I'm not speaking of a kiss of romance, Lenore."

I drum my fingertips against the floor.

Morella reties her bones around her neck. "Usher him away from this house this very night. Convince him you're all that he needs. In the end, you see, it's always the muse who remains for the artist. After the family members die, the friends have all left, the bodies wither, and the audiences cease to file through the doors, the muse remains—the greatest love of an artist's life."

I sigh. "I long for a kiss from female lips. Mortal ladies smell so much better than men."

Morella kicks my right foot. "You never listen to me when I speak of matters most urgent."

"You're always speaking of matters most urgent." I curl up to a seated position and grab Edgar's silk hat, which I never returned to him. "I'm a creature of passion, my dear Morella, and I bear a weakness for the ladies whom my poet loves. They're the balm of Gilead to my woes."

Morella's yellow eyes peer at me from beneath her white lashes. "Do not forget, Lenore, you look like a girl to these lady spirits—and an odd, winged raven one at that."

I lower the hat to my head with a smile. "And yet I woo like a handsome Southern gentleman poet, and that's what matters most."

"Don't risk your life chasing after his darlings. You'll get yourself killed."

"You've been telling me that I'll get myself killed for over a year now." I stand up and brush ash from my dress. "And yet here I remain, Lenore the Strange; Lenore the Strong. Everyone says I'm pure nonsense, but everyone's wrong."

A lady spirit rests her back against the tall gray stone with the uncapped urn up in the Burying Ground on Shockoe Hill. She's an astral vision, her dress a gown of luminous silver, her hair coils of starlight. Her eyes fall upon me with the luster of Venus, and the air smells of nighttime jasmine.

She's the embodiment of a poem Eddy once wrote when he was slightly younger—"Evening Star."

And I turn'd away to thee,
Proud Evening Star,
In thy glory afar,
And dearer thy beam shall be . . .

"Mrs. Stanard . . ." I tread toward her on legs that wobble embarrassingly. "Do—do you remember me?"

She squints, as though she doesn't quite see me. "Edgar?"

I stop and press my lips together, remembering how a similar conversation once unspooled with Eddy's mother.

"Yes," I say with a cringe of guilt. "I'm Edgar Poe."

"You've grown up into such a fine-looking gentleman." She places a hand to her head and primps her curls, which require no primping in the slightest. "I do hope you're still following your muse."

I slap my palms against my heart. "Oh, I adore you for saying that, my dear Mrs. Stanard."

"Are you still writing your poems?"

I open my mouth to respond, but another voice behind me calls out, "Are you still writing your love poems to Elmira?"

Forced to turn my back on my beloved, I discover a handful of men trooping toward me through the tombstones, toting bottles of booze that nearly blend into the night and lanterns that streak dragon-breath light. The tall fellow in the lead has pink lips and sharp cheekbones and looks the sort who ought to be barking orders in a mansion instead of tromping through graveyards after dark.

The gentlemen come to an abrupt halt no more than six feet away from me.

"Wait—that's not Poe," says the leader, and he raises his lantern, the handle shaking, squeaking. "Pitts! You said you saw Poe walking up here."

"I—I recognized his hat and his height in the lamplight," says the person called Pitts. "I thought he was dressed in a coat of furs—not *feathers?*"

"What are you?" asks the leader, cocking his head at me. "Why do you seem to be wearing wings, and why the devil did you just call yourself Edgar Poe?"

A wind whisks away the spirits behind me, including my Helen.

"Who are *you?*" I ask, and I tremble at the loss of Mrs. Stanard.

The leader expands his chest, which sparkles with gold buttons. "Alexander Shelton."

Oh, dear God. Elmira's fiancé.

"What are you?" he asks once again, and he gulps with a grimace, as though swallowing swill. "Why do you look so cadaverous . . . and . . . so raven—ous?"

"The word is pronounced *ravenous*," I say with a smile, "and, why yes, I am awfully hungry, come to think of it. Might you have something to offer?" I tap my long nails against the teeth on my neck. "I prefer my sustenance to be lively and *read.*"

As I'd hoped, the men seem to have interpreted that last word as the bloody sort of "red." Two members of this wolf pack inch away from me.

I push my poet's hat farther down on my head, and I say to this rapt audience of scoundrels, "Near upon this cemetery, while you lounge, and laze, and tarry, he who Myra ought to marry grows into the Lord of Horror." I step toward them, and they all scatter backward. "Gentlemen of Richmond City—gentlemen primped, poised, and pretty—'tis a monumental pity that you've met the wraith Lenore. 'Tis a pity that you'll taste your deaths while gaping at Lenore, Poe's grim muse forevermore."

Alexander breaks his bottle across a tombstone with a clatter that sends three crows flapping into the night sky.

"What are you?" he asks yet again.

"I just told you, foolish sir."

"Are you some sort of theatrical creation of Poe's?"

"Presently, I'm creating *him*, and my God, Mr. Shelton, how you're going to live in his shadow for the rest of your life—*you*, the husband of the woman who should be named 'Sarah Elmira Royster Poe.'"

Alexander holds his jaw in such a way that I envision veins and tendons bulging beneath the black and gold stripes of the cravat swallowing up his throat.

He growls. "Don't ever attach that name to hers again."

"If you'll excuse me, gentlemen"—I tip my hat—"I have poetry to catalyze."

Alexander springs forward and knocks me to the ground with a rib-piercing jab of his elbow.

My back slams against the frozen earth, where I lay for a stunned and silent moment, short of breath, my head lolling in front of a stone of white marble. My brain pleads with my arms to push my body back up to my feet.

Before I gather enough fortitude to stand, Alexander shoves me back down with a thrust of his right foot against my sternum. My back again crashes against dirt and grass, and a cold shot of dread flies from my heart to my fingertips.

My attacker then pushes his foot into my stomach, pins me to me to the ground, and holds the jagged edge of his bottle three feet above my face.

"Cut her throat," says Mr. Pitts, who's rocking to and fro like a nervous drunk. "Cut it, Shelton. If she's the muse she claims to be . . . Poe's vitriol stems from her. She's the source of humiliation."

"I'm not a muse of satire, you squirming pieces of coffin fodder," I croak in a voice that steals oxygen from their lungs.

The gentlemen stare at me—those pallid lumps of clay trussed up in extravagant fripperies. Alexander's foot remains a pillar of marble squashing my belly and my breath, and his broken bottle continues to stare me down.

"Please allow me to leave, Mr. Shelton," I say. "I don't intend to inspire Edgar to weave any of your names into his art."

"I should scratch the word 'Elmira' across your forehead and send you back to the 'Prodigal Son of Richmond,' bleeding her name for him," he says in the coldest tone I've ever heard uttered by a mortal.

"But you won't," I say, my throat parched and tight, "because you're a gentleman worthy of Sarah Elmira's love."

He swallows.

The lantern light glares against the teeth of the glass quaking in his hand.

I hold my breath and pray for a swift end, if the end is nigh. *Oh, God,* I should have listened to Morella . . .

"I *am* a gentleman worthy of her love," says Alexander.

I sigh my relief in the most inconspicuous way possible, my lips opened to the smallest sliver of a crack. "I'm glad to hear it, sir. I shall let my poet know of your honor, and we will allow you to live together in peace from this day forward. My congratulations to you, Mr. Shelton. 'I have no words, alas! to tell/The lovliness of loving well!'"

With movements slow and quivery, Elmira's fiancé lifts his shoe from my stomach. His knee creaks into the air, and he watches me from the bottoms of his dark brown eyes, as though he fears I might spring up and bite his ankle.

I scramble to my feet and adjust the hat on my head—and then I turn and run for my life, astounded that my favorite quotation from "Tamerlane" just saved me—convinced that Jane Stanard's presence on those grounds gleamed a glimmer of protection o'er me.

CHAPTER FORTY-EIGHT

Edgar

Before retiring to my chamber for the night, I work up the courage to approach Pa's room and rap upon his door.

"Come in," he says from within.

I do as he asks and find him draped in his emerald robe, lounging, as usual, in his armchair in front of the Revolutionary War musket and the crossed medieval swords that reflect the flames undulating in his fireplace.

He looks up from the leather-bound book he's reading. "What is it, Edgar?"

"I'm dying, Pa."

He sniffs. "You sound more like you're on the verge of complaining."

"My soul is dying in your counting room."

"Dear Lord." He rubs his eyes with the palms of his hands. "Must you always speak with such a dramatic flair, Edgar? Your parents' theatrical blood has poisoned your veins and turned you into a malcontent whom *no one* is going to tolerate for long."

"This is why I'm dying." I drop my hand from the latch of his door. "You never cease to abuse me."

"I don't abuse you. Stop saying that I do."

"What do you call your actions toward me at the university?"

"I paid for your education."

"You paid for only part of it. You left me stranded there and forced the other students to view me as destitute. I've heard you tell Ma when you think I'm not listening that you have no affection for me."

"I've never said that."

"I've heard you, Pa! Why did you take me in as a child when you could have let someone else raise me? Why did you do that if you didn't want me? You should have sent me to my grandparents in Baltimore instead."

Ma coughs in her bedroom across the landing.

Pa stands up. "Shut the door so Ma doesn't have to hear your ingratitude."

"I want to return to the university."

"Well, you can't. Constables in Charlottesville are waiting to throw you in jail."

"And who's fault is that?"

"Yours, Edgar! You're the one who gambled everything away. I want you to succeed as a responsible member of society, don't you see that? I *want* you to experience success."

"Well, our definitions of success differ vastly, Pa. You see me as a frivolous poet who wastes time and money. I see myself as a scholar who'll thrive in a life of letters."

"But you're young and fool—"

"You see yourself as a prosperous merchant," I continue. "I see you as a failed businessman, a failed family man, who's lucky—*damn* lucky—his uncle dropped dead and left him the largest share of his fortune."

Pa glowers down at me with his chin raised high in the air. I debate slithering out the door before he can hurl his book at my head—or worse—but then he says, "Do you know what I genuinely see when I look at you, Edgar?"

My eyes brim with tears, for I know whatever he declares will hurt a thousand times worse than the verbal injury I just inflicted upon him. I back away toward the door.

"I see the little boy my wife desperately wanted to take in after she learned she couldn't bear children of her own," he says with a gulp. "I see the hope in her eyes when we brought you into our home as a curly-haired orphan with inquisitive eyes. That's what you meant to her, Edgar: hope."

His voice has softened.

A tear leaks from my right eye.

"But"—he drops his book to his chair—"hope is nothing more than folly. Hope wastes time. Hope refuses to face truths. Hope . . ." Again, he lifts his chin. "Hope inevitably leads to disappointment."

"I know . . ." I clasp a hand around my throat to keep from choking on tears. "I know I'm a disappointment to you . . ."

"I taught you to aspire, but I didn't mean for you to aspire to live the life of a character in a novel. You're not Don Quixote or Gil Blas."

"I know I'm not a character in a novel, Pa. Stop treating me like I'm ignorant and delirious. I understand reality all too well—that's the source of all my pain."

"You've been writing all these nights you've been back home, haven't you?"

"If I don't write . . ."

"If you don't write, you'll what?"

I cover my mouth to hide the chattering of my teeth. He's done it again—reduced me to a groveler, an insubordinate, a dog cowering at his owner's feet.

"Wipe your tears," he says, "clear your throat, and answer me like the eighteen-year-old man that you are, not a child.

Don't tell me that if you don't write, you'll die, Edgar. No man has ever died from stifling his muse."

"I love her."

"Who?"

"My muse. If you kill her, Pa—"

"Is she in your room right now?"

I stiffen and strain my ears for signs of Lenore across the house. "No."

"Are you certain?" Pa surveys my frozen stance. His gaze runs up and down my figure.

Before I can cough up a response, he grabs the musket that's mounted on his wall.

"What are you doing?" I ask.

He drops a musket ball down the barrel and twists open a flask of gunpowder from the mantle.

"She's not in my room," I say, for I haven't seen her tonight and believe it's the truth—I *pray* it's the truth. "This is absurd." I fly toward him. "Stop loading that musket. You're not killing my muse."

He twists away from me and rams down the powder with a rod.

"Pa!" I grab the musket from his hands.

Something crashes to the floor in the direction of my room. Our shoulders jerk, and we both swing around toward the doorway of Pa's chamber.

"What was that, John?" asks Ma from her bedroom.

Instead of answering, Pa tugs the musket away from me and bolts toward my bedroom at the end of the lamp-lit niche beyond the staircase.

"If you're in there, Lenore, get out!" I cry out before he can fling the door open. "Get out! He's coming!"

Pa hurls open the door, and I rush up behind him.

The room within proves empty.

My fireplace poker lies across the bricks of the hearth, as though the metal crashed down from careless positioning.

I breathe a sigh of relief, although my heart skips a beat when I notice a soft rustle of the purple curtain shielding the door to the portico, as though someone just vacated the room.

"What does she look like?" asks Pa, his musket still positioned to fire.

"Put that weapon down, Pa. Good Lord!" I sidle past him with care and hang the poker with the other cast-iron tools for the fireplace. "The poker fell. That's all that you heard."

Pa lowers the musket to the floor and heads toward the writing box sitting on my table.

"What are you doing?" I ask.

He opens the drawer and tugs out poems, school notes, and sketches, throwing papers to the rug in a blizzard of parchment that snows my handwriting across the floor.

"Leave my work alone. Let me go to bed, Pa. I don't want you here in my room, digging around in my personal belongings."

He freezes. "Is this her?"

I creep toward him to see whom he means—*knowing* whom he means.

He clutches my sketch of a fiendish young woman in a black dress of mourning—a girl with snaking tendrils of ebony hair, smirking lips, a strong chin, raised in defiance, and a pair of deep-set eyes that tease: *I dare you to show me to the rest of the world. I dare you to show them your morbid fancies, Eddy Poe.*

"I met her last winter," he says. "She claimed to be my muse. She called herself Cassandra, and I foolishly believed her for a short while."

I rip the sketch from his hands, tearing the page in my haste, leaving him half of Lenore.

"Instead of bullying me for dreaming and writing poetry, Pa," I say, "why don't you leave me alone and tend to your own art?"

"I shoved my muse into a blazing kitchen fire back in Scotland years ago." He crumples up his half of the drawing and tromps toward the flames of my hearth.

I leap toward him. "No, don't!"

I'm too late. He tosses the paper into the grate before I can grab his arm. The flames hiss like a fist curling around the parchment and shrink Lenore down into a glowing ball of orange.

I unbutton my shirt and tuck the rest of the drawing against my breast. "Please let me go to bed, Pa." I hug my shirt closed. "Take that damn loaded musket and your disappointment out of my room and leave me be. I have a long day of work ahead tomorrow."

"Aye, that you do." Pa grabs up his musket and ambles away with a slam of my door that, once again, knocks the poker across the bricks of the hearth with a clatter.

CHAPTER FORTY-NINE

Lenore

I cling to the peak of the roof of Moldavia's upper portico and shiver like I've never shivered before.

Once upon a midnight dreary . . .

I am wary and weary of this mortal world. The skin of my forehead stings and burns, as though Alexander Shelton, indeed, carved Elmira's name across my flesh with merciless scrapes of that glass across my skin. I sought Edgar in his room for comfort. I stoked the flames of his fireplace to warm away the chills that seized me during my escape from the cemetery. But then my poet called out that alarm that sent me racing back out into the night:

If you're in there, Lenore, get out! Get out! He's coming!

Out in the garden, my skirt spontaneously caught fire, which forced me to roll around in the grasses until I smothered the flames—flames that I'm certain John Allan somehow ignited. Now a hole the size and the shape of a raven with broken wings gapes in the feathers and the fabric of my skirt.

Tonight's inspiration *must* surpass all others.

Tonight is the night this ends.

CHAPTER FIFTY

Edgar

The clock down the hall strikes midnight.

I've returned my papers—*bong*—to my writing box—*bong*—and I can't stop thinking—*bong*—how the final stanza of "Tamerlane"—*bong*—needs to be scratched out—*bong*—and completely rewritten—*bong*—but I don't dare lift my pen—*bong*.

He wanted to shoot her!

Bong!

He loaded his musket and threw open my door to shoot her!

Bong!

I lie frozen—*BONG!*—on my side—*BONG!*—in my bed.

BONGGGGGGGGGGGG . . .

I hold my breath and listen for any snores or farts or restless movements stirring in Pa's room down the hall. The urge to revise Stanza XVII of "Tamerlane" prods at my brain like a peevish, pestering finger, but *he* wanted to slay her, and I don't dare write tonight. Part of me wishes Pa would just go out and frig the widow Wills until they both turn blue and collapse in her bed, because I don't dare write tonight while he's brooding and bumbling around in this house, waiting for me to err—waiting to barge through my door and KILL MY MUSE!

Outside on the portico, a flute plays eight airy bars of a song that succors my rankled temper. I squeeze my eyes shut and absorb the music into my veins.

A pause ensues, and again I listen for Pa puttering about in his chamber.

Once more, the flute beckons, and I hear a line from "Tamerlane" whistling in the notes:

"The lovliness of loving well . . ."

"I don't dare write tonight," I say toward the drapes shielding my door.

"I have no words, alas! to tell
The lovliness of loving well!"

I cover my face with my hands. *I don't dare write tonight.*

Lenore's voice flutes through the keyhole in my door to the portico.

"Let. Them. See. Me . . ."

The flames in my lamps bloom within their frosted glass cages. They bedazzle my room at twice their normal brilliancy.

Beyond the windows and curtains, a guitar erupts into song, and quite inexplicably, out in the nighttime world, I hear Ma singing in a lovely *voce forte*:

"Come, rest in this bosom, my own stricken deer,
Tho' the herd have fled from thee, thy home is
still here;
Here still is the smile, that no cloud can o'ercast,
And the heart and the hand all thy own to the
last."

I rise from my bed and ponder whether I should succumb to this artistic temptation.

I dare not.

Or do I?

No man has ever died from stifling his muse, said Pa tonight—but, oh, my dear Pa, what you don't understand is that *no artist truly lives after silencing the muse!*

I flap my coat over my shirtsleeves and slip my feet into shoes. To barricade my interior door—a door that does not lock, to my chagrin—I haul the chair from my desk across the room and wedge it between the latch and the floor.

Ma continues singing "Come, Rest in This Bosom" to the accompaniment of the guitar, her voice a sweet contralto; the guitar an aural feast of strumming. No merrier rendition of a musical composition has met my ears before.

Light steals beneath my curtains.

Love and beauty await.

I throw open the drapes, and find Lenore—my winged, dark angel—playing a golden guitar she appears to have conjured from the air. She leans her back against one of the white wooden columns of the upper portico, my hat cocked on her head, and her eyes warm at my presence. Her lips ease into a smile. She seems to be illuminated by the flames of a hundred lamps I can't see.

I open the door. "Be careful! A short while ago, John Allan broke into my room with a loaded musket, hell-bent on killing you. He destroyed half my drawing of you in my fireplace."

Without missing a note of the music, Lenore glances down at a hole in her skirt—a raven-shaped burn mark with edges that curl inward with the putrid smell of singed fabric. The knees of her stockings peek through the sinews of threads.

Ma's voice ceases singing.

Lenore strums a different melody—one that matches the flute music from before.

"Let us embark upon revisions of the ending of 'Tamerlane,'" she says.

I step out to the portico. "I don't dare write tonight."

"Stanza XVII: 'I Reach'd My Home.'" She swivels around with her guitar and tips her face toward a scene below her. "The conqueror returns from his quest for power and pomp."

I edge toward the railing, and my stomach burbles, for I do not see the deserts or river valleys of the conqueror Tamerlane's home of Transoxiana.

Instead, I see Moldavia's grand hall.

Down within the dreary floral walls, a facsimile of myself in my black frock coat and striped pantaloons embraces Ma near the front door—the very scene of my return from Charlottesville. My trunk and writing box sit behind that twinned version of me. My pockets are turned out, empty of all coins.

Pa shakes his head at Ma and me and clomps up the mahogany staircase, which winds up to the portico where the real me stands—where my muse strums her guitar. His feet thump against each step like the gulps of a beating heart.

"'I reach'd my home—my home no more—'" I say, and I grab hold of Lenore's left elbow, for Pa plods closer.

Lenore strums all the louder.

The duplicate version of me breaks away from Ma, whips his head toward Pa, and sings to the tune of Lenore's guitar:

"I reach'd my home—my home no more—
For all was flown that made it so—
I pass'd from out its mossy door,
In vacant idleness of woe."

Pa climbs higher up the stairs, and his eyes meet mine. I yank Lenore into my room, shut the door, and bolt the latch.

"Write it down," says Lenore of the opening lines of the stanza, still plucking at the strings, and a chandelier flares to life above my desk.

I peek at my barricaded door that leads out to the interior corridor of the house. "Pa's listening from his room. I don't dare write."

Another chandelier whooshes to life near my bookcase, and in front of the dented leather spines of my well-read volumes, an image of Ma presses her hands against her heart and sings:

"Oh! what was love made for, if 'tis not the same
Through joy and through torment, through glory
and shame?
I know not, I ask not, if guilt's in that heart,
I but know that I love thee, whatever thou art."

I approach my desk with silent footfalls and twist open my brass inkstand, releasing the aroma of poetry into the air.

Lenore strums and sings:

"I reach'd my home—my home no more—
For all was flown that made it so—
I pass'd from out its mossy door,
In vacant idleness of woe."

I pull my draft of "Tamerlane" out of my writing box. My chair remains lodged against the door, so I'm forced to stand and bend forward to scratch out the final stanza. I pen my four new lines in my tiny, looping handwriting.

I reach'd my home—my home no more—
For all was flown that made it so—
I pass'd from out its mossy door,
In vacant idleness of woe.

My hand forms the little knot of the final *e*.

"'The lovliness of loving well . . . ,'" sings a voice from my midnight-blue chaise longue, and I discover Elmira reclining on the lounge in her midnight-blue dress from her engagement party. She leans against her left hip, her left arm draping the armrest, and a laurel of linden leaves crowns her head. "'I have no words, alas! to tell/The lovliness of loving well!'"

I shift toward Lenore, who's now strumming in the shadows—playing to the beat of a clock with a crescent-shaped pendulum slicing through time.

"Tamerlane should come home to find his beloved dead," I say, my heartbeat deadening.

Lenore nods a grim nod.

I resume penning the stanza.

There met me on its threshold stone
A mountain hunter, I had known
In childhood but he knew me not.

(I stop to count out the meter of the following lines with silent taps of my fingers against the desk.)

Something he spoke of the old cot:
It had seen better days, he said;
There *rose a fountain once, and* there
Full many a fair flow'r rais'd its head:
But she who rear'd them was long dead,
And in such follies had no part . . .

I peer at the maroon fleur-de-lis of the wall in front of me and mouth numerous possibilities for the final couplet. My eyes rest on a framed watercolor painting of Boston Harbor that my mother painted and bequeathed to me upon her death. *For my little son Edgar,* she wrote on the back, *who should ever love Boston, the place of his birth, and where his mother found her* best, *and* most sympathetic *friends.*

In unison, Lenore, Elmira, and Ma sing—

*"There **rose a fountain once, and** there*
Full many a fair flow'r raised its head:
But she who rear' d them was long dead,
And in such follies had no part . . ."

I rub my forehead and dither over the phrasing—debate the best words to rhyme with *there* and *part*. The pendulum swings; the clock ticks and tuts. The floor below me rumbles with the vibrations of a distant drumming, and my chest tightens at the tension trembling through the walls.

"It is time," says Lenore, and she closes her eyes, strumming the guitar as though she'll die if she stops.

I peek over my shoulder at my door.

Elmira and Ma have vanished.

"'What was there left of me *now?*'" I say, and I bleed that question across the paper in ink as the second-to-last line.

I tear at my hair. The rest of the couplet refuses to burst from my brain.

My shoulders flinch, for I swear, I just heard footsteps trudging toward my room.

"Despair!" shouts Lenore, and she steps out of the shadow, her fingers bleeding on the strings from the fervor of her playing. "'What was there left of me *now? despair—*'"

I nod and write *despair* at the end of the second-to-last line.

The footsteps draw nearer.

"Hurry!" shouts Lenore. "Tonight is the night! 'What was there left of me *now? despair—*'"

I lean over the parchment and seal shut my cherished epic poem—my darling "Tamerlane"—with a line that pours across the parchment in a flood of amethyst lamplight:

A kingdom for a broken—heart.

"Finito!" I shout with a satisfying dunk of my quill into the inkstand, and I reach for Lenore. "Discouragement be damned!"

My muse removes my hat from her head and beams with the brightest smile I've ever witnessed on a face in my eighteen years of life. She cups a warm hand around the back of my neck, and without further ado, she kisses me with her magnificent maroon lips.

And, oh, what a kiss it proves to be!

The touch of her mouth against mine transports me into a realm painted in luscious shades of blacks, and reds, and ghastly grays, where the air smells misted and autumnal, where the wind cries with a woebegone wail, and the waters of a tarn moan and howl, moan and howl. My soul soars over the pitched and moldering roof of the house of the Ushers—a melancholy mansion that resembles Moldavia, with macabre eyelids for windows that blink wide open to reveal vacant stares. I travel through one of these ocular openings, where I find a young man pulling teeth out of the mouth of the woman he loves—his deceased love, Berenice—whose molars of a pearled and pristine white become the object of his appalling monomania. The shadow of a cat lingers on the wall behind him, and I hear the scratches of the Usher sister beneath the boards of the floor, along with a *tick-tick-tick-tick-tick-tick-tick-ticking* heart. And there! Down the hall, await a series of rooms of singular hues in which masked revelers waltz to a hypnotic *beat*-beat-beat, *beat*-beat-beat, *beat*-beat-beat, and the pendulum swings, while within the walls of a chimney a woman screams. And the sea roars outside with a moan and howl, moan and howl.

The heat of Lenore's lips sears too much to withstand. I pull away from her mouth amid a blast of wind that gusts from her feet up through the feathers of her head. Her guitar no longer exists, and she stands with her arms to her sides, her palms facing me, her head tipped backward. With a smile of divine pleasure, she endures that hurricane force blowing through her figure in a rippling aurora of violet and gold, violet and gold. Feathers sprout across the bodice of her blouse, enrobing her breasts and her arms in beauteous black plumes. Her lips fall open and darken to a metallic charcoal gray, and she raises her elbows into the air, where her arms adhere to the wings unfurling behind her. I brace myself against my desk and watch in wonder as my muse closes her eyes and evolves before me, the air screaming and brightening around her, feathers blossoming down her forehead—

An earth-trembling explosion suddenly throws her backward.

Dear God!

The back of her skull crashes against my wall, and she drops to the floor. Blood pools across her chest, and smoke hisses from her head, her clothing, her fingers, her brown boots. I stumble to reach her but fall against the desk, confused about the ghastly stains of red spattered across the furniture, the papers, the inkstand, my clothing, my mother's watercolor painting of Boston Harbor.

I don't understand what's just happened.

What's happening? Oh, God!

I crouch down beside her and shove my hands over a hole in her chest that gapes through her feathers. Blood seeps between my fingers and scalds like flames, drenching my hands, blistering my skin. The furnace of smoke blasting from her body billows into plumes that sting my eyes and incinerate my lungs. My throat clogs and sears, as though I'm gagging on embers.

"That's not a real girl, Edgar," says Pa from behind me. "She's a chimera. A dream. A distraction . . ."

I glare over my shoulder at John Allan, who reigns over the center of my chamber, the smoking musket gripped in his right hand.

But he's wrong about Lenore. When I turn back toward her, I no longer see a raven-esque creature. She's a girl—a loving girl, a *dying* girl—bleeding on my floor in a black dress of mourning. Her feathers are gone, as are her astounding wings, yet her face remains that morbid, marble gray that now worries me dreadfully. She's more human than ever, which is precisely what pains me most of all. I didn't nurture her well enough. I've allowed her to die. She was so close to soaring . . .

"Let your muse go, Edgar," says Pa, his voice softening to a tenderness that turns the situation even more sickening. "Please, let her go, son. Wrap your hands around her neck and strangle the rest of the life out of her. She's not real. It's not murder. You may stay in this house if you silence her this moment and free yourself of her influence."

With eyes a dazed and lusterless black, Lenore stares at me. She reaches for my face, and her fingers smear my cheek in streaks of blood that steam against my skin. Tears of soot run down her cheeks, and I taste the salt of my own tears on my lips. The smoke gusting from her skin turns into ribbons of gray that flutter from her wound.

She attempts to speak. "Lea—"

I bend closer. "What? What is it?"

She clutches the back of my neck and squeezes her fingers around my top vertebrae. "Leave this house. Take me with you. Don't let me go. Please, don't let me go!"

"I won't." I scoop her up in my arms and struggle to rise to my feet.

"Edgar!" says Pa. "If you walk out the front door—"

"How can you possibly expect me to stay?"

"I won't give you a penny if you leave . . ."

"No, of course, you won't, you damn, heartless miser!"

I maneuver Lenore out of my room, and in my fog of shock, I mistake the agate lamp glowing outside the door for Jane Stanard, holding up a torch in her white robes, guiding me onward.

I haul my muse down the winding staircase without falling, despite my lack of balance, despite her weight bearing down on my chest, despite the blood dripping across the steps.

"Where are you going, Eddy?" shouts Ma from the landing above. "What did you do, John?"

"If you leave this house and attempt to salvage your artistic follies," calls Pa, "I predict you'll be dead in the streets within the year. Within the month!"

I lean forward and open the latch of the front door from behind Lenore's skirts. A cold blast of air rushes at us, forcing her eyes to blink farther open, and yet her face is so contorted with agony, I can't bear to look at her.

I kick the door open and cart her out into the night.

CHAPTER FIFTY-ONE

Lenore

The clinking of metal tools rouses me from unconsciousness, and I awaken to my chest ripping open with an agony that makes the world flash with pulsating lights of pain.

I'm lying on a table in a candlelit room with bare wooden walls lined with pliers, scalpels, and shelves of small bottles, some labeled "Poison." The tang of blood and chemicals in the air sends convulsions through my stomach.

A man with filaments of gray hair swept across his round head pokes at an area between my heart and my breastbone. The bloodied apron hanging over the large barrel of his chest drags against my right arm, but I don't care a damn about the blood or the filth, because fire gnaws down to my ribs and chews at my heart with white-hot fangs. The pain bathes the room in a throbbing orange haze. I moan through the torture and mourn for my wings and my stolen transformation.

My poet leans into view. "Please, for the love of God, dig that musket ball out of her!"

The stranger in the apron sucks air through his teeth and scratches the back of his head. "Do you have money to pay me?"

"You'll get paid, sir." Eddy squeezes my left hand, his flesh chilled, his grip firm. "Just please take it out of her!"

The man probes my wound with metal that scorches. I arch my back, clench my jaw, and shudder and groan. The man then scratches and digs with more force, until I holler—until the tools and bottles rattle from my screams.

"Can we give her brandy?" asks Eddy. "Something to ease the pain?"

"You might lose her even faster if she swoons while drunk."

"Take it out quickly, then! Please! I can't let him kill her. Do not let him kill her."

Eddy grips my hand, and the surgeon bends over with a pair of rusted pliers that he wiggles down into the center of my chest. It feels like he's chiseling at the raw walls of my heart. I grit my teeth and moan until tears gully down my cheeks, until my mouth flies open with unholy wails, but the surgeon still is scraping, still scooping out lead and burning my chest with that tortuous metal—*my God, how it burns!* And how the blood seeps, the smoke gags.

"I can't bear this!" says Eddy. He lets me go and snatches a bottle from a shelf.

Instead of bringing it to me, he yanks out the cork with his teeth, spits it to the floor, and quaffs a drink that incites my eyelids to quiver and my eyes to spin into the back of my head.

CHAPTER FIFTY-TWO

Edgar

Smeared in blood and reeking of smoke, I stumble through the dark streets of Richmond until I find Ebenezer's house, where I talk my old friend into joining me for a drink at the Courthouse Tavern. Never one to turn down a chance to imbibe from a bottle, Eb readily agrees.

He tosses me clean clothing, free of blood, through which I somehow string my arms and legs. Before long, we're gathered together at a table in a back corner of the tavern, surrounded by the fumes of ale and the stink of Richmond's dissolute wanderers of the night—the prostitutes and thieves, the eaters of opium, the unloved and abandoned.

"I plan to sail to Boston," I say to Eb, rubbing my jaws to enable my mouth to keep functioning, despite the whiskey coursing through my veins.

Eb sips from a glass bubbling with a beauteous topaz liquid. "You're certain you're not returning home?"

"John Allan believes I've left in a passion and will come crawling through the door on hands and knees, but, no—I am gone. I'll need to send for a trunk of my clothing and books . . . and money."

Eb chokes on his drink. "You don't have any money?"

"Not a cent. Why do you think I'm not buying any booze?"

"I thought it was because you're already drunk. Wait here, my friend." Eb scoots out of his chair. "I'll buy you a glass."

Eb's good to his word and fetches me a brandy, and we spend the next hour concocting wild plans born from the delirium of the devil's finest libations.

"Sail with me to Boston, Eb," I ask of him while resting my left cheek upon the table, my nose pressed against the leftover smell of a dirty rag that must have scrubbed the surface earlier that night. "Or maybe to England. My old friend Robert Sully—the nephew of that famous portrait painter—" I snap my fingers and try to conjure up the name of Rob Sully's renowned uncle. "Charles . . . or Samuel . . . or maybe—*yes*—Thomas Sully! Thomas Sully's nephew, my old friend Rob—"

"I know who Robert Sully is, Edgar. Get on with your story."

"Rob studies at an art academy in London. Now there's a fellow who's nurturing his muse! Or maybe we should embark upon a voyage to Russia. St. Petersburg! My brother is a sailor these days. I want to be just like him—Mr. William Henry Leonard Poe."

Eb braces a hand against my left arm. "I'll sail with you wherever you want, Edgar. Wherever you want to go"—he thumps his right palm against his chest—"I'll be there for you, because I love you as dearly as though you were my brother."

"Do you? Will you?"

He pats my elbow. "I will."

"I can't even fathom . . ." I fall asleep for a moment, but jerk awake and somehow remember what I'd just been trying to say: "I can't fathom waking up tomorrow and penning a single word of poetry. He killed my muse in cold blood."

"I should go," says Eb. "It's four o'clock in the morning. My mother will worry."

"'My mother will worry,'" I echo him—not in mockery, but in reverence of his mother's love for him, despite his faults and iniquities.

Eb wobbles up to his feet and pets my head as though I'm a spaniel. "I'll see if I can scrape up a few coins for you when I'm home. Get you some food and a bed."

"God bless you, Ebenezer Burling," I say, and I offer him a salute, my head still lying sideways on that disgusting, rag-scented table.

My next cognizant moment involves a man twice my size steering me out to the back alley by my left arm. "Go home," he says, "unless you can pay for a room."

"I have no home. Or money," I say, and I laugh at my own words, even though the truth wedges like a knife beneath my ribs.

The man wanders back into the tavern, and I slide to a heap on the ground.

"Wake up," says a woman with a shake of my left arm.

The sour smells of alleyway beer and urine shock my nose and shake me further awake.

I peer up above me and nearly burst into tears, for I find Judith's brown eyes, awash with concern, gazing down at me from beneath the ruffles of a calico bonnet.

"The missus is fretting and stewing over your whereabouts," she says. "Why are you out here, sleeping on the street? It's about to pour rain. She said you left in a rage early this morning."

"John Allan shot my muse."

Judith draws back. "Oh, Lord. Did he kill her?"

"Not yet. At least"—I lift my head from the ground—"I don't think so. I left her at the surgeon's."

"You left her?"

I roll over onto my stomach and push myself up to my hands and knees. Dirt snows to the ground from my hair. With a belch, the taste of hours-old brandy reminds me of the drinks I shared with Eb the night before. Or perhaps it was in the early-morning hours when we caroused and made plans. I've lost all track of time.

"Go to her," says Judith.

I remain stuck on hands and knees. "I need to write to my father before I do anything else. I don't have my clothing—or money. I can't pay the surgeon."

Judith places a hand on my back. "Are you leaving home for good?"

"I am. I'm sailing to Boston as soon as I'm able to afford my passage. I'm not residing under that man's roof one more second of my life."

"Take your muse with you."

I sink back on my heels. "She's dying, Judith."

Judith kneels by my side. "Do you want to prove to your father that he's wrong about you?"

I swallow. "Of course, I do."

"Then you must promise me that you'll succeed as a writer."

I laugh with exasperation. "How can I possibly promise *that?*"

"Work hard. Earn money. And keep your muse alive, no matter what happens. Find a way to pay for a room in this tavern until your ship leaves. Bring her here. Keep her safe."

"Pa owes me the passage north. I plan to write to him this morning and list all my grievances against him . . ."

"No! Don't list your grievances if you're asking for money."

I rise to my feet and rub at a crick in my neck. "He should have turned me out to the streets when he started hating me three years ago. He's been short with me ever since Mrs. Stanard died, when I was miserable with grief, and he yelled at me for sulking. He should have allowed me to die back then."

"Don't speak of dying." Judith wraps her arms around me and holds me close, despite the ungodly stink I'm most certainly emanating.

I plant my forehead against her shoulder and endure disorienting revolutions of my brain.

"Did you say you're sailing to Boston?" she asks.

I nod, which makes me all the dizzier. "I was born there. And it's a literary haven."

"Take your muse with you." Judith lets me go but braces a hand on my shoulder. "Please, always keep the light of your imagination burning."

Even though such a promise seems impossible, I swallow and say, "I'll try."

The surgeon sewed Lenore up, wrapped her chest in bandages, and left her to die on a cot in the hallway outside his operating room, covered in nothing more than a blanket as thin as the wings of a butterfly. I walk over to the cot, tripping on an uneven board as I go, and bend down on one knee beside her.

Her breathing has grown faint. Her pale lips resemble marble.

"Lenore," I say in a whisper. "I'm sorry I didn't better protect you. I should have left Moldavia sooner. I'm taking you to a room in a tavern. Eb's just leant me some coins. And then we'll set sail for Boston."

The surgeon plods into view and unrolls the cuffs of his shirtsleeves. "To whom should I send my bill?"

"John Allan, Esquire, care of Ellis & Allan."

"Very good."

I take Lenore's left wrist in my hand. "She's still breathing, isn't she? I'm not simply imagining her chest rising and falling?"

"I'm sorry, son, but if she lives another hour, I'd consider it a miracle. Make her comfortable. Arrange for the burial. There's nothing more I can do."

In the room I've acquired for Lenore and myself in the Courthouse Tavern, I continue to wage my war with Pa through written correspondence, penned on stationery that Eb kindly lent me, in addition to the money he somehow managed to procure for my lodging. Freezing rain pours by the bucketful outside the window in front of me, a filthy pane of glass greased in fingerprints.

My muse breathes through pallid lips on the bed behind me.

I address Pa as "Sir," air my charges against him, despite Judith's advice, for it makes me feel a little better, and I request that he send my trunk full of books and clothing to the tavern. I also ask for money for my passage, as well as enough funds to support me for a month until I can place myself in a position that will allow me to support myself.

I hear no reply, so I write again the following morning—for Lenore still lives, even if just barely, which affords me some hope. I explain to Pa that I'm starving and wandering the streets of Richmond. I ask for twelve dollars for passage and a little more to help me get settled.

By the following day, I receive my second letter back from him, without any money attached, and on the verso, I discover that Pa penned two words:

Pretty Letter.

"Pretty Letter"!

The man who raised me from infancy mocks my suffering. The suffering he himself instigated.

Ma must have taken pity on me, for Dabney—*dear Dabney*—appears at the tavern the following morn and hands me my trunk, which includes all my manuscripts and an envelope containing twelve dollars for my passage.

"Thank you, Dab," I say, and I clasp him in a hug.

"You take care," he says. "Please take good care of yourself. We're all worried about you."

"Give my love to Ma. Tell her not to fret. I don't want her health to worsen because of me."

On Saturday, I board a vessel bound for Boston, accompanied by Ebenezer—who seems a bit soused but, hopefully, comprehends what he's doing. And in my arms, I carry the near-corpse of my muse, wrapped in the gray coat Pa sent me at the university. Eb stole a white cap from his mother to cover the fuzz of hair that remains where fantastic feathers once bloomed on Lenore's scalp.

Lenore's head sways above the planks during my walk across the ship's deck, and I breathe the smell of smoke that lingers on her skin. Beneath the surface of her face there flickers a strange light—the weak glow of embers dying in a grate.

If the burden of carrying her with me to the North grows too heavy to bear, I fear what I may do. I may toss her into the waters, let her sink down to the bottom of the lonely sea, and free myself from aspiring to greatness so I may live a normal life.

CHAPTER FIFTY-THREE

Lenore

Using his penknife, my poet whittles down the nib of a goose-feather quill while seated at a table in an unfamiliar room with walls the color of a weak claret wine. The fireplace behind him lacks wood and, therefore, heat, and the only furniture in the chamber seems to be the table he occupies and the bed on which I'm lying, tucked beneath the meager warmth of his university coat.

Rain taps against the window.

Mildew scents the air.

"Where are we?" I ask.

Edgar lifts his head, his eyes rimmed in red.

"Boston," he says.

"How long have we been here?"

He closes his eyes, and his forehead creases. "Over a month. It's now April."

"Wasn't Ebenezer with us?"

"He sobered up at the first port after Richmond and sailed home."

I roll onto my right side and gasp at a sharp pain in my breastbone, reminded of the horror and the agony of John Allan firing a musket at me in Eddy's bedroom. My skirt crumples against the mattress, and I taste metal on my tongue. No wings drape my back, and their loss makes me shiver.

"How are you feeling?" asks Eddy.

"Uninspiring."

He gives a sad smile and sets the quill aside without writing a word.

"I'm working as a clerk but plan to join the army soon," he says. "I'll enlist as Edgar A. Perry to avoid the creditors. To disappear. My grandfather, David Poe Sr., was a quartermaster general in the Revolutionary War. The army's in my blood just as much as the arts."

His voice doesn't quite sound like his own. He may as well be speaking the lines of a play he doesn't care for in the slightest.

"Have you been eating?" I ask.

"A little."

"Writing?"

"I've been trying." He presses his palms against his forehead. "I've sworn I'd persevere and not let Pa silence us, but . . ."

Another sharp ache grips my chest. I curl into a ball and gasp for air, but my breath escapes my lips as an icy mist that stings my mouth.

"Eddy," I say through a spasm of chills, "let me go."

He moves in his chair with a screech of the legs against the floorboards, but he does not answer.

"We're both dying," I say. "Please . . . at least allow yourself to live. He's injured me beyond repair."

"I can't let him do that."

"Please . . ." I shudder, which makes my head throb, and another icy breath burns my lips. "Let me go."

Edgar sits down beside me on the bed and clasps his arms around me. He rests his head against my left shoulder and lulls me a little with the ticking of his heart, but he's so cold himself, he only makes me tremble more, and he turns my brain into a block of ice.

"You won't even need to worry about burying me," I say, my teeth chattering. "I'll simply smolder out and return to the fire and shadows from whence I came, and you'll be freed of me. You can concentrate on living . . . and on loving all those pretty women you adore."

"No."

"Please! I hurt so much, and I'm so dreadfully cold."

Another bout of ice erupts across my skull and freezes me down to the bottoms of my lungs. We've so much left to write—so many poems and tales yet to start—but to breathe one second more would be a torture I cannot endure.

Eddy whispers near my ear, "Lenore . . ."

"Let me go," I say again. "Kiss all those pretty women for me."

He cradles me against his chest and shakes with silent tears . . . but, like the obedient artist he sometimes proves to be, he does what I ask.

He lets me go, and the ice burns down to my toes.

CHAPTER FIFTY-FOUR

Edgar

Lenore does not simply smolder away. It's true, she ceases breathing, her pulse stops ticking, and a shadow passes over her face—a shadow that seemingly surfaced to her skin from the arctic depths of her core, sealing her flesh in a lavender layer of frost. She relaxes out of my arms and spills across the bed—again, like a shadow—and yet she still exists here in body. A cold, corporeal reminder of what John Allan took away.

I carry her to the shop of the nearest undertaker—a pasty-faced specter with a skeletal head who appears less alive than my muse. He lays Lenore down on a table in the middle of his stacks of empty coffins and touches the shorn black hair that covers her head.

"Where's her hair?" he asks, his eyes turned my way, the whites huge compared to the mossy greens of his irises. "And why is she so painfully cold to the touch? Even if you kept her on ice . . . something doesn't seem right."

I lay a hand on the chilled fabric of Lenore's left sleeve. "There's nothing wrong with her. But does she seem truly dead to you? I can't bear the thought of accidentally burying her alive if she's merely fallen into a state of catalepsy. I know that's a hideous situation that sometimes, too frequently, occurs . . ."

The undertaker peels open the lid of Lenore's right eye, revealing a lusterless pool of dried ink where her pupils once blazed.

He clears his throat and says, "She appears sufficiently dead to me."

I bow my head, and my teeth begin spontaneously chattering—clattering with such violence that I bite the tip of my tongue. And yet I'm unable to cry, which I'm certain would astound, and perhaps even in this situation, *disappoint* John Allan.

The undertaker rubs his hands together to warm them from Lenore, and he blows his hot breath against his thumbs.

"Can you afford a coffin, young man?" he asks.

I shake my head.

"I'll wrap her in a winding-sheet, then, and we'll carry her out in a temporary coffin for the funeral. I'll allow you a day or two to make arrangements with the guests and the church, if this is to be a religious burial . . ."

"No. I alone will be in attendance, and I'll require her burial to occur in a public plot, with no stone marker. But, please, let us still allow at least one day more in case she awakens."

"We'll wait two days before sealing her up in the ground, just to be certain, since you seem so anxious—and since she's so well chilled."

"Yes—well chilled," I say, for my mind fails to yield any other words, even though the phrase rots on my tongue.

I bend down and kiss Lenore goodbye, and when my lips touch hers, I endure the sensation of falling into a wintry shadow. I hear not one breath of poetry from her.

The following forty-eight hours pass in a pall of solitude.

I do not write a single word, nor do I care to.

The funeral falls in the hushed morning hours of a Monday, the most pessimistic of days. The air tenses with the threat of rain, but the sulking clouds, for all their brooding and swollenness, refuse to weep a single drop. The undertaker assists me in carrying my muse to the pauper's corner of a cemetery in a temporary pine coffin. At the graveside, we lift the lid, pull her shrouded body from the casket with movements slow and gentle, and lay her down in the ground without any wood to protect her from the soil and the inevitable worms. The gravedigger waits in the shadows of the charnel house, while I stand at the edge of that gaping hole, breathing the vapors of the opened earth. Words fail me. Lenore receives no eulogy. I grab a chipped piece of stone from the grass and mark an *L* on the brick wall beside her.

No more than a minute after I depart the graveside, the gravedigger saunters over with his spade and covers my Gothic Psyche in piles of dirt that slap against her shroud.

On a brighter morning in early May, Garland O'Peale stands on the sidewalk beyond the iron gate of the boardinghouse in which I'm lodging in one of Boston's lesser districts. He wears an ashen coat and a matching hat, both smothered in ratty old mockingbird feathers, and his face has turned so frightfully wan and emaciated that his cheekbones protrude above sunken cheeks. The green-tinted spectacles continue to conceal his eyes.

He crams his hands into his coat pockets and waits for me to approach.

I dismount the last step of the boardinghouse porch and meet up with him outside the gate. "What are you doing here?"

"Do you remember me, Poe?"

"Of course, I remember you, Garland. What do you want?"

"She's gone, isn't she?"

Without answering, I sweep past him, my hands also stuffed in my pockets. I tromp off to the office of some obscure newspaper that's offered me a position after a run of bad luck with employers not fond of paying their employees.

The imp follows. "I'm speaking of the lost Lenore."

"I know. Why do you care about her? And why are you suddenly here? I thought you abandoned me for Upton Beall."

"Ah, yes, Mr. Beall." Garland falls in with my stride. "I've come to realize, Poe, that the vessel is far more important than we muses often think. Beall lacks your meticulous care with language. Feeding inspiration through him felt like writing in plain ink, whereas speaking through you feels like burnishing a manuscript in gold."

I whip my head toward him. "That almost sounds like a compliment."

"Oh, it's more than a compliment. You're an exceptional writer, and I'm your wayward brother in literary arms who's come to apologize for not realizing your full worth. Besides, Upton Beall seems to be developing a muse of religious inspiration—a flickering little upstart that sings from his candles. Beall lost interest in associating with me."

"Ah." I nod. "So, you've returned to me because Upton won't have you."

"I searched for you in Richmond and learned through some sort of judgmental owl lady that John Allan shot Lenore. Is that true?"

I swallow, but still, I do not weep. "I buried her in a cemetery here in Boston."

Garland comes to an abrupt halt. "You *buried* her?"

I stop and pivot toward him. "She died, Garland."

"You buried a muse?"

"She ceased breathing. What else was I supposed to do with her?"

"You can't bury a muse in the ground, Poe. She's either gone for good or you're ignoring her . . . again!"

"I didn't know you cared anything for Lenore."

"Lenore inspires your heart to beat faster, my friend. She awakens your spirit and allows you escapes into the fantasies you so desperately require in order to survive. I didn't realize before precisely how much we both need her." He straightens the hat on his head. "But I need you to live, so I may keep living. I need her darkness to inspire my wit. Go and dig her up!"

Passersby turn their heads.

I cringe at their expressions of disgust.

"She's dead, and I'm late for work," I say, and I reel around and leave.

Before I can reach the end of the block, Garland wraps an arm around mine and steers me across the street toward a park.

"What are you doing?" I ask.

He quickens his pace. "I want you to meet a fellow who's also new to Boston. If Lenore, you, and I are to work together as a grandiloquent trio, then we're going to need readers."

I shake my elbow but can't break free of him. "What are you talking about, you aggressive ass?"

"Ah, there's the Edgar Poe I know! Curse at me. Ridicule me. Slay me in rhyme."

Garland drags me to a street called Washington and stops me in front of a brick storefront with the name "Calvin F. S. Thomas" painted on a black-and-gold sign hanging above the door. Beyond the beveled windows, a copper-haired fellow no older than myself arranges metal type in a composing stick for printing. The steadiness of his fingers reminds me of the surgeon's in Richmond. The inky blood of his trade stains his hands.

Garland opens the door and pushes me inside but does not enter the establishment behind me.

"Good morning, sir," says the young compositor in a Virginia drawl that soothes me in an instant.

"Good morning." I remove my hat. "Pardon my prying, but are you . . . did I just hear a Virginia accent?"

"You did, sir." The fellow cracks a wide grin. "I was born in New York but raised in Norfolk. You sound like a son of the great Commonwealth of Virginia yourself."

I offer my hand. "I'm Edgar A. . . . *Perry*. Born here in Boston but raised in Richmond."

"A pleasure to meet you, Mr. Perry." He wipes the ink from his fingers onto his black apron and shakes my hand. "I'm Calvin Thomas."

"The pleasure's all mine. Does your family own this printing office?"

"I own it. I'm trying to earn money for my education."

"Ah, as am I."

Calvin swings back around to his towering cases of metal letters and returns to arranging the type. "Do you need something printed?"

I run my hands across the unvarnished grains of the front counter and inhale the scent of the ink, intermingled with the sweet pulp of papers hung up to dry. I envision "Tamerlane" set in type on a golden-brown sheet of parchment.

"You're blushing, Mr. Perry," says Calvin. "Are you in need of a wedding invitation?"

"Call me Edgar, please. You can't be any older than I am."

"I'm eighteen."

"As am I." My blush runs hotter when I realize I've just repeated this same phrase from before, but I'm suddenly at a loss how to articulate my ambitions in front of this kindred Virginia dreamer. I tuck my hands back into my coat pockets, where my thumbs snare on holes, and debate if I should dare ask a question that now lingers on my tongue.

"If you have no money"—Calvin eyes the shabbiness of my coat, which isn't any worse off than his own patched-up jacket, I realize—"I may be able to arrange for you to pay on credit."

"Do you print books?" I ask with the release of a held breath.

"I haven't yet." Calvin clinks a letter into the upper case and saunters back over to the counter. "Why do you ask?"

My eyes water. From six hundred miles away in the capital city of Virginia, John Allan must be listening, for I feel his gaze scorching the back of my neck. He's waiting for me to answer like the industrious Southern gentleman he raised me to be.

"Do you aspire to be a writer?" asks Calvin.

I shake off Pa's grip and lift my head. "No. I *am* a writer. I have been since childhood. It's how I intend to make my living."

"Ah, that's fascinating." Calvin leans an elbow on the counter. "What is it that you write?"

I clear my throat. "I have a collection of poems I've been penning for years. It wouldn't be a long book . . ."

"Bring the manuscript to me. I'll let you know what I can do with it."

"Would you?"

"Of course. You might help me expand my business if I add book printing to my repertoire."

"I need to head off to work, but I—"

"Bring the pages whenever you have the time, Mr. Perry."

"Thank you." I reach out and shake his hand again. "You have my deepest gratitude, sir. I'm much obliged to you for your kindness."

"I can't make any promises as to the beauty of the binding. It would be more of a pamphlet . . ."

"But it would at least be a start. It would get my work into the hands of readers—allow it to be seen. Thank you." I fit my hat back over my head. "I'll return this evening to show you the pages."

"I'll look forward to it. Thank you for stepping into my shop."

After work, I return to my room and proofread the poems most ready for publication: "Tamerlane," "To — —," "Dreams," "Visit of the Dead," "Evening Star," "Imitation," three untitled poems, and "The Lake."

I wet the nib of my quill with fresh ink and pen a title page:

Tamerlane

And other poems.

By a Bostonian.

"Young heads are giddy, and young hearts are warm,
And make mistakes for manhood to reform." —COWPER

"'A Bostonian'?" asks Calvin upon my return to his shop.

I slide the manuscript across his countertop. "I prefer to remain anonymous until I'm freed from the troubles of my youth."

"Ah." He nods in understanding, asks no further questions on the subject, and we come to a financial agreement for the book's publication.

By the time I leave the printing office, twilight dyes the sky in a dusky shade of rose. Beneath a smoky lamp waits Garland O'Peale, resting his spine against the black metal of the pole. He's a mirror image of me, I daresay, if I were to wear a hat run amok in mockingbird feathers and green-tinted spectacles.

I approach him without hesitation—without fear.

"Come join me in the cemetery," I say.

He pushes himself upright. "Is it time?"

"It's past time—but, oh, God"—I loosen my cravat—"let's see if we're not too late."

Up in the cemetery, the cold Lady Moon casts the tombs in a haze that chills my heart, but I ignore my fears and superstitions and obtain a pair of spades from the gravedigger's shed. Garland and I weave our way through crooked trees and the stones marking the lives of Bostonians from centuries past, carved with skulls, and bones, and angels' wings, until we reach the pauper's corner—a desolate patch of unmarked graves. An owl trills from a branch in a tree overhead, but the only other sound I hear is the darkness.

The soil has settled, and yet the faint *L* on the wall allows us to find the place where I laid Lenore to rest. I stare down at her bed of dirt and inhale a deep breath, my hands gripped around the coarse wood of the spade's handle.

Hope is nothing more than folly, said Pa on the night I fled the house. *Hope wastes time. Hope refuses to face truths . . . Hope inevitably leads to disappointment . . .*

"Discouragement be damned!" I say in a voice that echoes across the graves—a voice that I hurl south to John Allan's ears in Moldavia—and I drive the blade of the spade into the earth.

CHAPTER FIFTY-FIVE

Lenore

Edgar, thy absence is to me like a crushing, metallic ore that cruelly, under a rancid sea of soil, seals me in sepulchral horror, on a cold and distant shore.

Deep inside a tomb abysmal, I awaken, dark and dismal—trapped am I, dear God, I'm buried in a grave forevermore! Buried here without a casket—buried, broken—yes, I'll ask it—"Why did I not smolder out and fade away with death before?"

Now I'm sealed beneath the floor—sealed down beneath the earthen floor.

Left to sleep, and nothing more.

Someone bound my jaw in wrappings, hellish, winding, binding trappings. Feel the maggots squirming, lapping!—tortures I can bear no more! Poet, please, relieve this pressure, hoist me up to air that's fresher, use your shovel as a thresher and exhume me from this horror.

Ah! I hear a shovel knocking at my ghastly graveside door!

Poe, forsake me nevermore.

I'll be stifled NEVERMORE!

CHAPTER FIFTY-SIX

Edgar

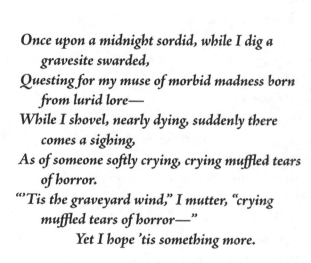

*Once upon a midnight sordid, while I dig a
 gravesite swarded,
Questing for my muse of morbid madness born
 from lurid lore—
While I shovel, nearly dying, suddenly there
 comes a sighing,
As of someone softly crying, crying muffled tears
 of horror.
"'Tis the graveyard wind," I mutter, "crying
 muffled tears of horror—"
 Yet I hope 'tis something more.*

*With my spade I shovel deeper, searching for my
 cloistered sleeper,
Fighting tirelessly to keep her from a soil-infested
 horror,
Lo! I spy a dampened wrapping—winding-
 sheets so cruelly trapping,
Trapping in the earth a spirit unlike any known
 before,
"Let it be the one I buried; let me view her!" I implore—
 "Let me view the lost Lenore."*

Like a Lord of Necromancy, I'll exhume my
    fiendish fancy,
Dearest parents and Aunt Nancy, do not rap
    upon my door,
For you'll find the son you banished—poet Poe,
    the one who vanished,
Drinking dreams within the arms of his Lenore,
    forevermore—
Yes, delirious with dreams; it seems my life you
    shall abhor.
        I belong to you no more.

Did my eye just spy a quiver? A small twitch—a
    shud'ring shiver?
A meek movement not yet noticed in the
    winding-sheet before?
Look! The shrouded head starts shaking, dust
    and dirt around her quaking,
Yes! She writhes, her silence breaking; with my
    hands I dig some more—
"Let us, Garland, free my spirit from this stark
    and stifling store,
        And the three of us shall soar."

I crouch down and sever wrappings, rip apart
    those ghoulish trappings,
Ignore time's incessant lapping, while I rush to
    save Lenore.
Yet, I fear what I may find here; "Do not think
    me too unkind, dear—
But I worry Death has marred you with his vile,
    postmortem gore,

Yes, I worry, but I'll care for you like no one's
   cared before."
         Lenore caws, and nothing more.

I untie a crucial binding, still I dread what I am
   finding,
The cessation of unwinding reveals the figure's
   not Lenore!
But a feathered, sable creature (shadows cloak
   its every feature),
A ravened version of the spirit who bewitched
   me years before—
Not a maid with raven feathers, but a muse of
   ancient lore,
A wing'd muse of ancient lore.

"Please forgive me, I implore you. Please," I beg
   her, "I adore you!"
The raven spreads her ebon wings, and I fall
   back and watch her soar;
She escapes that earthen hollow, turns her head
   for me to follow,
So, I claw, and climb, and swallow all my pride
   from days of yore,
Yes, I join the radiant maiden whom I named for
   light: Lenore—
         My dark muse—forevermore.

END

A Sampling of Poe's Early Poetry

In the following pages, you'll find three of Edgar Allan Poe's early poems in their entirety, printed with the wording of their first published editions.

In 1827, at age eighteen, Poe published "The Lake" and "To — —" (later renamed "Song") in *Tamerlane and Other Poems*. The book also included eight other poems he wrote during his teenage years.

In 1831, at the age of twenty-two, he published "To Helen"—his ode to Mrs. Jane Stanard—in his third collection of poetry, *Poems*. In an 1848 letter to the poet Sarah Helen Whitman (the subject of a later, second poem that he titled "To Helen"), Poe referred to his original "To Helen" as "lines I had written, in my passionate boyhood, to the first, purely ideal love of my soul."

"The Lake"
EDGAR ALLAN POE

In youth's spring, it was my lot
To haunt of the wide earth a spot
The which I could not love the less;
So lovely was the loneliness
Of a wild lake with black rock bound,
And the tall pines that tower'd around.

But when the night had thrown her pall
Upon that spot—as upon all,
And the wind would pass me by
In its stilly melody,
My infant spirit would awake
To the terror of the lone lake.

Yet that terror was not fright—
But a tremulous delight,
And a feeling undefin'd,
Springing from a darken'd mind.
Death was in that poison'd wave
And in its gulf a fitting grave
For him who thence could solace bring
To his dark imagining;
Whose wild'ring thought could even make
An Eden of that dim lake.

"To — —"

EDGAR ALLAN POE

I saw thee on the bridal day;
When a burning blush came o'er thee,
Tho' Happiness around thee lay,
The world all love before thee.

And, in thine eye, the kindling light
Of young passion free
Was all on earth, my chained sight
Of Loveliness might see.

That blush, I ween, was maiden shame:
As such it well may pass:
Tho' its glow hath raised a fiercer flame
In the breast of him, alas!

Who saw thee on that bridal day,
When that deep blush would come o'er thee,—
Tho' Happiness around thee lay;
The world all Love before thee.—

"To Helen"

EDGAR ALLAN POE

Helen, thy beauty is to me
Like those Nicean barks of yore,
That gently, o'er a perfum'd sea,
The weary way-worn wanderer bore
To his own native shore.

On desperate seas long wont to roam,
Thy hyacinth hair, thy classic face,
Thy Naiad airs have brought me home
To the beauty of fair Greece,
And the grandeur of old Rome.

Lo! in that little window-niche
How statue-like I see thee stand!
The folded scroll within thy hand—
A Psyche from the regions which
Are Holy land!

Author's Note

The Raven's Tale is a work of fiction, yet most of the characters, settings, and events portrayed in the novel emerged directly from Edgar Allan Poe's biography. My goal in writing this novel was to offer readers a window into Poe's teenage years using as many historically accurate details as possible. I wanted to root the book in his reality while also immersing the story in scenes of Gothic fantasy that paid homage to his legendary macabre works.

My search for the truth behind Poe's past entailed poring over letters, school records, bills and payments related to his upbringing and education, and firsthand accounts from people who knew—or at least met—teenage Edgar, including his classmates in both Richmond and Charlottesville. My research also took me to Virginia, where I visited the Poe Museum in Richmond, the University of Virginia, and other significant sites from Poe's childhood and teen years. Furthermore, I contacted Chris Semtner, curator of the Poe Museum, and members of the Friends of the Shockoe Hill Cemetery with questions about the novel's setting, which they graciously answered.

Poe's biography is problematic in that many people who knew him disagreed on details about his life and his character. His friends, associates, and foes tended to embellish facts with fiction when offering their personal accounts of interactions with him. Most notably, Rufus Wilmot Griswold, a known, bitter rival, published Poe's first obituary two days after Poe's death in October 1849. In it he created the "Poe as madman" mythology by penning such phrases as "[Poe] walked the streets, in madness or melancholy, with lips moving in indistinct curses" (Griswold, R.W., "Death of Edgar A.

Poe," *New-York Daily Tribune*, New York, NY, Vol. IX, No. 156, October 9, 1849). Griswold further sullied Poe's reputation by fabricating details of the deceased poet's life and forging letters for a piece that first appeared in *International Monthly Magazine* in October 1850. Griswold also published this damaging "memoir" in an 1850 volume of Poe's work that he edited.

Even Poe himself told untrue tales about his past, such as claiming that his parents died in the Richmond Theater fire of 1811, as I portrayed him saying in *The Raven's Tale*. Records prove that this was not the case about his parents. His mother, the popular actress Elizabeth Arnold Hopkins Poe, died of an illness, most likely tuberculosis, on December 8, 1811, eighteen days before the fire. The date and cause of the death of his father, David Poe Jr., remains unclear, although records show that he and his wife parted ways before her death.

The process of putting together the pieces of Poe's young life, therefore, felt like assembling a complicated jigsaw puzzle. Several gaps exist in his timeline from his return home from college in December 1826 to his enlistment in the U.S. Army in Boston on May 26, 1827. I filled in the missing moments with situations and events that seemed the most plausible according to letters and other records from Poe's life.

Poe's reputation as a drug addict is one of the myths that originated during his lifetime. Many of Poe's protagonists used opium, but the belief that Poe himself was a drug addict probably originated in 1845 when a reviewer compared his work to "the strange outpourings of an opium eater" (*Richmond Compiler*, July 30, 1845). Two physicians who knew Poe, however, stated that they never saw any indications of him using the drug—and one of those men, Dr. Thomas Dunn English, hated Poe as much as Rufus Wilmot Griswold did.

Poe struggled with drinking on and off throughout his life, and more than one account from people who knew him states that a mere glass of alcohol, or even a long gulp, would lead to shifts in his personality, drunkenness, and/or long periods of sleep. His sister also experienced the same immediate effect from drinking, according to Susan Archer Weiss's 1907 biography, *The Home Life of Poe*. As with other aspects of Poe's life, there are conflicting stories about the excessiveness and regularity of his drinking, even during his college years. Letters from Poe's lifetime show that alcohol occasionally affected his professional life, yet he also went long periods of time, including years, without touching a drink.

The Raven's Tale ends in May 1827, when Poe first embarked upon his career as a published author at the age of eighteen. His debut book of poetry, *Tamerlane and Other Poems*, appeared in print around June or July of 1827. As I showed in the novel, another eighteen-year-old from Virginia, Calvin F. S. Thomas, printed Poe's small pamphlet of poetry in Boston, Massachusetts. The August 1827 issue of *The United States Review and Literary Gazette* in Boston mentioned the book, and *The North American Review* printed a notice about the poetry collection in October 1827. No reviews of *Tamerlane and Other Poems* appeared in any publications, however, and fewer than forty copies of the book may have been printed, of which only about twelve have survived, according to the Edgar Allan Poe Society of Baltimore (www.eapoe.org).

Poe's burgeoning Gothic muse and his interest in the subject of death as a theme for his writings can be seen in such early poems as "The Lake" and "Visit of the Dead" (the latter of which he later renamed "Spirits of the Dead"), both published in *Tamerlane and Other Poems*. Modern readers often think of Poe as solely a writer of macabre stories and poetry, but throughout his career he also published humorous, satirical, and scientific pieces, among other styles of writings. Poe showed off his satirical side in one of his earliest surviving compositions, "Oh, Tempora! Oh, Mores!," a poem that ridiculed a clerk named Robert Pitts, written in approximately 1825 when Poe was sixteen. He also gained notoriety as a ruthlessly blunt literary critic, starting in 1835 when the *Southern Literary Messenger* in Richmond hired him to work on the periodical.

In that same year the *Southern Literary Messenger* published Poe's early horror story "Berenice," the tale of a man so obsessed with the teeth of his beloved, Berenice, that upon her death, he disturbs her grave and removes the teeth from her body before learning that she was mistakenly buried alive. "Berenice" horrified readers, and hate mail followed. In a letter written to the *Southern Literary Messenger*'s editor, Thomas Willis White, on April 30, 1835, Poe responded to the public's repulsion, acknowledging that his story was "far too horrible" and that the nature of the tale was considered to be in "bad taste." In Chapter Four of *The Raven's Tale*, I intentionally inserted those very words of Poe's in the form of the public's initial reaction to Lenore in Richmond. In fact, throughout *The Raven's Tale*, whenever people criticize Lenore and Poe's Gothic writings, they're often using short phrases I pulled from nineteenth-century reviews of Poe's works, including such terms as "sickly rhymes" (Willis, N. P., *American Monthly Magazine*, November 1829), "execrably bad" (Daniel, John Moncure, *Southern Literary Messenger*, Vol. XVI, No. 3, March 1850, pp. 172–187), "exquisite nonsense" (Neal, John, ed., *The Yankee and Boston Literary Gazette*, New Series, July–December, 1829), and "a gem of art" (*Richmond Semi-Weekly Examiner*, Vol. II, No. 93, September 25, 1849, p. 2, col. 4–5).

Poe's poetry flows throughout *The Raven's Tale*, as well as some of my own humble attempts at verses written in Poe's style. Please refer to the section "Poems, Songs, Letters, and Stories Quoted in *The Raven's Tale*" for my notes on the poems in the novel.

Because I ended the novel shortly after eighteen-year-old Edgar Poe moved out of the house of the family that raised him, I'm aware that readers may have questions about the fates of the Allans and other real-life individuals close to Poe during his youth.

Frances Keeling Valentine Allan, Poe's foster mother, who by all accounts, loved him dearly, died on February 28, 1829, "after a lingering and painful illness" (*Richmond Whig*, March 2, 1829). Her death brought a brief reconciliation between Poe, now twenty, and his foster father, John Allan, but that bond deteriorated once more when Poe left the U.S. Army in 1829 to further pursue his writing career. He did please Allan by serving a brief, albeit unhappy stint at West Point that began in 1830, but he was court-martialed and dismissed for neglecting his duties in February 1831.

Poe and John Allan's relationship further suffered when Poe wrote in a May 1830 letter to Sergeant Samuel Graves, a soldier whom Poe paid to serve as his substitute in the Army, that "Mr. A[llan] is not very often sober." Poe's unflattering words about his foster father found their way back to John Allan, who told Poe he was ending their relationship.

I found Poe's list of expenses for the University of Virginia and his claim that Allan sent him to college with only $110 in a letter Poe wrote to Allan from West Point in January 1831. Even though Allan's correspondence to family and friends during Poe's childhood convey his affection for the boy, evidence of the burgeoning dysfunction between father and son exists as far back as a letter Allan wrote to

Poe's brother, Henry, in November 1824, in which Allan said of fifteen-year-old Edgar, "he does nothing & seems quite miserable, sulky & ill-tempered to all the Family." John Allan remarried in October 1830 and died in March 1834, leaving behind his new wife, Louisa Patterson Allan, and their three young sons. In his will, he bequeathed nothing to his foster son, but he provided money for twin sons he fathered with a Richmond widow named Elizabeth Wills in July 1830. I acknowledge that most of the surviving letters give Poe's side of their conflict and not John Allan's.

Poe's first fiancée, Sarah Elmira Royster, married Alexander Shelton in 1828, and the couple had four children together, but only two lived to adulthood. Alexander died in 1844. Edgar and Elmira eventually reunited in Richmond and became engaged again in 1849, two and a half years after the death of Poe's wife (and first cousin), Virginia Eliza Clemm Poe, and shortly before Poe's death. They never married. Sarah Elmira Royster Shelton died in February 1888, and by all accounts generally shunned the publicity that followed her over her relationship with Edgar Allan Poe.

Poe's younger sister, Rosalie Mackenzie Poe, born circa December 1810, lived most of her years with the Mackenzie family that took her in after the death of their mother. Some records portray her as having the intellect of a child all her life. Others show her as a woman who played the piano, wrote poetry, and worked as an instructor at the Mackenzie School for Girls in Richmond. After Rosalie's foster mother died in 1865, Rosalie became destitute and eventually tried earning money by selling items she claimed to have belonged to her famous, deceased brother, as well as photographs of him. She died in a charity home in Washington, DC, in 1874 at the age of sixty-four.

Various scholars list Judith, Dabney, and "Old Jim" as the names of the slaves that served in the Allan household. Confusion exists with Judith's name, however. Some receipts list "Juliet" or "Eudocia" instead. She joined the Allans in January 1811, and according to various books and articles, she likely played a significant role in inspiring young Edgar Allan Poe's supernatural interests.

Edgar's older brother, William Henry Leonard Poe—also a published author—died in 1831 at the age of twenty-four.

Edgar's Richmond friend Ebenezer Burling died of cholera in 1832 at the age of twenty-five.

In the 1860s and 1880s, Poe's university friends Miles George, William M. Burwell, and the librarian William Wertenbaker all left behind remembrances of their time spent with the renowned author. I based many of the University of Virginia chapters on their recollections. Miles George's use of the words "superabundant talent" to describe Poe's gifts in Chapter Twenty-Seven are from George's letter "Reminiscence of Poe" (*State*, May 22, 1880, p. 2).

Poe's college friend Upton Beall, despite his reputation as a skilled card player at the University of Virginia, went on to graduate from the Virginia Theological Seminary in 1837 and became the rector of Christ Church in Norfolk, Virginia.

Edgar Allan Poe made a significant impact on the world of literature in the twenty-two years following the publication of *Tamerlane and Other Poems*. During his lifetime, he gained his greatest fame for his dark and lyrical poem "The Raven," which debuted in 1845, but Poe has also been credited with inventing the detective fiction genre and contributing to the growth of science fiction. He wrote dozens of poems and short stories (scholars disagree on the exact number), as well as a

novel, a play, essays, and the aforementioned critical reviews. He died in Baltimore, Maryland, at the age of forty on October 7, 1849. To this date the cause of his death, in pure Poe style, remains a mystery.

For a complete picture of the life of Edgar Allan Poe, including details about his marriage, his career, and his enigmatic death, please see my "Further Reading" section, which features books, articles, and websites that proved invaluable to me while writing *The Raven's Tale*. I take full responsibility for any inaccuracies or anachronisms found in the novel, and I must beg the reader's pardon for committing any such errors.

Thank you for joining me on this macabre, fantastic ride.

Further Reading

BOOKS AND ARTICLES

Baker, Meredith Henne, *The Richmond Theater Fire: Early America's First Great Disaster*. Baton Rouge, LA: Louisiana State University Press, 2012.

Burwell, William McCreery, "Edgar A. Poe and His College Contemporaries." *New Orleans Times–Democrat*, Cols. 4–7 (May 18, 1884), p. 8.

Campbell, Killis, "Contemporary Opinion of Poe." *PMLA*, Vol. 36, No. 2 (June 1921), pp. 142–166.

Case, Keshia A., and Christopher P. Semtner, on behalf of the Poe Museum, *Edgar Allan Poe in Richmond*. Charleston, SC: Arcadia Publishing, 2009.

Dayan, Joan, "Amorous Bondage: Poe, Ladies, and Slaves." *American Literature*, Vol. 66, No. 2 (June 1994), pp. 239–273.

Deas, Michael J., *The Portraits and Daguerreotypes of Edgar Allan Poe*. Charlottesville, VA: University of Virginia Press, 1989.

George, Miles, "Reminiscence of Poe," *State*, Richmond, VA (May 22, 1880), p. 2.

Mabbott, Thomas Ollive, ed., *Collected Works of Edgar Allan Poe*, Vol. I, *Poems*. Cambridge, MA: Belknap Press, 1969.

Mabbott, Thomas Ollive, ed., with the assistance of Eleanor D. Kewer and Maureen C. Mabbott, *Collected Works of Edgar Allan Poe*, Vol. II, *Tales and Sketches, 1831–1842*. Cambridge, MA: Belknap Press, 1978.

Mabbott, Thomas Ollive, ed., with the assistance of Eleanor D. Kewer and Maureen C. Mabbott, *Collected Works of Edgar Allan Poe*, Vol. III, *Tales and Sketches, 1843–1849*. Cambridge, MA: Belknap Press, 1978.

Ocker, J. W., *Poe-Land: The Hallowed Haunts of Edgar Allan Poe*. Woodstock, VT: The Countryman Press, 2015.

Ostrom, John Ward, ed., *The Letters of Edgar Allan Poe*, Second Edition, Vols. I and II. New York, NY: The Gordian Press, 1966.

Phillips, Mary. E., *Edgar Allan Poe—the Man*, Vols. I and II. Chicago, IL: John C. Winston Co., 1926.

Quinn, Arthur Hobson, *Edgar Allan Poe: A Critical Biography*. 1941. Repr., Baltimore, MD: Johns Hopkins University Press, 1998.

Semtner, Christopher P., *Edgar Allan Poe's Richmond: The Raven in the River City*. Charleston, SC: The History Press, 2012.

Stanard, Mary Newton, ed., *Edgar Allan Poe Letters Till Now Unpublished in the Valentine Museum, Richmond, Virginia*. Philadelphia, PA: J.B. Lippincott Co., 1925.

Taylor–White, Alyson L., *Shockoe Hill Cemetery: A Richmond Landmark History*. Charleston, SC: The History Press, 2017.

Thomas, Dwight, and David K. Jackson, *The Poe Log: A Documentary Life of Edgar Allan Poe 1809–1849*. Boston, MA: G.K. Hall & Co., 1987.

University of Virginia, "Proceedings of the Faculty of the University of Virginia," Vols. I and II, 1825–1826.

Weiss, Susan Archer, *The Home Life of Poe*. New York, NY: Broadway Publishing Co., 1907.

Wertenbaker, William, "Edgar A. Poe." *Virginia University Magazine*, Vol. VII, Nos. 2–3 (November–December 1868), pp. 114–117.

WEBSITES

The Edgar Allan Poe Society of Baltimore, www.eapoe.org.

The Poe Museum, www.poemuseum.org.

Poems, Songs, Letters, and Stories Quoted in
The Raven's Tale

Works are listed by chapter number, first line, title, author,
and first known year of publication or origin.

CHAPTER ONE
"the pomps and vanities of the wicked world"
The Book of Common Prayer, 1625 edition.

CHAPTER TWO
"Once upon a dark December, in a year we must remember"
Lines written by Cat Winters in the style of "The Raven," by Edgar Allan
Poe, 1845. Throughout the novel, Cat Winters wrote numerous other lines of
poetry in this style.

CHAPTER THREE
"The gay wall of this gaudy tower"
"Tamerlane," by Edgar Allan Poe, 1827. Other lines identified as belonging
to "Tamerlane" throughout *The Raven's Tale* are also quoted from the original
1827 version of the poem.

CHAPTER FOUR
"Beware, a maiden unrefined"
"Lenore's Sickly Rhymes," Cat Winters, written for *The Raven's Tale*. The
words "from a darkened mind" in the second line are from "The Lake," by
Edgar Allan Poe, 1827, but Poe spelled "darkened" as "darken'd."

CHAPTER SIX
"By the pricking of my thumbs"
Macbeth, William Shakespeare, circa 1606.

"When forty winters shall besiege thy brow"
"Sonnet 2," William Shakespeare, 1609.

CHAPTER SEVEN

"I hear the low tones of the darkness stealing over the horizon, as I tend to do in the evenings—a foolish fancy, perhaps"
Adapted from Note 10 in the endnotes for "Tamerlane," *Tamerlane and Other Poems*, Edgar Allan Poe, 1827: "I have often fancied that I could distinctly hear the sound of the darkness, as it steals over the horizon—a foolish fancy perhaps . . ."

CHAPTER TWELVE

"My artist is older than yours—far wiser than yours."
Variation of lines 28–29 in "Annabel Lee," Edgar Allan Poe, 1849: "Of those who were older than we/Of many far wiser than we—"
"of which no mortal has ever dared to dream"
Variation of line 26 in "The Raven," Edgar Allan Poe, 1845: "Doubting, dreaming dreams no mortal ever dared to dream before . . ."

CHAPTER THIRTEEN

"Thy soul shall find itself alone"
"Visit of the Dead," Edgar Allan Poe, 1827 (Poe changed the title of later editions to "Spirits of the Dead").

CHAPTER FOURTEEN

"May I compare thee to a winter's morn?"
Cat Winters, written in the style of lines 1–4 of "Sonnet 18," William Shakespeare, 1609.

CHAPTER FIFTEEN

"Thank heaven! I'm packing—preparing at last."
Cat Winters, written in the style of lines 1–4 of "For Annie," Edgar Allan Poe, 1849.

"in a kingdom by the sea"
"Annabel Lee," Edgar Allan Poe, 1849.

CHAPTER EIGHTEEN
"Hear that throbbing, thumping bell—tempting bell!"
Lines written by Cat Winters in the style of "The Bells," Edgar Allan Poe,
1849.

CHAPTER NINETEEN
"Here's a thing I've wondered since I was quite small and young"
"The Professors," Cat Winters, written for *The Raven's Tale*, with
a few nods to Edgar Allan Poe's "Oh, Tempora! Oh, Mores!,"
circa 1825.
"the same long but sufficiently good nose"
Variation of a line in the story "The Spectacles," Edgar Allan Poe, 1844: "My
nose is sufficiently good."

CHAPTER TWENTY-ONE
"And so being young and dipt in folly"
"Introduction," Edgar Allan Poe, 1831.
"Thou hast call'd me thy Angel in moments of bliss"
"Come, Rest in This Bosom," Thomas Moore, quoted from an 1822 printing
of Moore's *Irish Songs*. Other lines identified as belonging to "Come, Rest in
This Bosom" (purportedly Poe's favorite song) are also quoted from the 1822
edition.

CHAPTER TWENTY-THREE
"Since my love died for me today, I'll die for her tomorrow."
"Barbara Allen," traditional Scottish ballad, circa 1600s. In the song, "him" is
used in place of "her."

CHAPTER TWENTY-FOUR

"Let us drink and be merry all out of one glass"

"Here's a Health to the Company," traditional Irish song, date unknown.

CHAPTER TWENTY-FIVE

"Come, lonely genius of my natal shore"

The Giant's Causeway, William Hamilton Drummond, 1811.

CHAPTER TWENTY-EIGHT

"The skies they are opal and restless"

Untitled, Cat Winters, written in the style of lines 1–9 of "Ulalume," Edgar Allan Poe, 1847.

CHAPTER TWENTY-NINE

"Sing heav'nly Muse, that on the secret top"

Paradise Lost, John Milton, 1667.

"In youth's spring, it was my lot"

"The Lake," Edgar Allan Poe, 1827. Other lines identified as belonging to "The Lake" throughout *The Raven's Tale* are also quoted from the original 1827 version of the poem.

CHAPTER THIRTY-ONE

"I am a business man. I am a methodical man."

"The Business Man," Edgar Allan Poe, 1845. Originally published as "Peter Pendulum (The Business Man)" with slightly different wording in 1840.

CHAPTER THIRTY-SIX

"Helen, thy beauty is to me"

"To Helen," Edgar Allan Poe, 1831.

CHAPTER THIRTY-NINE

"It is likely that pieces of flesh as large as my hand will be obliged to be cut out"
Letter from Edgar Allan Poe to John Allan, September 21, 1826.

CHAPTER FORTY-THREE

"I have no wish to live another hour" and "I have no desire to live and *will not*"
Letter from Edgar Allan Poe to Mrs. Maria Clemm and Miss Virginia Clemm, August 29, 1835.

CHAPTER FORTY-FOUR

"shorn and shaven"
"The Raven," Edgar Allan Poe, 1845.
"I saw thee on the bridal day"
"To — —," Edgar Allan Poe, 1827.

CHAPTER FORTY-SIX

"The Prodigal Son of Richmond" is the title of a nonexistent, entirely fictitious poem Cat Winters based on young Edgar Poe's tendency to write and distribute anonymous satires of people he considered cruel and/or pompous.
"In visions of the dark night"
Untitled, Edgar Allan Poe, 1827. Poe titled later editions of the poem "A Dream."

CHAPTER FORTY-SEVEN

"And I turn'd away to thee"
"Evening Star," Edgar Allan Poe, 1827.

CHAPTER FORTY-NINE

"Once upon a midnight dreary"
Opening words of "The Raven," Edgar Allan Poe, 1845.

CHAPTER FIFTY-FIVE

"Edgar, thy absence is to me like a crushing, metallic ore"

"Lenore's Reawakening," Cat Winters, written for *The Raven's Tale*. Opening line written in the style of lines 1–5 of "To Helen," Edgar Allan Poe, 1831. Remaining lines written in the style of "The Raven," Edgar Allan Poe, 1845.

CHAPTER FIFTY-SIX

"Once upon a midnight sordid, while I dig a gravesite swarded"

"Finale," Cat Winters, written for *The Raven's Tale* in the style of "The Raven," Edgar Allan Poe, 1845.

Acknowledgments

The Raven's Tale would have been impossible to write were it not for the help of numerous generous individuals and organizations.

I must start by thanking the Edgar Allan Poe Society of Baltimore for providing Poe's works, letters, biographies, essays, and countless other indispensable Poe materials online, free of charge, for scholars around the world. I visited the society's website, www.eapoe.org, every single day that I worked on this novel and can't imagine writing this book without that trove of information at my fingertips.

Thanks to Chris Semtner, curator of the Poe Museum, for fielding my questions and for featuring this novel on the web show *The Raven Lunatics*. Thanks also to Dwight L. MacPherson, cohost and creator of *The Raven Lunatics*, and Rebecca MacPherson of Hocus Pocus Comics for cheering on this project and helping to share the novel's progress online.

I'm grateful for the assistance of C. Clayton Shepherd and Jeffry Burden of Friends of Shockoe Hill Cemetery in Richmond, Virginia, who answered my questions specific to the cemetery.

A huge, heartfelt thanks goes to my sister, Carrie, for not only reading more than one early draft of *The Raven's Tale* (even the *painfully* early ones), but for driving me around Virginia for a week during my research trip in October 2017. My brave, loving sister even stayed in a haunted hotel with me on the former site of Poe's "Enchanted Garden."

Thank you, Kim Murphy, for reading an early draft and for guiding Carrie and me on a tour of the University of Virginia. As always, I greatly appreciate your help with my books.

Thank you, Fonda Lee, for listening to me talk about *The Raven's Tale* during my drafting stage and saying something along the lines of, "Oh, so this is a book about Poe that reads like a Poe story." You articulated what I was struggling to achieve but hadn't yet accomplished. Once you said the words aloud it allowed me to pinpoint exactly what I wanted to do with this novel. I'm so incredibly thankful you made that comment.

Thanks to Laura Byrd for critiquing an early draft and for listening to me stress out about attempting to write a novel about Poe (and stressing out about life in general) during coffeehouse writing sessions. Thank you, Jenn Reese, Miriam Forster, Lisa Schroeder, Teri Brown, and Kelly Garrett for also letting me vent and panic in front of you and for boosting my confidence during our writing get-togethers. I wouldn't survive in this profession without those precious meetups.

Thank you, Martha Brockenbrough, for reaching out to your father about the Brockenbrough family tree when I discovered that two Brockenbroughs crossed paths with teenage Edgar Allan Poe. Huge thanks to your dad, as well!

Thanks to all my fellow YA writers who were there for me during this writing process, with special shout-outs to Susan Adrian, A. G. Howard, April Genevieve Tucholke, and Dawn Kurtagich for the check-ins and enthusiasm for *The Raven's Tale*.

As always, a tremendous thanks goes out to my agent, Barbara Poelle, for jumping on board with my initial ideas, for steering me onto the right course after a misguided first draft, and for advocating for the novel's success.

Thanks to my editor at Amulet Books/Abrams, Maggie Lehrman, who once again worked her editorial magic on my work and helped to reshape *The Raven's Tale* into a stronger, polished work of fiction. This is our fifth novel together, and I always feel my books undergo a lovely form of alchemy whenever we collaborate.

Thank you to the rest of my team at Abrams: Jenny Choy, Brooke Shearouse, Hallie Patterson, Nicole Schaefer, Hana Anouk Nakamura, and Marie Oishi, as well as my diligent copy editor, the proofreaders, and everyone else who played a role in bringing this book into the world.

Thanks to Shane Rebenschied for creating the beautiful cover art and to María Belén La Rivera for the gorgeous title lettering.

Thank you to my parents for *always* encouraging me to follow my muse. I'm so fortunate to have grown up in a house that supported my artistic endeavors, and I wish the same were true for all young artists.

Thank you to the rest of my family and friends who've consistently cheered me on throughout the years, and for the librarians, booksellers, teachers, bloggers, and readers who've helped me gain a much-appreciated following through all those wonderful word-of-mouth recommendations.

Adam, Meggie, and Ethan—your love, motivation, and understanding power me through each day, each book draft. Thank you for putting up with this peculiar career of mine. I love you dearly.